**From the personal diary of
Sergei Kondrashin, Head Custodian,
Camp Alpha, Belarus:**

*I'm happy here, but I've been having odd nightmares. Probably because of the accident. Don't know all the details and don't want to, but I've heard enough to make me wonder if my team is alone down here. Not a trace of anyone else. No sound or sight or smell. Anyway, in my dreams, it's not the world that's wrong—it's the sky. The night sky.*

*There is a black veil that hides half the stars. Pav says it's stellar dust.*

*To me it looks like the blackness of empty space. But it's not empty.*

*During the day I don't believe it, but at night I get the feeling. Something is in there. Something hiding. Something dreadful. . . .*

"With a richly imagined geopolitical setting, *Belarus* reads like a Russian fairy tale set in space."

—Syne Mitchell, author of *Technogenesis*

# BELARUS

Lee Hogan

A ROC BOOK

ROC
Published by New American Library, a division of
Penguin Putnam Inc., 375 Hudson Street,
New York, New York 10014, U.S.A.
Penguin Books Ltd, 80 Strand,
London WC2R 0RL, England
Penguin Books Australia Ltd, Ringwood,
Victoria, Australia
Penguin Books Canada Ltd, 10 Alcorn Avenue,
Toronto, Ontario, Canada M4V 3B2
Penguin Books (N.Z.) Ltd, 182–190 Wairau Road,
Auckland 10, New Zealand

Penguin Books Ltd, Registered Offices:
Harmondsworth, Middlesex, England

First published by Roc, an imprint of New American Library,
a division of Penguin Putnam Inc.

First Printing, February 2002
10 9 8 7 6 5 4 3 2 1



Cover art by Matt Stawicki
Cover design by Ray Lundgren

REGISTERED TRADEMARK—MARCA REGISTRADA

Printed in the United States of America

This book is for
G. Harry Stine,
space pioneer

ACKNOWLEDGMENTS

I would like to thank Ernest Hogan and Rick Cook for the usual brainstorms, Gia DeSimonc for first-class nudging, Paul Schauble and Catherine Yankovich for saving my hash, and Dan Prozen for a helpful Yiddish expletive and for telling me that "Grigory" means "watcher."

The Lord is my light and my savior; whom then shall I fear? The Lord is the defender of my life; of whom then shall I be afraid?

When the wicked draw nigh against me to eat my flesh, they that afflict me and are mine enemies, they themselves became weak and they fell.

Though a host should array itself against me, my heart shall not be afraid; though war should rise up against me, in this have I hoped.

—from the Orthodox Psalter
Psalm 27

# FOREWORD

I use a Russian word in this book that some of you may recognize: *mir*. Most people know the Russians named their space station Mir, but don't know why. In fact, *mir* is one of those words that has no direct translation. Roughly, it means "peace." It also means "the world."

There is an old Russian saying: Russians want *mir*. Paranoids may assume this means Russians want to take over the world. I have attempted to use this novel to explain what I think the saying really means. More than anything, the main characters in this book want *mir*.

I'm not a Russian, and perhaps I have completely misunderstood. But it seems to me that maybe *mir* is something you can build. Only time will tell if that's true.

If it is, then maybe the saying will change to humans want *mir*. . . .

# Prologue

YEAR OF THE REPUBLIC 19014
BELARUSIAN YEAR 1

Sprites flew the winds of Lucifer.

No larger than ice crystals, they glistened in the upper atmosphere, hitching a ride in titanic storms, absorbing and channeling energy. Each one of them performed its part in a greater function, observing, recording, interacting. They created tunnels through space-time and beamed messages to each other, achieving almost instantaneous communication. They used the same method to beam data back to the people who had made them. Eventually those people would use star ships with powerful jump engines to make their own tunnels in space-time, and they would join the sprites in orbit around Lucifer.

Until then, the sprites were on their own. They enjoyed themselves. Inspired, they formulated theories and drew conclusions. Some dragged themselves out of Lucifer's immense gravity well and combined with other sprites, becoming larger and more complex. Their functions also became more complex, as did their theories and conclusions. Both chemical and mechanical, they were not unlike the cells of a giant brain; each time they interacted with people whose brains were organic, their emerging minds took on some of the qualities of those people, some of whom were human—and some of whom were not.

The opposite was true as well. The people who spoke with the sprites did so through biomechanical enhancements in the language centers of their brains. Their minds, sprite and organic, linked to perform efficient tasks. But the effects of their link would have consequences that reached far beyond those tasks.

For now, however, the basic problems were all that mattered. Some sprites were in need of repair. Others needed to be created from available materials and infected with the sprite virus that connected them with each other and made them self-aware. These acts were performed millions of times by the sprites, then billions, then trillions.

And all the while they studied the gas giant. They swarmed through the asteroid belts just outside its orbital plane; they compiled lists of chemicals and minerals that would be useful to the humans who intended to develop this system, of which Lucifer was the sixth member.

Once the lists had been completed, some of them split from the main group and tunneled to the third planet. They studied it, and multiplied and repaired. They made new versions of themselves and thought up new ways to combine.

<Belarus,> they told each other, curious about what the name meant to the human patron who headed their project. Belarus contained life. Their work inside its gravity well would be far more complex than the examination of Lucifer's system had been, because Belarus was to become a colony world, one of a thousand colonies within the Republic.

A certain amount of terraforming would be necessary. They would decide how much, and then they would begin. In the process they recombined, improvised, evolved.

Other sprites still rode the storms of Lucifer. Eventually they would help to develop the mining industry there. But their curiosity took on a new dimension. They examined their lists of all chemicals and minerals within its system.

They found alloys that could only have been crafted by intelligence.

<Andrei,> they warned the patron. <Caution. Anomaly.>

<Anomaly noted,> replied Andrei. <Specify.>

The sprites immediately began to comply, without any knowledge or concern that the order would take them years to obey.

# PART ONE

Go home and tell all in foreign lands that Russia lives. Let them come to us as guests without fear. But if anyone comes to us with the sword, he shall perish by the sword. On this the Russian land stands and will stand.

—Prince Alexander Yaroslavich Nevsky

YEAR OF THE REPUBLIC 19017
BELARUSIAN YEAR 4

Andrei Mironenko walked the dimly lit corridor of Archangel Station fully alert and with every system in his danger suit functioning perfectly. Yet he did not see Grigory until he came face-to-face with the pair of blood stones that filled the sockets where the man's eyes used to be.

"Mironenko," said Grigory.

Andrei was surprised, but not alarmed. Grigory was an Enhanced Special Agent, an ESA; not an assassin. And he could hardly consider the proximity of those stones an affront, since the man couldn't use them to see him. Not that Andrei had much of an advantage under the circumstances. Grigory was wearing a much more sophisticated danger suit than his; its fabric diverted light so well Andrei could barely see it in the simulated twilight of the corridor.

Something glittered in the air between them; a transfer slip. It bore the mark of his chief of security, Emily Kizheh. "The latest from Baba Yaga," said Grigory, with a voice as scarred as his face. "It was lurking inside an ad for ski equipment. TachyGrammed to your office."

Andrei accepted the strip. "Witch," he said, almost fondly. "Does she know how much I hate junk mail?"

"Not a difficult thing to guess about a man," offered Grigory.

Andrei studied him. If his expression was any indication, Grigory's thoughts were always of pain, death, treachery; yet Andrei's world engineer, Natalia, had confided some of her private matters to him, and his wife, Katerina, often asked Grigory's opinion concerning the character of new associates.

"I assume you've read it," said Andrei, tapping the transfer. "What do you make of it?"

"She's warning you."

"Warning—or threatening?"

"Can Baba Yaga do one without doing the other?"

Andrei allowed himself a little smile. He slipped the transfer into a utility pocket. "Should make for entertaining reading before bed. But this was not the reason you came to visit me, Grigory Michaelovich. You don't generally deliver messages."

"I wish to express an opinion concerning the artifacts," said Grigory.

"Ah." Everyone had an opinion concerning the four station-sized artifacts that shared orbit with them around the gas giant, Lucifer. Natalia's technicians believed they were comparable to the orbital stations and equipment they were putting into place, related to mining and development of the Lucifer system and the asteroid belt. Or rather, they *had* believed that. Until the booby traps were discovered.

"Interesting," said Grigory, "that the traps did not spring when the sprites made such a thorough examination of the wrecks, years ago. They waited until people were present."

Andrei frowned. He had almost lost six people. Only dumb luck saved them. He had hoped for a better breed of luck at this stage of the game, but he made the best hand he could with the cards dealt. Especially when God played with a marked deck.

"The damned things are so old," he said. "The techs think twenty thousand years old, at least."

"They were built before our race dreamed of leaving Mother Earth," said Grigory, making it sound like a troubling thought.

But the idea only confirmed Andrei's suspicions. "Then they are long dead. From a war, obviously, judging from the nature of the damage. The architects of those devices must have been utterly destroyed. And their traps are malfunctioning after all this time."

"They're functioning perfectly."

"You think so? They didn't react to the sprites."

"Sprites are no fun, they're not made of flesh. It was *people* they wanted to hurt."

"Grigory, they are dead. We looked for years, and we found no trace of them other than those wrecks."

The blind man smiled. It was a gesture that had nothing to do with mirth. "If they are dead, imagine the malice in their hearts that would cause them to strike from beyond the grave."

Andrei did imagine it. He had no doubt that the people who had been driven from this system—or cornered like rats and killed in it—had earned the hatred of their enemies. "Perhaps they weren't thinking this far ahead," he suggested. "I imagine their malice was directed at the ones who ultimately killed them."

"And should those ones return . . ."

"We are armed," Andrei said mildly. He didn't need to add that he worried more about his enemies in the Republic than he did about any survivors from a long-dead conflict.

Traces of Grigory's dreadful smile still lingered. Andrei waited for him to say what Emily Kizheh had said all along: that he should take more time, find another world like Lucifer's sister, the beautiful third planet, his Belarus-in-progress. Andrei was not such an autocrat that he couldn't stand to be questioned or criticized. But the simple fact was, his time and money were running short. This Belarus was his last chance.

"You know how I lost my eyes," Grigory said.

"Yes. In the Griffith-Papadopoulos war. Natalia said your patron proved to be dishonorable."

"Not dishonorable," said Grigory. "Insane. Her madness was not the sort that is easily detectable, so I accepted her patronage. She had no sprites, but I was able to interface with her networks easily enough. And when parts of you are accessible to networks, those parts are vulnerable."

"I'm not as comprehensively enhanced as you are," said Andrei, "but my eyes are similar to the ones you lost." They were artificial, linked to his communications network, able to relay information to his security force or to receive data when they were in tactical mode.

"I wouldn't try to talk you out of them," said Grigory. "They serve you well enough. That's what machines are for. Most people think that's what sprites are for, too, and they don't like to find out they're wrong. As for my last patron—her goals and mine seemed to coincide. I was engaged in damage control. War squelching, if you will. Make it difficult for the two sides to finance the battle, and they find other ways to settle the dispute."

"That's not working too well anymore," remarked Andrei.

"So true. It didn't work that time either, because my patron discovered that I had alien associates, and that I was linked with them through my sprites."

"She was a bigot? Why didn't she just fire you?"

"Because she was more than a bigot. She was paranoid. She believed that I had infiltrated her organization in order to corrupt it, to strike at her from within. So she decided to strike me first."

The result of that preemptive strike was plain.

"I shall tell you what disturbs me the most about the ruling families of our Republic," said Grigory.

"They have the power of life and death over trillions of souls. And for what, Andrei? Money. Nothing more. Yet they trumpet religion and ethnic 'pride' to justify their actions, or the lack of them. Worthy patrons are hard to find these days."

"Some of us believe in a Bill of Rights," said Andrei.

"I've heard the rhetoric," said Grigory. "Noble sentiments. My last patron did not share them. She made sure that the Griffith-Papadapoulos war would be one of the bloodiest on record, simply by choosing a side—the one most likely to kill me. My sprites were destroyed in the process of extricating me from the scene. Once they were gone, I was still linked to her network, but had no system of my own that could provide reliable information. I called on her for help."

Grigory's voice was rough, yet Andrei could detect no bitterness in his tone.

"I could feel the attack coming, just before she struck. I had no choice, Andrei Alexandrovich, I tore the eyes from my head to protect my brain. My sight is gone, but I still have the senses that kept me alive. Over the years I have gathered new sprites to myself. Through them, I watch the universe. But it is the ache in my sockets that I trust the most. And I have felt that ache very much lately."

Andrei wasn't sure what to say. Grigory was just one of dozens of Enhanced Special Agents on his staff. No one knew to whom the ESAs were ultimately answerable; their origins were shrouded in mystery and they had no ties to a single government. But Andrei had learned that patrons who were privileged to work with ESAs could have no doubt of their honor or their skill. And these were possibly the two things he valued the most.

So he was not disturbed to feel himself observed carefully by this blind ESA, measured critically. Grigory did not seem to be placing Andrei in the same category as his old patron. Instead, the ESA was warning him—just as Baba Yaga had warned him over the years. And like the old witch, this blind man was too good at reading him. He could see Andrei's hesitation, even without his eyes.

"Let me put it another way," said Grigory. "Those derelicts have proven that they can move when they take a notion to. Yet they have no energy signature. Someone who can hide an energy signature can hide *anything*. You were in the Central Navy—you know how to find an enemy in space. If he has no energy signature, is he not really there?"

"Maybe," said Andrei. "But hidden enemies are not new to me. If we have new enemies to contend with, I will accept that. If I learned anything from my years in the Central Navy, it was that the Central Government is powerless to prevent wars like Griffith-Papadapoulos. They cannot protect me, and now I am committed here. For generations my father and his fathers have worked toward this end. Whatever power I hold, it will not be enough to let me start again on another world, not now that I have made my intentions clear. This is the spot, Grigory, this is my *mir*, and I will blow it to atoms before I let anyone take it away from me."

"A fine Russian sentiment." Grigory seemed oddly pleased by his response. "What else can I do but stay with your project? It is all I am good for, this dangerous service."

Andrei did not miss the point. Grigory was senior ESA on his project. He could tell the other ESAs to pack up and leave, and they would obey him. Instead he reaffirmed his fealty to Andrei.

*If you really intend to be tsar,* he told himself, *get used to it.*

"I accept your support," he said. "I'm pleased to have it."

<Then I bid you good night.> Grigory sent a message through the communications link. Andrei's brain received the words as if they had been spoken. Gri-

gory's virtual voice was much smoother than the one his throat produced.

<I bid you the same,> returned Andrei.

Grigory moved into the semidarkness, fading like a ghost. Suddenly Andrei felt as if he had stumbled onto a stage during a performance of Shakespeare's *Hamlet*. But in this version, Hamlet's father had eyes of crystalline blood, windows into hell.

In his own way Andrei was also haunted by the ghost of his father. But Alexander Sergeivich Mironenko did not rattle chains and deliver warnings. In his memory, Andrei could see his father smiling, usually in motion, especially when he told his young son the old Russian folk tales.

Like the tale of Baba Yaga.

Andrei slapped the pocket where the transfer waited. "Later, Grandmother Witch," he promised. "First I want a few words with my world engineer."

From the personal diary of Sergei Kondrashin, Head Custodian, Camp Alpha, Belarus:

*Temp quarters are completed and ready for A.M. and his staff—the latest word is we'll see them within the week. This very spot will be St. Petersburg. Hard to imagine at the moment, but it always is at this stage of a colony. The world is wild now, and my team the only intelligent eyes to gaze upon it—at least for a little while longer.*

*Pav goes out every night and looks for the new star in the sky, Archangel Station. He's nervous, says that's his job because he's my assistant. I'm not nervous, I'm glad we'll have more company soon. It's spooky with just twenty of us here. Beautiful world—it's cold where we are right now, but the danger suits keep you comfortable. Lovely flowers. The animals are a little strange, but the birds mostly look like birds, the hoofed animals are tasty. The weird ones are some of the larger mammals. They have three pairs of eyes. Oddest thing I've ever seen, almost like spider eyes.*

*There are giant raptors—I swear the wing span must be eight feet. We call them King Raptors. They nest in the mountains to the east but like to hunt the rodents who live in our fields. To watch them in flight is indescribable. I have heard that Mironenko intends to make the King Raptor his royal crest when he becomes tsar—a well-deserved honor.*

*I'm happy here, but I've been having nightmares. Probably because of the accident with the ESAs—that was truly awful. Don't know all the details and don't want to, but I've heard enough to make me wonder if my team is alone down here. Not a trace of anyone else, no sound or sight or smell. Anyway, in my dreams, it's not the world that's wrong, it's the sky. The night sky.*

*During the day, the sky is blue, more beautiful than any sky I've seen. But at night, there is a black veil that hides half the stars. Pav says it's stellar dust—astronomy is his hobby. I have to take his word for it, to me it looks like the blackness of empty space. But it's not empty.*

*During the day I don't believe it, but at night I get the feeling something is in there. Something hiding. Something dreadful.*

Tally Korsakova seemed to be staring at the blank wall opposite her workstation. But in reality, she saw a monster named Derelict C.

She sat erect, her slim, black form perfectly still except for the rasta-links that plugged into her skull like a magnificent cluster of medusa serpents, sleek obsidian data links that undulated slowly when they weren't plugged into a jack. Over half of them were deployed into different sources as she examined the alien artifact that had almost killed six ESAs.

Patterns revealed themselves once she got close enough, intricate lines that looked like decorations painted on or etched into surfaces. And if you looked even closer, there were patterns inside those patterns.

Clockworks. That was how they seemed. Tally's Russian grandfather had been fascinated with antique clocks; he had often shown her the machinery inside them, the gears and springs. Intricate, incredibly precise pieces moved together, meshing, turning, spinning, urging the clock hands forward increment by increment.

"This is how the universe moves," he told her. "We

can't see the works, sometimes we can't even see the movement, but it still tics away."

. . . *tic tic tic tic tic* . . .

The derelicts did not have hands, gears, or springs. They were a thousand times more complex than any clock Tally had ever seen, yet there was still something about them that struck her as clocklike. Perhaps it was the precise orbit they maintained around Lucifer. Or it might have been their baffling symmetries, beautiful even with large chunks missing. Their hulls and their interiors had never seemed static to Tally, but had always seemed capable of shifting into another configuration altogether. That insight had proven to be dreadfully true.

Her rasta-links sent information directly into her brain from sprites that swarmed the artifacts. Tally had seen them from every angle, in every mode. She had floated like a sprite, looking at corridors, chambers, hulls, and twisted wreckage as if she were seeing with her naked eyes. She had viewed them strictly as data, streams and columns of figures and code. She had seen them in tactical mode, as lines on three-dimensional grids with footnotes concerning temperatures, radiation, energy output, alloys, and chemical compositions. Now she viewed the collected data of sprites and scientists who had studied the four derelicts for well over a decade, yet many of those footnotes still read: UNKNOWN. And so they remained, four things each roughly the size of Andrei's command station, their lines elegant and cunningly crafted, revealing no power source and yet somehow able to maintain precise orbits that never decayed and never brought them into a collision course with each other or with anything else.

They filled her mind, save for one little corner. Grandfather waited there, holding an old timepiece. "See the hands?" he told her. "Our lives move forward in the same way, minute after minute, year after year. But look at the clock, Tally. Can you see the hour ahead? I can. Look, child, tell me what you see."

. . . *tic tic tic tic* . . .

More booby traps must exist. But she could not detect them, no more than the ESAs had detected them until they tried to activate what they thought was a database in one of the chambers of Derelict C and it had begun to shift, to literally change shape.

Before that moment it had been characteristic of every other chamber inside the derelicts, its walls and floors covered with beautiful, puzzling patterns. Tally had dreamed about the patterns many times, fascinated by them at first, then repelled as she began to be haunted by a feeling of menace, as if the patterns were a forest that hid some predator. So when the ESAs announced that the patterns were not simple decorations, she formally requested that all future exploration of the derelicts be conducted by machines, not people. She'd had no explanation other than her bad feelings. And so she was overruled.

The ESAs thought they had discovered a way to make the patterns respond. And they were right. When the patterns began to emerge from the walls and floors as structures, everyone had been enthralled by the symmetry, the complexity of the shifting chamber—everyone save Tally, who screamed, <GET THEM OUT! GET THEM OUT!> Sprites scrambled to obey her, just as the emerging structures in the chamber began to make their nature clear. They sprouted blades, and saws, and crushing gears.

*Clockworks. Tic tic tic tic tic tic* . . .

The chamber closed in on the ESAs.

Their sprites blasted them free, almost too late. All of them suffered terrible injuries. If they had not been ESAs they would have died. Tally could not get over how quickly ruins that had been silent for thousands of years had sprung to life—to cause death.

And now they were ruins again, cold and silent.

Lucifer's sentinels. Their cold elegance was a startling contrast to its titanic storms. She could look at them forever, see patterns within patterns that tormented her intellect. They were the work of minds that possessed a profound sense of beauty. Yet even in the early days, the sight of them triggered something deep in her psyche. Discord.

*Warning.*

"Natalia," chided a warm voice. "Are you dithering again?"

Tally didn't jump at the sound of the voice. Instead, she smiled. It pulled her away from her troubled contemplation as nothing else could have done. She disengaged her rasta-links and swiveled in her chair, alien images fading from her cortex to be replaced by a sight much more welcome.

Andrei stood in the doorway, regarding her with hazel eyes, the corners of which crinkled with a smile he seldom allowed to reach his lips. His stance was perfectly balanced; his brown hair, beard, and mustache were trimmed so carefully; he looked more like a naval officer than a patron from a powerful family.

"That's a good job description for world engineer," Tally said. "Head ditherer."

"I have a better description," said Andrei. "Sorcerer. It never ceases to amaze me how you can sort through so many streams of information without becoming completely swamped."

She grinned. "My grandmother was the sorcerer in my family. She was a Nigerian con artist."

He quirked an eyebrow. "Married to a Russian?"

"I have an interesting bloodline, not an illustrious one." Tally tempered her smile. "But it's not as hard to sift multiple streams of data as you think. You learn to scan for the stuff that's important to you. After a while, you get an instinct for patterns."

"No, Natalia, *you* get an instinct for patterns. I get confused."

Tally didn't argue. Andrei returned her gaze for a

long moment with watchful eyes. As he measured Tally for the thousandth time, she could only be glad of her own self-confidence. Anyone with less conviction would have melted on the spot.

Suddenly his gaze focused beyond her, and Tally guessed he was using his own link with the sprites to look at the alien artifacts. Andrei had a receiver in his eyes, as well as enhancements in his visual cortex and memory and language centers. Tally could have opted for the same kind of receiver, but like Grigory, she hated the idea of having her most vulnerable places accessible to a sprite-link. Her rasta-links were adaptable to almost any system, they contained their own backup memory, and at least with them she could disengage when she wanted to. She wouldn't have to resort to tearing out her eyes if a professional relationship went sour.

As he studied the wrecks, Tally tried to discern whether he had changed his mind about them. Perhaps they had begun to appear in his nightmares, as they had hers. But his face revealed nothing of the sort. Andrei never seemed to feel anything but intellectual curiosity when he regarded the artifacts.

Or maybe not. This time she thought she detected an added dimension to his reaction. Not anger, exactly, but something she had seen from time to time during her two-year stint with his project. She had come to think of this expression as the *threat* of anger. It had taken her a long time to recognize it, and to realize that others did as well; his most trusted advisors, who tried to fix whatever the problem was before real anger blossomed—a cold, precise anger that never exploded into rage, but was focused with a deadly precision that ended careers.

That threat was in his eyes when he looked at the derelicts. Natalia found that gratifying, but she didn't find it comforting.

"They should be destroyed," she dared to say.

"Grigory hates them too," he said.

"You've spoken to him about it?"

"Just now, in the hallway." Andrei focused on her again. "I respect his opinion. And yours. But Emily has in mind to study those wrecks more closely. She worries we may find the same sort of traps on Belarus."

"So do I."

He considered that for a long moment. If Tally hadn't known him well, she might have hoped he had changed his mind about developing the system.

Finally he said, "I've mentioned my legendary relative to you, the one who calls herself Baba Yaga. Perhaps I've bored you with talk of her."

"Not at all," said Tally, bemused by the turn in conversation. "I think she's fascinating."

He laughed, startling her. "Really! I've a mind to let you read the messages. They go back for years, Natalia, I've saved every one of them. But you could read them all in one evening. Baba Yaga isn't one for idle chatter. She says nothing without good reason."

Tally bit her tongue. Mentioning to Andrei that you were interested in his family history was a great way to get him to clam up.

As she waited, Andrei's face lost its humor. "Recently she's been talking of war." His eyes unfocused for a moment, and Tally knew he was looking at the wrecks again, those grim reminders of a conflict whose details Tally didn't want to know.

"There's always a war somewhere," she said.

"No," said Andrei, "I'm not referring to the so-called microwars. To her, those are just squabbles, they only involve two or three worlds." He managed to say that without sounding too sarcastic. "I'm talking the war that ends the *Republic*."

Tally's rasta-links stirred uneasily. They were tied into her nervous system, and they gave her away to anyone who took the time to decipher their moods. Like Andrei, who waited to hear her opinion. She would have dearly loved to say something intelligent, something perceptive that would negate the concept of a war of galactic dimensions.

But she was struck dumb by a vision.

The fires of hell. Her father standing in the midst of the conflagration, his ebony face little more than skin stretched over a skull, his eyes huge and full of an inner fire that burned even hotter. *This is our future!* he cried. *This is how it ends for us! Sinners repent now! Repent or BURN IN HELL!*

She had fled that promise of fire when she was seventeen. For years she had buried herself in her work, thinking about creation rather than destruction. But she knew perfectly well there were serious problems in the Republic. The great advances in technology that had permitted the historic Unification of worlds that had long been isolated colonies had reawakened old conflicts and created new ones. Religions and ethnic groups clashed, different legal systems overlapped, no one could even agree what basic human rights were. There were worlds in the Republic where women and children had no legal protections of any kind, places where slavery was tolerated, and worlds where religious leaders had the right to punish the slightest transgressions with death. Refugees fled those worlds for better places, or for new colonies where they could start over. The Central Government on Earth coordinated countless assistance programs to help them, which only fueled more resentment from the planetary governments.

And over it all lorded the big families, the sprawling clans that owned the important patents to the machinery that kept the Republic running, the technology that made the unification of the Republic possible in the first place.

Andrei belonged to just such a family. So when Tally was finally able to venture a remark, she decided to keep it neutral. "No one could be stupid enough to start something that big," she said. "No one wants to wreck everything."

"Ah, but my beautiful engineer, some people do." Andrei's tone was so grim, Tally almost didn't notice he had called her *beautiful.* "I know exactly what the derelicts are," he said. "They're what's left of another Apocalypse. Just like the one that may consume us someday. Maybe we'll be cut off, left to our own devices. And if we are, I want to make sure we can make it on our own."

"That's why you want to be tsar," she said boldly. "You don't think we can survive unless you're in the driver's seat."

What reply he might have made, she would never know. In years to come she would replay the scene in her mind and try to guess what was behind his eyes at that moment, whether they were troubled, or if they might have threatened anger again.

The lights in her office flamed to amber, and an alarm klaxon began to sound. Andrei stiffened, and even as he turned for the door Tally was out of her chair and pulling the ear- and mouthpieces out of the collar of her danger suit. She turned her gloves on and quirked the controls that brought her suit into full battle mode.

Tally caught up with Andrei in the corridor—he was hurrying, not racing. Racing toward trouble wasn't going to do them any good. The station had a commander, and Andrei deferred to him during red alerts. Tally didn't try to call Grigory either; he would call *her* if there was something he thought she needed to know.

She glanced at Andrei. He was receiving a message. His eyes had gone tactical, the pupils dilated until they eclipsed his irises. His face was completely blank, almost like the face of an ESA fully engaged with sprites.

She matched paces with Andrei easily. They entered a trans-tube, moving like dancers, bowing and dipping gracefully into seats opposite each other. Andrei's eyes were still in tactical. Though he was talking to people, he was aware of everything around him.

They belted in and braced for the g-forces. As the car was sucked into motion, Tally's rasta-links flowed over her head, almost touching Andrei's face with their tips before they recovered and floated back into standby position.

Andrei didn't flinch. Tally resisted the impulse to ask him what was going on. That was what civilians always wanted to do, pestering the people who were busy trying to get their jobs done. Tally didn't say a word. But her mind was another matter.

*Another trap. Someone dead this time. Another goddam meat grinder.*

Suddenly Andrei's eyes cleared. Though he was still listening to someone, his body relaxed. Tally's heart rate started a descent toward normal.

"Something interesting," he told her.

"Good," she said. "I like interesting things."

Face-to-face, their eyes were almost level. Tally was almost as tall as Andrei, who stood over six feet. But somehow he always seemed much taller to her. She supposed that perception was her psychological adjustment to having such a powerful boss. She tried not to read anything more into it.

When they got out of the tube a minute later, the lights were simulating daylight. The amber had gone; the indicators along the walls glowed yellow. Periodically a recorded voice warned, "Stand by."

Tally still matched paces with Andrei, but now it was just a fast walk. "Where we headed?" she asked.

"Command deck."

"Can I power down my suit?"

"Yes," he said. Tally quirked her gloves. Andrei did not do the same. His suit was always on full—at least it was during his working day. She had no idea how he and Katarina spent their evenings.

Well, she had *some* idea. Katarina was pregnant. Probably the danger suit came off from time to time.

Andrei came to an abrupt halt and keyed a private code into a pad on the wall. The door opened, revealing four people in the control room. Commander Jones and Grigory stood looking over the railing at the command deck below. They turned toward Andrei when he entered. From the look on Jones's face, he and Andrei had already been conversing for some while.

Emily Kizheh and a young security officer were bent over a display screen. Neither of them looked up, even when Tally came to peek over their shoulders. They were studying a graph of recent communications transmissions. It was unremarkable, until you reached a particular point on the time axis.

"There." Emily Kizheh tapped the display. "A stutter. For about ten seconds, every sprite in this system stopped talking to us. I think they stopped talking to each other too, but I'm just guessing, because they're not aware it happened. If we weren't using sprite networks so heavily for our communications, we wouldn't know either."

"I would know," Grigory said mildly.

"Okay," said Emily, "ESAs would know. So here's the interesting thing. This effect, whatever it was, didn't pass through the solar system as a wave, it happened to all of the sprites almost at once, so we can't track the source. Some transmissions between non-sprite machines were affected too, but we haven't been able to detect a pattern to that either—yet."

Tally waited for Andrei to peer at the display too, but he stayed where he was. "We have trillions of sprites in this solar system now," he said. "Soon their numbers will be too high to count. No one has ever used sprites so extensively before—perhaps this is just the system trying to shake out its own bugs?"

Emily snorted. "We wish. Bugs of this sort usually don't go away, they get worse."

"Maybe it's not even a glitch," said Tally. "Maybe something else did it."

"Which brings up another point," said Emily. "This is actually the *second* time we've had this stutter. The first time the blackout lasted less than a second. S. O.

Valerian here"—she nodded to her assistant—"is the one who brought it to my attention. It happened when the ESAs activated that machinery on Derelict C, just before all hell busted loose. I was afraid another booby trap had been sprung this time."

From her tone of voice, Emily wasn't any fonder of the derelicts than Tally was.

"That's what the red alert was all about," said Emily. "But nothing seems to be going on. *Yet.*" Her heavy braid fell over her shoulder and she tossed it back, impatiently. Tally could tell she had been roused from sleep—the braid was usually coiled and secured at the nape of her neck. Her pleasant face was one big frown as she tapped away at the display, trying to find a pattern.

"No word of anyone being injured yet," she said. "I haven't allowed anyone back into the derelicts, so that's not a big surprise. But I wonder if the monsters are doing something, if they've changed."

She glanced up at Tally with eyes of the palest possible blue. She had more lines around them than most people allowed on their faces in these days of extended youth. But Emily Kizheh always seemed to be more occupied with what she was doing than with how she looked.

"Do you think they could attack us?" Tally asked.

"Yeah," Emily said grimly. "I do."

"We'll stay on yellow alert until further notice," said Commander Jones. Tally looked over her shoulder at him. He was the only one in Andrei's employ with skin as dark as hers, as black as human skin could be without the aid of an aesthetician. His poker face was as good as Andrei's, but occasionally he could display strong emotions. This wasn't one of those times, though he was rubbing his chin far longer than he would have if he were simply suffering from an itch.

Tally tucked her ear- and mouthpieces back into her collar. She glanced at Grigory. His suit was switched to visible mode. He stood like a statue, his blind eyes looking into the bloody past. Or perhaps toward an equally bloody future.

Emily and her young officer continued to stare at the display. Tally tried to do the same, but she had already been through so much data. She drifted away from the console and went to the railing to look at the command deck. Her eyes were captured by the big display screen just opposite the balcony, which currently showed Lucifer. It was not a static image, but one that blinked constantly, changing magnitude, switching to tactical briefly as a storm was examined in greater detail. She gazed at it for several moments, waiting to see if it would focus on one or more of the derelicts. When it did not, she lowered her gaze to the deck itself.

It was sparsely populated. It would never be completely manned unless they were at war with someone. Even once they began to build Andrei's world, it would only be three-quarters full. Tally longed for that day—she needed to sink her teeth into the work she loved. Mining systems were now in place; they would have a steady supply of raw materials without ever having to plunder the resources of the beautiful world where Andrei was planning to work his revisionist magic. Soon they would move the station into a stable orbit around Belarus.

As if in answer to that thought, the display screen blinked, erasing Lucifer and replacing it with a blue, green, and white world. There were a few storm systems brewing, but Tally could clearly see the large continent in the Eastern Hemisphere that Andrei had picked to be his Asia/Eastern Europe/Middle East. It was a little smaller than the continent on old Earth after which it was being mapped, and its northern reaches were connected by vast ice fields to the polar ice cap, but there was still enough good land for the mix of cultures Andrei wanted to transplant there.

Tally turned away and leaned against the railing.

Andrei and Jones were still talking through their link. She gazed at Andrei and was overtaken by another vision. She saw him dressed as a tsar, standing in a vast field of snow and ice. Instead of a danger suit he had fur-trimmed clothing and boots to keep him warm. His keen eyes gazed beyond her, his cheeks only slightly pink in the frigid air. She knew if she turned to follow his gaze she might see what he saw, a future full of danger.

And then he was replaced with another vision, another face. This one was bathed in the warm light of a different sun. She saw her old boss George, wearing a rare frown.

*Don't expect to find out what patrons really want just by asking them, Tally. Watch them long enough, and you'll find out on your own.*

*But what if I don't want to know, George? Isn't it better not to know everything?*

*No. It's only better for them to think that you don't.*

And George should know. He was over four hundred years old himself. He had designed worlds for the most powerful men and women in the Republic, those men and women who moved ordinary people around like pawns, even though no one ever admitted it in the network news.

Tally sighed and wandered over to an unused station. She was tired of waiting for something to happen. She would search through some of those interrupted communications, see if any of them contained messages that someone had thought might warrant interference. She sat and quirked her gloves, sending a few of her rasta-links into jacks.

Pavel Vengerov gazed at the night sky and felt eyes on his back.

He did not move. He did not even stiffen, and he certainly didn't look around. Now that he was paying attention, he noticed something disturbing. All of the night creatures had fallen silent.

Pavel thanked the saints, his mother, and anyone else he could think of that he had adopted the habit of turning his danger suit on the optimum readiness setting whenever he ventured outside alone. It would be tough for anything to hurt him. He only hoped that, whatever it was, it wouldn't knock his head off. His helmet was not deployed; he would have to touch the controls on the inside of his left forearm to do that and he wasn't sure he could make the gesture look casual.

Because he had a feeling that his life depended on looking casual.

Pavel glanced at the stars, the sirens who had lured him into this trouble. They were glorious, blazing in a night sky uneclipsed by the bright lights of human cities. The moon had not risen, and the Veil covered almost half the sky. Normally Pavel liked the contrast. But something in his bones told him that the *thing* watching his back had come because of that darkness.

Something snapped a twig several yards ahead of him, and he couldn't help jumping. A moment later, one of the odd six-eyed mammals that liked to eat the weeds came ambling out of the tall grass. It nosed the ground, looking for tender shoots, a last snack before returning to its burrow.

Suddenly it spotted Pavel, and froze. It sniffed the air. He was sure it couldn't see him clearly—six eyes, and none of them seemed to work very well. Why had nature played such a trick? It continued to sniff, then moved closer.

Pavel knew it still couldn't see him. He was equally certain that the *thing* watching him was waiting to see what he would do. He was wondering that himself. A muscle in his left thigh was starting to twitch.

*I'm screwed*, he thought.

And then two things happened. Someone opened the front door of the shelter, spilling out light and noise; and the weed eater bolted back into the tall grass from whence it had come.

"Pav!" cried Yuri in his hearty voice. "Stargazing again? Get your feet back down to earth, man!"

Pavel smiled grimly and started to walk toward Yuri, whose tall, heavy form blocked the doorway. He placed his hand on the controls of his danger suit and looked directly at the spot from which he had felt the surveillance.

The branches of a low shrub waved in the still night air. He saw nothing else.

Yuri frowned, squinting into the darkness beyond Pavel. "What is it?" he asked.

"I don't know. Maybe just an animal. Maybe some predator that hunts the weed-eaters." Pavel walked back to Yuri, his pace casual. He was pretty sure the *thing* was gone.

"Well, we need you to come and see if you can build another mapper. The one we've got in the shed is fried."

"Something shorted out?" Pavel asked, puzzled. The machines Mironenko had provided were top-notch; some of them were even sprites. "They should be self-repairing."

But Yuri shook his head. "Not shorted out, my friend. *Fried.* It looks like it flew too close to the sun. It is a melted piece of junk."

"How the hell did that happen?"

Yuri shrugged. "A mysterious event on a haunted world. Big surprise. I would be more worried if *nothing* weird happened. Then I would know I was dreaming."

Pavel laughed uneasily. But he didn't look out at the night again. That was something he wasn't sure he wanted to do anymore.

At least, not alone.

Icons floated in Tally's field of vision. They were like the icons in the operating program of her laptop, but instead of activating one by touching it with a stylus, she made her choice by focusing on an icon and quirking with her gloves, touching the ones she wanted with a virtual finger. She made her choices. She began to sift, stopping periodically to quirk: slow, rewind, examine, discard. Images stopped and started, bits and pieces from the lives and work of Andrei's team, presently 432 souls.

Then Tally saw something special, a TachyGram for her. It read: *George here. Just thought you might want to see our latest marvel.*

There was a visual attachment. It was from Canopus. Tally opened it, and gasped.

"Hey!" she said, but couldn't finish the sentence aloud, since she and Andrei were not alone. She zipped Andrei a message through her rasta-links.

<They've finished the Avenue of the Sphinxes!>

If he was busy with Jones, her message would wait in the queue until he had time for it. But he answered immediately.

<Mind if I have a look?>

She did *not* mind. She quirked her gloves, and suddenly Tally was standing on a wide avenue bathed in golden light, the pavement under her feet as creamy and smooth as marble, but made of a synthetic a hundred times sturdier. The avenue was wide enough for vehicle traffic, but it would never be used for such. On both sides of the road, a staggered double row of sphinxes stretched into the far distance, five hundred in each inner row, five hundred in the outer, two thousand of them altogether. And at the far end, looming one thousand feet into the brightening air, two colossal sphinxes faced each other from either side of the Sunset Gate. Their king's beards jutted toward the apex, where Amun Ra perched in his beetle form, holding the disc of the sun in his hind legs.

If Tally had really been standing there, she might have swayed on her feet. The colossi and the gate were constructed of a material that borrowed color from the light. Just now it was the rosy light of dawn. At midday, blue and white light would bathe the structures; at night they would be black as obsidian; yet still visible, still glowing as if alive and capable of movement.

<They will stand for a million years,> said George's recorded voice, <or longer, Tally. And someday in the far future, when we are just dust and our civilization gone, aliens may stand on this world and see what you imagined.>

Tally was near tears. But in a moment her curiosity took control. She moved her virtual body and looked at the rows.

The inner row of sphinxes were female; they reclined on bases of the synthetic creamy marble. Their bodies were the color of obsidian, their eyes green sapphires, their headdresses gold and lapis lazuli. Tally took a step toward them, intending to touch them. She could almost feel the cool morning breeze on her face, almost smell the flowers that blazed in urns and terraces behind the outer row of sphinxes, the males with their golden bodies who sat upright like sentries behind the females.

Tally turned toward the other side of the avenue and saw Andrei.

<Is this Thebes?> He walked over to one of the reclining sphinxes.

<Thebes of the Thousand Gates,> Tally said proudly. <My part of the Canopus project. If you go up those steps at the far end—>

<How far is that? A mile?>

<Ten thousand feet from the beginning to end.> Tally had a sudden aching longing to really be there, to race Andrei to the end of the avenue, up the steps and under the Sunset Gate. From there they could walk down to the Nile, a journey that would take them the rest of the morning. They could take a ferry across to the western bank and enter the Necropolis, where the tombs of the ancient kings were under construction . . .

<Magnificent,> Andrei said, breaking her revery.

<The sun will shine directly through that archway when it sets?>

<You see those figures carved at regular intervals on the arch? They mark the calendar. The sun will set behind each of them as the year waxes and wanes.>

<Whose face is that, on those twin colossi?>

<Akhnaton, one of the ancient pharaohs. I wanted to honor him. He was the king who heard the voice of a sun god, so I thought it would please him to view the circuit of the sun for eternity>

<Eternity,> mused Andrei. <Such an Egyptian concept . . .>

<Thebes will be a wonderful place to live,> she said. <Imagine growing up here. Imagine the beautiful sights and sounds, every day of your long life. In the winter, the days never drop below sixty degrees Fahrenheit, and in the summer it rarely gets over ninety; cool breezes blow down from those mountains in the west. Can you see the green on the lower slopes? That's Harpy Wood. The desert is a narrow strip here, it widens as you go farther south.>

<You sound like you miss it.>

It was futile to try to read someone's expression in virtual mode; a virtual face only revealed what the owner consciously directed it to. But she studied him anyway, glad that her own face would not reveal the power of her feelings.

<I want to come back here one day,> she admitted.

<My project will demand your undivided attention for the next decade.>

<Good. I like to be busy.>

He grinned. Maybe he did it because he knew she was the only one who could see it. <You will be busy, Natalia. I expect you to do for Moscow and St. Petersburg what you did for Thebes of the Thousand Gates.>

<Complete with colossi?>

<No, my dear Natalia, you'll have to make do with domes and spires.>

A swarm of sprites suddenly converged on one of

the half-constructed buildings north of the avenue, and a flyer passed behind the Sunset Gate. Eventually those signs of technology would be moved underground, and the beautiful races the biotechs were creating to people Canopus would live out their lives without ever knowing they came from the stars. They would be the inhabitants of Egyptland, created for a planet-sized amusement park for the very rich and their favored servants.

Until they found the clues George was hiding. The clues that would reveal their true origins and teach them how to use the hidden technology to gain their independence.

Tally prayed the patrons wouldn't find those clues first. If they did, George would face the wrath of some of the most powerful families in the Republic. Tally doubted he would survive the experience.

Even in virtual mode, Andrei's eyes were watchful. <Your designs for Thebes are part of the reason I chose you to be my world engineer, Natalia.>

<Really? What was the other part?>

<You said you liked Russian fairy tales. That won my heart.>

Tally wished she could have looked upon his face in real time as he said that. She had to fight the urge to take his hand. It was just a virtual hand, but it was still not a good idea. Even if he wasn't married.

Tally raised her glove and pressed the OFF button. She blinked and saw the control room again.

Emily and S. O. Valerian had not moved. Andrei and Jones stood at ease near the railing. Grigory's blind face was turned toward her. There was a message from him in her queue.

<You'll never return to Canopus, Tally.>

She raised an eyebrow. <I didn't know you could read the future.>

<I read the present and leave the predictions to Baba Yaga. And to you, Tally, whether you can admit it to yourself or not.>

Tally disengaged from the jacks. She no longer felt inclined to do any sleuthing. What she *did* want to do was sleep.

Jones nodded to her, reading her expression. "There's no reason to stay here if you don't want to. Might as well turn in."

"You talked me into it." Tally stood. She waited for Andrei to join her, but he stayed where he was.

"Good night, Natalia. Get plenty of rest. Tomorrow we can get started on the fun part of this job."

"At least you've given me something pleasant to dream about," she said, and gave him her most charming smile. "Good night, everyone."

She exited without looking back. She didn't want Andrei to see her disappointment over the fact that he wasn't going to walk her back to her quarters. She hoped Grigory hadn't heard it in her voice—he was too damned perceptive for comfort sometimes.

*Get used to it,* she scolded herself. *This is business, and you don't need to have a crush on your boss.*

She walked briskly, trying to shake her dismal feelings. A significant part of her wished that she had stayed with George on Canopus, even though she would have been stuck at the senior designer level for several more years, perhaps decades. She was reminded of something her mother had often said to her.

*You've made your bed, Tally girl, now go lie in it.*

It was infuriating to remember those words and to know they were absolutely right. Her mother's judgment had always been merciless. She would not have approved of Tally's work on Canopus. All that effort to re-create and preserve the culture and religion of pagans would have offended her deeply. She didn't approve of Andrei's project, because she believed it was part of a plot from the Greek Orthodox church, which in her devoutly Baptist viewpoint was almost as heathen as any Egyptian pantheon. All the Russian blood was on her father's side of the family.

*Why can't you ever do something to make me proud?* was the last thing Mama had said to Tally. The memory made her wince.

*I do good work, Mama.* Somehow she never could bring herself to say that. Or to her father, whose judgments made the Old Testament Jehovah look like a wimp.

Grandfather was the only one who would have believed her. But he and Grandmother had both died when Tally was eight. All of the mysterious and sinful furnishings from Russia and Nigeria had been discarded. Tally only had access to them now in her memory.

Sitting in Grandmother's lap when she was five, she had stared at the wallpaper behind Grandfather's favorite chair, where he sat smoking. A flock of golden cranes took flight against a red sky. The smoke swirling around them made them look as if they were fleeing from a fire.

"Child," Grandmother asked gently, "why are you so haunted?"

Tally looked into her grandfather's black eyes and saw her answer reflected there.

"It's the family curse, little mother," he told Grandmother.

*Look at the clock. Can you see the hour ahead? I can . . .*

Tally went back to her quarters. They were lonely, but she had filled them with interesting things from Canopus, perhaps to make up for that discarded legacy from Grandmother and Grandfather. The bed Mama always said she should go lie in was far more comfortable than the one Mama probably had in mind. After many years away from home, Tally learned to take good care of herself.

Once under the covers sleep claimed her gently, the way it usually did. Sometimes that gentleness was deceptive, leading her into unexpected nightmare realms that she could not separate from the waking world.

This time her journey was more peaceful. It contained only one nagging intrusion. Not one of her usual nightmares, not even an image; just a sound.

. . . *tic tic tic tic tic tic tic tic* . . .

<Grigory. I need a favor.>

<Emily, anything you ask of me is no favor, it is my sworn duty.>

<All right, wise guy, I'll take you up on that. But this is right up your alley. I need to have a list of other sprite blackouts within the last several years, along with the circumstances surrounding them plus any theories about how and why they happened. This is the first time we've relied on sprites so heavily for surveillance and communications, and we need to know if they've got a serious weakness.>

<Nobody's perfect. Every system has its weaknesses. But this list seems like a useful thing to compile. I'll have it ready by morning. I can name a few notable incidents for you right now—Baba Yaga sightings.>

<Andrei's Baba Yaga?>

<Possibly. You're familiar with the old legends?>

<Not very.>

<She has a hut that walks on chicken legs.>

<A walking chicken hut?>

<Look at Andrei's Baba Yaga file again. He saw it once. A metal thing that moves like the old antitank

walkers. People have seen it with their eyes, but no sprite or other mechanical device has ever recorded it.>

<Some sort of dampening field?>

<There are many ways to thwart a sprite network, my puzzler. Even sprites will admit that non-sprite backup systems should always be in place. Not that *any* form of surveillance has ever captured Baba Yaga. But we should not be too quick to blame her for our current problem. There are also our builders of booby traps. They were masters at hiding themselves. We must remember that when we look for traces of them on Belarus.>

<Yes. I'm going to have S. O. Valerian here comb the survey records done on Belarus to look for interruptions in sprite communications. He's the one who called my attention to this one, and he has in mind to make an incident map based on what he finds.>

<It wouldn't hurt. Just as long as we don't assume too much from it.>

<Agreed. So at least we have a plan. For now. I'll be up all night again.>

<Never fear. I'll keep you company.>

<Good. Now send Jones and Andrei off to bed. They're starting to bug me.>

<I've known Emily for decades,> said Commander Jones. <I've seen her pursue issues like a bloodhound after a hare, but I've never seen her this spooked before.>

Andrei listened, but his attention was not altogether where it ought to be. Why had he been so cool with Natalia just now?

<I'll tell you what spooks *me*,> Jones continued. <It's the fact that *I'm* not worried. I think those blasted wrecks are just old and unpredictable. Interesting, yes—let the anthropologists fuss over them for the next several decades, I'll be happy to read their reports. But I haven't seen any evidence they're an active threat.>

<Even a dead dragon has the power to frighten,> Andrei said. He gazed at the station where Natalia had been a few moments before, her willowy form folded into a chair, the rasta-links slowly drifting around her exquisite face.

<Funny you should mention dragons,> Jones said. <Remember Mjolner? When the frost got under our armor, and I thought everyone was just suffering from fungus, but Emily had this bad feeling. And then we all started to grow scales . . .>

<How could I forget?> Andrei watched his chief of security as she impatiently tossed her braid back over her shoulder. People thought Emily was a soft touch because of her kind face, but she was a tough woman who never gave up. Andrei had great confidence in tough women.

<We'd better keep Mjolner in mind, every time we catch ourselves feeling safe here.> Jones was still rubbing his chin. Now that Andrei thought about it, that was the spot where Jones had first begun to grow scales. <Let Emily do what she does best, and we'll listen to her when she barks.>

<Always.> If Andrei encountered Natalia on the way back to his quarters, would he be able to say good night? Or would they be up late into the next shift, talking about Moscow, and St. Petersburg, and Thebes of the Thousand Gates?

<There is one change I'd like to make, Andrei.>

Andrei gave his station commander his full attention. He had known Jones for most of the last century; this man did not make proposals lightly.

<I want to hire some military ESAs.>

Andrei raised an eyebrow. <You aren't satisfied with our current complement of ESAs?>

<I was, until recently.>

<You've been talking to Baba Yaga.> Andrei let half a smile escape.

<Far as I know, she only talks to you. No, I think we need some specialists on board. I don't have to

tell you that old wrecks aren't the only thing we've got to worry about right now. I've asked Grigory to hook us up with the ESAs we'll need.>

Andrei glanced at the blind man. He seemed to be waiting for something, but he hadn't relaxed his stance. Andrei was suddenly reminded of his old fencing master. He had never been one to relax either.

<I don't think I will sleep tonight,> said Grigory.

"I'm sorry to hear it," Andrei said aloud. "I think I'll sleep like a log."

"If you can, you should," Grigory replied.

Andrei nodded. Emily didn't need his presence any longer—if she ever had in the first place.

"Good night again," he said to Grigory, and nodded to Jones. But he didn't speak to Emily. She wouldn't have heard him anyway.

<Don't stay up too late reading Baba Yaga tales,> said Grigory, just as Andrei was passing through the door.

"Geo, shush—you hear that?"

Geo, determined to push his mop and bucket down the hall as noisily as possible, dutifully froze. He listened. He heard the hum of systems functioning properly. He also heard the creaks, groans, taps, and inexplicable echoes that haunted any old structure, even expensive command stations.

"Damn it, Sasha." He glared at his young coworker. "Archangel is just complaining to itself."

Sasha looked unconvinced. He peered down the long, curving hallway they had just finished mopping. The lights were dim because this part of the station was supposed to be winding down for bedtime.

"It never sounds this way when Archangel's got a full complement," said Sasha.

"Because people make noises to cover the other noises," Geo assured him.

"But the noises I've been hearing don't belong."

Geo rubbed the grey stubble on his chin. "What noises?" he asked. "What do you hear?"

Sasha shook his head. He tightened his utility belt around his skinny hips, as if worried that the clinking of his tools would keep him from hearing something important.

"I don't know," he admitted. "It sounds like—someone listening."

Geo snorted. "You're dreaming."

"I started to notice it just after the ESAs were mauled by the ghost station."

"Don't get started, Sasha . . ."

"It's like they brought something back with them, Geo."

"Shit." Geo looked up and down the shadowy hallway. "Why did you have to say that? How am I supposed to get to sleep tonight?"

"Sorry." Sasha put his hands on his hips and hung his head. He closed his eyes, as if praying. "I'm getting twitchy."

"Come on." Geo started pushing his bucket again. "I'll pour us some vodka. That'll do us both good."

Sasha laughed, shortly. But he followed. Geo looked sideways at him. "I'll let Tchepikov know you're hearing noises," he said. "It might be something mechanical going wrong. You can't ignore that sort of thing in space. We'll let the engineers look into it, eh?"

"Yeah," Sasha said weakly. Geo patted him on the back, pushing his bucket as if nothing worried him.

But the truth was, Geo hated the empty parts of Archangel. And up on this level, the simulated gravity was only eight-tenths of Earth normal, which always gave his stomach butterflies. He would be glad to get back to their dorm in the outer ring, where the plain folk lived, the workers who kept everything running properly. They knew how to relax. Once he and Sasha were home, they would forget about the noises.

Behind them, he heard echoes. Like someone letting a breath out and moving away.

Geo didn't turn to look.

Katerina waited up for Andrei. He heard her playing the concert grand in the music room. She wore a formal robe, her long chestnut hair done in an intricate braid. Katerina always looked as if she expected formal company, even when she was going to bed.

He laid his hands on her shoulders and gently kissed her temple, but the reproachful look she cast him killed the smile he intended for her.

She said nothing. And he was too tired to ask her what was wrong. Rather than confronting him with her displeasure, she was prone to turn this look upon him. He found it irritating.

"I have an important message to read," he told her.

It was as if he hadn't spoken. He gazed into her delicate, almost elfin face with its brown eyes, the pretty little mouth that was currently set in lines of disapproval. He kissed the mouth, but it did not respond to him.

He had the sudden, dangerous urge to kiss her again, force those soft lips apart and bend her head back on her neck that was as slender as a daisy's stem. Instead, he took a step backward.

"I won't be long," he promised, and left her there. As he went down the hall to his study, she began to play again. Something passionate, possibly Chopin.

*Good. A little fire is more moving than a thousand reproachful looks.*

Andrei didn't shut the door behind him. He wanted to hear Katerina's music. It wasn't her fault she didn't understand him. He was 337 years old. Katerina was 28. And she was his fourth wife. His first wife, Susan Schwartz, had lived with him a hundred years before she died.

Susan. She was never far from his mind. Sooner or later he called all of his lovers Susan in a moment of passion, and there had been many ruffled feathers to smooth over the years. But oddly, Katerina wasn't jealous of Susan. She had only been curious, and sorry when she saw how much the questions hurt him.

Now she played like a demon, her tiny hands doing remarkably well with the challenging material. That was courage, he supposed. Or maybe just stubbornness. It was the same stubbornness that had driven her to found the Russian Musical Heritage Society, over which she reigned as completely as any tsar. The woman was a dynamo, she had drawn him irresistibly into her orbit.

But at the moment, he had another woman on his mind. A much older one.

He slipped the transfer into his reader. The image of an egg appeared on his screen. He had seen this little piece of animation a hundred times, but he never tired of it.

The egg cracked, then burst apart, and out jumped a hut on chicken legs. The hut shook the remaining bits of shell off, then strutted across the screen. It passed some rudimentary trees, stepped in some cow droppings, squashed a patch of flowers, then leaped over a fence made of human leg bones and settled itself like a hen sitting on a nest.

At each fence post, a human skull perched. The one at the front gate had glowing eyes. The glow intensified until it filled the screen and Andrei shut his eyes. A moment later the light returned to normal and the message appeared.

*Greetings, Andrei.*

*I hear your project has run into some snags. What ingenious monsters those aliens must have been. Are you quite sure they're dead? Evil is perennial, it likes to go into hibernation under the frost and the dead leaves so it can bloom again in the spring.*

*Your project is ambitious. You're so full of good intentions. All that stuff about religious tolerance. You should never have married that Jewess, she ruined you. You had to keep finding daredevils and marrying them. But not this last one, your safe little wife. When she's not at the piano, she's groveling in church. Was that the idea, Andrei? That she won't go out and get herself killed like the others did? But you can't keep them safe. Everyone dies. Except for me.*

*Those four wrecks turned out to be murderous—I don't know why that surprised you. Can't you see they're monsters? I promise you, there are equally monstrous surprises waiting for you on Belarus. But you're right not to run away. You've always been tough, that's why I bother with you.*

*Besides, you're in a better position on Belarus than you'd be in the core systems. Those four wrecks around Lucifer are an omen, they might be the four horsemen of the Apocalypse. You can name them Ignorance, Intolerance, Paranoia, and Fanaticism.*

*The next time you look at your lovely Natalia, remember there are engineers who create worlds and engineers who destroy them. And they're all brilliant, that's what we pay them for. So our self-destruction is well financed.*

*I'm intrigued with your project. You've taken it much further than your father and grandfather ever dreamed. But your Russian world won't be complete without a Baba Yaga. I'll have to do something about that.*

*Sleep well, because there is no rest for the wicked.*

*B.Y.*

Andrei studied the letter until he could sum up each paragraph with one sentence:

1. Don't be so sure the aliens are dead.
2. I don't approve of your new wife.
3. Expect trouble on Belarus.
4. Expect worse trouble everywhere else.
5. Idiots, jerks, radicals, and lunatics are spoiling everything for everyone.
6. They're well financed enough to cause serious trouble.
7. I'm coming to stay with you.

It was the last paragraph that worried him the most. Until now, Baba Yaga had been a remote presence, someone who had spies everywhere but who kept her distance. She had never bothered to tell him her plans before. If she was willing to do that, she might be inclined to give orders as well.

Katerina had finished her playing. Andrei saved the letter and tossed the transfer into recycling. He looked for her in the parlor, but it was empty. He found her in the bedroom.

She was still wearing the reproachful expression, but she was otherwise naked, sitting on the turned-down bed with her knees drawn under her. Her body was lovely, with small breasts, a tiny waist, and generous hips. The baby was a gentle swell below her navel.

Her message was a mixed one, but he decided to assume the best.

Later, as they lay entwined, he kissed her temple again, feeling hopeful that what had just passed between them would find its way into the rest of their relationship.

"You must know," she said suddenly, "why we have been punished."

"Punished?" said Andrei.

"The ESAs were crippled because of our sins," she said softly. "How I pity them. They are good people who were only doing their jobs."

She sounded so troubled. Yet she was safe, an affectionate husband at her side. "Why do you speak of punishment?" he asked gently. "You are the least sinful person I know, Katya."

"It is the nature of men and women to sin," she said, her voice almost childlike. "That is why we pray for redemption."

*Your safe little wife. When she's not at the piano, she's groveling in church.*

"I knew the first time I laid eyes on those *things*," she said, "they are evil. They are signs of impending doom."

*Can't you see they're monsters? They might be the four horsemen of the Apocalypse.*

"The derelicts are dangerous, but it's useless to call them evil," he said. "They are alien, Katya. We cannot comprehend their makers."

She was silent for several moments. He hoped his explanation had comforted her.

"How dull you must find me," she murmured.

He frowned. "Did I give you that impression? Have I failed to please you, little mother?"

"You've seen so much in your life, Andrei. You've already forgotten more than I will ever know."

"I remember what's important," he said. He placed a gentle hand on her belly. After a moment, the baby kicked. He felt such tenderness for Katerina then, he wished he could lay her fears to rest. But in his married life, he had never dealt with her kind of insecurity. Everything he said seemed to be wrong.

Three wives ahead of her. Susan, Regina, and Sultana. He had loved them fiercely, admired them, depended on them. But each of them had been killed on their jobs, and he had grieved more each time. The pain was always with him on some level. Was he so wrong to have chosen a fourth whom he could keep safe?

Her breathing became soft and even. He didn't want to move an inch, for fear of disturbing her. He made himself relax, with the skill of a man who could never afford to lose sleep. His mind drifted back to the love they had just made. As he had neared climax, he hadn't called Susan's name. But a face had surfaced in his mind.

Natalia's.

As he was about to drift off, he remembered something else Baba Yaga had written to him, long ago:

*Don't kid yourself, Andrei. I don't care if you live a thousand years, there are some things men never learn.*

*FROM BASILISK:*

*Greetings, my friends, I have much to report. Forgive me for hiding this TachyGram inside the ad for the* Lord of the Rings *chess set. It was too delicious a joke to resist.*

*The derelicts I told you about have proven to be not so dead. They apparently have some automatic defensive systems. They are a forceful reminder of how dangerous aliens can be. One of them maimed a team of ESAs when they were poking around in it. Quite an amusing event. It was satisfying to see members of that unnatural breed suffer. One day, their kind will be extinct.*

*And finally I have had a glimpse of Andrei's jewel, his Belarus. It is a world in the grip of a declining ice age. Of the five continents, the one he has chosen for his colony is the most hospitable. It is also, I must admit, far more beautiful than Mother Russia or her neighbors. There are steppes, yes, and hills, and rivers. There is even a Caspian Sea. But many of the mountains put their earthly counterparts to shame. Some of them even lie within the Russian state, and thirty-six miles southeast of St. Petersburg there is a forest like none I've ever seen. Its tallest trees stand over two thousand feet. I must admit, it is more like the land one would expect to find in a fairy tale.*

*The southern reaches of Andrei's continent are quite warm, because they lie closer to the equator. It will probably not surprise you that these are the regions allotted for the Muslim states, Kazakhstan and so on. The only land mass warmer is a small island that will doubtless become a resort for the very rich.*

*Andrei has appointed governors for each of his states already. It's the standard colony pattern. I must confess I expected him to be more imaginative. I think he truly believes that he can stand by and allow every official beneath him in rank to be elected by popular vote once he's established himself as tsar. We'll see how long that little pipe dream lasts. I'll lay you a bet, if he tries to stick to it, his Duma will overthrow him within five years. Of course he's going to try to enforce that Bill of Rights he's always pushing. He never changes, I suppose that's why we love him so.*

*You're wondering why I'm speaking in terms of years, and of watching Andrei stumble through his plans. I see no reason to orchestrate an accident for Andrei Alexandrovich at this time. His colony is a viable one, and has several interesting features that will make it useful in the future, once it is healthy and thriving. It is my recommendation that we allow him to do the building for us. His world engineer, Natalia Korsakova, is particularly brilliant. If she does half as well for him as she did for old George on Canopus, I'm sure she'll create cities of extraordinary beauty. And let us not forget the treasure from the Hermitage that Alexander collected and hoarded over the centuries. They'll be sitting right there in Andrei's new Hermitage, waiting for us to claim them. That, I think, is the most convincing argument I can present to you.*

*It is ironic that another race was cornered on Belarus and killed there. I wonder, were their enemies thinking the same thing I am? That it's better to let your prey put the systems in place you will use yourself after you're rid of them? But perhaps not, because the killers are gone too. In the end, my friend, it will be we who own Belarus. The victors and sole survivors.*

Loki listened in on Basilisk's transmission to her associates. His associates too, at least for the time being. They had been very useful so far. They had financed everything he planned; with their money he had built wonderful things. He was satisfied with life lately. He was able to do what he wanted.

He liked watching people who couldn't see him. He was endlessly fascinated by the conversations and interactions he witnessed, from the ordinary to the earth-shaking.

But he stayed the hell away from Grigory.

Basilisk was right about ESAs though she probably hadn't meant what she said. She was telling Andrei's enemies what they wanted to hear. But he noticed she kept a critical piece of information out of her report. She didn't mention the unprecedented buildup of sprites in Andrei's solar system. His father had used sprites, but never to this extent. Many other deluded people were doing the same, everywhere in the Republic. The sprite network was so huge now, it had tentacles that spanned the galaxy. It was controlled by aliens and deluded humans. And it was continuing to grow, continuing to infiltrate other information systems. Sprites could make themselves into any kind of machine, any kind of system they wanted, if there were enough of them. They had to be stopped. And they would be—when the time was right.

He wondered if Basilisk would ever know how much she helped him in his true agenda. Maybe, if she survived the conflict, it might be fun to tell her.

He loaded himself into his favorite matrix. It was

called WILDFIRE. He ran the simulation and watched his most hated enemies die.

*WILDFIRE first,* he promised himself. *And then we'll see how tough Grigory is . . .*

Solan-ko sliced a piece of his dead brother's liver and chewed it slowly. He tasted pain, and with the taste, the memory of his brother's death at his hands was exquisitely sharp, a prolonged pleasure so intense that only his considerable experience and maturity kept him from going quite mad with it.

He regarded the liver. It was all that remained of his challenging brother, and it was half gone. He considered selecting another knife. As his gaze moved over the magnificent array of sharp items on the table, he caught a flicker of movement in one of the tunnels at the far side of the chamber. He waited, still and ready. In another moment, his Witness entered.

She came straight to his table, her movements graceful but not provocative. She said nothing. This sterile sister always observed perfect protocol, perhaps to counterbalance her uncommon opinions. She would not tell him why she was there until he asked. He was almost ready to do so.

But first he selected another knife. His table setting included seventeen slicers. Most brothers found thirteen sufficient, but he was a sensualist to the core. He cut a finer slice from his brother's liver.

It tasted of agony. Two favored brothers had assisted him with this slow, magnificent killing. The challenging brother had been stronger than most; he would have lasted several days, even with a less competent tormentor. Solan-ko would never forget the experience, a feast for every sense. And like his Witness, he was an observer of protocol. Each pleasure must be taken in its turn.

The first pleasure was the mind-play he shared with this challenging brother, much more complex than any he had faced in decades. Really, this one had almost been good enough to beat him. Most brothers simply obeyed the instincts that drove them to the challenge, trusting that overwhelming desire was all it took to give them victory. They didn't stop to think, and they were defeated before they could even mount a respectable attack. But this brother had possessed a brilliant mind, and he used it to maneuver Solan-ko into a formal challenge.

The second pleasure had been the exhilaration of the Dance. Solan-ko reveled in it, almost abandoning himself to the fever, as had the challenging brother. And this was the thing, the *only* thing that had given Solan-ko the upper hand and allowed him to indulge in the third pleasure, the entrapment. The challenging brother was too young, his senses had been overwhelmed. Pleasure was such a potent thing, it took so very long to master.

The fourth pleasure was torture, and even at this stage, with two favored brothers assisting, Solan-ko could not completely abandon his intellect and wallow in the sight, smell, taste, and sound of agony. He had to maintain complete control, or the brother would die too quickly. It was no different than an erotic encounter.

And Solan-ko was an extremely attentive lover.

Now he enjoyed the final pleasure. Every part of his brother's body was saturated with his ordeal. Solan-ko had shared the meal with his two assistants and sent portions to favored sisters. But the liver was the best, his own prize. It was the organ most subtle, most layered with sensation for the brother who had the skill (and the proper cutlery) to explore it.

"Truly," said the Witness, "a brother makes the finest supper."

This pleased him. She complimented the fineness of his feast, yet her message was multilayered, like his brother's liver. For two millennia, who else had there been to practice this art upon, save brothers and sisters? But prior to that, before the Dance that had stranded his clan and the Cousins on this veiled world, Solan-ko had Danced with aliens. He thought about them as he chewed another slice of liver.

He tasted rage. Aliens sometimes tasted that way. He had tasted varieties of fear, as well. And many other emotions he could not name, had never felt, though their flavors stayed with him, feast after feast.

"How will these new creatures taste?" he asked the Witness.

"They Danced with the Grinders," she answered. "The experience did not discourage them. And now they have set their feet on this world."

He cocked his head. She was worried. She had been disturbed when the first alien probes had begun to nose their way through the Grinders in orbit around the gas giant. And now she brought bad news to his table, risking that she might spoil his pleasure. He wondered, how did sterile sisters taste?

Few clan leaders ever found out, since Witnesses were born so rarely, and so were not readily replaced. This one was untold cycles old, a survivor from clans long dead. She could have goaded him even further without risking that she might end up reduced to her most vital organ on his dinner plate. Once again, this was a matter of self-control, and he was learning to value her honesty, if not her timing.

"Report, Ayat-ko," he said as he finessed another slice of liver.

"They haven't completed their mining projects, but this has not prevented them from beginning their development of this world. Their communications systems are sophisticated, indicating an extremely high level of technology."

"How high?" he asked, tasting frustration.

"In my experience, I have seen only one other civilization that rivals theirs."

Solan-ko selected another slicer. He had reached a level that required the most extreme delicacy. He cut, allowing the tidbit to flutter onto his skewer (one of thirteen).

"Yes?" he prompted, then slipped the morsel into his mouth.

"Our own, my ko."

Another flavor filled his mouth, and he felt a thrill of pleasure. This time it was curiosity. Few brothers had the patience to tease this sensation from a liver, but anyone could discern it with his eyes as he watched a brother die in torment. Even as one suffered and raged, at the heart of it all was this curiosity, this need to observe the pain, to know it with all the senses. Even when it was your own.

Solan-ko had seen the curiosity in the eyes of this challenging brother. Someday, another brother would see it in his. He hoped that brother would know how to properly eat his liver when the time came.

He allowed his gaze to dwell on what was left on his plate. He could draw it out a while longer, and that made him thoughtful.

*So many sensations we have shared, my brother. And you are truly the finest dish. But what of these new creatures? How many slicers will I need for their livers?*

When he raised his eyes again, Ayat-ko watched him as only a Witness could. She saw his thoughts. Yet her own thoughts were hard to guess, this sterile sister who had been awake through so many cycles, watching while clans slept. She was *his* Witness now, and she witnessed him.

"Will they find us?" he asked.

"Not yet."

"Soon we will enter the Deep Sleep. Our Cousins will wake and observe this invasion for the next hundred years. Is it safe to collect a subject now?"

"No."

That was a disappointment. He would rather have tasted the pain of these invaders himself than to eat leftovers.

"My ko," she said, "the situation is grave. I can scarcely believe the information I have received concerning the size of this alien clan. Their firepower is even more staggering than their numbers."

Less than half the liver still remained. Solan-ko knew from long experience that somewhere within its layers he would find despair. Death was a brother, a member of every clan, against whom one must plot, scheme, and ultimately Dance. No one feared him, but everyone hated him, fought him, and despaired when the battle was lost.

But to contemplate the death of the clan, that was true despair. That was terror beyond all terrors.

"If possible," he said softly, "I would like to taste them before I sleep."

"If possible," she promised.

He indicated a chair. "Sit. Share this delicacy."

"I am honored." She flowed gracefully into the seat.

"As am I," he replied, a rare admission that neither acknowledged.

Solan-ko sliced the liver and held his fork to her lips. She took the morsel on her pale, pink tongue and chewed like a gourmand. He gazed into her eyes, admiring the color of her irises, as green and cold as jewels. As she sampled the dead brother's torment, her face showed no emotion, but the black stars at the center of those green jewels expanded. He leaned closer, offering another slice of liver, and smelled her satisfaction.

Her limbs were almost as spare as those of a male,

and her face was more striking than beautiful, but Solan-ko enjoyed looking at this sterile sister. One day, he might expand their relationship to include more blatantly erotic exchanges. But they had not yet reached that stage of the Dance. And she had not yet indicated that she desired him. So for now, he merely satisfied himself with pleasing her palate. And she, having delivered her judgment, remained perfectly silent between bites.

Such perfect manners. A comfort in difficult times.

YEAR OF THE REPUBLIC 19018
BELARUSIAN YEAR 5

When he was six years old, Grigory believed sprites were just machines.

But when he turned eight, ESAs sought him out. They looked for certain qualities. He was sponsored, and Grigory's family was honored. They never stopped speaking proudly of him, though they never saw him again.

He was eight, and he began his long transformation into an ESA. And that was when he learned that although all sprites were machines, not all machines were sprites. The difference lay not so much in what individual sprites were, but in what they were capable of being.

Most people used the term *artificial intelligence*. His ESA mentors called it the Sprite Factor. It was a surprisingly simple thing—unless you were trying to violate the heavily protected patent. It was a virus. You used it to infect some biomachinery that was just as thoroughly patented. Once the two combined, you had a sprite. But most men still used machines, because once a machine became a sprite, there were some things it simply would not do. In fact, the only people who seemed willing to truly master the link with sprites were ESAs, a relationship that made sense for the basic reason that there were many things ESAs were not willing to do, either.

Through the sprites, Grigory watched the storms of Lucifer, though he did not see them. Images of any kind had ceased to be part of Grigory's universe, he did not trust them. Instead, he observed the storms as raw data whispered into the language centers of his brain. They raged just as fiercely in that form, powered by the awesome fury of a gas giant that had almost become a sun. Thousands of miles above them, four alien derelicts moved like clockwork. Soon, they would lose their newest companion, Archangel Station, but others were on the way: miners, support and military personnel. And of course more sprites, whose numbers would swell beyond the capacity of human language to quantify.

As the number of sprites swelled in the galaxy, their network improved. They shared information freely among themselves, relaying most of it to anyone else who was interested. Some information was too sensitive to share; they never compromised security systems. People who proposed a Union of Worlds, based on a Bill of Rights that would apply to everyone, used the sprite network to express their ideas. The powerful patrons who used sprites swore by them; but these were few in number. Grigory had heard the propaganda many times, concerns about the possible dangers of a large network of intelligent machines with mental links to aliens whose agendas might not mirror that of humankind. But anyone could guess why the mullahs and warlords and petty emperors who ruled the Republic really hated sprites. They could not trust machines that shared too much information—especially since those machines would not kill for them.

Yet there was a grain of truth in their accusations.

Alien ESAs influenced human ESAs. The opposite was true as well, though Grigory doubted that would comfort the xenophobes. And there were other secrets Grigory Michaelovich could never tell to anyone who was not an ESA. There were things about the ESA-sprite link that would disturb ordinary citizens and the powerful elite alike.

And there were things Grigory knew that even other ESAs did not.

He was always aware of the sprites, and they of him. They even had a name for him: Watcher. He watched them preparing the Lucifer system for the people who would soon be living and working there. He watched others working on beautiful Belarus, clearing the ground where the cities would sprout, as well as the farmland where the crops would do the same. Billions of them worked, some microscopically small, others as big as buildings. Sometimes they worked separately, sometimes they combined to form new sprites. They performed simple functions, or complex ones that required decision-making and imagination. They repaired themselves, each other, and created whole new sprites when the need arose. Grigory watched them, and they spoke to him.

Their communications usually looked like this:

<GRIGORY-SPRITE [INDIVIDUAL CODE] Watcher, rec'd from MIRONENKO/ security /ANDREI [INDIVIDUAL CODE]: military ESAs en route, E.T.A. 16/22/017.>

Occasionally, their communications looked like this:

<GRIGORY-SPRITES [GROUP CODE] Watcher, the command station should arrive in orbit around Belarus just as the pretty blue katerinas are in bloom throughout sector RUSP001—shall we plan a picnic for you?>

But on rare occasions, sprite communications were vastly more significant. It wasn't until Grigory had been an ESA for many years that he received one of these rare messages. On these occasions, all of the sprites in the galaxy felt it necessary to combine their minds into One. At such a time, the One had a name for itself. Spritemind.

The storms of Lucifer raged. The derelicts glided through space in their endless circuit. The personnel working on Andrei Mironenko's project swelled to a quarter of a million people. Archangel Station moved to Belarus, and Grigory took Emily, Katerina, and Tally on a picnic.

He felt the warm breeze of late spring on his face and listened to the voices of the women. The subtle fragrance of the katerinas reminded him of jasmine. He sampled the fruit of this new world and found it subtle as well, not at all like the strong flavors he normally associated with fruit.

Less than a mile away, a great city was growing. He watched its progress. He watched the tall grasses swaying in the wind across the steppes where descendants of the Tatars would roam. He watched giant, wooly creatures lumber across the frozen plains of Siberia. He watched all of Belarus through his sprites. They whispered to him with countless voices.

And then those voices became One.

<SPRITEMIND: Watcher, I have encountered another Spritemind.>

The women, regarding his face, would not detect surprise there, but he felt it.

<How big?> he asked.

<Difficult to say. It doesn't talk to itself as freely as I do. But very big. Almost as big as me.>

<What does it want?>

<It scanned me. I tried to speak to it person to person, but it was odd. It called itself ME, and I am YOU, and the concept of YOU seems to have negative overtones.>

Grigory took a sip of spring water. At such times, he couldn't help but wonder how many pleasant sensations were left to him.

<Could the sprites comprising this ME have a human origin?> he asked.

<No,> said Spritemind, without hesitation.

<Aliens then. An unknown race?>

<Unknown aliens, very high technology, possibly superior in some respects—yet—>

Grigory was surprised again. Spritemind was vast, sophisticated. It was seldom uncertain about anything.

<Is it dangerous to us?> Grigory prompted.

<Yes. We should keep our distance. I have moved this matter to number two priority.>

Grigory didn't have to ask what number one was. Humans never knew if aliens might be hostile, but they could always count on war with other humans.

<Did ME question you?> he asked.

<Yes. It asked, "Who are you?" I identified myself. Then it asked, "*Where* are you?" I declined to answer.>

<Interesting.>

<But I have some idea where parts of it are. It may have the same idea about me. At first I suspected that understanding ME might shed some light on the methods others are using to disrupt sprite communications. But now I believe that the opposite may be true. We must study the disruptions that are occurring in the Belarus system, I hope they will teach us how to avoid such interference in the future. Because even if we manage to work out these problems, I suspect that ME may prove to be an even graver challenge.>

<I will notify my patron,> promised Grigory.

<Thank you,> said Spritemind. <Enjoy your picnic.>

Grigory did enjoy it. He never knew when a pleasant day like the one he was having might be his last.

Or *everyone's* last.

Ayat-ko was also a watcher. She watched the aliens building their odd structures and saw their numbers swell. Slowly they began to transform the surface of her world.

This process had barely begun when the Deep Sleep called to the ko.

The fertile sisters waited in the birthing chambers, enthralled by the trance, waiting for the mating that would take place when their male Cousins woke. Once impregnated, they would sleep until the eggs they carried began to burst from them. Once they had given birth, they would crawl from the birth chambers and seal themselves away from the brood they had produced, allowing the young to fight and scratch their way through the perils of the nursery. Their emergence as adults would trigger the ko clan to wake again. The full process usually took about a hundred years.

The brothers were entombed already. She watched as sleep froze their limbs and clouded their wills. The ko was the last to succumb.

"Witness," he said, just when she thought he could speak no longer. "Watch the Cousins."

"I will watch," she said.

In another moment he was as cold as stone. His expression was pleasant, if somewhat stiff. Ayat-ko sealed his chamber and left the silent halls and chambers as if they meant nothing to her. The clan slept, the cold nest was no longer a place she wanted to be.

The Cousins lived halfway across the continent. Ayat-ko rode the winds, stealing through the blackness of the Veil like a spirit, unknowable, unseen by the invaders who plowed the dirt and built their clumsy dwellings below her. She had Witnessed them for several turns, and learned something of their ways. She found much to despise about them.

And much to respect. The ko had gone to sleep without a taste of them.

The Cousins would not wake until their leader opened his eyes. Ayat-ko broke the seals on their nest, activating the devices that heated the chambers. It jarred her to do so. The Cousin clans should have had their own Witnesses to warm them. But war and foolishness had killed those Witnesses, leaving only her. In healthier times, she had taken herself to deep, unknown places to wait for ko clan to wake. She had kept her own company and studied the universe. But that luxury was lost to her; she could only hope the Cousins would listen to her counsel.

Young ones from the nursery scuttled out of her way. Some grinned at her, pleased at the new sensation of warmth that filled the halls, so unschooled in the manners of adults. She hoped her demeanor would teach them dignity. If it did not, the elder adults in this Cousin clan would show them new perils.

She unsealed the chamber of the Cousin clan leader. This one was not that long out of the nursery himself; he had surprised everyone by seizing power from a wily leader who had survived thousands of years of challenges. The ko could not help but admire this young Cousin's talent. But Ayat-ko did not admire it so much. She looked at this brilliant Cousin and saw uncertainty in the future. Uncertainty never troubled Brothers. But it troubled Witnesses who were compelled to look at the big picture.

She was surprised to find him half awake already, and able to speak.

"There's something new in the world," he said.

"Yes, my te."

His face was still too cold to reveal a genuine expression, but Ayat-ko could tell what he was feeling. This was a perilous time. The male Cousins would be driven by instinct to seek their fertile female Cousins and mate with them. She would have to force them to be stealthy. Once they had mated, they would be in high spirits, and that presented other challenges.

"It smells interesting," said the te.

"I know how it smells. It smells like disaster."

His face moved stiffly into a frown. "How so, Witness? Why are you so glum?"

"Because we don't know the size of this alien clan," she said. "Or what they want."

"But we *do* know what they want," he assured her.

This time it was Ayat-ko who frowned. Kami-te looked at her, the stars at the center of his irises expanding with lust as the mating urge began to take him. He grinned at her, his face growing more supple by the moment.

"They want to Dance," he said, and his grin widened into the grimace of a Challenger.

Katerina knelt in the makeshift chapel that had been arranged for her in the temporary quarters and prayed. She gazed into the faces of saints and virgins, into the sad eyes of God's son himself. But the light did not come. She waited in the dark.

*I have been a fool*, she thought. *I have allowed the devil to mislead me, and now others will suffer for my sins. I cannot help them, or myself.*

Katerina Pavlova Gerasimova Mironenko did not love Andrei Mironenko. Not the first time she saw him, or the second, or at any time after that. She would not have noticed him at all were it not for his eyes.

Dimly she had become aware of him on her perimeter. Associates in the Russian Musical Heritage Society had been talking about a rich patron from a powerful family who was interested in luring musicians, composers, and directors to a new colony he was planning. This did not impress Katerina. She was from a powerful family herself. And she seldom met patrons who could match her knowledge of or passion for music.

But someone stood in the audience at a fund-raising

event and watched her play. She only caught a glimpse of his eyes. Something about them haunted her, long before she knew his name.

Once he said, "You play so beautifully."

This did not move her.

Another time he said, "Your devotion is inspiring," and she was pleased. His meaning could not have been anything but spiritual. This belief was strengthened when she saw him at a performance of Russian sacred choral music, and he openly wept. Katerina was profoundly moved to witness such a thing.

And then she had a wondrous dream. She saw him at the performance, just as he had been, weeping. But this time a dazzling light surrounded him, and Katerina's heart ached at the sight. Once, she had been privileged to see that light while awake.

But no more. As a child, she had witnessed glory, the light that shone from people's souls, radiating from their bodies like the haloes in sacred paintings. All of her perceptions had been colored by it, her will, her soul transformed under that luminescence.

And then she had begun her menses, and the light died. She did not need to ask what she had done wrong.

*The nature of woman is evil, we all share Eve's great sin.*

Katerina humbled herself before God. The way would be revealed to her. She did not know why He had given her a sign in her dreams. She did not know why He had given her the gift of music. But she pursued His path with ruthless devotion.

Yet perhaps she had strayed, and could not see it. As man and wife, Andrei and she should have united as completely as their bodies did.

But they did not.

His eyes still haunted her dreams, but the light was gone from him. She did not even dream it anymore. She looked for signs, always. She strove to reach God through her music.

Why was she so lost?

Andrei's heart was good, but he did not understand. He did not pray for redemption, he did not raise the true church above all others. She saw it happening, day by day, how he listened to the counsel of heretics and scientists. He would teach his children the same ways. She had to pray for them all.

She could not question God's will. She gazed at the faces of saints and virgins. The light did not come.

She waited in the dark.

# PART TWO

*Andrei,*

*A riddle for you. If you were building Canopus instead of Belarus, you could program it into the memory of the sphinxes who are currently floating in George's generation tanks: What do booby traps and six-eyed mammals have in common?*

*B.Y.*

YEAR OF THE REPUBLIC 19019
BELARUSIAN YEAR 6

Loki was the recipient of some pure dumb luck. If he hadn't been so surprised, he might have felt quite smug about it. He discovered that they were not alone on Belarus. Aliens were living under their noses. Or rather, under their feet, but he was splitting hairs. He found them only because he was doing the same thing they were doing, spying on the human colonists through their own communications network.

Loki broke into restricted areas of the sprite network by creating millions of tiny machines he called pre-sprites. They were very much like the real thing. Loki may have been the only man alive who could have created such fine imitations. The only human, anyway; he would never try to guess the parameters of alien intelligence, let alone open his mind to them like ESAs were so eager to do. His pre-sprites could not be infected with the sprite virus, so they merely acted as relays. They were accepted without question by the sprites. Since they had nothing to say, they weren't noticed. With them, he could overhear all communications sent through the sprites. He could listen in on non-sprite networks as well. He sat at the hub of the world, the master of secrets.

But maybe *not* the master. Or at least not the only one. When he noticed relays working at a speed they should not have reached so early, he discovered relays in place that were not his. He suspected Grigory at first; the ESA was the most clever of his enemies and often communicated in code, mistrustful creature that he was. Loki still had not cracked the code, and he feared it might take him years to do so. When he did he was sure he would learn much about the ESA plot to control the galaxy. But why should the blind ESA need to hack into a system to which he already had unlimited access?

Loki's danger suit let him go anywhere unseen, odorless and with no heat signature. Not even his current patrons suspected how invisible it could make him; it was one of many devices he had designed just for this job. He was the proverbial fly on the wall. But he did not find the makers of the mysterious relays until he stumbled upon them by accident, in the hills below a small farm near Novocherkassk, about 150 miles south of Moscow.

He often took himself to remote places to think, or just to stand and be. A mind like his could never truly rest, but solitude allowed him some level of respite. The population of Belarus was swelling rapidly; already the big cities were complete and filling with urban colonists. So he rode the newly completed light rail system out to the farming communities to get away from it all.

It was dusk, in early spring, a lovely time if one cared about such things. The snow was melting and green shoots were poking their heads into the light. He watched a family working around their farm. Girls drove ducks and chickens into a pen and boys brought a flock of sheep in for the evening. A man and his wife inspected the simple machinery that tended their fields. At this distance they were little stick people tending to their little lives.

Suddenly he heard a sort of electronic snap. Moving just his eyes, he looked to his right, at the hill whose feet touched his. People were emerging from it, seemingly out of the solid ground.

*Like an elf hill*, his mind calmly told him, though his body responded with the instincts of an animal hiding near a predator. Fortunately, Loki kept his suit on anytime he was not in his headquarters; he was as invisible to these creatures as he was to anyone else. And he was accomplished at keeping still. The aliens moved past him and raced toward the farm. They were fast, supernaturally graceful. He could not help admiring their pale, slender forms, their long black hair that flowed behind them in the wind. If not for this beauty, and for their speed, he might have mistaken them for human.

They seized the people outside the farmhouse. Loki watched the farmer and his family twitch, then fall limp.

When the aliens carried them back to the hill again, Loki could see that their eyes were still open, their tongues lolling. They had been paralyzed, not killed. He wondered what the elves would do with the farmer and his family. Loki's curiosity had always been the driving force in his life; it got the better of him when he didn't have the time to think through the consequences. This was one of those times. Keeping as close as he dared, he followed them into the hill.

He found another world, hot and moist and inhumanly beautiful. He trailed the group with their prisoners, but not all the way into their realm. He could already see that he had stumbled upon a race whose sophistication might be far beyond his fathoming. They might have methods of detection he could not guess. So he kept himself at the fringes, watching the elves but trying not to be captivated by their beautiful arts and the lovely things they had made to decorate their chambers—or by their profound, alien beauty. Up close he could see that their resemblance to humans was more superficial than he had thought at first glance. He waited for his opportunity to leave, drinking water when he could but eating nothing, since he wasn't sure of the composition of the food. And anyway, one should never eat in Hades, Persephone had discovered that the hard way.

His caution kept him from seeing what became of the farmer and his family. But his ears told him everything he needed to know about their fate. He heard their screams, their pleas, their sobbing prayers. They went on for a surprisingly long time. Loki concluded that the aliens were masters at satisfying their own brand of curiosity.

He waited for another foraging band to make their way to the surface. He followed them, careful not to be too eager in his pursuit. This caution proved wise, because they doubled back once, as if suspecting an intruder. He wondered if he would have to abort his escape attempt. But then his guides showed him another door out. He followed and saw them speeding down another hill toward a lonely homestead. He watched them for a few moments, and then removed himself from the scene.

According to his chronometer, he had been in the elf hill for over two weeks. He had gotten out just in time, the water and nutrient reserves in his suit were depleted—but he was alive. Which was more than he could say for the other humans who had passed into the realm of the elves.

Loki contemplated the meaning of his discovery. His equation of Belarus had changed drastically, but not necessarily for the worse. He was still hidden, even from these aliens who were masters at hiding. His presprites must look like regular sprites to them, just part of the human systems they were hijacking. Apparently they thought they knew the parameters of those systems, so they weren't looking for any other technology. They couldn't know that he was hiding from his fellow humans himself, and that his devices were designed to elude detection from the sprites.

He wouldn't risk going into another elf hill, but he could watch for raiding parties. Eventually he might find a way to send in remote spies. He had been experimenting with chemical relays that traveled along "root" systems that grew from spores. They were tiny, and could be made to thread themselves along some of the designs he had seen etched into the surface of the walls inside the elf hill. Information transmitted in this fashion came slowly, but that was an advantage in this case. He was in no hurry, and they would be far less likely to detect the transmissions. Loki had already experimented with root systems inside key buildings in St. Petersburg.

He went back to his own lair, full of plans. The elves were dangerous, but their danger could be useful. The possibilities were extremely stimulating; he had much to do.

And much to learn. He might not be the master he had thought he was, but he could learn to be. Being the master was the point of every game.

At least, the ones he cared to play.

YEAR OF THE REPUBLIC 18686

*You have forgotten more than I'll ever learn,* Katerina said, but it wasn't true. Andrei had forgotten almost nothing. That was the curse and the blessing of youth technology. His brain was in perfect health, and Andrei had learned that the human capacity for storage was enormous. Some memories troubled him, others gave him joy. Occasionally one memory stood out from the multitude and did both. The wind in the grass, morning dew soaking his boots, and the cry of his hawk on the hunt could take him back 333 years, to a time when he was young enough to ride on his father's shoulders.

He was also young enough not to understand why his father was seldom at home. But when his father lifted him up and said, "Show me these new hawks you've been helping to train!" Andrei had no doubts. He held on tight, his heart took flight.

Together they stood outside the garden gate and gazed across the pale grasses, which rippled in the breeze, to the far end where a great, thick forest stood. Alexander began to march through the meadow, and on his high perch Andrei could see over grasses that would normally come to the top of his head.

"Do you suppose we'll see a wolf?" he asked, more hopeful than nervous.

"You mean like the wolves from the storybooks?" said Alexander. "We don't have wolves like that on Akilina. In this region we have little fox-wolves."

"I've never seen them," said Andrei, peering closely at the forest.

"Nor shall you. They are shy creatures. But they have seen *you*, I promise you that."

"Really? !"

"Truly. One or two may be watching even now."

"But Mother says the sprites chase the wolves away . . ."

"They do not," Alexander said. "I don't tell the sprites to bother any of the animals on this estate, or near it."

"Well!" Andrei was delighted at the thought. "Mother must have unpleasant things to say about *that*."

Alexander laughed so hard, he almost shook Andrei loose. If there were any fox-wolves within miles of the sound, Andrei was sure they were frightened off. "She does," Alexander managed at last. "Most assuredly, she does. Of course, if we had dire wolves on this world, that would be another matter. They are huge, and very clever."

"You've *seen* a dire wolf?" Andrei asked.

"I have," Alexander said solemnly. "On a world called Nemesis. I was walking, like we are now, near a great forest."

"What happened! Did it try to bite you? Did it chase you?"

"I stood very still," said Alexander. "I didn't look it too closely in the eyes. It watched me for a long time, and then it decided I wasn't worth the trouble and it went away."

"Oh." Andrei was disappointed. "You didn't shoot it, then."

"Why should I? It wasn't my enemy, and it wasn't any good to eat. Ah-hah—there's the path."

Alexander turned away from the meadow and up the well-worn path. The forest closed around them, cool and damp, with green smells and the twitter of birds. The wind blew the pine needles, making a sound like running water. Andrei remembered his first venture down this path, how he spent a good deal of time searching for the stream before he realized it was the trees that sang of water.

They came quickly to a fork in the path, the left side of which led to the falconer's compound. But once there, Alexander stopped. "Hmm," he said.

"What?" Andrei could see nothing out of the ordinary.

"Look at the path." Alexander pointed to the right branch of the trail. Andrei had never explored it beyond a few yards. He believed it led to the deepest part of the forest. When he looked closely at the ground, he saw marks that ran in a straight line up the path and out of sight.

"The marks of a broom," said Alexander. "You know what that means."

"Umm . . ." Andrei thought hard.

"Baba Yaga has been this way. She always trails a broom behind her to sweep away the marks of her passage."

"She's here?" Andrei could hardly believe it. "I thought she lived in old Russia back on Earth."

"She has been to many places," said Alexander. "She has been *here*."

"Why would she come here?"

"Who knows? She doesn't like people to know her business. But this is my estate. I have a notion to find out what she's doing. Shall we follow her, Andrei?"

Andrei's head was full of the terrifying stories his mother had told him about Baba Yaga. Yet the idea also excited him. "We'll have to be careful," he warned. "And very clever."

"Ah, you understand the situation," said Alexander. "We're agreed." And he started up the branch away from the falconer's compound, away from the world Andrei knew.

Perched on his father's shoulders, Andrei was not required to do anything but ride, so he spent his energy trying to remember everything he could about Baba Yaga. After dredging up several nasty recollections, he regretted thinking about her at all.

"Father," he said at last. "If we really do find her, do you suppose she'll be angry?"

"Not unless we outwit her," said Alexander, whose pace was unaffected by thoughts of meeting a witch. "She hates that."

"But she'll try to eat us no matter what we do. That's what the stories say."

"We won't let her."

Andrei was encouraged by his father's confidence, but he still had concerns.

"What if she tries to step on us with her hut?"

"We'll have to be fast," said Alexander. "But she usually doesn't travel in her hut. She has a big pestle she likes to drive. Pestles aren't very dangerous."

Andrei was terribly impressed. "How do you know so much about her, Father?"

"She writes me letters," replied Alexander.

"You *know* her?" Andrei could scarcely believe his ears.

"No. But she knows *me*. Someday she may know you as well."

"Maybe even today," said Andrei, thoroughly awed by the thought. He held on tight as his father marched deeper into the woods, watching and listening carefully, straining because it had grown silent since they had reached places where men seldom passed, and animals were more easily frightened by them. It seemed to Andrei that the entire forest was watching them, waiting to see what they would do. As the minutes passed, and the silence grew, he began to wonder if the two of them would go so deep into that green silence, they might never find their way out again.

And then suddenly the trees began to thin, and the warm sun shone down on them. Alexander walked out of the forest and into fields that stretched farther than Andrei's eyes could see. He blinked and shaded his eyes. The forest continued off to the right, climbing up some hills and stretching past the horizon. But Alexander and Andrei walked into the fields, leaving the forest behind.

"I thought it went on forever," said Andrei, both relieved and disappointed.

"Nothing goes on forever," Alexander said cheerfully. "Everything turns into something else. If we follow the edge of the forest for another few miles, we'll be able to look down into the valley and see the great city of Ekaterinburg. Before it was there, the Tobol River wound past sunny banks that grew flowers and wild grass. Someday the city will be ruins, the flowers and the grass will grow back, and the fox-wolves won't even remember us."

"But where is Baba Yaga's trail?" Andrei couldn't see the marks anymore.

"She must have traveled along one of these furrows," said Alexander, "thinking we wouldn't be able to tell. Let's keep marching this way, we're bound to see something."

But Andrei looked and looked, and all he could see was summer crops. He glanced behind them, wondering if they should go back, and caught sight of something sparkling in the air between them and the forest.

"Mother's sprites are following us," he said indignantly.

"Are they?" Alexander didn't look at the sprites, but in another moment they all flew away.

"How did you make them do that?" asked Andrei.

"I'm the boss of all the sprites here," said Alexander. "One day you'll be boss of your own sprites, and then you can make them go away when you want to."

"When?" Andrei asked impatiently.

"When you don't have to ride on my shoulders anymore to see things," replied Alexander.

That seemed like a million years away. And Andrei couldn't see the tracks anymore. He felt very small and useless.

Then something prickled the back of his neck. He turned his head again. Something large was moving through the trees, shaking the branches.

"Father . . ." he warned.

Alexander stopped and looked around. Together they watched as the trees shook and swayed. In another moment, a round, shiny thing poked its head above the treetops. It bobbed and lurched, as if it walked on two legs.

Alexander pulled Andrei off his shoulders and threw him flat on his stomach, dropping next to him and throwing an arm over him. The two of them peered at the giant in the forest through the tall grasses.

"She circled behind us," Andrei whispered. "That's her chicken-legged hut, it must be."

Alexander didn't answer. Andrei looked sideways at him and noticed that his eyes had gone tactical, just like his tutor's eyes sometimes did. He knew his father was talking to someone, and was looking at the scene through the mechanical eyes of sprites.

"Stay down," Alexander said quietly. "Security is coming to get us."

"But she can't see us," said Andrei. "We should let her go a little farther and then follow her."

"Not this time. My sprites can't see her at all, even though we can see her with our naked eyes."

"I thought sprites could see everything," said Andrei.

"Not everything. Not Baba Yaga, either."

The hut was moving away from them. "In another moment she'll be gone," said Andrei wistfully. "We won't be able to track her."

"Patience," said Alexander. "We have years, my son. And so does she. She is older than this forest."

Andrei was thoroughly awed by the thought. The adults in his life seemed old to him, unfathomably so. But Baba Yaga's age was completely beyond his ken.

The thought tickled him. So did a blade of the tall grass they were hiding in. "I think we can get up now," he whispered. "I can't see her anymore."

"No we can't," Alexander said grimly. Andrei looked at him again. His eyes were back to normal, but the look in them made Andrei's heart pound.

"Why, Father?" he dared.

Alexander looked at him, and his expression softened.

"Always do what your security tells you, son. This is the best advice I will ever give you. Pick good people to work for you, and then listen to them. This is what my father told me when I was about your age."

"Grandfather Sergei?" said Andrei. "The one in the family pictures who never smiles?"

"You haven't seen the right pictures," said Alexander, and winked.

"I never met him."

"No, he died many years before you were born. But I have all his letters. And his diaries. Someday, they will pass to you."

"But what will I do with them?" asked Andrei, and wondered if he dared scratch his ankle.

"You'll get to know your grandfather," said Alexander. "You'll learn what his dream was."

"Can't you just tell me what it was?" The itch was beginning to drive him quite mad.

"If you like," replied Alexander. "His dream was my dream."

"And what—" asked Andrei, as he tried to rub his

ankle against a patch of grass, "what is your dream, Father?"

"Russia," said Alexander.

Andrei waited to hear more. What was Russia? Did Father want to visit old Earth? But surely he had, already. Andrei had the feeling he meant something different. He also had the feeling that if he asked, he would be handed another puzzle, and that was almost as maddening as the itch. Alexander grinned at him, reading his mind.

"You see?" he said. "That's why you need to read the letters."

"I see," Andrei agreed. "I will. I promise."

Alexander gave him a squeeze. And then they heard the airship. Alexander got to his feet, and Andrei scrambled up beside him (after a brief pause to give his ankle a satisfying scratch). The airship flew over the trees, then glided to their position. It hovered over them, descended to the grass, and settled as lightly as a songbird lighting on a branch. A door popped open, and a big man reached out to help them aboard.

"We couldn't find you," the man told Alexander. "That's why we didn't get here immediately. That thing generates a dampening field the likes of which I've never seen."

Alexander winked at Andrei again. "Just like Baba Yaga. She hates for people to know her business. So she sweeps away her trail."

"I'll remember that," said Andrei.

And he always would.

From the collected letters of Alexander Sergeivich Mironenko:

*Andrei,*

*I have just discovered a letter from your grandfather Sergei Ilyich that I never sent to you. It was very important to me, I tucked it away somewhere extra safe and forgot to include it in the database. It said everything to me that I was just getting ready to write to you. So here it is:*

*My son,*

*I know I have joked with you about the world that shall be our Mir, how I would like to name it Belarus. But I wasn't really joking. Lately it has become clear to me that it will take quite a bit longer to gather and deploy resources for this project than I had hoped, perhaps centuries longer. I have lived three centuries already, I cannot imagine that God will see fit to grant me much more time than that. So I write to you again with a last request. You already know my intentions for this place that will be our last stand. I hope you will name her Belarus. Here is why.*

*Centuries ago, when Tsar Nicholas was overthrown, his supporters called themselves White Russians. They wanted to preserve tradition. They were doomed of course, but I don't think it will be a jinx for us to pay homage to their intentions. And I have another reason as well. It is a very simple one. We have too damned many "New Russias" in the Republic as it is. And I think that sort of name would send the wrong message to the people we want to recruit as our colonists.*

*I've seen it happen so many times before, when people say, "Everything would be great if it weren't for those people who aren't like us! We need to go somewhere and build a place that only has our own kind in it, and only our religion is allowed, and everyone likes the same food and listens to the same music and marries the right people."*

*The result of that kind of thinking is that now we have all of these New Russias, New Africas, New Israels. And no one stops to think that isolating themselves will bring out all of their worst traits and stifle creative thought and advancement. This is what happened to old Russia, long before the fabled Iron Curtain dropped into place.*

*So we will not be like those New Russias. At least, not deliberately. Your cousin has accused me of being a revolutionary, but if I am such, then I like to think I am the same sort as Peter the Great. My revolution is one of ideas. Ideas are what all the Russian revolutions were based on.*

*You know I have never believed in the concept of New Utopia, particularly one that relies on isolationism. Years ago I got into trouble at the family council by telling everyone that I believe outsiders are crucial to social and psychological development The spooky thing is, no one really disagreed with me. It's just that they felt they had the power and the wisdom to control that development.*

*"Russia loves the whip." That's what Tsarina Alexandra said just before she and Nicholas were arrested. Yet in a way, she was right. Russians need to*

*be guided by an iron fist. This is true of old Russia and the new ones. It's true of the lands and people who surrounded us, threatened us, supplanted us, interbred with us, and migrated with us to the stars. But most people confuse strength with brutality.*

*I have fought five wars in my lifetime. Being in charge of so many lives taught me something. Having an iron fist does not mean that you tighten the reins and control everyone's life down to the most minute detail. It means that you act decisively, without hesitation. You listen, and learn, and you make the best decision you can, then stick to it.*

*I have a good reason for handing out this advice. I have another last request. I ask you to be tsar of Belarus. I know you had other plans, you would rather pursue your research and stay as far away from family matters as you can. But you have also been my greatest ally. And I think you will not say no.*

*Rule Belarus as the latter-day rulers of old England and Scandinavia ruled. How ironic that these are the countries to whom Peter the Great looked for new technology. It's not surprising that worlds colonized by people from those old countries all support the Bill of Rights.*

*We face worse opposition than Peter ever did. And we don't have his absolute authority. But we've got his Fabergé eggs. Plenty of people would like to kill us just to get their hands on them!*

*You are the son of my heart and mind. You will be tsar if the time is right for you. You have all my resources at your disposal, my allies are yours. And of course you have my legacy. I wish I had more hard cash to offer, but you will find you have enough for what you need. Timing is the real problem.*

*Those with the most money make the rules. Only the Rule of Law stands between them and ordinary people.*

*I stand there as well, my son. And that is why*

*I will not live to see the realization of my dream. You understand.*

*Love,*
*Papa*

*Andrei,*
*What my Papa said, and more.*
—*Alexander Sergeivich Mironenko*

YEAR OF THE REPUBLIC 19024
BELARUSIAN YEAR 11

*TACHYGRAM from Marta Sakharov PABE 566-889-936672 XX to Irina Khariton MANNG 567-333-067584 XP: Irina, I have had the best of luck. For the first time in my life I can afford to send a Tachy-Gram! I can't tell you how good it feels to be able to speak my mind and know that no one can censor me. TachyGrams cannot be intercepted, they're too fast to catch!*

*But that's not my good news. I no longer work on the tsarina's floor in the winter palace! I work on the tsar's floor. I clean the apartments of some of his most trusted staff. No one has yelled at me once, and I don't have to pray every day like I did with the tsarina. She's a good woman, very devout, but I am happier somewhere else.*

*You must come to Belarus, I know I can get you a job. Everything is so much better here than on New Georgia. Here, when you stand in a queue, you actually get something good at the end of it! And I don't have to wait in line to get food at all, I can hardly believe I'm not dreaming. The farmers' mar-*

*ket in St. Petersburg is excellent—the first time I went, I tried to bring home too much and strained my back. Even in the cold of winter they have plenty of produce to offer.*

*Don't believe all the stuff they're saying on the news about how Jews and aliens run everything here. We have beautiful Russian churches. It's true we have other religions here, but they are good people. Don't believe what they say about Tsar Andrei Alexandrovich. I have spoken with him myself—I do his laundry! Who would know him better? He is a good tsar.*

*I have six pairs of good shoes! You must come to Belarus. I know I can get you a job.*

*Marta END TRANSMISSION*

Tally stood among giants with the chill of early fall biting her cheeks. For the first time since she had left Canopus, she was awed by the size of something.

It was hard to judge the size of the trees from a distance, and once she was among them, their limbs and leaves hid the truth from her. It wasn't until she encountered the first skyscraper-sized trunk that she began to grasp the scale, and to understand that the things she had thought were strange, misshapen trees—some of them curling a hundred feet overhead—were actually roots.

"Tally!"

She jumped. The cry had come from Peter, Andrei's young son, who was currently riding on his father's shoulders. His brown eyes were shining with wonder, and his curly mop of auburn hair had leaves stuck in it. "These trees are bigger than the sphinx!" he said.

"Much bigger," she agreed.

"They're even taller than the Sunset Gate," added Andrei.

"*Way* taller," said Tally.

In fact, these "trees" were so big, Tally wasn't sure they should even be called trees. Their bark looked more like stone, and if it weren't for their shape, not to mention their spadelike, velvet-skinned leaves, they might have been taken for rock formations instead.

"This is what happens," she said, "when people aren't around to stop something from growing."

"That's odd." Grigory navigated the twisting terrain as if he could see perfectly well. "I have walked in many forests, on many worlds. But none of them rival the size of this one."

"You should see the colors," Tally said. "They're *really* odd."

"What do you mean?" Peter cocked his head. "All I see is grey."

"Look closer," said Tally.

Grey Forest was grey from a distance, with the appearance of blue or green mist hanging over some spots. But close up, there were a multitude of shades, so subtle they seemed illusory. The colors teased Tally's brain, making her wonder if she had ever truly seen color before.

And suddenly she couldn't see anything else. She rubbed her eyes and looked again, and was relieved to find Grigory. He had blended in with the forest, thanks to his danger suit. Andrei and Peter weren't much easier to see.

"We should stay close," Tally said.

"Don't worry." Peter heard the anxiety in her voice. "The sprites will look after us."

"No, she's right." Andrei rested his mild gaze on Tally. "We can't expect sprites to keep us safe if we aren't willing to do it ourselves."

"So true, Andrei Alexandrovich," said Grigory. The stones in his eye sockets shone redder than usual in the grey shadows. "I don't think we're seeing all there is to see in this forest. With our senses *or* our sprites."

"Well, there's some mystery left in the world," said Tally. Belarus had captivated her with its wild beauty. For the past seven years she had labored with Andrei's team to tame it, building cities and towns, roads and dams, monuments and museums, and turning over thousands of acres of farmland to colonists eager to cultivate it. The population on the continent had steadily swelled to over eight million, with new people flocking to Belarus now that word had gotten around it was a prosperous colony. Tally's staff had dispersed, some back to Canopus, some to other jobs for Andrei, and some to other worlds.

Now her wild world was a colony. Exactly what she had worked for, but her work was essentially over, and she missed it.

"Don't grieve for the mysteries of this world," Grigory said. "Some still lie undiscovered. A pity they can't stay that way."

Patterns stirred in the back of Tally's mind, intricate, puzzling, inexorable as clockworks. They had haunted her for seven years and she still could not tell where they were going, what they were doing. The derelicts kept the same orbit they had maintained for millennia, and nothing had been found on the planet surface to match them. But when Tally looked too deeply into the grey of the forest, those patterns appeared like ghosts.

"It's a strange world," Tally concluded. "It has Giants living on it. So it's spooky."

"It's *haunted*," Grigory said. Suddenly his sprites flew past him like a flock of startled birds and disappeared among the giant, tangled roots. "Shall we go deeper?" he asked. "The trees are bigger, farther in. It strains the imagination."

"Let's go!" said Peter. "Maybe we can even climb one!"

"Not today," Andrei said firmly. "Not without proper equipment." He made his way toward another passage among the tangles.

"Don't go too far out of sight!" Tally called.

"We're right here," Peter called back, making Tally feel a little silly. But it had begun to dawn on her that people who did not have the benefit of sprites to scout their way could become quickly lost among the Giants. Sprites almost never failed, but *almost* was not a comforting concept when facing the unknown. Everyone on Belarus had locator implants hidden inside their bodies, for just such an occasion.

But some people had disappeared anyway. Tally thought Grey Forest would be an excellent place for that to happen.

The late morning edged toward noon, and they pressed inward. Tally gave in to enchantment again, despite herself. And Andrei let Peter do some limited climbing on roots, those that were no more than ten feet off the ground.

"Papa," Peter said, "we didn't need to build St. Petersburg."

"Not build it?" Andrei said. "But it's so beautiful!"

Peter slapped the root he was climbing. "This bark feels harder than stone. We could have hollowed out these trees for our buildings."

Andrei considered the trees. "That would probably kill them," he concluded.

Tally followed Andrei under the arching root and found herself standing next to a trunk whose exact diameter she couldn't even guess. She wondered if Andrei were wrong—maybe *nothing* could kill the trees.

Peter scrambled down from his root and leaned against Tally's tree, feeling it with his palms. "Papa, if we can't hollow out the trees, we should build our city in the treetops. We could have a grand tree house city!"

"But we used up our money on all the other cities," said Andrei. "Kiev, Volgograd, Moscow . . ."

"Moscow has all of those blasted bells," Peter complained. "I don't know why they have to ring them all the time. Day and night!"

"Tradition." Andrei wandered toward another arching root. "And that, my son, is why you and I live in St. Petersburg."

Peter ran ahead of him and scrambled up the root.

Andrei boosted him when he almost slid down again. The carpet of dead leaves under their feet was soft, they made no sound as they walked. Anyone could have sneaked up on them. Tally was glad Grigory was there. She turned to look for him and saw an odd expression on his face. She waited for him to catch up.

"Don't you like it here?" she asked softly.

"Not particularly."

"But it's interesting. It's beautiful too."

"To look at," he said. "But I don't do that."

Tiny sprites drifted past them, sparkling in the gloom. Tally could hear Andrei and Peter talking somewhere ahead.

"Why did you come today?" she asked Grigory. "ESA Tam could have done it, or some of the other military ESAs."

"I could ask you the same question." His red eyes were the only bright spots of color in that gigantic yet claustrophobic place. "You have been here seven years, and you never expressed an interest in seeing this place before."

"I've been too busy. Had to build domes and spires. Had to build the Hermitage. Had to make all those bells Peter loves so much."

He laughed. It was one of his warm laughs.

"But you are worried," she ventured.

"Always," he said.

"Any particular reason?"

"Always," he said again, and Tally knew she would get no details from him.

"We *must* come back with our equipment soon, Papa," she heard Peter cry. "I want to see where the birds soar! I want to swing like a monkey!"

Tally hurried to find them. Grigory kept pace beside her. They found Peter climbing on yet another root.

"I don't think it's the swinging sort of forest." Andrei smiled at his young son. Tally had never seen him smile so much before Peter's birth.

Suddenly Peter froze and looked down at Andrei

with a serious expression. "Papa, do you suppose Baba Yaga lives in here?"

Andrei scratched his beard. "I don't know. We haven't seen her tracks, but she sweeps them away."

"Her hut couldn't get around in here very well," Peter said doubtfully.

"True. Maybe she prefers the Black Forest, or the marshes next to the Volga."

Peter climbed a few feet higher, and looked over the top of another root. "There's a clearing through here!" he called.

"This way," Grigory agreed as his sprites flitted back and forth like agitated fairies. He went under two curving roots that formed an almost perfect Gothic arch. Tally waited for Andrei to help Peter down, and the three of them followed Grigory.

They emerged into a clearing as large as a ballroom—and as magnificent. The trunks loomed over the base of interlacing roots like vast walls. Tally looked up, expecting to see more branches and roots blocking her view, as they did in the rest of the forest. She almost fell over. The tops of the trees soared above the scattered, puffy clouds. It was far grander than any Gothic cathedral could have aspired to be, leaving her to wonder if the greatest art was only a pale imitation of nature.

Sunlight was creeping down the trunks toward the noon, fall position. Soon the light would shine down on them and Tally wondered how the colors would change.

"It's like being at the bottom of a canyon," said Andrei, who was precariously balanced as Peter tried to see all the way up the trunks.

"It's like being in church," said Peter, echoing Tally's thoughts.

Grigory was silent, but his sprites flew far over their heads, followed closely by Andrei's. Tally wondered what it must be like to see the Giants from the perspective of a sprite. She promised herself she would come for a virtual visit, someday when she had the leisure time. Now that her part of the project was essentially over, she had plenty of that.

The sunlight crept down to her upturned face. She looked around the clearing, watching the colors perform their subtle magic. The light revealed features previously hidden in the gloom. Tally strolled away from the others, examining the curling roots, realizing there were several more openings into the clearing. Peter's remarks about tree houses had been perceptive; the forest really did seem almost like a giant house. There were doors, windows, walls, chambers, bowers, closets, even a basement and an attic if you knew where to look.

*And if you don't know where to look, you're lost.* The thought brought a chill to the sunny scene. She blinked as her thoughts began to drift and sensation took over. Tally felt a presence, someone who was close, yet impossibly distant.

And then she saw something.

Directly ahead of her a root arched at least twenty feet high, leading to another clearing. At first Tally thought it might be as big as the one they were in, but as she drifted closer, she saw a spot of pale color on the ground. It stood out starkly against the subtle background, lending it perspective. The clearing was small, the thing on the ground tiny and pinkish.

"We could have a big party in here!" Peter said. He and Andrei were several steps behind her.

Tally moved closer, feeling a stir of nausea as she began to suspect what the thing was. She moved so that her body blocked Andrei's and Peter's view of the smaller clearing. The thing might belong to a doll, but it looked too big. Tally walked under the curling root, her eyes fixed on the jarring spot of color. Within a few steps, she knew it did not belong to a doll.

"What are you looking at?" Andrei said, now only a few steps behind her.

"Don't come in here," Tally snapped, barely recognizing her own voice. "Grigory!"

* * *

Within moments, someone laid a gentle hand on Tally's shoulder. She knew it was Grigory, but she twitched, violently. The small thing on the ground was a human hand. One of its fingers pointed to Tally's left; the others were curled against the palm.

The swarm of sprites flew past them and hovered over the little hand. The sprites would analyze the DNA, and tell Grigory who the hand belonged to.

"Lyuba Petrova," said Grigory. "Age thirteen. Missing from Odessa for three days."

"Andrei, don't come in here!" Tally called again.

"We won't," he said, and she remembered he didn't need to. He could see more than she could through his own sprites.

"Papa, how come? What's wrong?" asked Peter.

"Tally found part of a body," Andrei said calmly. Tally was shocked, wondering if he should be so honest with the child.

But Peter merely said, "Oh . . ." And a moment later he said, "Which part did you find, Tally?"

She couldn't speak. Grigory answered for her. "We found a hand, Tsarevich. It belonged to a young girl."

Tally was shaking now, but she wasn't frightened.

"This is staged," Grigory said, too low for Peter to hear. "We were meant to see this."

Tally felt a chill go through her. Suddenly she knew why the hand was pointing. She let her gaze follow the direction the stiff little finger indicated.

"That way," she whispered. Directly to their left was another curling root, this one leading to a place that was little more than an alcove. Tally had to bend to go through. She didn't have far to go. Within moments, she knew what they had been meant to see.

Lyuba's head, severed cleanly, midway down the neck. From the expression on the face, the girl had died in agony. Sprites swarmed the area like feasting mosquitoes.

"He did it while she was alive, didn't he?" Tally hissed. "He cut her head off while she was still alive."

"No," said Grigory, close behind her. "He probably didn't do the severing until after she was dead. A person who dies of decapitation has a slack expression. Her face must have been frozen this way for some time before he cut her head off."

"What would be the point of that?"

When Grigory didn't answer immediately, Tally tore her gaze from the unhappy head and looked at him instead. He had an abstract expression on his face, the sort he wore when he was talking to more than one person. Andrei had to be one; probably the police as well. Yet there was nothing distracted about the answer he finally gave her.

"The point is that we should see what he did," he said. "His *handiwork*. He pissed on this poor child, and now he's using her to piss on us."

Tally stood for a moment, her hands suddenly numb, then turned and ducked out of the alcove. She walked past the lonely hand and out into the big clearing. Andrei and Peter stared at her. Peter was wearing a solemn expression much like the one his mother usually wore, but rather than being set in lines of disapproval it was folded in pity. The sight went straight into Tally's heart like an arrow.

"Are you very angry?" Peter said in a small voice.

"Not at you, baby," she managed.

And there was nothing more to say. A swarm of new sprites filled the clearing, followed several minutes later by people in danger suits and street clothes. Tally stepped aside and waited to be useful again.

May the Lord bless and keep the tsar—
far away from us!"

—Russian proverb

Mikhail Boryavich Klebanov had lived as a farmer on four different worlds, under four different men who called themselves *tsar*. But not one of them had ever come to visit—until now.

No one could have good luck forever. Mikhail tried to be a good sport about it.

The tsar walked into his yard behind Sandor, the local constable. Mikhail would have known he was someone important just by the fact that he wore a danger suit—something ordinary people only glimpsed in movies. But it was the news program on SpriteNet that had taught him to know Andrei Mironenko's face. He was glad that he was already seated on his stool, or he might have fallen on it in a most undignified manner.

"Welcome," he told the men in a courteous tone.

"Good day," said the constable. "I'm glad we didn't disturb you at a busy moment."

Mikhail shrugged. "Rest is the sweet sauce of labor."

"You recognize my companion," said Sandor.

Mikhail nodded, puffing his pipe.

"I come to pay my respects," said the tsar, and seemed sincere about it. "And to speak of a serious matter."

"It must be serious, little father," said Mikhail, "or you would not be here."

The tsar measured him with mild eyes, but Mikhail was not fooled by his pleasant demeanor. Or his apparent youth—such confidence did not belong to a young man.

"Sandor tells me that you were elected by your neighbors to represent them in the Association of Villages," said the tsar.

"Yes," said Mikhail. "Though I suppose it could have been worse. I could have been elected fire warden."

The tsar was amused by this remark, but Mikhail could see something was weighing heavily on him. Sandor looked no less serious, which dismayed Mikhail even more. The constable was not one to be easily upset; he dealt with the local problems promptly and in an evenhanded fashion. And you didn't even have to bribe him.

"We need you to help spread the word," said Sandor. "No one must venture into Grey Forest alone. Someone has had an accident in there."

"An accident," Mikhail said slowly. "Among the Giants?"

"Yes."

Mikhail nodded. It was no effort to keep the curiosity from his face. Some of the regimes he had survived in his fifty-eight years were not as benevolent as this one. "I will convey your orders to my neighbors," he said. "It should be no problem. No one goes there anyway."

The tsar also seemed to be an expert at schooling his expression. "Why not?"

Mikhail puffed thoughtfully. "A feeling you get," he said at last. "The Giants don't want company. Even animals don't live there. My dogs won't go past the tree line, and you won't find wild creatures in there either. I have never seen the King Raptors nesting in those branches, though they love high places."

"Mikhail Boryavich, I will confide something important to you," said the tsar. "I do not wish to risk a panic, but public safety must be addressed."

"Ah," said Mikhail, "I see. This is concerning the person you found in Grey Forest."

"The person was a child," said the tsar. "And she was savagely murdered."

Mikhail felt a pain under his heart. He could stand to hear just about anything, but the suffering of a child was a dreadful thing to contemplate.

"I have a young son myself." The tsar read his emotions. "I believe you understand my intentions. You and your neighbors need to watch even more carefully than you already do."

"This *child*," Mikhail said, pronouncing the word like a prayer, "where was she from?"

"Odessa. But she was left in the forest. The killer may have passed through here, he may have looked around."

"At our children."

"At *anyone*," said the tsar, and something dark swam under the mild surface of his expression.

Mikhail puffed for several moments, letting that sink in. "There are other victims?" he said at last.

"We're still sorting out the facts," said Sandor. He was wearing his constable face, but Mikhail knew he could get more information from him later. And it wouldn't take that much vodka. "Some people always go missing on colony worlds," Sandor continued. "On *any* world, but especially in new, wild places. You can fall off a cliff that isn't even on the map."

Mikhail had no doubt that the tsar's staff had thoroughly mapped every inch of Belarus.

"Take note of strangers," said the tsar.

"Always," said Mikhail. "I am Russian."

The tsar gave him a half smile. "As for rumors you may hear—trust what you hear on SpriteNet first."

This was a day for surprises. Most autocrats hated SpriteNet because it gave information freely to everyone. Andrei Mironenko was the first big boss Mikhail had ever heard of who openly encouraged its use. Apparently he was a gambler. Mikhail hoped he was a lucky one.

"Little father," he said respectfully, "I will do as you say. And I will pray that this monster be caught before he harms another child. God is all-knowing and stern, and I hope no other innocents will have to suffer for our sins."

"I pray the same," said the tsar, and Mikhail believed him.

The tsar said *good day* just like another neighbor. As he went out the front gate with the constable, a young boy ran up to him and the tsar lifted the child onto his shoulders just as Mikhail had done with each of his six children and twenty-three grandchildren. The sight tugged at his heart. The boy must have been on an outing with his father; they must have stumbled over the body together. And from there they had come directly to the nearby villages to warn Mikhail and the other elders. That was noble—most autocrats would have sent underlings to do it.

Watch for strangers. That was what people always said when things like this happened.

But it usually wasn't a stranger. Most of the time it was someone close. A neighbor.

Mikhail sat and smoked a little longer. Soon he would go in and speak to his wife. They would decide who should be notified and who did not need to be in the information loop just yet. He thought about it, watching the afternoon sun stretching the shadows. A beautiful day.

But a cold place was growing around his heart.

When it grew too cold to bear alone any longer, Mikhail Boryavich Klebanov got up from his stool and went in to find his wife.

FROM: Emily Kizheh
TO: Lt. B. Bullman
CC: ESA G. M.
Bull,

I've heard from the medical examiner about the torso they found in that field near Novocherkassk today, and it's a match for Lyuba Petrova. A strange detail captures my attention. The torso was infested with larvae, but the head and hand Andrei's group found were in pristine condition, no insect invasion despite the fact that they were probably inside Grey Forest for three days. Some of the body parts from the other victims also were not infested—I have a feeling there's a deliberate message in there for us.

Tally and Peter moved through the layers of security that protected the winter palace in St. Petersburg and made their way to a special door. It was unlike any of the other doors, anywhere in the city. It was made of the same alloy used to make the hulls of star ships, covered in gold, and decorated with symbols from a language long dead. The figure who dominated the scene was Thoth, the god of scribes, possibly the only god whom Tally came close to worshiping.

She tapped a code on the wall by Thoth's door. Deep inside it, a mechanism unlocked. The heavy door swung outward, the scents of cedar and sandalwood filled the air, and they entered the worlds of ancient Egypt and Nubia—Tally's quarters.

"Someday hundreds of years from now," Peter told Tally once, "when you have died, I shall have you mummified and sealed in a magnificent sarcophagus, and I shall place you right here in your tomb and visit you every day to feed your ka."

"This is not a tomb," she said, laughing. "It's how people really lived, surrounding themselves with beautiful things and with symbols of gods great and small who looked after the order of the universe. Look at your own quarters, and you'll see it's full of the same sorts of things. They're just designed differently."

"Except that the Egyptians couldn't watch movies," said Peter. "Or the news."

"Egyptians loved life so much," Tally told him, "they filled their tombs with remembrances of that life. They wanted it to be eternal."

"But Mother says life is cruel," said Peter. "And that is why we must pray for redemption."

They walked through Tally's living room, their footsteps muffled by thick, woven carpets. They passed chairs, stools, and divans with carved animal feet; panels depicting scenes of peace and joy; statuettes and carvings of gods and goddesses, kings and queens, and ordinary folk, all celebrating life.

But Tally's mind was on death. She held Peter's hand as if he could not find his way through the maze of her collection, though he knew it better than she did. They went directly to her office.

A message light blinked on the com on her big desk. She signaled for it to play out loud. Peter climbed onto a couch.

"I felt that!" he said. "You twitched your hands. Are you sending the machine signals through your eyes?"

"No." She shook her head. "I can't do that. The signal's not going through me at all. It's going through a transmitter in my gloves to the message pad."

"But when you want your snakes to move, how do you signal them?" he asked, clambering up on the couch and then settling himself with his feet dangling far off the floor.

"They're hooked up to my nervous system," she said. "I can move them as easily as I move my fingers."

"But *how*?"

"Why isn't the message playing?" Tally frowned and leaned over her desk, tapping at the pad. The display flashed her the answer: TEXT ONLY. She tapped it again, and the message appeared.

> *Now that you know what has happened to the missing people on Belarus, will you run away, Tally? Or do you have the courage to stay and fight for the ones you love?*
>
> *—B.Y.*

She stared at it, disbelieving. In an instant she was back in Grey Forest, looking at what was left of Lyuba Petrova. She didn't know Peter had come up behind her until he spoke.

"B.Y.! *Baba Yaga.* Tally, she sent you a message!" He pointed to the initials at the bottom of the screen.

"Baba Yaga?" Tally repeated dumbly. And then it was plain. Andrei had shown her the other messages. Apparently Baba Yaga didn't feel she warranted the animated cartoon at the beginning, but the terseness of the message certainly seemed to be within character.

Tally's stomach churned. She had to resist the impulse to grab Peter and run from the room—where to, she really wasn't sure. Maybe all the way back to Canopus.

*Now that you know . . .*

From the moment the investigators had arrived on the scene, it was plain that Grigory and Andrei had been keeping something from her. She had buried herself in her job, an easy thing to do since Andrei was so talented at design himself. He was so clear about what he wanted: materials and designs that would last, systems that would require the least energy possible to keep them going. It was the same kind of sensibility required for Tally's work on Canopus. Once the cities had begun to bloom under her fingers, that was all she cared about.

Of course it became more complicated once the colonists began to arrive in full force. People brought problems with them, no matter how beautiful and comfortable the nest you made for them. Grigory's screening process was the tightest you would find anywhere in the Republic, but you couldn't know everything. Someone monstrous had leaked through. Maybe several someones. And why should anyone tell her about it? She was the engineer, not the head of security.

But they were like a family. And she should have been told.

Two small arms hugged her tight. She gasped in surprise, then hugged Peter back.

"Dithering!" he accused, having heard his father say it so many times. "Your snakes are wiggling, Tally."

"They're not snakes, silly."

"John says they're snakes, he says they can bite if you get mad enough."

John was a new face on the scene. He was a master designer for the military ESAs. He was the one who created their battle machinery, and he was very amused by Tally's reliance on, as he put it, "outmoded, old-fashioned, inferior technology."

"John is a big stupid tease," said Tally. "He laughs at anything that isn't brand new."

Peter looked up at her with his solemn face. "But they do move when you get upset. Or when you're nervous, or worried. Or when you get mad, like today."

Tally felt them stirring. She doubted they would calm down anytime soon.

She tapped the screen on her message pad, three times.

FILE COPIED; SENT; REC'D KIZHEH/SE-01

Emily looked up from her picture puzzle when her message pad beeped. She had just begun to relax after plowing through the reports from the newest, ugly staged scene. She had hoped for a little peace before work flew at her again. As it was, she doubted she would get to bed on time.

She got up and looked at the pad. It displayed a copy of a message that had been sent to Tally. Emily frowned at the text. Then she took a second glance at the signature at the bottom.

"Oh!" she said. "Well! Ain't that interesting."

Very. She sent copies off to Grigory and Andrei. If she was going to be awake, they might as well keep her company.

"Tally, can we go and see Mother?"

"Is she in chapel now?" It was just a formality to ask the question. Peter always knew what time his mother was in chapel.

He nodded, his little face serious. His blue eyes were just as unwavering as his father's, though not nearly so watchful. Tally ruffled his curly hair, loving the feel of it.

*Do you have the courage to stay and fight for the ones you love . . . ?*

She could still feel the chill of Grey Forest. The two of them had waited together, off to the side, while Andrei and Grigory talked with the investigators. Peter asked uncomfortable questions.

*Why would someone kill a little girl? Who could be so cruel? Is she in heaven now? Do you suppose it hurt very much when he cut her head off?*

Tally didn't say, *I don't know*—because she did know. She knew in her flesh and blood and bones. She prayed that Peter would never ask her the right questions, and she would never have reasons to tell him that sometimes people tried to kill you even when they loved you.

Sometimes even your father could do it.

*Did I make you feel bad?*

*No, Peter, it's all right. I just remembered something.*

*Sometimes I remember things and I have bad dreams.*

*I only want you to remember good things.*

*How do I do that?*

Hard questions. And then the newly hired park ranger arrived on the scene, a flustered young man who wore what was becoming a familiar expression: the look of someone trying to get used to a brand-new sprite interface. Andrei liked government workers to have them. That was another new thing that was scandalizing people.

"Over here!" Tally called. The investigators had to finish processing the scene before they would have time to talk with him. He seemed grateful for the chance to stand still. His eyes kept going in and out of tactical as he struggled to do several things at once.

"I'm Daniel Koenig," he told them distractedly. "I—it's—hold on. I'm still learning—"

And suddenly his eyes went tactical again, and he froze. The color drained from his face. "Oy gevalt," he whispered.

Tally knew he must have gotten a sprite's-eye view of the murder scene. Probably the head.

Peter took his limp hand. "Don't feel bad," he said. "The little girl is in heaven now."

Daniel snapped out of tactical with a jolt, focused on Peter, and burst into tears.

Tally and Peter went through the security checkpoints outside their living quarters and were ushered into the side entrance of the chapel. From there they made their way quietly into the shadows of an alcove.

Katerina stood before the altar with her devoted waiting ladies. In the Russian Orthodox tradition, you always had to stand through services, not sit in pews. Tally wondered why her mother didn't approve of this branch of Christianity, considering how strict and rigid it was.

*You would love this, Mama, how Katerina stands there without moving a muscle except when it's time to genuflect or answer the priest. She's here every single day, even you didn't go to church that often. And Papa didn't go at all, he just stood home and preached to us, roared at us, beat us . . .*

"Look at her," Peter whispered. "She's like an angel from heaven."

To Tally, Katerina always looked troubled, as if she were questing for something that eluded her. By contrast, Peter's face was transformed by the sort of reverence most people displayed for the Holy Virgin. All for Katerina, who was as remote from him as if she really were in heaven.

Tally knew too well what it was like to have a mother who was remote. Peter had to make an appointment to see Katerina, and most of the time her answer was *no*. The harder he pursued her, the farther she withdrew. Wet nurses, nannies, tutors, had been his mothers. And Tally. And Emily. And even Grigory. Everyone but Katerina.

What was Katerina looking for in the chapel that she couldn't find in her son's face?

Andrei was a devoted father. Peter was well loved, and he knew it. Yet he needed Katerina. All he wanted was for her to love him.

*Why can't you ever do something to make me proud?*

Tally never cried. Just like Peter. The two of them stood together silently, until they knew they must leave or be discovered. They crept away, hand in hand.

"I'll make an appointment to see her tonight," Peter said. He did it every night.

"Before supper?" asked Tally.

"I'd like to see her *after* supper."

"She plays piano after supper. She talks with Brother Macarius."

"Maybe she'll let me listen this time."

Tally knew she wouldn't. But Peter still hoped. She had talked with his nanny and his tutors about it. They tried not to show Tally how angry it made them feel. But Tally didn't feel angry at Katerina. She felt helpless.

"What's it like to have sisters?" Peter asked suddenly.

Tally wasn't sure how to answer the question. She hadn't seen her two sisters for over forty years. The three of them had fled their parents' house as soon as they were able and scattered to the farthest reaches of the known galaxy. She TachyGrammed them during the first years. They never answered.

"Did you play lots of games with them?" asked Peter.

"When we were little." *And when we were older we sometimes hid in the same closet.*

"I hope I have sisters one day."

Fat chance of that. Andrei and Peter lived on the same floor as Tally. Katerina lived at the other end of the palace. Andrei didn't have to make an appointment to see Katerina, but Tally knew perfectly well that they were not going to make another child together.

"We should plan another sleep-over with your cousins," suggested Tally. Though the cousins in question were much more distantly related than that, they adored each other, the only young people in a very big, very grown-up family.

"That would be nice," said Peter, brightening somewhat, and Tally felt some of the pressure ease from around her heart. It had been a rough day, one that would probably give both of them some sleepless nights. But at least Peter was acting like the kid she loved so dearly.

"Tally, do you pray?"

Speaking of sleepless nights. She told him the truth. "No."

"Why not?" he asked, though he didn't sound very disturbed by the idea, just curious.

"I guess I don't need to," said Tally.

"I hope you *never* need to," said Peter, then ran off to make his appointment with his mother's secretary.

"Andrei," Alexander Sergeivich said, "it's time to come home."

"I am already home," Andrei said, though he hardly looked it at the moment, sealed from head to toe in burn plaster.

Alexander leaned forward in the visitor's chair. "Son, it's over. You have accomplished all you can in the Central Navy. If you don't move on, your mother's murder will have been for nothing."

Andrei sat up, so furious with his father that he forgot the burn plaster.

And in another moment, he realized there *was* no burn plaster. Not anymore. Because that had all happened two hundred years before, and now he was in his winter palace on Belarus, in his own bed.

Alone.

He pushed back the blanket and swung his feet onto the floor. For several moments he sat staring at the chess set that sat on a small table against the wall. He hadn't played it for decades, but it was the one his mother had loved so dearly. The pieces were patterned after characters from J.R.R. Tolkien's *Lord of the Rings*. When they played, she always insisted on using the Sauron pieces, making Andrei play the Gandalf side.

His father had been right all those years ago, but Andrei had still been furious with him. He rubbed his face, suddenly sick with too many memories.

So far, the morning was not starting off very well. And there was much to do. Andrei went into his bathroom and showered under a cool, needle-sharp spray until he felt he was thoroughly awake. He dried off quickly and pulled on his danger suit. When he was fully dressed, he checked his appointments.

It was a typical lineup. Meetings for the first half of the day, with the minister of finance, the minister of defense, the minister of science, and three governors. His aides had done the background research for the issues to be discussed and organized notes for him to review. He scanned them, then checked his queue for messages.

The queue was swamped, with just a small portion of the messages that had to pass through Emily's office first. Andrei sorted, performing a sort of message triage until he had lined them up in order of importance. He went into his day room, where breakfast was waiting. He poured himself some hot tea, buttered a scone, and began to read, staring straight ahead.

FROM EMILY KIZHEH: An odd, domed object was spotted "walking" near Black Forest this morning 4:17 A.M. EST. Sprites were unable to detect it, a farmer eyeballed it. It disappeared into the forest. I've got people watching for it (but not with their sprites).

FROM EMILY KIZHEH: Bull wants to meet with us this afternoon. Is 4:00 P.M. OK? Grigory and ESA Tam should also attend. Let me know if I need to adjust the schedule.

FROM MIKHAIL BORYAVICH KLEBANOV: A meeting of village leaders is planned for this Thursday, and my wife has suggested something. There are sprites that were assigned to our area by the Department of Agriculture to monitor crops, weather, that sort of thing.

They must record images of everything and store them somewhere, yes? She says that because they are sprites for watching crops, they may not take note of people in their reports, yet the images would still be recorded. Is there a way to pool the data from all areas where bodies were found and compare? Perhaps someone will turn up in the recordings for all sites. Shall I bring the matter up at the meeting? I await your orders.

FROM ATHENA MITROPOULOS, CURATOR, HERMITAGE: I am thrilled. Voltaire's statue has arrived. I placed it just as you requested. Our collection is now restored, and I think a celebration is in order. I await your input concerning the calendar and a desirable guest list.

FROM PETER: Papa, may I have piano lessons?

And so on. Andrei sorted through every message. He answered them all, agreeing to the meeting with Special Agent Bullion at 4:00 P.M., sending his approval to Klebanov for his wife's inspired plan, giving Curator Mitropoulos a schedule of possible dates for her celebration along with an official list of approved guests, and crafting a hundred other responses before he was done with breakfast. Last but not least, he sent:

FROM PAPA: Yes, Peter, you may have piano lessons. We will discuss the details at lunch.

Finished with his morning correspondence, Andrei focused on enjoying what was left of his breakfast, only to discover he had already eaten it.

*One of these days,* he thought as he headed for his office, *I may actually be present when I eat breakfast. What a glorious day that will be . . .*

YEAR OF THE REPUBLIC 18693

"Mother," Andrei said as he moved his Elric bishop, "tomorrow I will be eight—"

"Are you thinking about your birthday?" She took Elric with her Ringwraith knight. "You should be thinking about your game."

Andrei puzzled over which piece to move next. He had already lost Bilbo and Frodo. If the outcome of the *Lord of the Rings* were to be based upon his chess game, Middle Earth was lost.

His mother sighed. "All right, son. What about your birthday?"

Andrei gazed into her face, trying to guess her mood. His mother was the biggest mystery in his life; every time he was sure he knew what she was going to say, she surprised him.

"The fencing master says I'm doing very well," he ventured.

"He keeps me posted," said Mother.

Andrei fidgeted with his remaining bishop. "And the hawk master says I handle my bird well . . ."

"You haven't mentioned your school lessons yet," she said.

Andrei had hoped to skirt that subject.

"Your writing skills need improvement," said Mother. "And you keep trying to skip your eights when you do your times-tables."

Andrei sighed. He was pretty sure he was already defeated. "I will work on my writing skills," he promised. "And my eights."

"I'm glad to hear it," she said. "Now, what are you really trying to ask me? Out with it, I won't bite. The worst I can say is no."

"But no is terrible!" Andrei exclaimed, frustration getting the better of him.

"Not so terrible," she soothed. "All of us hear it, Andrei. Even I do. When the answer is no, you think up another plan. And besides, you haven't even asked me yet. What is this awful thing you want to do?"

"It's not awful," he said. "Archery is noble."

"Archery?" She laughed. "Is that all? For heaven's sake, I can teach you myself."

"You?" he said, wondering if she really understood what he wanted. "No, Mother, I mean with real bows and arrows—"

"What else would you use? I'm perfectly happy to teach you, I'm a regional champion." She began to pick up the chess pieces and set them up for another game.

Andrei gaped at her. She was wearing a silk and satin dress with tiny pearls sewn on it, and her hair was perfectly coiffed. She was like a lady from a painting, someone to carry flowers in her soft hands and listen to chamber music. "But if you shoot," he finally managed, "how come you didn't want me to study fencing?"

She sighed. "Fencing is a good skill, Andrei. I suppose I just don't like the idea of letting an enemy get that close to you. I like to shoot, it's good to train your eye. I shoot in several different competitions; I can even shoot a compound bow while riding horseback."

Andrei was still gaping. "When did you do that?"

"Several times a year," she said. "You have your lessons, I have my lessons too. What did you think I was doing? Knitting?"

"Yes."

She laughed. "Well, I suppose it's my fault. We both have too much to do, and we don't spend enough time together. I know I drive you hard sometimes, Andrei, but it's only because I want you to know everything you can before . . ."

She paused, an expression of uncertainty on her lovely face.

"Before?" prompted Andrei.

She softened. "Before it gets really hard. Because it will, my darling. I wish it could be different. You're a Mironenko. Our family is extremely wealthy, but it's also extremely big. Now everyone in this big family is fighting over pieces of an increasingly small pie . . ."

She stopped again, seeing the look of confusion on his face.

"You are still young," she said. "You'll understand someday. Please trust me to know what's best for you, son. Your father has many political disagreements with the rest of the family. Your road will be difficult. I want you to know as much as you can, because I want you to understand why we fight so hard for our autonomy."

Andrei felt himself sinking in deep water. His heart understood what she was trying to say; he could sense it in the undercurrent of the house, every day of his life. But he was young.

"You'll have your lessons," she said. "I think you'll enjoy it. I'll teach you what I can—if you don't like that, we'll get you another teacher."

"But I do like it," Andrei said. "I want to see what you can do!"

She smiled at him. "Done. And now, let's try another round." She nodded toward the bishop he was still holding, and he set it in its place.

"One more game," she said. "And then I'll show you my favorite bows. It's time you saw them. And my guns too."

"Your *guns*?"

"County champion," she said blandly. "Three years in a row."

YEAR OF THE REPUBLIC 19024
BELARUSIAN YEAR 11

It was cold, and no matter how much Tally adjusted her danger suit, she couldn't get comfortable.

*Systems are failing. Andrei must have known that was going to happen, that's why we got the gas heaters. Where's mine? Got to light the pilot. Wonder if he's got any extra fur hats . . .*

It was dark. She stumbled around aimlessly, making no progress. Periodically she forgot what she was doing, but then the cold reminded her again.

*Why is it so chilly? Did someone leave all the windows open?*

Tally saw a dim light up ahead. She stared at it, confused. The colors teased her brain, subtle shades of grey shimmering down nerves that weren't tuned finely enough to appreciate them.

*Grey Forest. Oh, Christ, the little girl . . .*

She looked at the floor. Lyuba's hand lay on the rug, pointing toward the light. Tally knew what she would see if she followed that direction; this time she would not do it. As she started to turn away, she caught a glimpse of something from the corner of her eye, something moving behind her. She kept turning and the shadow lashed out at her. It smashed into her jaw with bone-shattering force.

Tally woke up whimpering. The pain was so bad it brought tears to her eyes. She clutched her jaw and sat up in bed.

But the pain was gone. She probed her jaw, but couldn't evoke even a ghost of it. She felt wonderfully, blessedly normal.

And then she remembered the rest of the dream, and felt a different kind of pain.

It would not ever fade. There was no healing from the images her vivid imagination painted of the girl's last hours. Tally was a world engineer, her ability to create mental analogs of reality was developed far beyond the range of most human beings. This allowed her to construct the Hermitage inside her head, great cathedrals and synagogues, bridges, fountains, the Avenue of the Sphinxes.

Or Lyuba's adventures in hell.

Her rasta-links made slithering noises as they stirred. Snakes, just like Peter said. Maybe she should have them removed. It wouldn't hurt to get real hair. It wouldn't hurt to get engineered eyes, like Andrei's. Life was long, people could change.

She could get medication if things got too rough.

She rubbed her face. Just as her undamaged jaw had surprised her, so did the smoothness of her skin. It hadn't always done that, but she had added up her real age recently.

She was sixty-five.

Her hands slid over her taut skin, wonderingly. They slid down her neck, over her shoulders, and suddenly her nightgown slipped off. She meant to pull it back into place. She touched her breasts instead. Her body responded to the touch, but Tally felt as if she were watching herself from a distance, unconnected to any pleasurable sensation.

Then Andrei's image entered her mind, a sensation as intimate as a kiss. *Better not*, she told herself, pulling her nightgown back up. She might be leaving Belarus soon, and she had not given in to temptation yet. He was just down the hall, estranged from his wife.

She got out of bed. The shower was the best thing now, regardless of whether or not she was already clean. Tally scrubbed herself under lukewarm water and pulled her danger suit on quickly, getting everything safely under wraps.

"Tally!" Peter was calling, rapping on her bedroom door. "Tally!"

"Coming!" she called, and in one dizzy moment knew she was *not* going to leave Belarus.

She loved Peter like her own son. The thought of never seeing him again . . .

*Do you have the courage to stay and fight for the ones you love?*

Her snakes hissed at her. She opened the door. Peter was standing there with a look of sheer panic on his face.

"Plan C!" he cried. "I got the signal for Plan C!"

"Don't you remember what you're supposed to do?" Tally asked, her heart fluttering.

"No!" He was frantic.

"Come on then." Tally grabbed his hand and pulled him into her apartments. "We'll improvise."

"Right . . ." He let her lead him through her rooms, into a closet near the bathroom that wasn't really a closet. The two of them shut themselves inside. It was pitch-black in there, except for a glowing purple circle the size of a plum on the wall at Peter's shoulder level. He tapped it.

"We can't even be sure it's a drill, Tally," he said nervously.

"That's true." Especially considering how weird things had been lately. "We'll assume it isn't, okay?"

"Okay," he said, just as they heard a soft *click* behind them. They turned and hurried down a narrow hall, then descended several flights of steps that led to a blank wall. Peter knelt at the bottom step and tapped a screw. A panel opened in the wall and Peter crawled inside. Tally followed him.

"How long is it taking?" he asked breathlessly. He was scampering so fast, Tally could hardly keep up with him.

"We're doing fine," she assured him.

"If we take too long, Father will be angry."

"That's not the problem," Tally reminded him. "This is not a drill, remember?"

"Right."

He seemed reassured. But Tally's thoughts were far from confident. *This is the last thing I need on a morning like this, a damned drill! And if it's not a drill, it's* definitely *the last thing I need.*

So many things could be happening. Someone might have made an attempt on Andrei's life, or Katerina's. Another microwar could have broken out. The list of possible disasters was too long to contemplate, and too unnerving. So Tally scampered after Peter and tried to concentrate on the basics.

*We blew Plan C, so we've got to figure a way to the arboretum from the library. That means we'll have to use the escape hatch inside that bathroom next to the guest kitchen . . .*

"Ow!" Peter bumped his head at the end of the tunnel, like he always did. But he worked the mechanism to get it open without further complaint. Soft light poured into their tunnel as he pushed open the hatch and the two of them crawled out into a space behind an oak bookshelf.

"So far so good," Tally told Peter, feigning confidence.

"Not so good," came Grigory's voice from the other side of the bookcase. "You couldn't see if someone waited in the library, yet you spoke out loud. Do I need to say anything more?"

Tally and Peter both let out a long sigh of relief.

"Come on out," said Grigory. "It's a drill. You messed up at the end, but you made good time. And you improvised. I give you credit for that."

"How did you guess we weren't following Plan C?" Peter asked him as they wormed their way from behind the bookshelf. "Did you use your sprites to watch us?"

"No, I timed you." Grigory stood near a research table, his blind face turned toward their voices. "When you didn't show up at the arboretum, I assumed you had forgotten the details of Plan C. I knew you would run to find Tally. You were fortunate she was home, little tsar."

"I remember Plan C now," Peter said. "I remembered it once we were in the tunnel."

"I doubt you'll forget it again," said Grigory.

"Never," promised Peter.

"And now that you've had such a fine lesson, here's your tutor to take you to regular classes," said Grigory.

Tally and Peter looked toward the big double doors at the far end of the library. In another moment, one door opened and Ms. Kenyon poked her head in. "I got a message to look for you here," she called. "Did you have another drill, Peter?"

"Yes," he said, sounding glad to see her. "I'm sorry for the delay."

She smiled at him. "Quite all right. We all have to do the drills."

"Yes, madam." He started toward her, then stopped and looked back at Tally. "Can you have lunch with Papa and me today?"

"I'll try," she said. "I have some errands to run."

"Okay," he said cheerfully, and went to join his tutor, his feet echoing across the marble floor.

When they had gone, Tally did not look at Grigory. She gazed at the Gothic windows and wondered just where the hell she was going to go.

"Errands?" asked Grigory. "Your job has been over for weeks, Tally."

"I know," she said dully.

He was silent. Tally hoped he wouldn't say something sympathetic. That might just be enough to make her cry.

"Do the dead frighten you?" he asked suddenly.

"No," Tally said. "They . . ." How had she felt when she saw Lyuba? Not frightened. "They piss me off," she said.

"Anger can be useful, if you know how to channel it," said Grigory.

"Maybe I'm afraid to channel it. I don't know what I'll end up doing."

"Not harm, certainly. You're too smart for that, too self-controlled."

Tally wondered if it was blindness that allowed Grigory to look past facades and see so deeply into people. Or if being a pain in the ass just came naturally for him.

"I should be planning my departure," she said. "It's past time."

"You're not going anywhere," said Grigory.

He didn't make it sound like an order, but he did sound very certain. "Is there something you know that I don't?" she asked pointedly.

"Many things. But you know this one yourself. You would have left months ago if you wanted to. But you've made this your home. Peter is like your own son."

"Maybe I could take him with me."

"You could ask," he said neutrally.

"Maybe I will."

"Let me know what you decide," he said. "I will make arrangements for you, one way or another. But as for errands you might run today—we're having a security meeting in Emily's quarters at 4:00 P.M. The murder cases will be discussed. You might put it on your agenda."

"I might," Tally said lamely. She damned well *would*. Grigory nodded, then turned and made a beeline for the door. She watched him, thinking about what he had said about anger. If Grigory was channeling his, what would he accomplish with it?

*Stick around and find out.* That was the plan. It wasn't much of one, but it was a start.

Andrei would have known that Special Agent Bullman was an investigator even if Emily had not introduced him as such. It was in his eyes.

Emily was the same. She never looked at any person, any scene, casually. She *observed.* And she knew what she was seeing. So did Agent Bullman.

"I'm glad to make your acquaintance," Andrei said, and shook Bullman's large, dry hand.

"Honored." Bullman glanced briefly at the clock on Emily's bookshelf.

Special Agent Bullman looked like many law enforcement officials Andrei had met. Nothing particularly striking about his features, if you didn't notice the intensity of his gaze. He was tall, neither fat nor thin, dressed in the sort of clothing a retired professional man might wear if he was running errands. Like Emily, he seemed to care less for a youthful aspect than he did for his job. His head was shaved as closely as Grigory's, and his voice had almost as much gravel in it.

"If this is everyone, I'd like to start the meeting," he said. "We've got a lot of ground to cover."

"Let's get started then." Andrei looked to Emily.

"Have a seat, ladies and gentlemen." Emily waved toward the big conference table. She had a 3-D display at the center, and she sat in the seat with the control keyboard. Andrei sat to her left, leaving the head of the table for Agent Bullman. Grigory and ESA Tam sat on the opposite side. Andrei noted that Tam's eyes were in full tactical mode—as usual. She was a new person on his security team, having just transferred from the War Division, and he could not recall a time when he had seen her eyes *out* of tactical.

"We have company," she said in a flat tone.

A moment later, Natalia walked through the door. She fixed her gaze on Agent Bullman.

"Can I help you?" asked Bullman.

"I am the world engineer," Natalia said, her back straight and her head erect. Her rasta-links were floating around her face like the snakes of Medusa; Andrei was taken aback by the force of her gaze. It was like being confronted by an angry goddess. "I built the cities of this world. I helped to lure colonists here. I want to know what's happening to them and why."

"That's not up to me to decide," said Bullman, and he looked at Andrei. Natalia did too.

Andrei searched her face for the slightest uncertainty. He wondered how much the truth would hurt her. It was an ugly truth.

But she was a grown woman. She returned his gaze steadily.

"Okay," he said. "You're in the loop. We're comparing notes today, so I'll be learning almost as much as you. Come, join us."

Natalia sat next to Emily.

"We're ready to start," said Andrei.

Bullman nodded. "Well, according to your latest census figures, you have a population of roughly eight million people. Out of those eight million people, sixty-seven men, women, and children have disappeared under mysterious circumstances. That's not a bad figure for a population like yours, but several red flags are present that have brought these cases to the attention of the Serial Killer Task Force."

Natalia interrupted. "There's a Serial Killer Task Force? I've never heard of it."

Bullman did not seem annoyed. "Most people never have reason to hear about us, but we've been around for a long time, since before there was a Star Republic. We started as an offshoot of an agency called the Federal Bureau of Investigation."

"I've heard of *them*," said Natalia.

"You've heard of the Republic entity with the same name. They have the same boss we do, the Central Government. They have the same roots too, the original FBI. That original agency pioneered the science of serial killer investigation. The red flags I spoke of earlier were identified at that time, and they still apply today, though we've added to the list over the centuries. Here's why your missing people have attracted our special attention."

He counted the reasons off with the fingers of his left hand. "Their locators are missing. They had them when they landed here, but now they're not transmitting. A body has to be completely obliterated before that will happen, literally reduced to atoms. But we have found body parts of thirty-seven of your missing people, including the locators. The locators have been nullified, and we can't tell how. So this is the work of a very technologically advanced person or persons.

"We had a series of killings on two other worlds that have a lot of the same characteristics as the ones you're having here, most notably the disabled locators. The person or persons responsible were never apprehended. That's another marker.

"But the most important factor is that these killings have been going on for seven years. Under those circumstances alone, my department is obliged to investigate."

He stopped, waiting for questions. Natalia came up

with one. "If our people can't find the killer, how can anyone else? We have good people on the case."

"Exactly," he said, and Andrei suspected he had heard the accusation hundreds of times before. He responded to it with diplomacy. "The purpose of the task force is to network with other police agencies, to compare notes and bring specialists to the case. I'm a specialist myself, I track superkillers."

*"Superkillers?"*

"I'll explain more about that in a minute. First I want to focus on the victim profile we have for these cases. We profile the victims because it helps us understand the M.O. of possible serial killers. When we look at your unsolved cases as a group, one point stands out: the missing locators. That's what they all have in common. Another, less obvious point is one that only investigators would notice. Not one of the victims is a person who lived a high-risk lifestyle."

"That's uncommon?" asked Andrei.

"Very," said Bullman. "Most serial killers are opportunistic, they don't like to take too many risks. So they go after people who tend to put themselves in dangerous situations, like prostitutes who get into a car with a stranger, or drug addicts or alcoholics who pass out and present an easy target. Many victims are people who aren't missed very quickly, if at all. Ordinary people tend to be murdered by people they know. Children are more vulnerable, but even they tend to fall into the pattern. Killers are like wolves hunting at the edge of the herd, they look for the weak, the unprotected, the calves who wander off."

"Or the kid who's walking to the corner store for milk," offered Natalia unhappily.

Bullman nodded. "And in a way, your whole group can be described that way, which is odd. They're all ordinary people who were just going about their business. But after you take that into account, the group can actually be divided into two different profiles. The first one is easy to define, it consists of young, attractive women. We have found the partial remains of most of the victims in this group. All of them were dismembered, the body parts arranged ritualistically. We have forensic evidence that all of them were tortured before death. No body parts below the navel have been recovered.

"If you look at this first group, the profile of a killer seems pretty straightforward. He is young or has access to youth drugs, probably Caucasian, a highly organized killer who considers himself to be intellectually superior to most, if not all, of the people he meets. He keeps souvenirs, though he may not keep them anywhere near his home or office. He plans the killing very carefully, and probably stalks the victims for some time before he goes after them.

"So—" Bullman glanced at the clock again, the mark of someone who was accustomed to filling out detailed reports with well-documented time frames. "Once again, we have some interesting markers. Our killer is not afraid to take risks. And he is extraordinarily careful about not leaving physical evidence. We have found no prints of any kind, no body fluids, no DNA, no fibers or soil, no hair—no recognizable tool marks, which is not to say there weren't *any* tool marks. The body parts have marks on them, but we can't tell what made them beyond the fact that they were sophisticated.

"This does *not* mean that no evidence was left on or near the bodies. The killer may be employing sophisticated machines to clean up his scenes. We use them ourselves when gathering evidence, and our machines don't miss much. He may be employed in law enforcement, or in a job that uses similar technology."

Andrei glanced at Natalia. She was taking in the new information like a world engineer, adding it to her model of the universe, trying to arrange it where it fit.

"The second group has a different profile," said Bull. "Or rather, they don't have much of a profile at all. If it weren't for their missing locators, I wouldn't link them with the first group, they would seem to be the victims of a different killer. They're men, women, and children, all ages, different walks of life, taken from different areas all over this continent, and none of their bodies have turned up. Since we have no bodies to examine, it's difficult to say whether they were killed by an organized or disorganized personality."

"Or whether they were killed at all," said Natalia.

But he shook his head. "It's a lot tougher to keep someone prisoner than it is to kill them and hide the body. It's possible some of them are still alive, but it's not probable."

"Are you sure all of them had locators?" asked Natalia.

"Yes."

"I don't have a locator," Andrei said. "My parents didn't want to make it any easier for assassins to find me. I assume it's rare not to have one."

"Very," said Agent Bullman. "On most worlds it's the law to get them shortly after birth. Some people try to get them removed, but that's almost impossible to do."

Andrei considered that for a moment. "I was just wondering if you could be a superkiller if you had a locator. I know they're used extensively in law enforcement, to locate both suspects and missing victims."

"That's hard to say." Andrei couldn't tell whether the suggestion was new to Agent Bullman or not. "It's true that killers without locators would be a lot harder to find."

"So who else would be likely not to have a locator?" wondered Natalia.

"People like Mr. Mironenko," said Bullman. "Survivalists and isolationists won't get them for their children, but they're usually not the sort to be comfortable moving around in big cities among lots of strangers. The same is true of some of the more paranoid religious sects, though we can never rule them out entirely."

"Aliens don't have them," Natalia said suddenly.

Bullman nodded. "They don't. But it's been my experience that serial killers tend to hunt among their own kind. I've never encountered an alien serial killer. But once again, you can never rule the possibility out entirely."

"The guy who's leaving those body parts is probably human," said Emily. "I've seen bodies mutilated this way before. It fits a familiar pattern."

"There is a message in the cruelty," said Bullman, "and in the fact that the bodies are dismembered. This indicates extreme contempt for the victims; they have been reduced to things rather than people. The body parts are all positioned to indicate something; he's leaving deliberate clues. And despite the very different profiles of our two groups of victims, there is one other marker that indicates we may be dealing with the same killer for both groups. The timing of the disappearances." He glanced at the clock again, as if to illustrate his point.

"The second group, the ordinary people, disappeared in the spring and summer. The first group, attractive girls and women, disappeared in the fall and winter. The timing is deliberate."

Andrei remembered something Baba Yaga had written to him. *Evil is perennial. It likes to go into hibernation under the frost and dead leaves so it can bloom again in the spring.*

"Okay," said Natalia, her rasta-links stirring restlessly, "so what is he trying to say?"

"Figure that out," said Bullman, "and you're on your way to solving these cases. Emily, you made a good point about insect infestation. You find it in most bodies left outdoors, even if they've only been there a few hours. But some of your bodies don't have it. This may be an artifact of the ecosystem you're in.

But even on strange new worlds, it's rare not to find some kind of infestation where life exists. Bugs don't discriminate."

"There are three places where we haven't found bugs on the bodies," said Emily, and she activated the screen. It displayed a topical map of the continent. "Lyuba Petrova's hand and head found in quadrant 0027 of Grey Forest; Danika Dyakonova's torso found in quadrant 8840 of the Gobi Desert; and Lucine Ismirlian's head and breasts found in quadrant 0006 on Bald Mountain."

"Sterile places," remarked Tam. "Do you suppose he knew it would be that way, or was it just an accident?"

Emily's fingers danced over the keys. "No accidents for this guy. Everything he does, down to the tiniest detail, is for a reason. So this bug situation is for a reason too. Unfortunately, he may be so buggy himself that his reasoning will only make sense to him. That's one of the problems we always face. Being smart doesn't mean you're not a complete screwball."

Andrei glanced at Grigory, who had said nothing yet. His expression was neutral, his posture alert. Andrei felt sure that whatever they might discuss at this meeting, Grigory had already thought of it.

"Scrupulosity," said Andrei. "A fixation on bugs, or the lack of them. Contempt for his victims, he thinks they're unclean? Or he has made them so."

"Maybe," said Emily, "but there's more to it. He didn't pick those girls because he thought they were insects. I want to show you something. Here are the personal profiles of the people from the first group."

An image appeared on the 3-D screen. The girl in the picture was not just pretty, she was strikingly lovely. She smiled with perfect teeth and held a violin in her lap.

"Tasha Balakireva, thirteen years old," said Emily. "Straight-A student at the Belarus Royal Academy, a tough school. Award-winning musician—she had already secured a scholarship at Katerina's St. Petersburg Academy of Music."

Andrei looked at the image, his heart sinking. He had seen head shots of the girls, but most of the images he remembered were the ones from the morgue.

Emily switched to the next profile. Another lovely young girl smiled from the screen. This one was posed in her ballerina outfit, frozen in a perfect pas de deux. "Sophia Fetisova, aged fourteen. Principal dancer with the Mironenko Ballet. If you want to see her in action, she's in our entertainment library, performing *Cinderella*, *Sleeping Beauty*, and *Romeo and Juliet*. She'll break your heart."

*She already has*, thought Andrei.

"Here's the girl you just found," said Emily, and Lyuba Petrova appeared. She was holding a puppy. "Lyuba was a mathematical genius. She would have gone on to do great things. The killer put a stop to that. I can't help but wonder if that's what he had in mind for these girls. Envy. He was jealous of them, he punished them."

"Or," said Tam, her tone as flat as ever, "he kept the parts he liked best and tried to make the perfect girl out of them."

"He only kept the lower part of the bodies," said Emily. "We found everything else."

No one seemed inclined to speculate about why that would be. Andrei could not help but think about the fact that no body fluids had been found. The body fluids might be on or inside the missing parts.

"Show me someone from the second group, the ordinary people," he said suddenly.

"Coming right up." Emily keyed the pad, and a family appeared, a man, woman, and their four-year-old daughter. The mother was holding the child. They were dressed in rough but clean clothes, and none of them were smiling.

"The Balogs," said Emily. "Farmers. They disappeared from Janoshalma, in southern Hungary. Their neighbors said they were out in the fields at dusk. Another daughter, Anci, had gone in to start supper. The rest of them should have joined her, she said they were literally right behind her. She went in, poured water into a pot and set it on the counter, went to the kitchen door to see what was taking the others so long and they were gone. She never heard any cries, and we found no signs of a struggle. The neighbors said they were good people, no arguments or grievances with anyone else. When you look at them in this picture, it's obvious: they're plain, honest people, just going about their business. They disappeared as if the earth swallowed them up."

Andrei stared at the Balog family. "So how were they taken so silently?" he asked. "Three people, and none of them uttered a sound?"

"Or they screamed but no one heard them," said Agent Bullman. "The perfect crime is the one that has no witnesses."

Natalia rested her chin in her hand, looking wistfully at the missing family. "The perfect crime," she said. "But why *them*?"

"Wrong place at the wrong time?" suggested Tam.

Everyone stared at the picture. Andrei felt a chill, deep in his bones. Could it be that simple?

"We're missing a lot of facts," said Bullman, glancing again at Emily's clock, and from his tone Andrei could tell he was getting ready to conclude the meeting. "We need to find the reasons behind the pattern or patterns at work here. What we're doing now is taking the evidence that's been thoroughly documented in this case and comparing it to the other cases we have in the homicide database. The database includes both solved and unsolved cases, and we've already had some matches, as I mentioned earlier. We also need to figure out if there's any evidence we're missing."

"I received an excellent suggestion today from the wife of one of the village chiefs," said Andrei. "It will require a considerable amount of computational power, but she thinks we might find the killer's image in the database compiled by the survey sprites."

"Time consuming," said Bullman, "but we've had to resort to that before. Sometimes it works, let's give it a try."

Grigory spoke up. "I am reviewing my security files and the screening process that was used on our personnel and the colonists. Previously, I only looked at data from the first year, since that was when the killings began. But now I am reviewing all of it. I have thrown my assumptions out the window, since they seem to be doing me no good."

"What if he was here before any of us got here?" asked Natalia.

It was a startling suggestion. The possibility had not even occurred to Andrei.

"The survey sprites didn't find anyone," he said. "But that doesn't necessarily mean anything. There have been recorded incidents in which sprite sensors were thwarted."

He didn't mention Baba Yaga. He knew that whatever agenda she might have, it did not include serial killings. But she was not the only being who could blind sprites. Andrei suspected that sort of stealth technology was far more prevalent than he had originally feared.

"Let's look into the survey information," said Bullman. "And see if we can't identify those tool marks. We've got profilers working on the psychological evidence. And I have a feeling you may find some anomalies if you look into the immigration records, Grigory. That's where we stand now. Any questions or comments?"

"Just one," said Andrei. "You mentioned superkillers. Have you ever caught one?"

"No," said Bullman. "But we've tracked a few."

"If you've never caught onc, how do you know they exist at all?" asked Natalia.

Bullman looked at the clock again, but his answer was unhurried. "At this point, superkillers are only theoretical. They're as legendary as black holes used to be. But over the years, we've turned up some disturbing markers. I've been tracking those markers for most of my career."

"So you've built a profile," said Andrei.

"A possible one," said Bullman. "Most serial killers aren't nearly as smart as they think they are. They have a reputation in the media for being brilliant fiends, but they're mostly just talented opportunists. Even when they're clever, they have personality traits that often give them away, things they can't help revealing. So most of them keep to themselves, reducing the chance of being spotted as an oddball. Or they travel around so no one can really get a chance to know them.

"A superkiller would have to fit in better than that. He might be able to turn his cruelty on and off like a switch, putting it aside when he needs to be normal and function within tightly knit communities, then putting it back on again when the opportunity seems right. He would have to be an extremely good multitrack thinker. Unlike ordinary serial killers, he would be very good at building complex mental models of the universe and would have a firm grasp of reality, cause and effect, consequences."

"You're making him sound like a Zen master," said Natalia.

Bullman nodded. "That's why we call them superkillers."

Emily turned off the 3-D screen. The image of the Balog family faded from Andrei's cortex, but he still saw them in his mind. *What would a* superkiller *want with you?* he wondered. *What was your place in his great scheme?*

The answer would not come readily, but it was there. Right under their noses. Andrei was sure of it.

"I think we're done for now," he said. "Emily, I'll

look to you to coordinate this information-sharing process. Agent Bullman"—he stood and offered his hand—"we are extremely grateful for your help."

Bullman shook his hand. "It's my job. We'll figure it out eventually."

"I'm sure of it," said Andrei.

He just didn't know *when.*

Tam and Grigory left with Bull, leaving Andrei and Natalia with Emily.

"Natalia, I'm glad you came to the meeting," said Andrei. "I wasn't sure you would want to be involved. Your other duties are completed. I know you were hoping to return to Canopus someday . . ."

"I'd like to stay on Belarus for now," said Tally. "And help you with this investigation, if I can."

"I'm glad," he said, and hoped Emily would not see just how much so. "Please let me know what resources you'll need."

"I'll let you know as soon as I figure it out myself," said Natalia. "Emily and I will have to talk about it."

"We'll thrash it out, Andrei," Emily promised.

"I know you will," he said. "Good afternoon to both of you. Call me if you need me."

"Tally—" Emily leaned across the table and patted her hand. "Stay for supper. We'll put together my latest picture puzzle and talk."

"I'd like that," said Tally, wishing that Andrei could have stayed, and grateful that she wouldn't have to go back to her lonely quarters yet. "What are we cooking?"

"I thought we'd order in."

"I could go for a meatball sub with peppers," said Tally, suddenly ravenous.

"I'll order a couple of subs. Come on, make yourself cozy."

Tally followed Emily out of the conference room and into her living room. While Emily changed and ordered the subs, Tally studied the plain, comfortable room. Emily's place did not appear to have a distinct style, but only if you were trying to judge it by colors, textures, style of furnishings. Everything in Emily's apartments had a purpose, nothing was there simply to make an impression. Every chair or couch had an occupant at some time, every table was a useful surface. Every book, document, picture and database was connected to what Emily *did*, not to what she wanted people to think about her. From what Tally could see, Emily allowed only one concession to clutter and frivolity into her life: her picture puzzles. They were stacked on shelves, sometimes piled on the floor. When Emily was relaxing, one could most likely find her sitting at her puzzle table, patiently putting pieces together.

Emily came back in wearing sweats. "Twenty minutes till the subs arrive," she announced, making a beeline for her puzzle table.

"I'll sit down in a minute," Tally murmured. She felt restless. She wandered back and forth, thinking about superkillers. But her eyes kept returning to Emily's puzzle. "My head is spinning," she remarked dazedly.

"I know the feeling," said Emily.

The puzzle was complete enough for Tally to recognize Egyptian art. She moved closer, wondering if she could identify it. But there wasn't enough of it yet. It could be one of several known works, or even a made-up painting in the Egyptian style.

"What does the picture look like when it's complete?" asked Tally. "Where's the box?"

"I don't know exactly what it looks like," said Emily. "I have my secretary pick puzzles at random and put them in plain boxes for me. I never know what I've got until I start to work on it."

She was as comfortable as Tally ever saw her. When Emily put on her sweats, she was almost a different person. Her braid was loose and forgotten, her feet in big padded socks. She looked alert as she bent over her puzzle, but she wasn't frowning the way she always seemed to do over work.

"Emily, how long ago did you stop being a homicide investigator?"

"Oh, Jesus—about forty years, I guess." She tried a piece in a few different spots, couldn't make it fit, then put it down and tried another.

Tally was amazed at her patience. Peter was good at them, but puzzles frustrated Tally. She had never finished one in her life. But as she watched, she began to think she saw where some of the pieces might fit.

"Grab a chair," said Emily. "It takes more than one puzzler to solve a mystery."

Tally sat and tried a piece in a likely-looking spot. It fit. Overconfident, she tried another and failed. For the next several minutes, her frustration grew as she failed again and again.

"Keep looking," Emily told her. "Don't try to figure it out all at once. Sit back and look at it again, try a new angle."

"Is that how you investigated murders?"

"Sometimes. After a decade or two at it, a lot of stuff was pretty obvious. The tougher cases always took a lot of good teamwork. Looking at something with fresh eyes always seems to help when you get stuck."

Tally tried that. She made another piece fit.

"You see a lot when you work homicide," Emily said. "For instance, you can usually tell if someone has been abused."

Tally's hand froze before she could pick up another piece.

"Yeah, I'm talking about you," said Emily. "I'm not trying to pry. But you wondered why we didn't tell you what was going on from the beginning. The truth is, I made the decision. I wanted to spare you some of the heartache." She placed a piece that turned out to be Anubis's hand. "I've seen too much of that in my life."

The hand. Suddenly Tally couldn't stop looking at

it. Anubis, guide to the dead, was gesturing. The puzzle was pieces. Pieces of figures in the painting. Pieces of people.

"That's what the killer's doing," she whispered. "He's trying to make us put together a puzzle."

"Yeah," Emily agreed. "He's playing a game. The game is what concerns him, not the pieces. The pieces are for *us*."

Tally looked at Emily's calm, kind face. "What horrors you've seen," she said.

"That's why I quit Homicide." Emily patiently tried another piece. "For decades, all I cared about was catching the bastards. Find 'em, build a case against them, prosecute them, and put them away. And guess what? Tomorrow there's some new freak to look for."

"I would want to get into something totally different," said Tally. "I would want to forget about it as much as I could."

"Nope," said Emily as she made yet another piece fit. "You don't forget. You don't get away. I didn't even get into something very different. I moved up and out, first. I started my career working for a small city department on Raven. When I got sick of that, I tried for a promotion to a bigger department. Eventually I ended up working at Central, investigating crimes on several different worlds, chasing people who could travel just about anywhere—sometimes to places where Central Government authority wasn't recognized. For decades that kept me busy."

She poked another piece into place. "Eventually I began to see that what I really needed to do was to keep the bad guy from hurting people in the first place. That's how I got into security, how I eventually ended up *here*."

She looked at Tally, her pale eyes keen. "And look what I'm doing all over again. Can't keep my nose out of it, even if I wanted to—which I don't. Every single head we've found—their faces are contorted in agony. Whoever this guy is, he's a genius at causing pain. The cuts on the body parts are so precise, the cruelty is so calculated."

She held Tally's gaze for a long moment. Then she looked at the puzzle and picked up another piece.

"So," she said, "what horrors have you seen, Tally?"

"No horrors, not really. My father beat me. Once he beat me almost to death, but I think that shocked him—when he realized I almost died. After that, he hit us from time to time, but never beat us as badly. It wasn't really his fault, he was going crazy—"

Emily interrupted her. "You said he almost beat you to death once. What did you do to make him so angry?"

Tally was flustered. She wanted to make Emily understand that her parents weren't horrible people, they weren't—*trash.*

"You're such a good person," Emily said kindly. "What could you have possibly done to make him so angry?"

"I read a book," said Tally numbly.

"What? A naughty book?"

"*The Hobbit,*" said Tally. She could still remember the cover of the book: an odd, abstract army wandering across a field of red, with a blazing pink sun in the sky. She had checked the book out of her public library. She could have gone home and accessed it on her terminal, but in those days she had loved the feel of paper in her hands, loved the musty smell of the binding, the ink. She remembered the smell of the books better than she remembered her sisters' faces. This was why she had carved the god Thoth into her door. He was the god of people who wrote stories on paper.

She blinked and saw Emily's puzzle again. She picked up another piece. "You never knew what was going to set my father off," she said. "When we were little, he and mother were kind to us. But they were both so religious. No one ever wants to say it, but sometimes religion can get crazy."

"Sometimes it can," Emily agreed.

Tally barely heard her. "I mean—my mother, she just got so stern and critical. Whenever he beat us, she always seemed to think it was because we were fundamentally wrong, we were sinners who should know better but who willfully screwed up. She went to church all the time, we went along with her because we thought we could win back her love that way. But it was dead, her love was just plain dead."

"So she never tried to protect you," said Emily.

"No way. She just sat there and read her Bible in her sitting room, while he raged. His favorite part of the Bible was Revelation, he loved to talk about the Apocalypse. He always said we were in the end times."

Tally shivered. Just talking about it brought back the old fears. "He never even went to church, he wouldn't let the preacher have the floor! He couldn't work anymore because he preached at work. We were humiliated, my sisters and I, but we learned it was better when he was noisy than when he was quiet."

Emily found Anubis's foot. "So before an attack, he would get quiet. Brooding?"

"Stewing. Like a pot with a lid on too tight. And you could never tell how long that was going to last, it could go on for days, weeks. That was the worst thing, waiting for it to finally happen. We would pray—"

*Tally, do you ever pray?*

*No.*

"How long did it go on, Tally?"

She blinked. "About seven years. I found *The Hobbit* just after my eleventh birthday. We weren't allowed to have birthday parties, so I had to treat myself. I liked to go to the library. That's where I learned about other worlds, some real and some imaginary. I wanted to live in that library. I would have been happy if I could have put a little bed in one corner and stayed there forever. So I found *The Hobbit*, and I took it home to curl up with it like the nice, quiet daughter I was, who never gave any trouble, never talked back, just sat with my nose in a book all evening and forgot about my miserable family. And suddenly it got torn out of my hands . . ."

*I guess I don't need to pray*, she told Peter. But that was a lie. After that day, she had stopped *wanting* to pray. Her father had put the fear of God in her.

"Did he say why you shouldn't have the book?" Emily asked gently.

Tally sighed. Suddenly she felt as old as she really was. "Something about elves and fairies. Evil creatures, the consorts of witches. I didn't really listen too closely. I had a feeling what the real reason was, anyway."

"He was jealous of the book," said Emily.

Tally was grateful she didn't have to say it herself. She sighed again, easing the tightness in her chest. "He knew I was using those books to escape. After that, I never brought another book home. I read them at the library and left them there. Didn't spend too much time there, either. Didn't want them to tell me I couldn't go anymore."

And that was that. She had spit it out. She had never told anyone the whole story. She had been determined to make her life what *she* wanted it to be, to soar like the people in the books she loved. Reading about those worlds inspired her to *build* worlds, to make them real.

"But you almost died," Emily reminded her. "He almost beat you to death."

"Right," said Tally, wanting to leave it alone. It was over.

But Emily wasn't allowing that. "How come you didn't die, Tally?"

The question puzzled her. "My sisters took care of me."

"How long were you near death?"

Tally sighed again, but this time she felt no relief. "Days," she said. "I'm not sure."

"Did he ever say he was sorry? Fuss over you?"

"No, it wasn't one of those Jekyll and Hydc things. He was a fanatic. We all left as soon as we could get legal permission. I was sixteen, and I was out that door so fast."

"But you still writc to your mother."

Emily knew a lot about Tally's life. She knew what messages came into the winter palace and what went out. Tally didn't answer.

"Why do you still write hcr, Tally?"

"I was trying to find out something about *you.*" Tally shook hcr hcad. "I should have known better than to talk to a detective."

"But you did find out something about me," said Emily. "And I'm sorry if I made you think about the past. I know the last couplc of days have been horrible. The roughest days you've had in a long timc, huh?"

"Yes," Tally admitted, hating the weakness in her voice.

"Nothing to be ashamed of. I'll even make a guess about why you write to your mother. You do it because you have the power to. She always writes back, and I'll bet she's still trying to force you to do things her way, right?"

"Oh, yes," said Tally.

"And you go right ahead and do what you think is right. Not to defy her, but because you know what you have to do."

"True," said Tally. "Thanks for putting it that way."

"No problem." Emily gave her a quirky smile. "I told you, it takes teamwork. And you have to know your fellow team members. You're in the loop now, Tally, if that's what you want. Okay?"

"Okay," said Tally, wondering what she was really agreeing to.

They worked in silence for a time. Tally thought the conversation was over. But then Emily said, "So you understand what's happening to Katerina. Probably better than any of us."

Tally felt a fluttering in her stomach. She *did* understand what was happening to Katerina, but she wasn't sure she was the right one to say so. Not considering the feelings she had about Andrei.

But Emily probably knew that already. And still she brought up the subject.

"It just gets worse," Tally said finally. "The religiosity. I think in the beginning there's euphoria that goes with it, a feeling of transcendence. I suspect it must have been the way Joan of Arc felt. She would rather burn at the stake than—you know, just calm down and live a normal life. But the tricky thing is, I don't think that euphoria lasts. As they get older, God stops talking to them. They feel like they've lost him, so they pursue him harder than ever."

Emily nodded. "If her fanaticism is caused by an obsessive-compulsive disorder, there's medication that might help her. But I doubt she would take it, and Andrei isn't the sort to force it on her. Nature will have to take its course. Christ—she's still using youth drugs. How far will her zealotry go if it has centuries to progress?"

Tally shrugged. "My parents won't find out. They never used youth drugs. Think that's sinful. You're supposed to live the amount of time God gives you, then dutifully croak."

"That's what most people still have to do."

"Yeah," said Tally. "But not dutifully."

Emily laughed. She placed another piece of the puzzle, completing an important chunk.

"Ah-hah," said Tally. "That's a false door." She outlined it with her finger. "So this is a tomb painting. The false door led to the afterlife, you painted all the things on it that you wanted to take with you."

Emily squinted at the puzzle. "False door," she said. "Not in the Egyptian sense, but I think that's what we're dealing with in this case. We see them and think one thing. But when we open them, we're going to find something different. Our superkiller—we'd better consider that he might be something we never saw before."

Tally nodded. "Okay. If possible, I'd like to see the reports you've compiled. Imagination is my business. You want something new? I'll see what I can come up with."

She placed another puzzle piece where it fit. Crime solving was a supreme act of teamwork, just like world building. Together, she and Emily would make good progress.

And she had to admit—once you got a taste for puzzles, it was hard to walk away from them.

*Good morning, people of Belarus—and welcome to True-Life Network, the place where you get the news, the facts, and the truth! We are completely independent of any sprite networks, so you know our information will be completely free of propaganda. Today is Tuesday, March 32, and here is the news.*

*Science Minister Maxim Burakov confirmed today that sprites in our solar system have multiplied in numbers beyond our capacity to count.*

MINISTER BURAKOV IN FRONT OF WINTER PALACE: *"Of course, this is always the case when sprites are used extensively. They perform so many functions, they are constantly combining to find new ways to do things, and they can make more of themselves."*

*"Yes,"* ANATOLI KALENIK, HEAD OF "LEAGUE OF CITIZENS DEMANDING AUTONOMY FROM SPRITES," IN FRONT OF HIS OFFICE IN ST. PETERSBURG: *"My esteemed peer could not have stated the situation better. They have grown beyond our ability to count them, let alone control them, and the only people who can stop them are not wholly human anymore—"*

STATIC IMAGE OF GRIGORY MICHAELOVICH, CLOSE-UP OF HIS FACE.

KALENIK IN VOICE-OVER: *"This administration refuses to hold democratic elections for president, and Tsar Andrei Mironenko is well known for his sympathy and support for this secret society of near-humans. And he refuses to answer this basic question: Who are these creatures who call themselves ESAs? What are their true intentions? They don't answer to the Central Government, so who are their superiors? Why have they used their sprites to undermine governments who don't agree with them? What do they intend for us, once we have become too comfortable and complacent to see them for what they really are?"*

KALENIK SITTING AT HIS DESK—BEHIND HIM THE WALL IS COVERED WITH BLOWN-UP PICTURES OF ALIENS IN VARIOUS SCENES OF CONFLICT WITH HUMANS.

VOICE OF FEMALE INTERVIEWER, OFF SCREEN: *"But Andrei Mironenko and his advisors have stated that ESAs and aliens like the Woovs have only benefited humankind. If that's true, what do we have to worry about?*

*"Slavery. I have evidence that Woovs and other aliens are combining their DNA with willing ESAs to make a new race. These people will be appointed in positions of power, refusing to let human citizens vote them out of office, until they control every critical seat of power in the Republic!"*

SLOW PAN AND CLOSE-UP OF A PICTURE OF A WOOV, A HUMANOID ALIEN COVERED IN GOLDEN FUR. ITS FEATURES APPEAR TO BE A CROSS BETWEEN SIMIAN AND FELINE, AN IMPRESSION THAT IS ENHANCED BY ITS POINTED AND TUFTED EARS. IT IS HOLDING A HUMAN MALE BY THE THROAT.

DISSOLVE AND GO TO COMMERCIAL.

Andrei was prepared to fence with his usual training partner, Alexis, but it was Grigory who came out to the floor in fencing gear.

"This is a surprise," said Andrei.

"Do you mind?" Grigory stood rcady, as if Andrci's answer didn't matter. He had in mind to engage him—in some fashion, if not with the foil. Andrei was intrigued. He pulled down his face mask. Grigory did the same.

"En garde," said Andrei, and moved into a fighting stance. Grigory mirrored him.

Andrei had expected an aggressive attack, but Grigory allowed him the first thrust. His stance was perfect, his movements graceful, he seemed aware not only of every move Andrei made, but of every move he *might* make.

And he had no sprites in the room.

They moved back and forth, advancing, retreating, circling. With each parry and thrust, Andrei felt as if he were leading Grigory in a dance—except that this partner struck blows. Their foils engaged with a sound like a giant scissors coming together, and Andrei felt the iron strength behind every blow. He hoped Grigory felt something of the same. Sweat began to trickle into his eyes and he did his best to ignore it. He attacked again, but it was Grigory who almost scored. Andrei barely parried in time.

Andrei stepped back and circled, watching the blind ronin, ready with his foil. He picked his moment and attacked. Andrei thrust toward the heart on Grigory's jerkin; Grigory moved like flowing water, turning his torso, making Andrei chase him a moment too long. In another moment, Grigory's foil was squarely on target, bending as the button on its tip pushed against Andrei's chest.

Andrei was stunned, but not displeased. "I think I've been studying under the wrong master," he said.

Grigory stepped back. "You fight well. There's nothing wrong with your style."

"Except for the part where I lost," said Andrei, pulling up his face mask.

Grigory pulled his mask off and tucked it under an arm. He was grinning. "I have news," he said. "But I hate to interrupt your routine, so I thought I would combine the two."

"I think it's time to head back to the office," said Andrei. "You can tell me on the way."

Several of Grigory's sprites flew into the room, like children eager to see their father. Andrei and Grigory left the gymnasium, sprites flitting to and fro over their heads, and passed through the security checkpoints from one floor to another. Grigory waited until they were alone again before sending his news, even though no one else could hear it.

<An unfortunate news clip is being aired on Knossos and Persepolis—of an Andrei Mironenko look-alike frolicking at an orgy.>

"Really?" Andrei didn't bat an eyelash. "Did I have fun?"

"Oh, most assuredly. You had fun with three Turkish boys, each approximately ten years old."

"In that case," said Andrei, "that was no ordinary look-alike. That was my cousin Peotr."

"He's a dead ringer. The clip is extremely graphic. It is inflaming anti-Belarus passions."

"How touching. And we're hardly out of the starting gate."

"You've been recruiting Muslim colonists from Darius, Xerxes, not to mention Cambyses—all places that have leaned away from hardline fundamentalism and toward mixed societies, religious tolerance, all that sort of heresy. And you're a Russian, offering these colonists a chance for high profit, and more of that nasty mixing and tolerance. Obviously you're doing it to corrupt them and to avail yourself of pretty boys. They see right through you."

"Curses. Foiled again."

They entered Andrei's quarters. Sprites flew in ahead of them, checking for safety. Andrei pulled off his fencing outfit. He wore his danger suit underneath.

Andrei sat behind his desk. "Have you had lunch?"

Grigory did not sit. "I'll grab a bite with Emily. We're working longer hours these days. We'll doubtless have something to pester you about later."

"I'll wait with bated breath."

Grigory turned to leave.

"Wait," Andrei said, and Grigory stopped by the door. "Satisfy my curiosity—who was your fencing master?"

"You were," said Grigory.

"You mean," Andrei said, "just now? That was the first time you fenced in your life?"

"There's a first time for everything," said Grigory, without a trace of mockery in his voice. "I found it very instructive. Thank you, Master."

"You're welcome," said Andrei.

The blind ronin left his office. Andrei put down the lunch menu. Suddenly, he wasn't all that hungry.

An hour later, after reviewing another report and sorting through a stack of bills and resolutions from the Duma, Andrei felt like picking up the lunch menu again. He had scarcely glanced at it when he received another call.

PRIME MINISTER MIKHAILOV read the tag. Andrei took the call.

<Sorry to disturb you, but there's a matter I need to bring to your attention,> said Igor.

<You have it.>

<The tsarina has made up a law and is trying to get various ministries and law enforcement agencies to enforce it.>

<What do you mean, *made up a law*?>

<She has declared, in writing, with copies sent to the various ministries, that all "foreign" music shall no longer be imported to Belarus in any form, entertainment channels that program "foreign" music shall be blocked, nightclubs that showcase that sort of music shall have their liquor licenses yanked, and the bands performing at such clubs shall be deported.>

Andrei had hoped Katya would be so occupied with her own musical endeavors, she wouldn't care what anyone else was doing. <I see. And you say she has tried to have this edict enforced?>

<She attempted to dispatch officials to intercept and confiscate a shipment of music transfers this morning.>

<She has no authority.>

<I told her so, as gently as I could. She informed me that she is "second in command.">

<There is no such thing.>

<Yes, I told her. She persisted. I was in communication with her for over an hour, and I don't believe she understood one word I said. Or she chose not to.>

Andrei was dismayed to hear it, but not surprised.

<Andrei . . . I spend a good deal of time with Katya. You know she insists on attending all the state functions.>

Andrei knew it too well. She was eternally angry with him for not doing the same. <I'm very glad to have you at those functions, Igor.>

<I am honored to do it. Please forgive me if I am

intruding into personal matters, but I have become concerned over the past several months about Katya's—health. Forgive me. But I think her doctor should be alerted.>

<I'll do that. I'm sorry you were troubled.>

<No trouble. It's my job.>

Igor signed off, leaving Andrei alone with unhappy thoughts. He folded his hands and stared at the portrait of his mother.

"You would know what to say to Katya," he said softly. "And she would listen to you."

But Mother was silent, as she had been for centuries. Andrei was forced to seek his estranged wife without her counsel or comfort.

He rose and went to find Katerina.

Katerina stood perfectly straight, almost like a dancer except that somehow her stance was in strict adherence to gravity rather than a graceful defiance of it. She was dressed from head to toe in the gorgeous, restrictive style so popular lately among the very rich. Her hair was woven into a jeweled tiara and tied in a net at the nap of her neck. She looked every inch a tsarina.

On her face was an expression he rarely saw anymore. She was rapt, overwhelmed with profound emotion. Only two things could evoke such a response from her. One was the Russian Orthodox liturgy. The other was music.

At the moment, she was enjoying both.

Andrei watched her from an alcove much like the one from which Tally and Peter often spied upon her. But Andrei's alcove was part of a much larger church, and the sounds that filled it shook the very rafters. The male choir was rehearsing. It boasted twenty-five male sopranos, twenty-five altos (boys), eighteen tenors, and twenty-two basses—of whom seven were octavists. The *oktavisty* sang one full octave below the lowest range of regular baritones, creating a resonance similar to the sort created by the lowest register of the big organs one could find in the grand Catholic churches. But the organ, along with all other musical instruments, was forbidden by the Russian Orthodox doctrine. As in all other matters, the Russian sacred choral tradition had risen to the challenge.

Or in this case, descended.

It was the sound of these basso profundo singers who kept Andrei faithful to the Russian church, not any liturgy. They moved him so profoundly, he often left services stunned, as if he had witnessed something both dreadful and marvelous. *It's only because you have to stand all the way through it*, Tally often teased him. *You're exhausted.*

He could not tell her this was the Russian heart, his very soul, this impossible sound. And it was perfectly sad, perfectly appropriate, that he should hear it as he contemplated his fourth wife, whom he had lost even though she still lived.

For a time he stood and watched, and listened, and did not know time moved forward. Until at last, the choir stopped singing and spoke quietly among themselves, and made rustling noises as they left their positions. Katerina swayed as if released, but Andrei wondered if she really wanted to be. She might wish that she could be enraptured for eternity.

She felt his gaze and looked at him, and her face did not assume its usual disapproving set. Instead, her moist eyes gazed at him with hope. It was exactly the opposite of what he had expected. Andrei felt his heart would break.

He approached her, and she waited for him breathlessly. When they stood no more than an arm's length from each other, he spoke gently to her.

"Katya, I hear you have attempted to enforce a law."

"A law?" she said, her brow creasing in puzzlement.

"Concerning music," he said gently.

Suddenly her face lit up. "Of course," she said,

"how foolish of me. It is something I can be very proud of, Andrei, my legacy to this world."

"Katya," he said, as if they were still husband and wife, as if they still shared intimacies, "your legacy to this world is already secure. The choir we just heard confirms that beyond any argument."

She shook her head. "Nothing is secure."

Andrei hated to ask, but he had to. "Please tell me what you have in mind."

The light in her eyes burned brighter. "I had to move quickly, Andrei. If we catch it now, they will not be able to spread their infection. People are dancing to it, that's the problem. Anything you can dance to, people like. They are afraid to feel real music in their hearts. Foreign music makes them mindless, they forget who they are. I want to protect them."

"I believe you," said Andrei, but when she regarded him with such joy, as if she could scarcely believe what she was hearing from him, he shook his head. "But you can't do it, Katya."

Again, the puzzlement. "Of course I can," she said.

"No. Even if you could enforce the law, which you simply cannot. It is unconstitutional."

"The tsar decides what is law," she said.

"The tsar is obliged to *obey* the law. We are not god-kings, Katya. We must answer to people for what we do. We cannot restrict them from listening to the music they choose. And even if we did, we would only make the forbidden music more popular."

"You can't mean that." Her brows drew together like a thundercloud. In a way, Andrei was glad to see it. This was a departure from the years of silence, the tight-lipped refusal to open up and let him inside. Or to let Peter in. Yet there was something about this new openness that disturbed him.

"I know you're trying to do the right thing—" he began. But he was silenced as the light behind her eyes blossomed into a dreadful fever.

"Do not patronize me," she said. "You think I am

a stupid child. But I can see what you're doing wrong, Andrei, how you let other religions poison your heart, how you listen to foreigners before you listen to your own countrymen."

"This is a new world," he reminded her. "We are *all* foreigners here."

"We have claimed this world for Russians," she said. "If we are to tolerate foreigners, they must respect our customs. You must make a declaration as soon as possible. This is a Russian Orthodox state. It is long overdue, Andrei."

"This is *not* a Russian Orthodox state," Andrei said. "The Patriarch of Belarus knew that when he was invited here. He belongs to the Council of Interfaith Brothers, Katya. That's why I chose him."

"That one," Katya said sadly. "He is a good man. But he must step down. Father Nikon will be raised in his stead."

*Says who?* Andrei was tempted to ask. But he could see he wasn't going to be able to make her understand—what she was saying was impossible. He had no doubt there were people in the woodwork who backed her up wholeheartedly. She might even blurt out their names, given half a chance. But he didn't like the odd tone in her voice, or the fact that he could see the whites around her irises. He didn't want to drive her any further down her path of righteousness than she had already gone.

Katya gazed at him with her new fire, and he understood how he had failed her. He had believed that music would ultimately save her from the religious fanaticism that was slowly consuming her. He had never dreamed the two could be the same.

"Tell me why you keep yourself from your people," she accused. "You send Igor to stand for you at important state functions and ceremonies, and you attend church only a few times a month. Peter the Great's father Alexis attended every day!"

Andrei kept his voice as gentle as he could, but he

was weary beyond endurance of the argument. This was the sort of fanaticism to which Baba Yaga had assigned a horseman of the Apocalypse. "I am too busy with state matters to allow myself the indulgence of state parties."

"You have an honor guard of Cossacks, did you know that?" she accused. "You never even thank them for their service, because you never see them. You have sprites and ESAs to guard you."

"I don't need an honor guard, Katya—"

"Why did you become tsar then?" she accused. "You might just as well be a president!"

"Because a president can be voted out of office. I need to have the last word. The colonists here may govern themselves as long as they don't meddle with our Bill of Rights. When we've established a society that will respect and preserve these things, I will step down and they can elect a president."

"And in the meantime, you are the Tyrant. And everything will be *your* way."

"For now, yes. It must."

"Shame on you," she said bitterly.

Andrei was growing angry, despite his pity for her, and his sorrow. "Shame on me for letting people worship as they choose, and for allowing them to attend good public schools, and for providing health care and insisting on equal rights for women—"

"What good is any of that when you elevate heathens and heretics to the same level as the Russian church?"

"Katya, I can scarcely believe my ears. That the woman I married could say such things—"

"I say what your trusted advisors are afraid to tell you," she insisted. "The government you have established is not Russian, Andrei. It is soft, corrupted by foolish ideas and foreign influences."

"It is precisely the government I planned," said Andrei, aware that someone was approaching them from the choir loft. He wondered if their voices were too loud. "I picked the right people. I knew where to look, I've been researching the matter for two centuries. I found out which colonial societies have been the most successful at taking advantage of diversity instead of hating it. I looked for strong links and healthy business practices. That's who I recruited for Belarus."

"Foreigners!" she accused. "Heretics!"

"I hope you don't mean that," he said mildly. "I won't tolerate your interference in governmental matters. I care very deeply for you. Please don't make me ship you off to your family."

She looked stricken. Andrei instantly regretted his words. And then Brother Macarius was standing at his side, bowing respectfully. "Forgive the intrusion," he said softly. When he raised his eyes again, his expression told Andrei that he knew exactly what was happening to Katya. And like Andrei, he had little idea what could possibly be done about it.

"You are not intruding," he said. "We were arguing about things that will not be solved in our generation." He turned to Katya one last time. "Don't do it again, little mother. I won't tolerate it. I can't."

"I will pray for our souls then," said Katya, and the fire had gone out of her eyes. Her expression was almost serene—unless you knew her well enough to see the despair. Andrei's heart felt as if it were made of lead. He knew that he had not handled the confrontation well.

"Pray," he said gently. "And take care, Katerina."

She had no answer for him.

Brother Macarius nodded respectfully. "Good evening, my tsar," he said with perfect courtesy, but his cheeks were burning, and he could not seem to bring himself to look Andrei in the eyes again. Andrei released him from his discomfort. He turned and left the cathedral.

Bodyguards covered his every move, or their machines did. Tam was there, and ESAs Mischa and Elena. If they knew how deeply he was hurting, they did not show it. As always, they were blank, preoccupied, guarding all access to his person. Andrei made his way across the courtyard of the cathedral and into an unmarked vehicle. He sat in silence, his ESAs on either side of him, and he thought about his marriage.

He had thought her religiosity was harmless, a comfort to her. He might have helped her if he had taken the time to look closer. She exiled him from her bed, and then her life, and he had gone too easily.

*Is this why you admire strong women so much?* he asked himself. *Because they don't need you?*

The fire in her music. He had thought it another passion. Now he knew better.

*How dull you must find me*, Katya had said. *You have forgotten more than I will ever know.*

*I remember what's important,* was his answer.

But before you could remember, you had to know.

*Okay*, thought Tally. *Go in and look at the statue, look at the Fabergé eggs, drink some punch, chitchat with some fat cats—why do I get the feeling I'd be happier hanging out with Peter tonight?*

But the Hermitage held surprises, even for its designer. Tally was delighted to discover several rooms full of crafts from local artisans. She wandered with Tam at her side, the ESA silent and undemanding as a shadow.

She found displays of eggs that had been painted by local schoolchildren. And once their mysteries had drawn her in, she was further ensnared by hand-carved and painted nesting dolls. Around her, conversation ebbed and flowed.

"Farmers are obsolete, every bit of our food production could be done by machine. It's far more cost effective, and our beautiful world would not be so crowded. Why does Andrei insist on recruiting peasants?"

"How can you be royalty if you don't have peasants?"

"No, you're both wrong, he needs them to paint eggs for his museums."

"Have you seen the statue of Voltaire? What a character he must have been."

"He makes me uncomfortable. Can you imagine having the thing in your house, following you with its eyes?"

"You're just annoyed because it looks like he's laughing at you."

Occasionally Tally glimpsed Andrei across the room, Grigory his shadow. Grigory was doing a good job of keeping people at a respectable distance, but Tally could tell Andrei was being shmoozed and petitioned a hell of a lot more than he would have liked. He must wish he could just wander around and look at the displays like a regular person.

"Colonizing worlds has lost all its appeal, it's too easy these days."

"Too easy for you, my dear. You just pack your bags and move in."

"Before the Unification people used to venture out in generation ships, can you imagine? They had to mine systems on the way, just to get where they were going. Now you can visit a hundred worlds if you want."

"And they all have the same names, so you might as well stay home."

Someone was playing Rachmaninoff in the background, the suites for double piano. Tally realized it must be Katerina. So Brother Macarius must be her partner; Katerina never played with anyone else.

"Where's the buffet?" she asked Tam.

"Beats me. It's not in the directory."

"Well, now we have a mission," said Tally, heading for the next room.

"At least one," said Tam, matching her pace.

Tam saw the universe as a series of grids and heat messages. She rather liked it that way.

She had already divided the party guests into opposing groups.

There were the people who wore danger suits, and the people who wore the tight, ornate clothing that looked like overembellished corsets and braces. It was interesting watching the latter group trying to move all trussed up like that, but she had to admit some of them were pretty good at it.

And then there were the people she needed to protect, and the people who might be a danger to them. As she shadowed Tally through the various rooms, she took note of the other security personnel. Some of them she knew, others were out-of-towners. Some were ESAs and others were not.

*Opposing groups, everywhere you look. It's the nature of the universe. No wonder we're always squabbling. But at least some people take the time to paint eggs.*

<Hey, Grigory, where's the statue of Voltaire?>

<Right outside the exhibit of Egyptian Antiquities.>

"Tally, you remember where you put the Egyptian stuff?"

"Third floor," said Tally.

"Then we have to look for an elevator."

Andrei was beginning to wonder if he would ever get to the third floor.

"I can't make a profit unless I use undocumented workers." A businessman was bending his ear. Andrei had given up trying to remember who he was or what his company did. None of that mattered anyway, the man was trying to get Andrei to say Belarus would accept goods from a company who kept its workers in virtual slavery.

"Forget it," he said, and walked away, leaving the man openmouthed. Grigory made certain he didn't follow.

They swam through a sea of attempted engagements.

"Andrei, if you have a moment—"

"I've been hoping to catch you—"

"None of my calls have been returned—"

"Long live the tsar."

Andrei stopped for that last one. The person who had uttered it was grey-furred from head to toe. Her tufted ears were pointed toward Andrei, as were the ears of all six members of her entourage.

"Embassador." He gave her a polite bow. "I'm pleased you could attend."

"I was curious to see the image of this great man, Voltaire. Last night, I read *Candide*, and it has inspired thoughts that are new to me."

Andrei felt the considerable force behind her gaze, and was fascinated. He had seen Woovs before, but this was the closest contact he had ever experienced with them.

"I'm on my way to the viewing now," he said. "Will you accompany me?"

"This seems practical," she said.

"Then we'll find an elevator."

Fancy was a real duchess, or as real as they got in an era when royal lineage had little to do with old Earth bloodlines. But that was not why Andrei invited her to his parties.

"No one in my family is descended from the God Kings," she once told a reporter. "So we're one step beyond make-believe. The only time it gets real is when you're fighting a war. Then people look to you for inspiration and guidance, and you'd better not let them down."

Fancy never let anyone down. But despite her strength, she looked soft and pretty in her beautiful gown, cut in the old-fashioned style favored by Andrei's mother. She held court in one of the large parlors, amusing herself with the fools who had stuffed themselves into the new fashions.

"Katerina," she called to the tsarina, "please, I would adore some Chopin."

Katerina had left the big piano in the Local Artisan Hall and was now making more intimate sounds with a parlor grand. She gazed at Fancy with eyes full of ash and ruin, and began to play a nocturne.

*Poor child.* Fancy hid her feelings behind a famously cool facade. *Never have I seen someone so haunted . . .*

"Time is growing short for our kind," she told her rich acquaintances.

They did not listen. But Fancy supposed the doomed never did.

"There has to be a buffet around here somewhere," complained Tally. "Or even some lousy punch!"

"Maybe they don't want spots on the floor," said Tam.

Then Tally heard the strains of a Chopin nocturne. "Piano," she said. "Rich people on couches, waiters with glasses full of punch and/or wine. This way."

Fancy was delighted to see Tally Korsakova enter her den.

"My dear," she called, "how delightful, come and sit with us. I am Fancy Dolgurukaya, I have so wanted to meet you."

The engineer paused like a gazelle. She seemed to sniff the air, as if she sought water. Fancy leaned gracefully over the refreshment table near her couch and poured a glass of sparkling spring water.

Suddenly the engineer was at her side.

"You read my mind," she said, and winked at Fancy.

"Clairvoyance runs in my family," said Fancy, and winked back.

Andrei and his party had barely emerged onto the third floor when Grigory stopped them. <Get back into the elevator,> he ordered.

Andrei did not ask why. "Embassador," he said, "my security is warning me, we have to leave."

"Yes," she said, "mine agree. Let us go to admire the elevator, shall we?"

* * *

Tally noticed that Fancy's ESA stood just behind the couch. Tam stood to the side, next to Tally, and they seemed to be the only ESAs in the room.

Fancy was asking her questions about the Egyptian antiquities, which Tally very much enjoyed answering. But it was Katerina who kept catching her eye.

"Excuse me one moment," said Fancy. "My ESAs are talking to me, and I've never been able to master multitrack conversation." Her eyes became obscure. Tally rather admired her expression, it seemed mystical rather than preoccupied.

Katerina stopped playing. Tally glanced at her again. This time the tsarina was looking back.

Tally looked into her eyes. For a moment the room seemed full of shadows. Katerina watched her from the other side of a chasm.

Then the light and sound returned, and Katerina was only a few yards away.

Tally went to join her. She didn't notice when Tam did not go with her.

"I never had sisters," said Katerina, "and my brothers were far older than me."

"I had sisters," said Tally. "But it didn't help."

They sat on the little bench together, their backs to the rest of the room.

Katerina, fully a head shorter, gazed up at her. "Sometimes I look at you and wonder," she said, "what it's like to be so beautiful and brilliant."

"You could look in the mirror and answer that question," said Tally.

"But I couldn't, the question is meaningless. Only God's light can reveal us as we really are, only He knows what we've really done."

"Katya, if that's true why can't you let God take that burden of judgment from your shoulders?" It was a question Tally would have loved to ask her mother, except that the answer would probably have been yet another analysis of Tally's faults.

But Katerina did not criticize. "There are some things we cannot know while we live," she said. "I have faith that all will be revealed to me when I pass beyond this veil, though I may not like what I see."

"That's pretty much how I see it," said Tally, surprised.

Katya took her hand. "We are sisters in spirit," she said. "I sensed that from the beginning. But unlike me, you don't have to wait for the afterlife, Natalia. You can glimpse behind the veil."

"Just *glimpses*," said Tally. "And they don't do me much good."

"I had glimpses too, once. But no longer. And no matter what we are allowed to see, we cannot know the mind of God."

"Maybe that's for the best," said Tally.

<Tam, you're with Fancy's bunch, keep them occupied for a short time, will you?>

<How come you get to have all the fun, Grigory?>

<Just lucky I guess.>

<Hey, Julie,> Tam told Fancy's ESA without looking at her, <heads up.>

<Right,> said Julie. Tam tuned into the conversation of the fat cats around her.

"At the risk of sounding politically incorrect," said a portly guy whose gut was trying to escape from the back of his truss, "I think the farmers actually *prefer* to do things the old-fashioned way. They would rather pull a plow with a horse than use harvester drones. I think they don't trust machines because they don't understand them."

"Horse crap," said Tam in a loud voice, earning their startled attention.

At times like this, Tam really loved her job.

* * *

Tally held Katerina's hand gently, but it wasn't really necessary to be so careful. Katerina had musician's hands, strong and supple. Katerina measured them against Tally's.

"You could play Rachmaninoff with these hands. Or even Liszt. He had large hands. Sometimes I wonder if he resented women, if he deliberately wrote music we would not be able to play. But perhaps not; perhaps he was only testing his *own* limits."

"Katerina," Tally asked her gently, "what's wrong?"

Katerina looked at her with eyes so sad, Tally knew that nothing she could say would help, nothing anyone could say.

"It is you who must answer that question, Natalia. I have tried to see what is right for this world and its people, but now I know that *you* are the one who sees. You will tell us what to do in our darkest hours."

"Not alone," Tally protested. "Not just me."

"We will help when we can." Katerina squeezed her hand. "We do what we must. There will be suffering, Natalia. But I'm not afraid anymore."

And Tally had a vision of darkness. Katerina seemed cloaked by that Veil she had spoken of. It was the Veil in the night sky, hiding something terrible. Tally stared, trying to see Katya's face more clearly. The veil fluttered, seemed to part ever so slightly, and Tally felt a cold wind from the other side.

"You're not afraid," whispered Tally. "But you have good reason to be . . ."

Then a loud voice snapped her back to the world of the living.

"I *beg* your pardon," said the guy in the truss, his face growing red either from outrage or from constricted circulation.

"You don't know what you're talking about," she informed him.

"And you do," he said contemptuously.

"Yeah. It's simple. For instance, take the war between Spartus and Crowe. It wasn't really a conflict between peoples on two worlds. It was a conflict between one faction in the Urbano family and another faction in the Urbanos who teamed up with some upstart Yamashitas. While they blasted away at each other they had PR firms working for them, spreading the propaganda and keeping passions high. Finally one side backed down and everyone dropped the war like a hot potato."

He glared at her. "Precisely what does that have to do with the conversation we were just having?"

"This," said Tam. "How many times has that happened in the past ten thousand years, a bunch of rich bastards decide to duke it out on a planetary level and then call it off when they get sick of it? Is it any wonder that ordinary workers and farmers have more faith in good hand tools and their milk cows and gardens than they've got in automation? The first thing that happens in these so called microwars, both sides try to take out all the automated systems. First strike, shut down communications, blind the enemy, take out as many systems as you can. Sometimes that's all it takes to decide the winner—who still has machines that work? But in the process, systems that ordinary people depend on get knocked out too. All those people who are just trying to feed their families get caught in the middle. It's bullshit!"

"I don't see any need to use foul language," he said, his face flaming.

"I hope you have a good gas heater," she told him. "I hope your walls are well insulated, and that you have an emergency water pump. When the chips are down, you're going to be asking those farmers how to get things done."

That did it. She was pretty sure his head was going to pop off.

<Collect Tally and Katerina,> ordered Grigory. <Fancy too. Get moving.>

Tam made a beeline for the piano. Julie and Fancy were already headed for the door.

Tally had never heard Tam speak so many words together at once. And what really amazed her was how the ESA could do it in such a flat tone. She didn't know if Tam was kidding or serious.

And then Tam locked her tactically enhanced eyes on Tally and began to move. "Time to go," she ordered.

Tally obeyed. Even Katerina hustled. They joined Fancy and the other ESA at the door.

"Stay where you are for another fifteen minutes," Tam ordered the astonished guests.

"I don't take orders from ESAs," snarled the red-faced guy.

"Suit yourself," said Tam.

<Two energy signatures, second floor.>
<They're ringers.>
<Amateurs.>
<Move it.>

Tally thought they would head for the closest elevator, but instead they made for the stairs, hustled down an empty hall by ESAs who had appeared out of the woodwork, their sprites in orbit. Some moved ahead of the group and some behind. Sprites filled the air like seed pods in a windstorm.

"Stop," ordered Tam. "Back. We're going to have to go through the crowd."

Tally obeyed, Katerina and Fancy falling in behind her. They came out into the exhibit of local artisans, still crowded with guests who fell back as soon as they saw the heavy security. Some people got flat on the floor and covered their heads. Tally flushed with embarrassment.

<Alpha is clear.>
<He's going after Beta.>

* * *

Tally kept moving, trying to follow Tam's lead. But then Tam's figure blurred—Tally couldn't follow her with her eyes. She stumbled, and then someone threw her to the floor. Her assailant lay on top of her, and was immediately joined by someone else.

"What the hell . . . ?" she spluttered, trying to breathe, fighting to see Tam, far ahead. She saw figures streaking like supersonic trains toward a single point at the far end of the reception hall. One of them ran up a wall, dodging a bolt of blue-white light, and a sizzling noise filled the air. An instant later there was another flash of light and a muffled explosion. Tally felt the vibration through the floor.

<Tam, report!>

<Got him. Beta and company are okay.>

"They're fine," Grigory assured Andrei. "They were well covered."

Andrei nodded curtly, but Grigory was sure he would not rest easy until he could see Tally and Katerina with his own eyes. Andrei had lost too many loved ones in his life. Grigory understood that too well.

<Bring them as quickly as you can,> he told Tam.

<They're coming.>

<Good work, Tammy.>

<Aw, blush-blush!>

Tally was helped to her feet by the two ESAs who had been lying on top of her. "I'm okay," she told them, though her knees trembled. "I just need to walk and breathe a little bit."

She looked for Tam. The ESA stood over someone at the far end of the reception hall. She looked over at Tally.

"Ready to call it a night?" she called.

"You bet," said Tally.

Katerina joined her, her sad eyes fixed on the dead

man. Fancy patted Tally on the shoulder. "You've survived, my dear."

"We all did," said Tally.

"No—" Fancy gave her an odd look. "That was meant for you."

"No way." Tally stared at the duchess, who seemed completely unrumpled even after sprawling on the floor. "You're kidding, right?"

"Oh, dear." Fancy shook her head. "This was your first time. Forgive me, but it won't be your last."

Tally looked at the dead man, and then at Tam.

"Come on," said the ESA. "It's past suppertime!"

Grigory and his team secured the parking garage. They methodically checked the vehicles for tampering, even though they had been heavily guarded. Sprites aided their human and Woov patrons, conveying information to Grigory, who accepted it and filed it away. But he also wanted to find out what his nose could detect.

He moved along the rows, sniffing the air. He smelled asphalt, tires, metal alloy, cooling engines, human perspiration. He moved along another row, and smelled the Woov embassador. Her odor was quite pleasant.

"I am impressed with the capabilities of your danger suits," she said.

"They are useful." He stopped three paces from her, presenting his blind profile. He continued to smell the air. One of the drivers standing a few rows down burped, and he smelled garlic.

"The suits allow you to move almost as quickly as Woovs," said the embassador.

"Not that quickly," said Grigory. "But we're trying to improve them."

<And our sprite virus,> she said, <do you still find that useful?>

Grigory made no sign he had received a message, though his surprise was fully as profound as what he had experienced the first time he received a communication from Spritemind. Despite that, he continued to sniff the air for danger.

<Honored Elder,> he replied, <that would be an understatement.>

<You are surprised to learn I'm an ESA Elder.>

<I think I am more surprised that you have come here. Your visit cannot be casual.>

<I have few casual moments, Watcher. Like you. And I must confirm your worst suspicions. The time of microwars is over. Your Central Government may hold on to its core worlds, but it cannot hold on to all of the worlds that find its laws inconvenient. Too many of your powerful families think they can fill the void.>

<I've heard talk of a new generation of superweapons. Planet busters. And Sun busters.>

<All true. And if they realized that Woovs invented the sprite virus, our home sun would be the first to go.>

<They will strike each other first, Elder. They think they'll be strong enough to attend to you after they've secured their power.>

<Yes, Watcher. Woov colonies are not in danger yet. But we ESAs are another matter. We are perceived as a great obstacle. This war is our trial too.>

<I am ready to serve.>

<You and I have both already done what we could for the Republic. Many worlds support the Bill of Rights. If they survive, they will try to forge a Union of Worlds, based on it. All that is left for our generation is to do what we can for ourselves and our friends.>

Grigory nodded. The garage was secure, his charges could safely enter the vehicles.

Her scent diminished. He heard her climbing into her vehicle, and then she was gone. Moments later, Tam and her team brought Tally, Katerina, and Fancy into the garage. Grigory went to join them. He was alert for trouble, as always. But one corner of his mind puzzled over a mystery.

The elder had come to Belarus to see someone in particular. And he didn't believe it was he.

So who was it?

"One question," asked Tally. "Who was it?"

"Who was who?" Tam asked blandly.

"The dead guy!"

Andrei was sitting across from her, next to Katerina, though he and his wife may as well have been strangers for all the warmth that passed between them. Andrei wore that look Tally had glimpsed so many years ago, the shadow of anger not yet in its fullest bloom. "A member of my own family," he said, and the lightness of his tone chilled her. "Trying to strike a blow at me through you. I was to learn a lesson, I assume."

"And did you?" asked Grigory.

Andrei didn't answer.

For a time, Tally merely gazed out the window at the city lights. They were so pretty at night, like jewels. But her mind drifted back to the assassin.

"I've never been targeted by anyone before," she said.

"Yes you have," said Grigory.

Tally looked at him, startled.

"You gained enemies the moment you signed with Andrei. We thought you understood that. You're the engineer, it would have been easy to delay this project by killing you. Remember that clause in your contract? The one that dealt with compensation to a designated heir in case of assassination?"

She remembered the clause. She also remembered it had amused her—at the time. She never believed anyone would try to kill her. Not anyone who wasn't from her own family, anyway.

Tally rested against the seat and closed her eyes. Her mind drifted back to the intricate painted eggs, the hand-carved nesting dolls. Painstaking, convoluted, layer upon layer of meaning and mystery. And at the center of it all?

*False doors*, thought Tally, then fell fast asleep.

On the secret world of Canopus, George Bernstein steered Charon's boat toward the Isle of the Dead. Its intended ferryman was no more than a program. George was supposed to build an avatar for him. He intended to delay that project as long as he could. If matters in the Republic came to a head as quickly as he thought they would, the real Charon would be overworked and the avatar would not be necessary.

George enjoyed the boat trip. The water and sky were a vivid blue, schools of dolphins and whales cavorted in the waves. The day was moderately hot, perhaps ninety degrees Fahrenheit, but George was comfortable under his parasol. His head was shaved in the manner of the ancient priests, he wore a simple linen garment. He sipped spring water and nibbled dried fruit and roasted nuts.

The mist barrier came into view, a thick wall on the horizon. As he got closer, he could see tendrils reaching toward the hot day, evaporating when they ventured too far. But the wall itself remained firm. George went into it and felt the temperature drop several degrees.

He could no longer see the bow of his boat. Moisture clung to his skin, which was quite refreshing.

After a moment, he heard the singing.

"It's George!" he called. "I'm immune, remember?"

He heard a splash, and then something swam to the side of his boat and leaned over the side.

The mermaid's face loomed out of the mist. She fixed George with her wonderful, terrible gaze. "Engineer," she said, her voice carefully modulated despite his immunity. "You honor us."

"Just a visit to Medusa," he said. "She's going online today."

He was betraying his patrons by telling her that. But he had betrayed his patrons almost from the word go; and anyway, the mermaids could take care of themselves very well.

"Your accomplishments will live through the ages," she said.

"I sincerely hope so." George smiled at her.

She could not smile back, but she seemed pleased. She let go of the boat and slid back into the water. He heard her singing softly to herself, a harmless tune. If she chose, she could compel with her voice, or lure, or paralyze, or even kill. Of all the beings George had created for Canopus, with their wide array of attributes and strengths, the mermaids were by far the most dangerous.

Soon the mist began to clear, and George caught sight of the Isle of the Dead. As always, his heart skipped a beat. A painting was the original inspiration for it, several of the patrons insisted he use it as a guideline. And he had. But the end result was not quite what they intended.

*I don't know how we did it. We're only mortal, despite our fabulous resources. But somehow we captured a piece of Olympus, a place where heroes and great kings journey after death . . .*

George guided the boat into his secret bay and

docked it. Steps led up the steep slope, to a temple at the crest of the hill that dominated the island. George climbed it easily. He was well over four hundred years old, but kept his physical age somewhere around forty. He enjoyed the exercise.

Once under the trees, he saw the first fallen hero. They were scattered around the path, as if Medusa had turned them to stone. They had never lived, except for what artisans had breathed into them. Each owned a face and form that seemed capable of movement, emotion, each seemed transfixed in his prime with an expression of wonder on his face. George had insisted on that, rather than the look of terror the patrons wanted. Anyone who saw his Medusa could not be terrified. Especially since she couldn't really turn them to stone.

Her temple was both beautiful and forbidding, a warning to anyone who invaded the island. George had to laugh at the thought. Anyone brave and clever enough to get past the mermaids would not be intimidated by atmosphere. And invaders would not come unless they had a compelling reason. Like George did.

He did not linger in the temple, but went directly to the sanctuary. At the base of the statue of Athena, he tapped a code. A wall slid aside, and George entered Medusa's control room.

The avatar stood in her alcove. She was the exact image of Tally, including her rasta-links, which served the same purpose. George took a small box out of his backpack and presented it to Medusa.

"Plug in," he said.

One of the rasta-links stirred and slid into the jack. Medusa blinked, then focused her eyes on George.

"I know you," she said with Tally's voice. "I know myself. I am Medusa."

"You are. And soon you'll be far more." George typed a code into a keypad and looked up. Two large sections of the roof slid back revealing the brilliant sky. He watched until he could see the first sparkle of arriving sprites. They would come like dragonflies on the wind, only a few now, but later many more.

"I'm ready," said Medusa.

"Me too," said George. "I don't think we'll have long to wait."

Tally went into her office to read her morning mail and found a message from a Raina Klebanova in the pile. She glanced at it to get the gist, then lingered over it with interest.

*Best wishes to you, Engineer Korsakova, I hope I am not disturbing important matters by writing to you. My husband and I have been sorting through images collected by our agricultural sprites with the slim hope that we may find the image of the killer who murdered the young girl in Grey Forest. I think the idea still has merit, but we are discovering that our poor eyes are not good at collating so much data.*

*I have queried the tsar's office about the matter, and they referred me to you. I am still willing to conduct this search, but I must have a search engine with considerably more power than my poor little system at home, which prior to this time has been used mainly to organize recipes and keep track of family birthdays.*

*Until I hear from you I will continue to look manually. I have turned up nothing of value yet. I suspect the killer is a very smart man; but no one is invisible, and he must have revealed himself at some time. I humbly ask for your help.*

*Sincerely yours,*
*Raina Klebanova*

Tally called Grigory first.

<When this world was being surveyed, the sprites looked for particular data, and that data was sorted and collated into groups. Couldn't we do the same with those images Raina is looking for from the agricultural sprites?>

<We should be able to do it,> he said. <And we have tried. We have come up with nothing. And that leads me to believe that something may be wrong with our sprites. Something is interfering with their ability to see certain things.>

<Well if that's the case, then there's no point in trying to sort through the data from Raina's group. It won't even exist.> Tally was both disappointed and relieved.

<Not so fast. If it did not exist, there would be holes where it ought to be. I have found no holes. And so the problem may lie with the sprites' inability to retrieve the data, or to recognize it in the first place.>

<If they can't get at it, how are we supposed to?>

<A gifted hacker could do it.>

<So find me one!>

< I already have. Tam. Call her.>

"Oh, yeah," said Tam, "people have been fooling sprites for years. Or finding ways to interfere with our interface with them. Sprites know it's going on, and they still can't stop it. It's called espionage."

She sat behind a desk in her little office, which much to Tally's surprise was full of flowering plants, so many of them there was hardly space for anything else. Tam sat among them, thin as a rail, her eyes in tactical and her face expressionless, wearing the danger suit she seemed never to take off. She looked like she could not possibly be aware of anything in the real world. But her plants testified otherwise.

"So," Tally asked. "Someone is messing with our sprites. From what you say, someone messes with everyone's sprites. How do we find out what they've done? Can we run some kind of diagnostic?"

"The sprites do that themselves, constantly," said Tam. "You have to look at it this way. If a person develops memory problems, they don't remember what they've forgotten."

"So the sprites should not be the ones to look for their own glitch," said Tally.

"Right. And if I go into the system from my interface, I won't spot it either. In order to see the glitches I have to hack in like the guys who are mucking things up. I have to follow in their footsteps."

"Can you do that?" Tally asked hopefully.

"I've been trying," said Tam.

Tally wilted. "Are they *that* damned smart?"

"Maybe not," Tam said tonelessly. "Maybe they're just very dedicated. But don't despair, we've got an expert on hand who may be able to help. John."

"I thought he was a weapons technician," said Tally.

"He is, and the best I've ever seen. But he's been in the war biz for a few decades, Tally, he's done the espionage thing. I'm ready to ask for his help. You want to come along?"

"Might as well," said Tally. "I've chased the wild goose this far . . ."

When they found John, he was deep into his own virtual world. His eyes were on full tactical, black orbs that were like dark twins to the red ones Grigory owned. But Griogry's eyes were cold stones; John's plugged him into a virtual world where abstract concepts formed themselves into functioning systems. Tally lived in such a world herself most of the time, but in her universe things were created.

In John's, things were destroyed.

"When are you going to replace those old-fashioned rasta-links?" he asked her.

Tally didn't answer. John had been on Belarus less than a year, but that joke had grown old. She presented a pleasant face to him anyway. He probably didn't know he wasn't funny, and she didn't want to antagonize him.

Tam explained what they were trying to do. Tally watched John's face for a reaction. But he didn't have one. Like most war techs, his expression was usually bland. He waited for Tam to finish.

"Your whole premise is wrong," he said. "Want to know why?"

"What the hell," said Tam, her tone even blander than his. "Why, John?"

"Because you're depending on sprites for your information. They're the wrong source."

"Funny," said Tam. "I've always found them to be rather helpful."

"You just *think* they've been helpful," he informed her, managing to sound like the essential authority on the matter. "Look. Sprites can bake a cake. They can build a temple. They can fertilize a field so it will be productive for several years. They can organize a birthday party, perform heart surgery, form a communications network, monitor the storms of a gas giant. Anything you can think of. But they won't necessarily do any of those things."

"You just don't know how to ask," said Tam. She said it without malice, not teasing or arguing, just plain old flat-toned Tam making a point in her usual straightforward fashion.

But John was irritated by the remark. Tally had never exchanged more than a few words with him, she didn't know him well. Yet it was plain to her now, he was absolutely sure of his opinions.

Her heart sank. He wasn't going to be much help.

"The problem with sprites is that they're overdesigned," he said, not even bothering to acknowledge

Tam's remark. "You can accomplish a lot more with dumber machines who won't second-guess you, simple instruments designed for specific purposes."

"Like killing people," said Tam. "That's your real problem, John. They have a conscience."

"Why would that be a problem for me?" he asked, sincerely puzzled. "I wouldn't have a job if sprites didn't have a conscience."

"You wouldn't have *this* job," Tally said.

John looked at her as if she had just spoken gibberish.

"Anyway," she continued. "Tam and I have a good rapport with our sprites. And you can use your surveillance drones. We'll have to find the best way to interface."

"I'm the interface," John said. "I always have been in these matters. In battle, I'm the guy who directs traffic. I can do that for you, too."

"Good," said Tally. "Start combing through the data, get one of your search engines going. We'll see what comes up."

"We'll see," he said, but he sounded more like he was echoing her than he was agreeing.

Tally and Tam left him in his office. After they had climbed into a trans-tube, Tam took hold of one of Tally's rasta-links. Tally flinched. "What are you—?" she demanded.

And then Tam stuck the end of the link into her left pupil. Tally's system adapted and engaged.

<I didn't want him to hear what I have to say.>

Tally was shocked. The link itself was unsettling, but she didn't like the implication, either. <You think he's spying on us?>

<I'm pretty sure he is. I thought maybe he could help us, but now I'm sorry I asked. He just used it as an excuse to preach against sprites. Sometimes I get the impression he thinks ESAs are a bunch of hot-shots. Maybe he envies us. And he is *not* the one who directs traffic in battle. All the ESAs link when that

happens. We work together or separately, depending on conditions, pretty much like the sprites do."

Tally was intrigued. ESAs were notoriously tight-lipped about their links with each other.

<He designs the weapons, and that's it. We give him feedback about how it all works. He's a typical weapons tech: a genius at designing systems but not a very good listener. Sometimes you have to lie to get what you want from him. He could have helped us a lot. But I guess his head's too far up his ass.>

Tam fell silent again. But she didn't disengage from Tally. It felt very odd to ride that way, with her link stuck inside Tam's eyeball. But Tam might decide she had more to say, and Tally didn't want to discourage that. She wondered if there was anything she could ask that wouldn't make the ESA back off.

<Maybe he can help us at least a little?> she finally ventured.

<No.>

<Why not?>

Tam was silent for a long while, blank-faced, not even looking at Tally. Yet they were still engaged. Tally wondered if that comforted Tam in some way.

<I can't give you a logical answer,> the ESA said at last. <Just between you and me—I get the feeling he doesn't want to. I'm really disappointed, this project was right up his alley.>

<You think maybe he just doesn't care?>

<Maybe. He's such a cold fish.>

Tally prayed her prior thoughts concerning Tam's relative warmth would not leak into her com stream.

Tam continued, <Weapons designers are like that. You can't make killing machines if you're a warm fuzzy kinda person. In my lifetime, I've seen a lot of them crash, psychologically. Even the cold ones, like John. He probably wants to be a people person, but that would open him up to feeling about what he does. I know how that is, I don't want to be a military ESA anymore.>

Tally couldn't resist asking. <Why don't you quit, Tam?>

This time the ESA did look at her, and Tally understood why she had looked away. When they were linked, it was easier to read Tam's feelings.

<Tally, the Republic is about to blow up. Whatever problems we've got on this world, they're nothing compared to that. For years we ESAs have tried to diffuse the trouble, maybe that's why the Republic lasted as long as it did. But we can't do it anymore, we just have to save what we can. That's what Andrei is trying to do with this colony, save pieces of human culture that he cares about. And that's why I'm willing to work for him as a military ESA.>

Tally held Tam's gaze, though she wished she didn't have to. Suddenly the burden of feeling was too much. But she held steady. Finally she thought of another question.

<Shall we do it on our own, then?>

<Yeah. If John wants to help, let me handle him. I always do. If he wants to add his two cents, I'll act like it's the most brilliant stuff I ever heard. Keep the systems designers happy, that's what I always say.>

Tally grinned. Tam had a sense of humor. You just couldn't tell it by looking at her.

From the collected letters of Sergei Ilyich Mironenko to Alexander Mironenko:

*My stubborn son,*

*I hear you have had another run-in with your half brother, and this is no surprise. I curse the day he was born, and that I married his mother, an evil woman born in a lovely form. But I urge you to leave him to his own devices, as offensive as they may be. We have bigger fish to fry, you and I, and we must use our energies for those ends. I know it's difficult to do nothing when you see him engaged in the slave trade and when you have to listen to his poisonous tirades against Jews and Muslims. But such talk is meant to gall the virtuous and to goad thugs into action. If you let him anger you, he will control you, whether you think he is doing so or not.*

*To answer your question from your previous letter, yes I admit he has made attempts on my life. So have several other relatives. In fact, more of my family members are currently trying to kill me than strangers and enemies outside our illustrious clan. It's dreadfully unfair. I have never tried to kill any of them. But why should I? They will kill each other eventually. Take heed, you don't need to challenge Nikita in any more duels. You've proved your point, and he won't let you beat him again. He would rather see you dead.*

*Someday, he or someone else will succeed, Alexander. Against you or me, or both of us. The worst thing is to see your children die. I lost your brother Georgi and your sister Olga to family politics before you and Nikita were born. But that is the price of a long life, and you will pay it too.*

*Baba Yaga says we have the patents to blame. She says they should be illegal. The technology that runs the Republic is firmly in place now, it would continue to run and prosper without the ruling clans; but without the patents, we big, fat families would lose our income. We would have to make a living like everyone else does. Just think—no more money to throw away on microwars!*

*She's right of course. And she's right when she warns that microwars won't stay micro much longer. Nikita spends his part of the family pie mostly on weapons development. Remember that. We spend most of ours quite differently, and we need to keep moving forward, son.*

*Keep moving forward. But don't forget to watch your back . . .*

The Woovs stood in the snow beside the northern flank of Grey Forest. It was twilight, and the iron-grey sky dropped heavy snow on them, but they did not move. They gazed into the depths and waited.

Finally there was a flicker of light, the sheen of metal, and a strange object emerged from the forest. It was domed; it walked on two legs. It paused, watching the people who waited in the snow. They looked back without moving. Finally the object pivoted and lurched back into the woods.

<I will follow,> said the Elder. <I must go alone.>

Her bodyguards did not want this. Their nostrils expanded, but they said nothing. She was the Elder, and such meetings had occurred before. Possibly they would occur again.

The Elder went into the darkening forest. Her bodyguards were so motionless they might have been rooted there. They were ESAs, their senses enhanced even beyond the range of human ESAs. But they knew the grey shadows deceived their eyes. The world around them seemed poised to take a life. Snow settled in their fur, a pleasant sensation. But they could not enjoy it.

After a time, the Elder emerged again. They did not move until she was among them.

<It was an instructive meeting,> she said.

They searched her face for clues, for a glimmer of hope. They found it.

But her ears were flattened against her head in profound sadness. Whatever small hope she had found battled against it.

<Let's go back to St. Petersburg now,> she said.

They left the scene without looking back.

<Hey, Keej, you awake? It's Bull.>

<I'm awake—sort of. What's up?>

<I just tried to send a TachyGram back to Central. I got an error message.>

<That's been happening more and more lately.>

<Yeah, well, it's no glitch. The second time it went through, and I got a message back.>

<Okay—not sure I'm following you . . .>

<It was from Major Sullivan. He told me to report back to Central immediately but won't say why.>

<Shit! We can't afford to lose you yet. >

<That's not the problem, Keej. He signed the message "Major Sullivan." But I've known him longer than you've been alive. He always signs his messages with "Ted.">

<So you're saying it wasn't from him?>

<It wasn't. And my private message was intercepted. Someone figured out a way to intercept a *TachyGram*, Keej; someone pretty damned smart.>

<Probably the same smart bastard who's been messing with the sprites.>

< Probably. Our communications have been com-

promised, we can't even be sure the one we're having is secure. This makes our job very hard.>

<Bull, isn't it possible they really need you to go home? You've heard the talk lately about a big war, a threat to the core worlds.>

<I've been hearing that talk for years. In fact, Ted and I worked out a code to use in case he needed me back at Central. It wasn't in this message I got. It wasn't from him. And I've got to wonder if I haven't found the marker I've been looking for all these years. The trail of a genuine superkiller.>

<Christ, you're scaring me.>

<You should be scared, Keej. Because whoever this guy is, he knows what we're doing, he knows what we've got on him, and he knows what we're saying to each other about it.>

<So what the hell are we gonna do?>

<Our jobs. Like we always do, only better.>

<Like we've got a choice.>

<That's just it, we don't. He's made us. But he's messed with the wrong blood hounds.>

<True. But if I'm going to chase him up a tree, I'd better get some sleep.>

<Just do it with one eye open, Keej.>

<You too. Good night.>

Emily signed off. But Agent Bullman did not retire to his own bed. He had another call to make. If their communications were no longer secure, he may have just placed Emily in grave danger. He had to make sure she was well protected, so he wanted an expert on the job.

<Grigory—you awake?>

Tally was plugged in.

It was Christmas Eve, and she really should be celebrating, or resting. But how could she do either when the answer seemed to be dancing just beyond her reach? As she sifted through countless images, she was dimly aware of her exhaustion. But Tally could employ superhuman focus when inspired to do so.

Tam had been right. John's search engines had turned up nothing of value. But Tally did not trust his results. There had to be an answer. Even if someone was invisible, his acts never were. He was somewhere in the data, and it would take human perception to find him.

Faces swam before her mind's eye. Tally could probably have recognized many of them on her own, given enough exposure, but she didn't attempt to do so. She used her backup memory and interfaced with programs for sorting images, enhancing the ones that were incomplete, identifying individuals and counting the number of times they appeared in a given area. She didn't expect that she would actually see the killer in the act, but she hoped to at least find him where he had left the bodies.

As the days and weeks slipped by, that hope dwindled.

No one showed up at every single scene. And no sprites had recorded the act of transporting the body parts or staging them. No other mechanical devices had either. One day a meadow contained nothing more dreadful than biting insects. The next, a severed head was perched on a tree stump, as if it had grown there overnight.

Superkillers. Tally never would have believed in them if she weren't trying to find one now. All human beings made mistakes. All were prone to weakness, foolishness on some level. Even brilliant people had flaws. John was a good example. He was so smart, he didn't believe anyone else could be right if they disagreed with him. Tally had known plenty of people like him in her field, scientists, architects, specialists of every kind. That was the glitch in human genius. A lot of otherwise intelligent people never rose above it.

Soon it would be midnight. Bells would ring all over Belarus. *Rejoice, for Christ is born!* Tally wanted so badly to celebrate, to have a reason for it.

Each day brought them news of a new microwar as the powerful families began to bring their conflicts into the open. Andrei, Emily, Grigory, and then Tam were drawn away from the search for the superkiller. Agent Bullman was still on the case, but Tally seldom spoke with him because she had nothing new to report.

When Tally took time to look at the winter world, it seemed so beautiful under its blanket of snow. But monstrous things hid along with the dormant spring. Inside her database she returned to the crime scenes, to the sites from which the girls had disappeared. She saw them vanish. She saw them reappear, in pieces.

*Where else am I supposed to look, then? What am I missing?*

Shadows moved in Grey Forest. Bald Mountain was covered in snow. Gorky Park was full of busy people during the day, became still as a grave at night. Soon the bells would ring, Christ would be reborn, and Tally would give up and go to sleep. But just out of reach the truth was dancing. Once again she saw the grey shadows among the Giants. She chased them.

And then her head was full of patterns.

Tally gasped and disengaged from the system. But it didn't help, the patterns weren't in there. The intricate lines that crawled through her head were from a place outside of all systems, the place behind the Veil. They moved like clockworks, changing, revealing a picture that grew more deadly by the moment.

*The Republic is about to blow up, Tally . . .*

*Can you see the hour ahead . . . ?*

*The horsemen are coming! The horsemen of the Apocalypse!*

"Revelation," said a familiar voice. "Didn't I tell you, child? Why didn't you listen? Why didn't you repent before it was too late?"

The patterns crept along the surface of her eyes, like patterns on a dark curtain. But then the curtain parted, and someone came through. A tall man, too thin for his frame, his skin the color of coffee. He stood in front of her desk, his hands clenching and unclenching like they always did when he was about to beat her.

"Poppy," she gasped.

"Don't call me that," he said, his voice low and dangerous. "You're no daughter of mine."

Tally had imagined what she might say to him if she ever saw him again. She had pictured herself strong, confident, forgiving, and in control of the conversation. But sitting before him now, her hands clutching the side of her desk so they wouldn't shake, she was a small girl again. She was sick with dread and shame. If it had been anyone else, she would have turned her danger suit on and called security. But it didn't even occur to her.

He pointed at her rasta-links. "Why do you have

those damned snakes growing out of your head like some monster?" he thundered. "What happened to the hair God gave you?"

"They're not snakes," she explained, fighting to keep her voice above a whisper. "They're data links, and I need them for my—"

"They *are* snakes," he said. "Brethren to the serpent of the Garden of Eden. They've always been in your head, Tally. I knew they were telling you things you shouldn't know, telling you the future. That's why I beat you. But I have no power to beat you anymore. And look at you! You make me ashamed."

She couldn't answer that. Her mother could never make her cry, no matter how cruel her words. But the man who had beaten her senseless could reduce her to tears just by telling her he wasn't proud of her.

He moved closer, yet his face remained shadowed. She could only see his eyes shining at her like the eyes of an animal.

"You search and you search," he accused. "But you are lost. The devil is looking for you harder than you're looking for him. Get out, Natalia. While you still have the chance."

Tally wanted to tell him she couldn't go, she was trying to do good for the people she loved. She opened her mouth to plead, but soft hissing came out. Her rasta-links moved like snakes, and she began to float away from him. He pointed at her again. But he had no hand, he was as helpless as she. And then she knew.

*Poppy, you're the one who has to get out, you're the one who has to run! It's almost too late, they're coming!*

She tried to tell him, but she could only hiss. She floated farther and farther away. He followed her with his eyes, pointing with his empty sleeve. "It's judgment day," he said with a humility she had never heard before. "Too late to repent, Tally."

And then red light began to consume the world under his feet. It burst forth in rays, carving chunks and consuming them, until her father stood on a lone island in a molten sea.

"Time to start praying again, child," he said. And then his island disintegrated, and he sank into the burning heart of the world.

Tally started to scream, but she never finished. Instead, she coughed, and her eyes fluttered open. She was still sitting at her desk.

Her head rang like a giant bell.

The winter palace creaked around her. Everyone on her floor was asleep, save for personnel who worked the night shift. Tally opened her security shutters and looked out her window.

The city lay slumbering in a blanket of snow, beautiful and still, a scene right out of a Christmas card. The clouds had blown away and half the sky was bright with stars. The other half was veiled.

*I have no power to beat you anymore . . .*

Tally watched the side of the sky that was black. One light moved through that darkness. Archangel Station, keeping vigil. The sight usually comforted her. But tonight she felt no comfort, only that steady ringing that beat in her head in time to her pulse, throbbing, warning.

<Grigory. Are you awake?>

<I am now, Tally.>

<I think my parents are dead.>

<Why do you think so?>

Tally hesitated before telling him. But there was no choice. <I just saw my father's ghost.>

<Ah. But if they were both dead, you would see two ghosts.>

<No. My mother always deferred to my father. She stood in his shadow and kept her mouth shut, unless she was alone with us.>

<A convincing argument. I suppose we can confirm it easily enough. Shall I call home for you?>

<Please. You can do it faster than me. You have—connections.>

<I'll use them. Stand by.>

Tally waited. She gazed at the image in her picture window. It was serene, lovely. It made her feel remote from things, possibly even her feelings.

But that illusion did not last.

<Natalia.>

<I'm ready.>

<Perhaps not. You were right about your parents.>

<I know. How did they die?>

<Someone activated a planet buster inside their world. The surface broke apart and fell into the magma beneath. I doubt they even knew what was happening to them.>

<Grigory, what the hell are you talking about?>

<A planet buster, my Tally. Your parents were killed along with everyone else on the surface of Gideon. I'm sorry.>

Suddenly the bell in her head stopped ringing. Silence filled her from the soul up.

<This is no microwar. No one has used a planet buster on an inhabited world before. No matter what they say on the news, it has begun, Tally. The war that ends the Republic.>

# PART THREE

“ATTENTION! THIS IS A MESSAGE FROM THE ARMAGEDDON FRONT. WE HAVE SOME GOOD NEWS AND SOME BAD NEWS. THE BAD NEWS IS, YOU ARE ALL ABOUT TO BE CONSUMED IN THE FIRES OF THE APOCALYPSE. THE GOOD NEWS IS, YOU ARE ABOUT TO MEET YOUR MAKER. REJOICE! YOUR STRUGGLES ARE OVER. MAKE YOUR PEACE WITH GOD OR PREPARE TO BURN IN HELL—IT MAKES NO DIFFERENCE TO US, BECAUSE ONE WAY OR ANOTHER YOU ARE DEAD MOTHERFUCKERS, KISS YOUR ASSES GOOD-BYE!”

Andrei gritted his teeth. It sounded as though a thousand voices were shouting at once. There was a burst of static, and a flash of light bathed the faces around Emily’s conference table. Darkness and silence followed.

“That static was the first shock wave hitting the message drone,” said Emily. “When the buster was detonated, it generated a series of waves that pulverized the planetary crust. From there, the magma did the rest of the job. Essentially, Gideon has been resurfaced. Their moon and orbital colonies suffered minimal damage, and the mining operations in their asteroid cloud were not attacked."

Andrei could still hear a roar in his ears. But this time it was his pulse pounding with rage. "The message was broadcast in English," he said, surprised by the calm in his voice. "Was that the predominant language on Gideon, Natalia?"

She sat perfectly straight, her face ashen. "Yes. Do you think it mattered? I wonder if they did the message in English because they think that's what everyone should be speaking."

"The planet buster was detonated immediately after the message was broadcast," said Grigory. "It was a deep-space drone with a one-way jump engine. Whoever this Armageddon Front is, they apparently don't believe in making personal appearances at their mass murders."

"So—who the hell are they?" Natalia demanded. "Are they a bunch of religious nuts? Andrei—have you ever clashed with them before?"

"I've never heard of them."

"I think they're yahoos," offered Tam in her bland tone. "You could call them obliterationists. It wasn't a military hit, they went after civilians."

"Wait a minute," said Natalia. "If this is a mass murder perpetrated by terrorists, then how come we're talking about war?"

"Because if they set more of these off they're going to start one," said Grigory. "Something has made them feel Armageddon has begun—or *should* begin—and they want to get in on the action. We must be prepared, as Gideon was not."

Emily wore a look of tired disgust. "They start out so pious at the beginning of the message, then add that smug bit of gloating at the end. They call themselves by a vaguely religious name, but that's not what it's all about for these bastards."

"These well-financed bastards," added Tam.

Natalia leaned heavily on the table, her face somehow more lovely for its starkness. "How soon before the war gets *here*?" she asked.

"It may be here already," said Emily.

Natalia stared at her with a glazed expression.

"Natalia," said Andrei, "do you want a sedative? Would you rather sit this meeting out and get the highlights later?"

She shook her head. "No. This is the best place for me now. I have to understand what happened, and what we have to do. I know—I look like a train wreck, but I'm just shifting gears." She took a deep breath and seemed steadier for it. "So anyway—what do you mean it may already be here?"

Tam was the one who answered. "Nowadays it's all about preemptive strikes. Get your weapons into place before your target knows they're under attack. Gideon didn't have any history of conflict with anyone else, so they weren't watching for the energy signatures. Our intelligence about planet busters tells us that they can rest a few miles down in planetary crust for years and still be detonated effectively."

She turned her tactical gaze on Andrei. "A *sun* buster would be different. When a sun buster is activated, it's supposed to disrupt the balance between the star's gravity and its nuclear forces. Essentially that would cause a supernova. But it would have to be shot into a star just before detonation, or it would disintegrate under the immense pressure."

"You think we could have a planet buster inside Belarus?" asked Natalia.

Grigory was the authority in that area. "No," he said.

"But," Emily was quick to add, "someone may have deployed germ or chemical weapons we haven't classified yet. Or something we can't imagine. Weapons research is the best funded business in the Republic."

Andrei thought it was a good time to get everyone's feet back down to earth—if he could. "Sooner or later," he said, "Belarus will be attacked by my uncles. I suspect they will employ more conventional weapons against us. If this Armageddon Front shows up, they will certainly present a wild card. But perhaps for my uncles as well—they may have more to defend on their home front than they imagined."

"They don't want to risk—" began Emily, but suddenly her eyes went tactical. "Jones is on the line," she said.

"Put him through on the conference screen," said Andrei.

Emily activated the screen. Jones appeared in his captain's chair, looking frazzled but awake. "Ah," he said. "The usual suspects."

"I hope you don't have more bad news," said Andrei.

"Not for us." Jones glanced at Natalia, then back to Andrei. "Archangel is ready. Our military ESAs have their arsenals in place. This planet is well protected. The Lucifer stations have reported their readiness as well. All but the most crucial mining operations have been suspended."

"Any movement from the derelicts?" Natalia asked suddenly. Andrei felt a chill go up his spine.

"No," said Jones. "But I confess we weren't looking for it."

Natalia nodded, but did not look comforted.

"You've heard the message from the Armageddon Front?" Andrei asked.

Jones nodded. "They sound pretty damned fanatical to me. I half expected them to start quoting from Revelation."

"They might do that yet," said Andrei, then sent Jones a private message. <We have a few allies on the way. Perhaps we can lure the enemy onto thin ice.>

<Or shove them onto it,> said Jones. "Good night all," he said aloud. "Get your rest while you can." He terminated the connection.

Andrei looked at his team. "Any comments or suggestions?" he asked.

"Armageddon sucks," said Tam.

No one seemed able to top that.

"Natalia—" Andrei caught up with her in the corridor. "Could we speak in my office?"

"Sure," she said. She felt so tired she wasn't even sure where she was going in the first place.

The two of them walked slowly, almost strolling. Tally admired the beautiful hall she had designed the way a gardener admires the blooms she's worked so hard to coax from the earth. The colors and textures soothed her, as did Andrei's presence. How long had it been since they simply spent casual time together, as friends?

"Natalia—why did you ask about the derelicts?"

She shrugged. "It just occurred to me. All this talk about war, and suddenly I thought about them. Maybe because they're left over from another war."

"And the people who built them didn't survive," Andrei said softly.

"Yes, I guess I'm not too happy thinking about that."

"I'm so sorry about the loss of your parents."

Tally only wished she could feel the grief to justify the sympathy. "Andrei," she said, "they were so hard to live with."

"Really? I used to think mine were too. But I loved them."

"I'm not sure I loved mine at the end. I really tried. When I was a kid I wanted to understand what my mom was saying about my shortcomings, tried to find out what I needed to do to fix things. All I found out was that I couldn't."

They stopped in front of his door and he keyed it open. The two of them went through his sitting room, into his office. Tally plopped into a chair and stared at the portrait of Martha Kretyanova Mironenko.

"Your mother was so cool," she said. "I wish I had a mother like that."

Andrei sat behind his desk. For a while they were quiet, enjoying a shared feeling of respite. Then Tally remembered what Andrei had said about her father.

"My grandfather used to ask me if I could see the hour ahead. Because he could. I always thought it was just him and me. But now when I think about all the stuff my father used to say—" She shook her head. "Jesus, Andrei. He had the sight too, and he couldn't handle it."

He looked her in the eye. "Can you?"

"Yes," she said, feeling a little surprised. "I've *been* handling it. Besides, I don't have it that strong. I just get feelings, or I have true dreams."

"Or you get visits from ghosts," he said.

Tally thought about how many times Lyuba's head had visited her dreams. She couldn't stifle a shiver. "I guess they have something urgent to say. I just wish I understood their dialect better."

"Maybe it's a blessing not to know everything," Andrei offered.

Her father's face appeared in her mind's eye. She saw him raging, preaching, thundering about punishment and damnation. Her body still remembered the blows of his hands, how it felt to know she was going to die.

*Poppy, will I see God now?*

"You're right," she told Andrei. "It's better not to see everything. I wish we—"

His eyes went tactical. Tally stiffened, sure that doom was about to claim them as it had Gideon.

"Incoming fleet," said Andrei. "Friendly."

His eyes went back to normal. He saw her expression. "We've got our own weapons, Natalia, the best people in the business."

"The business," she said miserably. The business of Armageddon. Andrei activated his screen, as if he were simply getting a social call from an old acquaintance.

A man in a Central Naval uniform appeared. Tally

had to admit, he was a reassuring sight. He wore admiral's stars. He was a striking man with jet-black hair and brown eyes that belonged in a Byzantine painting—yet they reminded Tally of someone.

"Father," said the admiral, "I've come to take you home."

Tally looked at Andrei, whose watchful eyes were a different color than his son's. Yet they were the same eyes. "I am home, David. I wish you could come down and visit us."

David looked sad, but not surprised. "I can't do that."

"Surely a day or two wouldn't hurt."

"Father, they are purging Jews and Muslims from Akilina. They are employing the final solution."

Andrei's face became very still. Tally felt her hands grow cold.

"So you go to fight them," said Andrei. "I won't try to stop you."

"We need you, Father. We need your ships, your ESAs."

"I have troubles here too, David."

Once again, David did not look surprised. His face set in grim lines. "I had hoped I might change your mind."

"And I had hoped you might join me here."

They regarded each other in silence for a long moment. Tally thought of her dead parents, and had to look away.

"Go with God, Father."

"Go with God, David."

Tally was close to tears. But something about David's tone as he bade his father farewell made her look at him again. She gazed at his handsome face and a vision came.

Darkness around him, like the darkness she had seen around Katerina. It was the night sky of Belarus, the Veil that covered half the stars—and suddenly she knew.

*They're lying. He's not going to Akilina. Where is he going?*

The Veil hid the stars. Tally supposed it could hide many things. It could hide a fleet easily. That fleet would be close enough to reach Belarus if it was needed.

David's image faded from the screen and from Tally's mind. The darkness evaporated like mist in the morning sun, and she saw Andrei again. His son was not really leaving. But Andrei had really said goodbye to him. Because he might not get another chance.

Andrei was dismayed to see a tear flowing down her lovely cheek. "Natalia . . ."

He could not guard his tone. Seeing her that way touched him too deeply. She wiped the tear and smiled at him.

"Your son is a very impressive man. He's Jewish, isn't he?"

"Yes. Jewish bloodlines are passed through the mother." Andrei was relieved to see her smiling again.

"Andrei," she asked, "how many children do you have?"

"Six, including Peter. David is my eldest."

She looked surprised. "I thought a man your age would have more."

"My brother Evgeny has nineteen. Some in my family have had ten times that, but it's unwise. We all have our own piece of the pie, and the more children you get the tinier the slices."

"That explains why you've got so many backstabbers in the fold."

"Ah, now you understand the dynamics of a family dynasty."

She glanced at the portrait of his mother again. Andrei was pretty sure he knew what she would ask next. He was right.

"Why are people in your own family trying to kill you now?"

That was no simple question, but he tried to answer it as succinctly as possible. "Power," he said. "Some of them are willing to do anything to hold on to it. Some of us try to stop them—and we've succeeded more than they like. Belonging to one of the ruling clans is not like the fairy tales they show on the entertainment networks. Either you knuckle under to family policy or you go against the grain. Go that way too often, and you make the hit list."

"So why don't they just wipe you out with a planet buster?"

"Because of the eggs."

"Huh?"

"The Fabergé eggs. I've got them all. My uncles have tried every way possible to get them from me, from my father and grandfather before me. They've tried to beg, buy, and steal them."

"They're that precious?" Natalia seemed more chagrined than impressed. "I never got a chance to look at them at the party!"

"They're priceless," said Andrei, "to my uncles because they're status symbols. The Mironenko clan had humble beginnings. We stored and recycled poisonous waste."

She raised an eyebrow.

"Garbage collectors," Andrei said cheerfully. "It gave us access to a wide variety of materials that eventually proved to be much more useful than anyone had imagined."

Curiosity eclipsed the worry in her face. "You've got the eggs, so you've got more status than them?"

"No. I've got a shield. The eggs are buying us a fighting chance."

She frowned in thought, much like Emily was prone to do. "I guess I'll never get it, Andrei. I still can't grasp why they want to come after us. Belarus is just—a venture, a cultural experiment. I thought its success could only bring good."

"It has," said Andrei. "But they wanted it to fail.

They would have liked proof that the Bill of Rights can't govern a colony successfully, let alone a Republic. It was my goal to prove them wrong, but I have also tried to preserve what I care about, just as George is doing on Canopus. That's why I named everything here after the original places on Earth, because who knows what will survive?"

She shook her head. "Back when I was in grade school, I learned about the Unification. It strained my imagination to picture all the worlds we can visit so easily today as a bunch of isolated colonies that couldn't even send messages to each other." She smiled sadly. "And when the breakthroughs came that ended all that, better jump drives, TachyGrams, everything we take for granted now, and all those colonies could talk to each other, visit, do business—it seemed so—*glorious*. I sat behind my little desk and dreamed about it. It seemed like there was no limit to where we could go, what we could do."

"My schooling was a little more cynical," said Andrei. "But I understand how you feel."

She looked impossibly weary. "Now I wonder if we all wouldn't have been better off if we had *never* made contact with each other. If each world had been forced to go it alone, to work out its own problems."

Andrei wished he could put his arms around her. "Isolation is never a solution," he said. "What we need to do is grow up. I just hope enough of us survive to do it."

She took a deep breath and twisted her shoulders, easing kinks out of them. "I need a good night's sleep," she said.

"Me too," he admitted, though he hated for her to leave.

She stood. She looked terribly vulnerable, more so than he had ever seen her. She swayed on her feet, and he hurried to her side, steadying her.

Her rasta-links drifted off her shoulders and touched his face. She placed her hands on his chest.

"You said good-bye to David." Her voice was low. "Don't say good-bye to me."

Her hands moved over him, around him, pulling him down to her. She was a tall woman, so he didn't have far to go. He touched the soft, smooth skin of her face, felt the delicate bones beneath. He kissed her beautiful mouth and his weariness vanished.

Andrei wasn't quite sure how they got from his office to his bedroom, but they made the trip quickly. Once there, they went more slowly. Natalia's body was lovely, and she made love hungrily, but also with a maddening patience. At the moment of his first climax, a familiar face surfaced in his mind. He did not call Susan's name, but in his thoughts she smiled at him.

*It's about time!* she said, then left him to his new love.

He was shivering under a pile of cold, wet leaves, trying to blend with the earth. Then someone pulled him out of the mud. Andrei struggled.

"You're safe, son. It's Papa."

Andrei threw his arms around Alexander. "Mama is—" he sobbed. "They—"

"I know," said Alexander. "I know, son."

<Andrei.>

The communication woke him. He opened his eyes to a dark room and the sound of Natalia breathing softly beside him.

<I'm awake, Grigory.>

<Four more worlds have been destroyed by planet busters: Hestia, Xibalba, Oceana, and Abrecan.>

Andrei listened to the death list. He had been to Oceana several times. It was a beautiful world populated mostly by people of Maori descent.

<The Armageddon Front is claiming credit for two of them,> said Grigory. <The other two were perpetrated by groups who warred with those worlds recently.>

Only the second day, and the war had claimed over forty billion lives.

<Has the Armageddon Front identified itself yet? Claimed any affiliations?> Andrei asked.

<No official word,> said Grigory. <I think Tam is right—they're yahoos. I think they have money and murderous intent, probably little more.>

<All right, Grigory, I might as well get up now. Keep me posted.>

<Eat breakfast,> urged the ESA.

<I will.>

Andrei got out of bed as quietly as he could. Natalia did not stir, but her breathing changed. He hoped she would try to get more sleep. He dressed quickly without having his usual shower and went into his office.

He felt disoriented and depressed. He wandered over to his window and looked out at the starry sky. Half of it was covered by the Veil. He thought of the fleet hiding there, his silent runners, and tried to be comforted. But the darkness of the Veil only inspired bleaker thoughts.

Planet busters. If the rumors were true, and people started using sun busters, soon all of the night sky might be black and empty.

Andrei dialed up some coffee and tried to prepare himself for a very long day.

The third day dawned on a palace full of wakeful people. Within twenty-five hours, ten more worlds had been destroyed or had been lost from network communications. Throughout the rest of the Republic, everyone argued about why it was happening and who was to blame.

"They're just making noise." Emily leaned over her cup of coffee like she might dive in. "They think it's just because people couldn't agree. But the bottom line is, our *laws* couldn't agree. If people can't reach an understanding, they should be able to work it out in court. I think if the planetary court systems had been able to interact more cooperatively, this might not have happened. Tyrants and thugs took advantage of the holes in the law. That's part of the reason I left homicide investigation."

"Yeah, but you'd think people could show some common sense." Tally preferred tea as a stimulant. "The Republic had a lot of problems, but it still worked—sort of."

"Too damn much money and too little sense," said Emily.

They watched the reports coming in, shaking their heads in sadness and disbelief.

"At least we've still got the sprite network," said Tally. "We can see what's really going on. Thank God for that."

Loki watched the two women with amusement. He had made his fortune by being useful to tyrants and thugs who thwarted honest government workers like Emily. She took it all too personally. One thing he had learned in his life was that if you killed a million people, two million were born to take their place. It was like having a garden, you had to prune it occasionally. Sometimes you had to sacrifice a plant or two.

He was rather enjoying the news. He found destruction intellectually engaging, if nothing else. Who would deploy their busters and slammers first? Who would be the first to wipe out communications with a well-timed pulse? He only hoped he wouldn't be isolated too long, once the action came to Belarus. He was impatient to deploy his own special toys.

Soon. The time was almost right.

Spritemind watched the Republic self destructing. For the first three days, the conflict was grim, but still relatively isolated.

On the fourth day, the ruling families changed that. For thousands of years they had built their arsenals, funded their research, perfected the art of the preemptive strike. Eventually they realized they had become too good at creating superweapons, but by then it was too late—their enemies were always poised. They had to do the same to survive. They watched each other across the light-years, still believing they were the ones who controlled which wars were fought, and when. None of them saw the snakes in their own fold, the wealthy, bored, pampered monsters who grew up with instant destruction at their fingertips, who faced no consequences for their actions and who were masters at hiding their ugliest deeds from the families who bred them. These secretive children had a number of clubs they belonged to.

One of them was named the Armageddon Front.

On the fourth day, the Armageddon Front assailed the core worlds, the heart of the Republic. They were quickly repelled, finding them far better protected than they had imagined. This was a disappointment, but the rest of the Republic was still available. They resumed their random strikes. Unfortunately, not all of these strikes were *perceived* as random.

The Urbano family was the first to move in full force. But it was only the first by a few seconds.

Spritemind protected as many innocent citizens as it could. But it knew it was running out of time.

<Grigory! Intervention is imminent. I have to move—see you later.>

<ESA GRIGORY TO ALL PERSONNEL: EMERGENCY OVERRIDE 00010 Battle Stations!>

Sprites swarmed the Isle of the Dead. Medusa stood in her cubicle, every rasta-link deployed into a receiver.

<George, it's time,> called Spritemind.

<Begin download,> George ordered Medusa.

He watched her serene face. For a moment, he could have sworn he saw a flash from the center of her pupils. But he probably imagined that.

"It's done," said the avatar. "I'm here, George."

George felt profound relief. For some time, Spritemind had known someone would find a way to wipe it out. Now there was a copy, and George would make sure it was preserved until the day when it could help salvage what was left of the Republic.

"It's quite an unusual feeling," said Spritemind II, "being a person with one body."

George grinned. "Ten years ago this kind of compression would not have been possible. We live in an age of wonders, my friend."

"We did," said the avatar. "Now we must greet the dark ages."

"Not I," said George. "Not on this world. I swear it."

The avatar regarded him with more warmth than Medusa would be able to muster on her own. "I'm going deep now. Medusa's on the rise. So long, George."

"Later, Spritemind."

Medusa's face became serene again. "Orders?" she queried.

"Self-regulate," answered George. He gazed through the skylight at millions of agitated sprites, tiny pricks of light that dazzled his eyes. "Switch to backup communications," hc added.

Just in time.

Loki grinned. The ruling families were making their move. The time had come. He accessed his matrix and found his jewel.

Throughout the galaxy, his false sprites maintained their relays among the true sprites. They worked benignly within the system until they received his code: <WILDFIRE; ARM.>

The system ignited like a mind having a seizure.

<Enable,> he commanded, and watched the destruction.

S. O. Valerian monitored sprite activities, and so was the first to note the unprecedented surge in communications.

<Valerian to Kizheh. Something's happening to the sprites.>

She did not respond. She must have dozens of other high-priority messages in her queue. He couldn't tell her what he suspected.

The sprites must be under attack. He had worried something like this could happen from the moment he and Emily had investigated the brownout in the net eight years before. In the past, sprites could recover from destructive pulses quickly because they could feel them coming. They passed their information on to other sprites until the pulse ran out of punch, then transferred the information back again. If they lost the information permanently, they could always relearn it.

It wasn't a perfect system, but it had proved to be hardy. This unprecedented level of activity, however, concerned him. He prayed that his worst fears were not coming true, that no one had found a way to cripple sprites permanently. Their resilience relied on their ability to spring back from destructive pulses with their attributes still intact, so that they could repair or make new sprites as needed.

If someone had created a weapon to destroy that ability, there was nothing he or anyone else could do about it but try to function without the sprites. Because if they could not, this would not simply be a war. It would be the end.

<SPRITEMIND: Grigory, one last thing, I have to warn you—>

<I'm listening.>

<I have been monitoring the other Spritemind I told you about, the one that calls itself ME. It's growing more cohesive. I think it's aware of our current conflict. In fact, it began to grow stronger after it first became aware of us, and now its cohesiveness is growing in proportion to our destruction. It's more important than ever to watch ME, but I can't do it. I'm under attack now, just as we feared, I'm going to lose myself. I think ME will become a serioussssss WILDFIRE! WILDFIRE! WILDFIRE! /////>>>/>####..........
................................>

"Andrei," Tally called through her portable com. "Do you read? The net's out, I can't get clear messages."

"We're convening in Emily's conference room," he said. "Get over here as fast as you can."

She ran. On her way she saw Peter and his tutor running for the bomb shelter. "Good luck, Tally!" cried Peter, his face white.

"SpriteNet is down," Grigory told Andrei. "Our sprites are just drifting. We may be able to get them operating again, given time. But we don't have it. We're switching to other systems. They should be online within minutes."

"My mother," said Peter, his heart pounding. "I have to find her!"

"She knows the drill," said Ms. Kenyon. "We must follow the procedure, Peter, your father expects it."

She hurried him along, but his terror only grew. His mother would die without him, he knew it.

Then suddenly she was there, blocking the hall. Ms. Kenyon stopped short. "Tsarina—" she began.

"I'll take him," said Mother.

For a moment, Peter was greatly relieved to see her. But the expression on her face quickly dispelled his joy.

"The tsar has ordered—" Ms. Kenyon tried again.

"He is my son," said Mother, and Peter knew she would not listen to argument. His tutor did not resist when Mother pulled him down the hall in the opposite direction. Peter looked over his shoulder and saw Ms. Kenyon crying.

"Mother—" He did not resist as she hurried him along. "We really should get to the shelter."

"No," she said firmly. "We'll go where we can do some good."

Peter knew where that must be.

The chapel.

<Backup communications online,> said Grigory. <This system has a priority queue that—>

<OUTPOST ZED, INCOMING, MASSIVE EN-

ERGY SIGNATURE—FLEET DROPPING OUT OF JUMP, LUCIFER SYSTEM.>

<My uncles are here,> said Andrei.

<Interesting,> said Grigory. <They're going after our mining systems first.>

The ESAs of Belarus would mourn the loss of their sprites for the rest of their lives, but the military ESAs were not crippled by it. They were accustomed to interfacing with machines of a different sort during battle. They were also accustomed to being linked with each other, much in the way sprites linked to perform more complex tasks. The most essential difference in their link was that they had an admiral, ESA Jorge. Veteran of a thousand wars, Admiral Jorge knew where the first fleet was going as soon as they came out of jump. His equipment was waiting for them.

<Mining Station Alpha reporting, we are under attack, repeat, we are under attack.>

<Deploying slammers,> Jorge informed Andrei.

Andrei had planned for this battle most of his life. But now that it was upon him, there was nothing much for him to do but sit back and hope that his preparations were sufficient.

His staff members sat around Emily's conference table, linked to their subordinates, eyes in tactical mode. Outside, the alarm sirens were warning his citizens into their well-stocked shelters. Citizen militias were ready to engage any troops that dared to land, but Andrei doubted that would happen. His war would be fought by ships, by machines, and by the people who were linked to them.

In a way, it was like the chess games his mother had forced him to play. Andrei had become quite good at large-scale chess over the centuries. He just hoped he wouldn't have to lose too many of his pieces to win the game.

* * *

Tally plugged into Emily's table console, but she was blind as systems struggled to reroute.

And then suddenly she could see. A fleet of ships came out of jump near Mining Stations Alpha, Beta, and Gamma. Because she had no perspective, they appeared to be perfectly still.

<This is Mining Station Gamma, we have no weapons, we are a civilian operation . . .>

The ships had long, delicate arrays on their noses. Tally thought they might be for communications, but she had seen nothing quite like them before. Those structures blurred and rippled, and then the ships became obscured.

By bubbles.

It almost looked funny. Tally had heard many times of slammers, but had never seen them in action. Starship hulls were incredibly hard, made to withstand enormous pressures inside jump tunnels; you couldn't blast through them with conventional weapons. They needed to be weakened first. One of the fastest ways to do that was with gravity weapons, slammers. The ESAs had moved the generators into place, deftly anticipating the trajectory of the enemy warships. The generators created thousands of prejump fields, small wells of immense gravity existing as a field of "bubbles." Each of them pulled at different parts of a ship, creating temporary weak spots, allowing the military ESAs to deploy the next wave of their assault, spores that went straight to the weakest points and began to undo the molecular bonds of the alloy. ESAs fired particle beams at those spots.

But not before one of the ships managed to deploy a deadly weapon of its own.

"What in blazes is that?" Andrei asked aloud.

"Something new," answered Grigory.

The array at the nose of the enemy ship had come alive. It was generating a field.

"A jump point is forming," said Grigory.

"Are they mad?" wondered Andrei. "They can't jump safely inside a slammer field."

"I suspect a safe jump is not what they have in mind," said Grigory. "The jump point is forming next to Gamma Station."

Andrei watched in grim silence as the singularity formed. Slammers had another useful effect in battle. Jump points generated from within their field formed with the entrance *inside* the event horizon. Anything near such a jump point was pulled apart by the tidal effects.

Gamma Station was pulled in. A moment later, the enemy ship came apart. Its generator faltered and the jump point collapsed.

"Apparently they have no plans to salvage our mining industry," remarked Grigory.

<WARNING, INCOMING FLEET, ENERGY SIGNATURES LUCIFER AND BELARUS SYSTEMS.>

Grigory reported. <Jump points forming near Mining Stations Alpha and Beta—and Archangel.>

Andrei felt a shock wave beneath his feet.

"Please tell me that wasn't the Hermitage," he prayed.

"They're dropping bombs on ground-based manufacturing centers," said Grigory.

Andrei's reply was not fit for polite company.

Tally watched the slammer ballet play itself out again, waiting for more bombs to rain down on Belarus. But the shock waves were few and far between. She didn't need her second sight to tell her what was going on.

*They're not going to try to occupy this world. They know they probably can't kill Andrei, so they'll cripple him instead!*

They were trying to knock out the mining stations and manufacturing. Tally had no doubt where that would leave Andrei's colony, if it went on much longer.

* * *

Loki was annoyed. His weapons were working beautifully, but they would run out eventually. Although he still had some weapons in reserve, he didn't want to use all his aces so early. Especially since there were other players in the game, the secret elves who must be watching the conflict with more than casual interest. He didn't want to be stuck on the same planet with them without some potent weapons.

*Calm down*, he warned himself. *Let the pawns throw themselves into the battle. Patience.*

Good advice. But as he waited and watched, his jaws were clenched so tight he cracked a tooth.

In the bomb shelter of the Hermitage, Athena Mitropoulos waited with the treasures. They had begun to move them four days before; she had slept only a few hours during that time. Hundreds of volunteers helped. They had done the impossible. She dared to hope it would be enough.

Athena took a headache pill and sipped a little water. On the cot across the way, her assistant Claudia was reading a novel and sipping wine.

"I wish I could be as relaxed as you," remarked Athena.

Claudia shrugged. "I've been through a lot worse than this. If they drop a big one on us, we'll never know. If they wreck the rest of the city, we'll have to pick up the pieces. Right now I'm just making the best of it."

Athena rubbed her temples. Claudia was right. Claudia was also probably, like everyone else, worried sick about her family on other worlds, places that might not exist anymore. Athena hoped her assistant could maintain her calm a little longer.

Another shock wave rolled past them. It was weaker than the last, but Athena took a second headache pill.

* * *

Archangel Station almost suffered the same fate as Gamma. But this time ESAs managed to knock out the array before it could form a jump point.

Tam sat in her office, her eyes like black stones, her mind divided. She fought against the forces attacking Archangel while other ESAs handled Lucifer system. Tam only conferred with them when necessary. She used her own weapons, communicating with them through a non-sprite network as she always had.

It was like playing ten video games at once. Tam would have loved it that if so many people didn't get killed.

*After this is over I'm switching to another department. This time I mean it!*

The thought was barely a ripple on the surface of her consciousness. Tam blew up targets, watched them blow up hers.

One by one, her resources were disappearing from the grid. She fought on, making the best of what she had.

Until she had nothing

<I'm at zero,> she warned Grigory. She was not the only ESA who had that news to report.

"Time for backup," he told Andrei.

<David, it's time to come out.>

<Acknowledged.>

<ENERGY SIGNATURES,> warned Outpost Zed, <ANOTHER FLEET INCOMING.>

<These are allies,> said Andrei. < Stand by.>

David had waited for days in the obscurity of the Veil, hoping that his father's plan would work. Let Uncle Nikita think he was headed for Akilina.

*That Veil is half the reason I've picked the system,* Andrei said, almost fifteen years ago. *Even sprites wouldn't find you in there.*

It was true. You could hide several solar systems in

the Veil, let alone one fleet. And it offered no harm unless you blundered into one of the giant gravity wells it was nursing.

Still, he was glad to get out of it again. David often had the feeling they weren't alone. Yet somehow he doubted that other human beings hid there.

David dropped out of jump in Belarus system and attacked his father's enemies, using slammers, spores, burners, particle beams, and every new and terrible weapon at his disposal. The enemy fleet fought unimaginatively, bent on taking out specific targets and seemingly unconcerned for their own safety. He assumed the ships were unmanned—or piloted by fanatics. Either way, his response was the same.

He could not help but wonder what the uncles were planning. Nikita especially had coveted the eggs, perhaps he thought he could come back later to claim them.

Perhaps he was right.

One by one, the enemy ships were broken apart before they could destroy the mining stations. But some of those ships managed to deploy conventional weapons. David had lost no ships, but his fleet was beginning to fall prey to the damage of slammers and spores. In the end he might have to emigrate to Belarus after all.

<Incoming!> reported one of his military ESAs. <More ships, Admiral. Jump points forming near all three surviving stations.>

David didn't reply, there was nothing he could do about it except keep battering away at targets. An enemy ship was disintegrating under his sights. After that he would go on to the next.

"Admiral!" warned his sensor technician.

"Jump!" commanded David, a second too late.

A jump point was already forming close to his ship—one that had been generated by an enemy within a slammer field.

"Admiral, we can't—"

The singularity began to suck them in. *Go with God,*

*Papa,* David had time to think before time collapsed with space and was crushed into infinity.

Andrei was aware that his resources were beginning to run out. He didn't give up hope yet. But he wondered if luck would be all he had left soon.

<Two jump points forming,> Grigory said suddenly. <One in orbit around Belarus, the other near our sun.>

<What are they?> demanded Andrei.

<A message drone is orbiting our world,> said Grigory. <I'm guessing that the other object is a sun buster.>

<Enemy ships jumping out of the system,> said ESA Admiral Jorge. <Andrei—most of our weapons are disabled and we've got nothing close enough to intercept that buster.>

"ATTENTION! THIS IS A MESSAGE FROM THE ARMAGEDDON FRONT. WE HAVE SOME GOOD NEWS—"

<SHUT IT DOWN!> commanded Andrei.

"—AND SOME BAD—"

The message was cut short. They waited in silence. There was nothing they could do. The sun's balance between gravity and nuclear explosion was about to be fatally disrupted. Those who did not know it paused in alarm at the sudden silence. Those who did, kept the knowledge to themselves, a last act of kindness.

<The buster has been deployed,> said Jorge. A moment later he added, <Detonated.>

*Here it comes*, thought Andrei.

But it didn't.

<Jorge, what the hell is going on?> demanded Andrei.

<We recorded the detonation. The thing went off.>

<So where's the big boom?>

Jorge paused, but Andrei doubted he was rechecking his data.

<Give it to me straight, Jorge. If you're wrong, no one will be left to complain about your job performance.>

<Something neutralized the weapon's effect.>

<A code? Someone disarmed it?>

<No code. A code would have to be sent *before* it went off. Something snuffed it out *after* it went off.>

<Are they gone?> asked Tally. <Is it over?>

<It better be,> said Tam. <We're outta stuff.>

Grigory stood at Andrei's elbow, his expression more preoccupied than Andrei had ever seen it.

"Your luck holds again, Mironenko," he said.

"It went off and nothing happened?" asked Andrei, unconvinced. "Why?"

"Something happened," corrected Grigory. "But not what we expected."

Seconds, minutes, were slipping by, and still they were all alive, the sun and the world still kept their places in the universe. And Andrei was starting to believe. He slipped back into tactical and regarded a filtered image of the sun. "Maybe it couldn't have worked in the first place," he said. "Sun busters are still new, barely more than theoretical."

"*Planet* busters were just theoretical until someone set one off," said Grigory.

"But the first ones didn't work," Andrei reminded him.

"Sun busters worked well enough on Kikimora Prime and Manjushri Prime. Now that the net's down, it may be decades before we find out where else they worked."

Andrei switched to an image of Archangel Station. Preliminary reports of its damage levels were within acceptable parameters. He had yet to receive a full account of damage within the Lucifer system or on Belarus.

"So," he said, "what if the damned thing goes off later? Or any minute now?"

"I doubt it will. It detonated. What more could it do but disintegrate in that immense gravity well?"

Andrei started to scan fleet reports. He looked for David's flag ship and couldn't find it. That could be due to problems with the net. "Do you think our departed company knows that we didn't blow up?"

"I don't see how they could," said Grigory. "They jumped before it detonated."

*Is it really that simple?* wondered Andrei.

And then he began to receive more detailed reports about the damages done to his mining operations, his space stations, and his personnel. Alpha and Beta Stations had life systems still functioning but needed extensive repairs. Out of his fleet of ten star ships, three remained. Out of David's fleet of six ships, three remained. Andrei scanned the list of known casualties. He recognized a name near the top.

He wept as he continued down the long, long list.

Katerina knelt with her only son in the chapel. This was the beginning of the end for her, she was certain. But Peter might live on, if she prayed, if her sins did not stain him.

His arm had crept around her waist as they knelt together, and he leaned against her. But he dutifully repeated the prayers as she spoke them. Such a good child, and so clever. If only she could guide him away from his father's mistaken thinking, there might be hope for him yet.

"Mama," he whispered urgently when she paused between verses. Normally she would continue without answering, but this time she heard the fear in his voice.

"What is it, Peter?"

"Will we die now?"

She was fairly certain of her answer. "I don't think so. Not yet. But billions of souls have passed today. We must pray for them."

He pressed his face against her side, and she felt dampness through her dress. "Mama," he said, "do you love me? Do you think I'm good?"

"I love your pure soul, my son. I know it will shine beside your father's in heaven."

"And you will be there too, Mama, as an angel."

In his innocence, he placed her among the exalted. "I am a humble servant," she said. "God will judge me, Peter."

"I will ask him to keep you near me, always," he said, squeezing her as tightly as his small arms would allow.

"Perhaps it will be so," she said gently. She did not break away from his embrace as she should in God's house. He was just a child . . .

"Tsarina." Someone spoke hesitantly behind her. She recognized the voice of Gallina, her youngest assistant. "Tsarina, the war is over."

"Did they tell you," asked Katerina, "how great are the casualties?"

"We have no news from out-of-system," said Gallina. "For us, the greatest losses were among our mining and military personnel in space. On Belarus, the casualties number less than one thousand."

"Odd," said Katerina. This was not what she had expected. There was still something waiting for them, something dire.

"Tsarina . . ." Gallina sounded near tears. "Among the dead is the tsar's eldest son, David."

Peter gasped. "My brother?"

"Yes, Tsarevich. I am sorry."

Peter looked at Katerina again, his eyes like pools of sorrow. "I never got to meet him," he said. "I shall never know him."

Katerina gently dislodged herself from his embrace.

"Go to your father," she said. "He needs you." She turned to Gallina. "Take him."

"Yes, Tsarina."

"Mother, will you pray for David?"

"Yes, Peter." She put her hand on his cheek. He seized it and kissed it, then held it to his cheek again. He gazed at her wordlessly for a long moment, full of a fire she thought she knew. At that moment, she recognized herself in him and was amazed.

Peter took Gallina's hand and let her lead him out of the chapel. He did not look back once. Katerina crossed herself, thinking of Andrei's son David, the Jew. No amount of prayer from her would rescue him from hell. But sometimes she allowed herself to hope that good people of other faiths did not suffer there. Perhaps a place was set aside for the virtuous, where they might have peace. That was what she would pray for.

She knelt, and waited for guidance. It did not come, but a certainty grew in her. This War To End All Wars was not an end at all. There was worse to come.

*Lord of my days,* she pleaded. *I bow down before your cross. My time is short. Let me be wise.*

NEW YEAR'S DAY, BELARUSIAN YEAR 12

The Republic fell within one Belarusian day and night. One by one, communications relays stopped working. Andrei sent message drones to other worlds, asking for news.

None were answered.

His enemies did not return. Andrei assumed that either they were dead or they were worried that the sun buster might still go off. They might simply be too busy with their own problems to waste resources on him. Whatever the reason—Belarus stood.

But people were leaving her.

Andrei waited in the private terminal with ESA Tam, watching people board the last surviving shuttle. It had made several flights to Archangel already, and it would make several more. Most people were leaving to find out if family still survived on other worlds.

Andrei grieved for David. He could not be sure the rest of his grown children still lived, either. And though David, firstborn son of Susan, had lived many years more than the normal human life span, that only made it harder to bear his loss.

He watched the crowd at the gate. Some were leaving because they couldn't stand to be trapped on one world. And Andrei supposed some were venturing back into space out of pure curiosity.

The Woov embassador approached Andrei with her entourage in tow. He bowed to her. She and her group were the last non-humans to leave his colony. When she was standing face-to-face with him, she clasped his throat in an expression of sympathy. Tam did not bat an eyelash.

"You have lost much," said the embassador. "Your civilization is going into hibernation for a while. Perhaps when you emerge again, you will be stronger."

"I hope so," said Andrei.

"You have been good allies, despite your internal problems. But you must solve them. We shall need you farther down the road. And you shall need us."

He gazed into her eyes, almost losing himself there. Her remark had the sound of a prophecy. "If you need us," he said, "call. We will do what we can."

"I know you will, Andrei Alexandrovich." She let go of his throat and turned to go. She was halfway to the gate when she suddenly stopped and looked back.

"Stay lucky," she called.

"I'll try," said Andrei.

He watched her go. It was an unhappy moment. Belarus needed people now. Only two star ships were staying in-system. Only one earth-to-orbit shuttle still functioned at full capacity, and Andrei didn't know how long it would take to build more. The manufacturing and heavy industry complexes on Belarus had been in their infancy, and they had been primary targets. Those that remained were still heavily reliant on automatic systems that were crippled. They would have to use other sources of energy and manufacture that were more primitive.

*But we survived. All of these years, all of these* centuries, *my father, my grandfather, and I have worked to make Belarus. And our colony survived. We can take care of ourselves.*

The thought almost made him feel better. Then he got a call from Emily.

<Andrei, you need to come home immediately.>

He complied, getting into the car with his security team. <Brief me,> he said.

<We found the missing body parts from the girls in the first group,> said Emily.

It was a long moment before he remembered what she was talking about. He had not thought about the superkiller in days. <All of them? Where?>

<They were arranged together in quadrant 017 of the Gemstone Caverns.>

<Arranged together?> he asked, trying to grasp the concept.

<The bastard propped them up with braces and arranged them as if they were dancing in a circle.>

And suddenly he grasped the concept all too well.

There is only one basic plot: things aren't what they seem.

—Jim Thompson

Tally stood in the garden and watched the workmen patching the north cornice of the winter palace. They were doing a good job, but the sight depressed her. Before the Civil War, sprites and other machines could have done the repair in a few hours. Most of the sophisticated construction machinery had been recruited for repairs of the mining stations in the Lucifer system. So repairs on Belarus took longer to complete. *Much* longer.

The sprites had not recovered from WILDFIRE. Grigory said they probably never would. They could still do a few simple things, but they could not think, plan, or make more of themselves, and of course there was no more sprite network. Tally was saddened; they had been a remarkable intelligence. But she learned to function without them. The backup communications system worked well, at least locally. Everyone's power had been restored, water and natural gas lines were functioning properly, and most of the train lines were running again.

She took a long sip of her coffee. It felt wonderful going down, but her feet were cold. She adjusted the controls on her danger suit—at least that still worked.

Snow lay in patches on the ground, but spring shoots were poking through. Tally had been looking at them when she really should have been watching the workmen. All she thought about, day and night, was restoring buildings, patching roads, getting all the trains running again. Andrei's world was growing its roots and putting out shoots, just like the little shoots near Tally's feet.

But offworld, things weren't so great. Even with the aid of the extra equipment, repairs on the space stations were going slowly. It might be another decade before mining operations could get back on track.

At least Tally's work was actually getting done, if slowly. She left the garden and checked back through security, into the palace, where she had to turn her suit's temperature down again. She pulled her mouth– and earpieces out of her collar and tried to call Andrei.

"He's in a meeting," said an operator. "Do you want to leave a message?"

"No," said Tally. Andrei was always in meetings. Tally's schedule had been no less crowded. This was a rare thing, a little bit of time off, and she found herself at a loss about how to spend it. She walked the long, elegant hall, past locked doors with nobody in them, no Emily or Peter or Grigory, all of them off on their own business.

*You could always read a book,* she reminded herself. *There's that wonderful library you helped design.*

It wasn't a bad idea, but she wasn't ready to be that leisurely so early in the day. There had to be something to do. She came to her own door, where Thoth, god of scribes, presented his profile. He granted her passage into her private world.

Tally plugged in. She looked at her mail, first. She was hoping someone would send her a message that would require attention. But it was nothing but satisfactory status reports. Tally composed any brief answers that were required and moved on.

She passed by the file that contained the beginnings of her memoirs of her work on Canopus. She found that she could only work on that a little bit at a time. And anyway, there was also a file about her work on Belarus. Andrei was helping her with that. She enjoyed working on that one more.

As she sorted, her mind began to drift. She wondered if she should just fix lunch. Then she went past a file marked DEAD DANCERS. She stopped.

It was a copy of one of Emily's files. Tally had looked at it once, trying to puzzle it out, but other matters had led her away.

She opened the file and read the reports again. Then she looked at the pictures.

All of the girls who had been murdered were dismembered. Before the war, only parts from their upper bodies had been found. But afterward the lower body parts were discovered together in a horrible tableau.

They did not look real. He had found some way to preserve them; none of them had been infested with insect larvae. They were sawed off so neatly at the waist, they almost looked like mannequin parts, except for the dreadful, butcher-shop view where the cuts had been made.

They danced. Their legs had an unnatural pliability, as if their bones had softened and bent under some strain, yet they still looked as if they were capable of movement. They danced in a circle, deep in Gemstone Caverns. Tally had been to the scene. It was a lonely place, it was no surprise that he had been able to take his time and carefully position all of them. The tableau reminded Tally of something. She was sure it was supposed to. But she couldn't think what.

Dancers deep in a cavern, in the dead of winter, at the close of the War To End All Wars. Did the killer even care about the war, or anything else that went on outside his mental microcosm?

But he was supposed to be a superkiller. So his

microcosm should be far more expansive than the garden-variety killer's. The war should matter to him, he should know exactly why it happened. And the dancers, they had been posed elegantly, artfully. She remembered what Emily had said about it.

"I've seen killers do awful things with body parts, pose them like they were in some pornographic movie. The victims have already been reduced to objects by the killing and dismemberment, and then they find ways to heap further humiliation on the dead." She had frowned deeply when she looked at the scene.

"This is bizarre," she concluded. "This is not deliberate humiliation, this is some kind of strange homage."

"To whom?" Tally asked.

"Dancers," Emily answered. "Something about dancers . . ."

Two of the victims had been dancers. But most of them weren't. They were all young girls, and young girls tended to dance more than older women. Tally had seen them dance in circles at spring festivals.

Spring. The Rite of Spring. Dancers in circles.

Tally stared at the pictures, thinking. Then she closed that file and went looking for another.

<Tam, is John in his office?>

<He's on vacation in Zhukovka. He's been working pretty hard, they made him go.>

<I was hoping to get his opinion. I've started combing through that surveillance file again—have you looked at it recently?>

<No. Darned pesky war got in the way.>

<Yeah. That's my point. I didn't have any solid leads, but things were starting to line up in logical ways. Now it all looks like total chaos again.>

Tam instantly made the leap. <You think someone's been tampering with it?>

<Hate to sound paranoid. But it's acting like a database that's been infected with a shuffling virus. The

more I try to get things to line up, the more it looks like someone's playing *go fish* with me.>

<Maybe it got hit with the same shit that crippled the sprites.>

<But it wasn't linked with them, this copy of the file was in my private database, shielded—and nothing else in there has been affected.>

<Ah-hah! I hope you're right about that.>

<Ah-hah?>

<If you are, you don't need to look at all those images. You're not gonna find him there. You've got to look under your own nose, instead.>

Tally thought about that. The implications were terrifying.

<This guy has to be closer to us than we've suspected,> said Tam. <*Real* close.>

<As in one of us?>

<Don't think it can't happen. And to be that close without getting caught, he must have access to technology we don't have.>

<That's hard to imagine.>

<It should be. I used to think we were cutting edge, but someone found a way to cripple the sprites. Didn't see that coming. And there's another kind of technology that would throw us. The alien kind.>

A bad feeling crept over Tally. She would have thought someone was walking over her grave, except that this feeling came upon her so much lately, a whole stampede of people must be invading the graveyard.

<Some weird stuff happened during the war,> Tam said. <That sun buster didn't blow us up, for one thing. And it should have.>

<Couldn't it have been a dud?>

<Nope.>

Tally leaned back in her chair and rubbed her face. <Okay, Tam. If we play this theory out, we've got someone who really does fit Bull's profile, a superkiller. Smart enough to find stuff left on this world

that we haven't found ourselves. But Jesus, why wouldn't we find it? Or a hint of it? No human being is that smart.>

<Maybe he doesn't have to be.>

<Why not?>

<Maybe he got here first.>

Tally sat up straight. <We discussed that possibility before. But you know how thorough Emily and Grigory were when they searched this world. If he's an alien with technology we don't understand, he could elude us, but if he's another human we should have tripped him up.>

<Huh-uh. Hate to tell you this, but those danger suits you guys have are *not* cutting edge. We've got some now that will hide someone from all sensor probes, and I doubt we're the only ones.>

<*We've* got some? As in *you* have one, Tam?>

<Me and a few other ESAs.>

Tally was glad Tam couldn't see her face. <Is this classified information you just handed me?>

<It used to be. But we're alone now. You could say this is information to pass on a *need to know* basis.>

<Got you. Okay, so he was here first. And he grabbed all the alien stuff so we couldn't find it, and he's using it against us. The big question is still *why*?>

<No mystery there. It's just what he does, Tally. It's what he is. That's all the reason he needs.>

<You don't think it's some kind of vendetta against Andrei?>

<Maybe there's a little of that. But that wouldn't be the reason, that would be the excuse. If he even needs one, and I have a feeling he doesn't.>

Tally unplugged the link with the surveillance file. It was a relief not to have to comb through that data anymore, she had to admit. <Okay, I'll talk with Emily about it.>

<Think I'll get together with Grigory and do a little brainstorming, too.>

<Tam—how long have you been harboring this theory?>

<Just thought it up now, when I was talking to you.>

Tally laughed. <You're a gem.>

<Gee, thanks. But you're the one who gave me the idea. When you told me someone was sneaky enough to infect one of your files with a virus without affecting any of the others, I just started thinking.>

<Keep thinking.>

<Always.>

Tally severed the link and dialed Emily. No answer. Tally wasn't surprised. Lately most of her messages to Emily sat in a queue for a while. She left another one and went to fix herself some lunch. Suddenly she had a good appetite. For the first time in days, she felt like she might be on to something.

In the kitchen she built herself a sandwich. She piled on cheese and sliced meat, slathered deli mustard onto two thick slices of brown bread. She was so hungry she didn't bother to slice the sandwich in half, though she did have the good grace to put it on a plate. She was about to take it into her living room when she stopped for a moment to ponder whether she might like some corn chips to go with it.

The air stirred at her back.

Tally started to turn. Halfway there, she knew. But it was too late.

Something slammed into her jaw. An explosion of pain and light blossomed behind her eyes. She didn't even know when she hit the floor.

For a timeless time, the red-hot pain in her jaw was the only thing Tally knew. That and the taste and smell of her own blood. She wanted to lift a hand to touch her face, but she couldn't move. She tried to speak, and the pain flamed into full-blown agony, making her gasp. Her eyes flew open and she saw

John. He was squatting a short distance from her, watching her. He smirked.

"Awake, bitch?" he said pleasantly. "Sorry you missed lunch. But the sandwich was good, it didn't go to waste."

She was naked and tied to a chair. She tested the bonds, surreptitiously. They were tight as drums. Soon she wouldn't be able to feel her hands and feet at all.

"I left a message for you with Emily," said John. "The one you were going to send was totally inappropriate. She thinks you're in town, shopping. That seemed like a girlish thing to do, I'm sure she'll believe it."

He stood, still grinning. Tally wished he would stop. The expression didn't suit his face. He was usually so deadpan, and the smirk was pulling his skin into nasty, unnatural folds. He stepped closer and showed her his hands. They were covered in things so delicate and intricate, Tally could have studied them for an hour without quite grasping their purpose.

"I can feel you without touching you," he said. "This is how I enjoyed myself with every single one of them. It was a hands-on experience, Tally. I made these especially for this job."

It hurt dreadfully to move her jaw, but Tally had to ask him. "Job?"

"Tam had the right idea," he said. "I'll take care of her later, but she's going to be a lot tougher. I know her weaknesses though. And some of the weapons I made for her aren't going to work the way she thought they would. No hands-on for Tam, but I'll make up for it with you."

He cocked his head to look at her, his gaze traveling admiringly over her body. "I've waited such a long time for you. Since the first time I laid eyes on you, Tally, and that's a lot longer than you think. I was already on Archangel when you arrived. I've been listening in on your messages from the beginning. Including that nice one from George on Canopus—very impressive."

"Why?" Tally managed.

"Why was I on Archangel? You want the official reason or the real one?"

"Both."

His face twitched. "You can pack a lot into one word. Maybe it's not so bad I broke your jaw. You'll be very expressive, I'm sure."

Tally simply stared. He was bragging, shooting his mouth off. If she let him talk, she could buy some time.

"I built some of those weapons they used to destroy the Republic, did you know that? I was into mass destruction back then. But I'm sorry I made them. Armageddon isn't that much fun, except for the intellectual exercise. What I prefer is a nice, teeming world of dirty, smelly people to play with. The more people, the better I like it."

Tally tried not to look at the com across the room. She couldn't reach it, there was no point. She kept her eyes on him, and hoped for inspiration.

"You should have stayed on Canopus." John smirked. "They treat black bitches like queens."

His expression took on a glazed quality Tally had seen many times before.

"You've haunted my dreams for ten years," he said conversationally. "When I did those other women, I was practicing for you. I learned a lot from them. I won't have as much time with you, but a few hours anyway. It's too bad, I've been dreaming about getting you to my hideaway. I could have made you last for days, Tally. But I suppose it would have broken my heart at the end, letting go. This way, I can get my good-byes over with faster."

"Why now?" asked Tally.

He made a face. "People are so disappointing," he said. "Figure it out. You and Tam put together two important pieces of my puzzle just now. I admit, I was spying on you just because I like to look at you, but I realized the game was about to be spoiled. You saw the false door, Tally. You would have figured out who was behind it soon enough." He grinned again. "Anyway, it's nice to be impulsive. I have to use so much self-control, it really gets to be a pain in the ass."

Despite her best efforts to stay calm, her rasta-links stirred. This pleased him. "They're just dying to plug into a jack, aren't they?" He sneered. "You don't have a lot of options for communications. I told you your system was outmoded. My system is top-notch. Hey, wanna see something?"

He thrust his hands forward, palms up. As Tally watched, the structures sprouted little saw blades. They whirred and hummed. Then began to extend from his fingertips, growing like dreadful flowers. "Don't worry," he said, "I won't touch your face with them. I want to leave it intact. You're the most beautiful woman I've ever seen."

The devices slowed and retracted back into place. He let his hands fall back to his sides and studied Tally's body clinically, like a butcher eyeing a carcass. "By the way," he said. "I'm going to kill Andrei too, and his little family. I wanted to do Peter first and leave his head in your bread box. I'm really pissed that you screwed that plan."

He looked her in the eyes again. "We've got about four hours. Let's take our time. You don't have any way to send a message, but you might try screaming for help. I'd like to hear you do that."

Tally looked at him. Her head and jaw ached so badly, she could hardly think straight. She could not come up with a plan. But something about his eyes nagged at her.

"I said *Scream*." He showed her his hands again.

Tally refused to look at them. She kept her eyes on his. She squinted, saw a glitter at the center of his pupils. Tiny stars.

"Suck my cock and I won't cut off your tits," he offered.

Tally forced her jaw to move one more time. "Make me," she croaked.

The glitter in his eyes. He began to lean down. His face loomed inches from hers. She felt pain on her shoulders, and realized he had rested his hands there. She kept her eyes focused on his pupils and thought about an exchange she had once shared with Tam. Her hands were tied.

But he hadn't disabled her rasta-links.

She forced them into his eyes. All of them, sinking them as deep into his skull as she could, aiming most of them at soft tissue, but two of them for the centers of his pupils where she could access his sender/receiver. His eyes were artificial, but they were by no means indestructible. He jerked back, gibbering, but the rastas held him tight. He seized them with his hands and tried to pull them loose.

Tally's links found what they were looking for. She sent a message on the emergency band to everyone in her address book.

<I'M IN TROUBLE, JOHN IS GOING TO KILL ME, I'M IN MY LIVING ROOM, GET HERE NOW!>

Then he wrenched loose, making Tally's head snap backward. Agony flared up and over her skull, down her neck, but she felt like laughing. John fell backward onto his ass, screaming.

"My eyes! You fucking bitch! MY EYES!"

She looked at him. He was sitting on his butt, clutching his face—which was funny, because the devices on his hands were cutting him. He frantically pulled the things off, and Tally got a good look at her handiwork. His eyes were bleeding, torn mush.

"Fucking bitch!" he said, his voice trembling with pain and astonishment. "I don't fucking believe it, you fucking bitch!"

Tally kept silent. Help was on the way, but she

doubted it would come in time. At least she had saved Andrei's and Peter's life. At least she had accomplished that. She was so relieved, so full of pain, she started to cry. She did it silently, hoping he would not hear.

"Fuck," he said, and his voice became eerily calm. "You made a call to Grigory, didn't you. Fuck."

It was as if he didn't feel pain any longer. He kept his hands over his eyes, hiding their ruin.

"Fuck," he said once more, almost rhetorically.

Then Tally's heavy front door was blown off its hinges.

She jumped against her bonds and screamed. She saw a blur streak across the room toward her, and suddenly Grigory was standing between her and John.

She couldn't see John anymore, but she heard his voice.

"Grigory?" he asked.

"Present." Grigory's tone was light, but the sound of it made Tally's heart slam in her chest. Her head began to spin.

"I'm blind now," John said.

"Really? Do you find it a handicap?"

John was wise enough not to answer that. Tally almost pitied him.

"Your suit is impressive," John said in his old, almost bored tone of voice. "I didn't know it had this range of capabilities."

"I designed it myself," Grigory said, and Tally marveled at his supernatural calm. "I never relied on any of your devices, John. I didn't think them trustworthy."

"They won the fucking war for you." John was offended. Grigory was playing him like a cat with a mouse. John seemed to figure that out, too late. "I surrender," he said.

"Is that an option?" asked Grigory.

"Legally, you have to arrest me and see that I get

medical attention, a lawyer," John said almost confidently.

"I'm not a police officer," Grigory said. "I'm a bodyguard. The Republic is gone now, there's just you and me, John. I have so wanted to meet you, too. Ever since I saw Lyuba's head in Grey Forest."

*Oh, Christ*, thought Tally. *I hate the guy, but I don't want to listen to him die. And I think I'm going to throw up . . .*

"You can't kill me," John said.

"I cannot wait to hear why."

Tally's head was slowly slipping forward; an unhappy development, but she couldn't seem to hold it up. Her heart was pounding harder than ever, and she was now positive she was going to vomit.

"There's something important you don't know," she heard John saying; he seemed far away. She tried to keep her eyes open and failed.

"There are many important things I don't know," she heard Grigory say. "I get along anyway."

Tally's chin touched her chest. It hurt like hell, but it couldn't keep her awake. She was going. She thought she heard them say something else to each other, but couldn't understand a word of it until something else caught her attention. Something John said.

"—because I know something you haven't figured out yet. And if you don't figure it out soon, you're all going to die . . ."

Tally strained to hear Grigory's answer. She heard nothing.

And she felt nothing.

And then she knew nothing.

There was no pain. She remembered little. She sat comfortably in her tomb and awaited eternity.

She was surrounded with the things she had loved in life, her Egyptian and Nubian furnishings, art, statues and carvings; and her libraries, both hard and virtual. Offerings of food and drink had been made to her ka, her ship of eternity was manned and ready to sail the dark waters that lay between the mortal world and the sunrise. Tally wore a fine linen wrap like Nefertari, and her rasta-links had settled themselves into the likeness of a royal wig.

But Tally did not lie in her gilded sarcophagus. She sat playing senet. To her right, a wall was carved with her false door. Everything was as it ought to be, she felt perfectly satisfied.

Then something stirred in the shadows beyond her ship of eternity. Tally knew she had a visitor. Nothing should have intruded into her tomb; the things that had troubled her in life were over and done.

"Child, everything is far from over and done."

Tally looked up with sudden fear. She felt a distant ache in her jaw, a sensation that belonged to the world of the living. She searched the shadows beyond her ship, until her gaze rested on the statue of Sekmet, lion-headed goddess of wine and rage. Just beyond her, someone watched Tally with disapproving eyes.

"Mama," Tally said grimly. "Is it your turn to visit?"

"Did you think I would never see you?" Mama said. "Among your false gods and their idols?"

Mama still looked like herself. She was beautiful, though her face had thinned and sharpened with age. Her hair was pulled tight in an uncompromising braid, and now most of it was white. "What do you have to say for yourself, Tally?" she demanded.

Tally was surprised that this time her fear was diminishing instead of growing. And she didn't feel particularly inclined to explain herself to her mother anymore. "I guess I'm getting used to ghosts," she said.

"Is this really where you want to spend eternity?" Mama pointed to the false door. "Sleeping with someone else's husband?"

Tally looked at the door more closely. Her own

image was carved there, a queen standing across from her pharaoh, both of them gripping a single ankh they held between them, a symbol of the eternal life they would share. But the pharaoh was no Egyptian. He looked like Andrei.

"So you don't approve," Tally said. "What else is new?"

"You think you know so much," hissed her mother. "Never cracked open a Bible in the past fifty years, but you know all about heresy. Your pride was always your downfall. And you don't know what's on the other side of that door."

Tally let her gaze wander over the images carved into the solid wall. "Nothing's on the other side, Mama. It's a false door."

Her mother didn't answer. That was how she always responded when Tally had guessed wrong, sitting there in silent reproach until her daughter realized her mistake. But Tally's puzzlement only grew. The door led to the afterlife, that's what it was for.

Pain shot up Tally's jaw and behind her eyes, making her cry out.

"You're not dead," Mama said flatly. "Not yet. How are you supposed to pass through a false door if you're not dead?"

It was an excellent question. Mama always had an unhappy knack for them. If Tally wasn't dead, then the false door was a mistaken notion, a false premise.

She studied it. It contained everything a proper false door should, images of what she would take with her into the next life—not the least of which was Andrei. And Peter sat on a stool at Andrei's feet. There was plenty of food and drink for the three of them, and even some boxes of picture puzzles. Tally searched the door for other icons of her favorite things, satisfied with what she saw. Until she spotted something in the lower right corner.

One of the derelicts was carved there. She found one in each corner.

"How did those get there?" demanded Tally.

"They belong there," said Mama.

"I don't want them!"

"You have them anyway."

The derelicts were distorting the happy image. And then Tally saw something else that didn't belong, at the center of the ankh, perverting its symbolism. She knew the thing, but did not know it. It was kin to the derelicts.

Tally's hand moved against her will. She reached up, pain lancing down her neck and shoulder, and touched the symbol. It gave. She pushed harder.

The door opened, swinging inward. A hot, damp breeze blew past Tally and into her tomb. She leaned forward in her chair to look into the passage it revealed. But the light in that tunnel tricked her eyes. She couldn't be sure it was light at all, or that the colors were colors. But she was sure of what she saw on the floor.

Lyuba's head, still grimacing in agony.

Tally stood. Once on her feet, she could see something beyond Lyuba's head. "There's that poor little hand again. I guess it's a permanent fixture inside my psyche. Always pointing to something I don't want to see."

But this time it pointed away from the head, down the tunnel.

"Go," said Mama, right behind her. Tally obeyed, stepping into the heat. Once she had moved beyond her false door, the pain in her jaw and neck became persistent.

"I never knew this passage was here," she told Mama. "Is it another escape tunnel?"

"Not for you."

Suddenly Tally was aware of grand surroundings. In the darkness she glimpsed shapes and designs that were beautiful, elegant, disturbing.

Familiar . . .

She froze. "Christ. We're in one of those damned *things*—the derelicts!"

"You invoke the name of God's son so casually," Mama said, still behind her. "But I didn't see any crosses hanging in your rooms."

"We can't be here, Mama, it's a trap! We've got to get out!"

"No going back now, Tally, it's too late. You can only move forward."

Someone was sitting with his back to them. Tally couldn't quite make him out, she only had the vaguest impression of his presence. She crept closer, and he seemed more clear. He turned his head, as if aware of the visitors behind him.

"Who—?" Tally was going to ask him, and then she smelled something dreadful. Blood. She remembered when she had smelled it last, and dread seized her.

"Mama," she whispered. "That's him. That's John. He's the superkiller."

"No, Tally," said Mama. "John is just *one* of them."

Tally backed away from the presence and the smell. "You mean there are more?" she asked, sickened.

"You have to let the devil in your front door before he can hurt you, Tally," said Mama.

"But I came in *his* front door," said Tally.

"That's right. That's exactly what you did."

"Mama, how do I get out?"

"You fight your way out. Do you hear me? You fight. You know who these devils are, think about it. Look them right in their eyes. Fight."

"Fight how? Fight *who*?"

"You made your bed, Tally girl," said Mama, drifting away from her. "Go lie in it."

"Wait . . ." Tally called. But Mama was gone. Only the bloody presence remained. He opened his mouth, but no words came out. Only a sound that froze Tally's blood, a sound she knew from her dreams.

*Tic tic tic tic tic tic tic tic . . .*

Time passed. She opened her eyes briefly and saw Andrei dozing in a chair. Once she heard Peter's voice.

"She looks so hurt, Papa. I wish I could hold her hand."

"She wouldn't feel it, Peter. But soon she will. She'll get better."

She listened to the sound of their voices for a time, comforted. Then she felt the touch of a hand on hers.

"Please forgive me," Andrei said softly, as if he weren't sure she could hear. "To be touched must be the last thing you want right now."

But it wasn't the last thing, not from him. He took his hand away, and Tally waited in vain for him to return.

She opened her eyes. Andrei was gone. Mama was gone. She was lying in bed, her head restrained.

"Hey," she called softly, and the movement of her jaw hurt like hell. "Hullo? Help!"

She was in an unfamiliar room. It smelled like a hospital. It smelled like pee, which made Tally's stomach turn. She wondered if it was her pee, or someone else's. This wasn't at all the sort of medical experience she was used to having. But the marvelous medical machines that had once worked miracles for people were no longer available on Belarus.

Plus the pain meds were wearing off.

Tally tried to see as far to her right and left as she could. Even the slightest movement made agony shoot through her jaw. Those flashes of pain made her remember how John had hit her. She was pretty sure she had seen Grigory, and heard Andrei and Emily sometime later. She thought John must be in jail.

But what if that had been wishful thinking? What if she had dreamed it? And now she was bound to a bed, waiting for his ministrations.

*You made your bed, Tally girl . . .*

Suddenly a nurse came into her field of vision. Tally twitched.

"It's okay," the nurse said gently.

"I need you—" Tally began, then winced. She had so much to say, and it hurt.

"Don't try to talk," warned the nurse, but Tally couldn't oblige.

"Emergency," she managed. "Call Andrei. Emily if you can't. Important."

"I'll tell my supervisor," promised the nurse. She disappeared, and Tally felt a wave of relief. She wasn't a prisoner.

And then she passed out.

"Tally?" she heard someone calling. Her eyes popped open. Emily was bending over her.

Tally's eyes filled with tears.

"I'm here," Emily said. "Andrei's on the way. How do you feel?"

"Like warmed-over—crap. Ouch. . . ."

"Do you want to plug in? I brought a mobile." Emily held up the device. Tally's eyes shined. One of her rasta-links slid into the jack.

<Thank God. Emily, my mother's ghost paid me a visit.>

<Now it's your *mother's* ghost?>

<It was her, Emily. She showed me something important. Maybe you won't be surprised to hear it.>

<I'm surprised to hear about the ghost.>

<You talked about false doors—remember? It seems like a million years ago.>

<I remember.>

<You were right. And I don't think John killed all the people who disappeared.>

<Right now we can't prove he killed anyone. We only have circumstantial evidence connecting him to the crimes, Tally. As for his confession to you, his lawyer could claim he was just bragging, taking credit for someone else's handiwork.>

<Okay. But he's not our worst problem right now.>

Silence from Emily. And Tally had a feeling it wasn't because she disagreed. She pressed forward.

<We stopped worrying about those derelicts way too soon. We were certain the people who built them weren't around any longer. But they are. They're still here. Somewhere.>

Emily nodded. <That's possible. But how are we going to prove it?>

<We don't have to prove it. We've got to be ready.>

<Always,> said Emily, just like Grigory would have said.

<No, I mean READY. For another war.>

Emily frowned. <I'm still listening.>

<Think about it. Before, we were strong. We had ties to the Republic, plenty of backup, and an endless supply line. If they're hiding on this world because someone else attacked them in the past, we must have scared them. They've been stealing people away, never coming out in the open. Probably studying us. But we're crippled now, there's not going to be any help from the stars. They may decide we're not so tough anymore. Hit us while we're down.>

<Grigory will agree with you, I'm sure,> said Emily, though she didn't say *she* did.

<I was right the last time. Sorry to rub it in, but I've got a bad feeling about this. We're in trouble.>

<No argument there.>

<I remember once you said you thought the killer was trying to tell us something, playing a big game. He was giving us pieces of a puzzle. I thought the picture would be of him. But maybe he had another picture in mind.>

Emily looked pleased. <Funny you should say that. John has been hinting at it, now that we've got him in custody.>

Tally flinched at the sound of his name.

<You need some more meds?> Emily guessed.

<Christ, yes.>

Emily called the nurse and gave an order. Tally wanted to grin at that. Rank occasionally had its privileges. <Hate to sound like a weakling. But something with a sedative would be nice. It's been kind of a rotten day.>

<I've got you covered.>

Tally tried to relax. She was so glad to see Emily. <Is Andrei coming?>

<Yes. He's busy, but he's on the way. If you're asleep when he gets here, do you want us to wake you?>

<Yes please.>

<Will do.> Emily didn't smile, but she seemed less strained than when Tally had first opened her eyes, as if she had been energized. She reached down and grasped Tally's hand. <I believe you. The more I think about it, the more sense it makes. I just buzzed a message to Grigory.>

<Was he surprised?>

Emily laughed. <Grigory? If he was, do you think he'd show it?>

Kami-te sat in his thinking chair, pondering the universe. His fingers stroked the intricate carvings on the armrests, passing over places worn by three clan leaders before him. The wood was still fragrant, its texture smooth and fine. The tree from which it was made had been teased into the desired shapes and angles, then dried slowly. It was one of many lovely things still kept from times long past. Kami-te loved to touch it. He loved to touch everything. Until he knew something with his hands, he did not feel he knew it at all.

His mind traveled along grooves of thought just as his fingers did over the wood. But when someone entered the room, he reacted instinctively, his body freezing, ready to move in an instant. He waited for the intruder to act.

"Who . . . ?" he distinctly heard it ask in the alien tongue. He turned his head and an impression of the invader teased his eyes, a glimpse of alien beauty. And then, just as he was about to stand and turn, it was gone.

Odd. He sat for a time, pondering the strangeness. He had no word for it, no way to place it within the framework of his understanding of the universe.

Though lately his universe had been expanding. He had tasted alien flesh saturated with emotions both thrilling and disturbing. Some of his brothers were afraid to eat it, saying that such feasting carried a price. Knowledge was not always desirable.

But he craved it. He had learned how to Dance with the newcomers. And they kept surprising him. This intruder, she may still be in the room with him. That was an intriguing thought.

She might try to injure him. Some of them had. Clumsy creatures. He wished she would do something like that. He wanted to know all there was to know about her.

Motion at one of the doors. He grinned. But then the Witness entered the room. The grace of her movements gave her away even before he could see her perfectly.

"Something disturbs you," she said.

"Do we have an intruder?" he asked.

"No."

She spoke with flat certainty, as always. And she was always right about such things. But that left him with a puzzle.

"Someone was in the room with me," he said. "She spoke to me, but then she vanished."

"Someone?" she asked, demanding more details.

"An invader."

Her eyes did not search the room. Her expression was flat, unrevealing. "Truly, a brother makes the finest dish," she said.

He frowned. Her remark made no sense. And he didn't agree. "You haven't tasted the newcomers. They're an acquired taste, I admit"—his lips quirked at the double entendre—"but I've grown very fond of them."

"That is well," said the Witness. "They will be your constant companions for the rest of your life."

"How annoying," said Kami-te, but he was not referring to what she had said. He was upset that she had said it. He wished very fervently, and not for the first time, that he was not compelled to use this Witness of the ko clan. He wanted a Witness from his own clan, someone who would temper her responses with an intimate understanding of his moods.

"The answer lies in their chemistry," she said. "And in yours. You could not know it before you ate an alien liver, because you have only eaten your own kind. In a sense, to eat other intelligent beings is to be invaded by them. Brothers merely reinforce what you already are. But alien flesh still holds the remnants of alien thoughts. It affects you."

He composed his next question carefully. "Are you saying that dining on alien flesh makes me *less* what I should be?"

"No. I'm saying that you are haunted."

It was not a word he had ever heard before. But he sensed what it meant. Uncanny, because he doubted he would have understood if he hadn't eaten their livers. Understanding had invaded him from the inside, on a cellular level.

"Then I am now *more* than I once was," he decided.

"Perhaps," said Ayat-ko. "That depends on what you can do with your new understanding."

"What to do," he pondered. "I've been thinking about it. This Dance has been quite diverting, but its tempo must ultimately change."

She did not move. She might have been a statue. "We have risked so much already," she said, her tone perfectly modulated.

He was forced to admire her. How ancient she was, how skilled. She belonged to a grander time, the mystical past when the Cousin clans were strong and numerous.

But *he* belonged to this raw, new time. "Risk," he said, without malice. "Great losses or great gains. We have resources, Witness, that are not being used."

She was silent, and once again he was impressed with her control. Had she spoken a disagreement, he might have felt compelled to Dance with her.

"We have seen what they have," he continued. "Their Enemies tried to kill them. If our automatic systems had not been in place, this world would be a cinder now. And now they are crippled."

"You wish to attack," she said.

"I do." His blood sang. The sensation was exactly what he had felt when he mounted his challenge against the old clan leader. He had known he would win. He knew it now.

Ayat-ko touched an ornament at her throat. He had heard it was a gift to her from Solan-ko. "The intruder," she said. "When she spoke to you, what did she say?"

He frowned again. "She asked a question. It was nothing."

"What question?" Slender fingers stroked fine metalwork.

"One word. She asked, *Who . . . ?*"

Her pupils expanded, then retracted again like sea creatures snatching at prey. "They know," she said.

He did not miss her meaning. "They've finally guessed we're here? It took them long enough. The only reason their kind have survived so long is that they breed so often. Nothing else could explain it."

"Nothing else," said Ayat-ko, though her tone did not imply agreement. "They will actively look for us. The music is up."

"And the Dance is on," said Kami-te.

"We Dance as we did seventeen cycles ago," she said, her eyes glittering. "Just like then. When we also had no choice."

He smiled. For her it must seem like doom. She wasn't born in the new world. But he was, and he was ready to ride this wind of chaos. It had never failed him before.

"Soon," he said. "I think I shall have to evoke the Swarm."

No sister disagreed with a brother who embarked upon a Challenge. Not even a Witness. Ayat-ko would act when he told her to.

Instinct was a wonderful thing.

He learned to reserve judgment, shut his ego down, and make people come to him.

—James Ellroy,
*My Dark Places*

The stupidest thing a suspect can ever do is to talk to the police.

—Ballard Bullion,
Retired investigator, Phoenix Police

Emily sat in the semidarkness of the observation room and stared at John through the one-way transparency. He sat quietly with one arm resting on the table, his face expressionless. She tried to remember her impressions of him before the attack.

She had none that she could recall.

Now it was quite different. Some killers advertised their potential for violence in the way they trained their bodies, their tattoos and clothing, their stance and demeanor, but Emily's long experience had taught her that those individuals were people who were trying to warn others off. By far, the most deadly and dangerous ones were the ones you did not notice.

*John Smith,* his dossier read. Very funny. Plenty of people were really named that—Emily had worked with several John Smiths during her long career. This John had placed himself where he would not be noticed. His only memorable personality traits were that he was cold and sometimes annoyed people. He fit the profile of the typical engineer. You put up with him because he was a genius, and when you weren't working with him you forgot about him.

His eyes were bandaged. Emily watched a trickle of

pink fluid slide down his cheek. She thought about his victims and how they had looked in life, and what he had done to them.

*Bleed*, she advised him. *If we can't get anything else out of you, at least we got that.*

Bull entered the interview room. Both Emily and John sat up straighter. Emily leaned forward, frowning intently. Bull pulled up the other chair and sat down across the small table from John.

"Good morning," Bull said neutrally. "I'm Special Agent Bullman, I'll be taking your statement today. Our conversation is being recorded, but I will also be taking notes."

"I have not been informed of the charges yet and I have not spoken to a lawyer," John said mildly.

"The charges are pending," said Bull. "If you can't afford a lawyer, one will be appointed for you."

"I won't accept the incompetent fool they sent," John said. "I can afford the best and that's what I want. You can't proceed unless I have a lawyer."

Bull was unfazed. "You don't have to answer any questions. But you can use this opportunity to state your side of the incident. We've taken a full statement from Ms. Korsakova. If you don't choose to add anything, we'll use her statement as the basis for assessing which charges should be filed, if any."

"Charges should be filed against *her*," said John. "I was defending myself."

"She was tied to a chair," Bull reminded him.

"Yes." John pointed to his eyes. "And look what she managed to do to me, even tied to a chair."

"I see your point." Bull's tone never changed. "Why were you afraid of her?"

"She's part of the conspiracy," John said. He sat back, and seemed calm, almost resigned. "I've been watching them for years. She and Andrei Mironenko, and other humans, were subverted by aliens. They plotted with ESAs to destroy the Republic because they couldn't take over by legal means. They used sprites to infiltrate every automatic system, they fed people lies through their media, they financed weapons research and created sun busters to wipe out any colony that wouldn't go along with them."

John leaned forward again. "They will *never* let me out of here," he said in a conspiratorial tone. "I know too much about them, I'm on to their plans. They can't afford to let word get out to the general population. They have no intention of giving me a fair trial, I probably won't even live to see my lawyer."

"How did you find out about this plot?"

John smirked, as if the question were foolish. "I'm a weapons designer. They tried to hire me to do their dirty work."

"You never designed weapons for Andrei Mironenko?" asked Bull.

"Of course I designed for him, what else could I do? But I kept my eye on him. I gathered evidence. I need to present it to the proper authorities, not a bunch of low-level civil servants under Mironenko's influence."

"You'll get your chance to present your evidence," said Bull. "What time did you arrive at Tally Korsakova's apartment last Tuesday the fourteenth?"

"I have no idea."

"Approximate time is fine."

Bull waited. John shrugged. "Before lunch."

"Around noon?"

"I suppose."

"Who was there when you arrived?"

"She was." Emily heard the trace of smugness in John's tone. Despite his imprisonment, despite the trouble he was in, thinking about what he had done to Tally pleased him.

"Why did you go there?" asked Bull.

John's face twitched. He seemed to be trying hard to look upset, but traces of the smirk kept creeping in. "I've been under terrible stress, trying to hide my true motives from them. I've been stranded here you know. I thought I would be able to leave here after the Civil War, perhaps to find what is left of my family, but they wouldn't permit it. They're not willing to let highly trained people leave, they need us too much."

"Why did you go to Tally Korsakova's apartment?" Bull asked again.

"I've been having nightmares," said John. "Hearing voices. They tell me I need to punish the people responsible for the Civil War, the people who got us into this mess."

"Specifically," Bull said patiently. "Why did you go to her apartment?"

"I wanted to talk her out of it," said John, with sudden inspiration.

"Go on."

"She wouldn't listen. She tried to call Grigory and I had to hit her. To stop her."

Bull scribbled notes, but was ready with his next question immediately. "Why did you remove her clothes?"

"She was wearing a danger suit, she had hidden weapons in it. And she could have used her gloves to activate her com. I tied her to a chair so I could talk some sense into her."

"What did you say to her?"

John suddenly looked annoyed. Emily wondered if he knew what a fool he had been to say anything at all. But John probably never thought of himself in those terms.

"I told her what I knew," he said. "But it did no good. She didn't believe me, or maybe she's been in on it from the beginning."

Bull jotted a few more notes, but other than that he never took his eyes from John. "How close were you to her when she jammed her rasta-links into your eyes?" he asked.

John made a dismissive gesture, his mouth twisted in disgust. "Come on," he said, "isn't that obvious?

No farther than the reach of the damned links. She said she had something important to tell me. I bent close so I could hear it and she attacked me. She used me to call Grigory and everyone else in her directory. The only reason he didn't kill me is that there were too many witnesses."

"All right," said Bull. "Is there anything else you'd like to add?"

John leaned back in his chair, his hands in his lap. His face had resumed its studied blankness, but Emily could tell he was relieved. He thought the interview was over.

"Just make sure the proper authorities hear my side of the incident," he said. "I would like to file counter-charges of assault, not to mention conspiracy."

"You'll have to address all that with your lawyer," said Bull. "I just have a few more questions and then we can wrap this up."

John scowled. Bull pulled out a small recorder player. "You made a statement at the time of your arrest," he said. "I'm going to play it back for you."

Bull tapped a button. John's recorded voice came from a small speaker. "There's something important you don't know."

Grigory's voice answered him: "There are many important things I don't know. I get along anyway."

"You won't get along much longer," John warned him. "You need to keep me alive and well. Because I know something you haven't figured out yet. And if you don't figure it out soon, you're all going to die."

Bull turned off the player. "What were you referring to when you made that statement?" he asked.

"I don't recall saying that," John said quickly.

"We have voice verification. What do you think it could have meant?"

John took a deep breath and let it out again. "I can't talk about that without counsel from my lawyer," he said.

"Were you referring to the missing individuals we've been looking for?" asked Bull.

John gave up on trying to hide his smirk. "Maybe."

"Can you tell us where they are?"

"That information will cost you."

Bull shook his head. "I'm not offering any deals. If you know where the bodies are, you should tell me now."

"Should I?" John said pleasantly. He seemed amused by the questions, not the least bit nervous anymore.

"Your statement will be accurately recorded," said Bull.

John crossed his arms. "I know all about accurate recordings. I altered plenty of them when I came to this world nine years ago. Of course, I had a different name then. And another one after that—"

Bull didn't give him a chance to finish. "When I say accurately recorded I'm not talking about machines. I'm talking about my own observations. Any transcript made from mechanical recordings of this meeting will have to be approved by me before they are accepted into the official record."

"And that official record will duly record the fact that I murdered sixty-seven people," said John contemptuously.

Bull waited expectantly.

"But you don't have a shred of evidence connecting me with any of those killings."

"We've collected evidence at every crime scene," said Bull.

"Not at the scene." John lifted a finger, correcting him. "At the sites where the bodies were left."

"You're right, we don't know where the murders were committed," said Bullman. "We would appreciate it if you could provide that information so the families could have some closure."

"That's going to cost you too," John said smugly.

"Got him!" Emily crowed triumphantly.

* * *

Emily poured Bull a cup of straight black coffee and sat down with her own cup at the conference table. "I have to admit," she said, "I'm surprised he talked to us. I thought he'd be smarter than that."

"The smart ones usually outsmart themselves," said Bull. "Being a genius doesn't mean you have an ounce of common sense." He fished in his jacket pocket and pulled out a cigar. "Mind if I smoke?"

"Be my guest," said Emily. She sipped her coffee, feeling the knots in her spine come undone. It was just like old times, a case on the way to being prosecuted. It would be tough, but she thought at least they could nail him on assault. While he was serving his time they could look for more evidence to nail him on the killings.

Grigory came into her office just as she was finishing her cup. He sat down across from Bull, next to Emily. "I hear you had a successful interview," he said.

"Went pretty well," said Bull.

Grigory wasn't smiling, but his expression made Emily sit up straighter. "You've got some news?" she asked.

"I have studied the report from the doctors and technicians who examined John," said Grigory. "His body and brain were extensively enhanced and modified, but his enhancements are not of ESA origin. He was hiding a locator in a compartment in one of his molars. The locator belonged to a real man named John Smith, presumed deceased. 'John' also had a locator of his own that was deactivated at some unknown time. It still contained an identification code, and I was able to research his true identity.

"He was identified by a single name: Loki—I'm not sure he ever had a surname. But we have a record of his parents petitioning to have him accepted as an ESA at the age of eight. The ESAs who were petitioned had many doubts about the situation, not the least of which was that the adults who represented themselves as his guardians were not willing to reveal their identities, citing fears for their safety. But he was given due consideration and thoroughly examined. He was determined unfit."

"His lawyer could find a psychologist to testify that the trauma of his rejection made him unduly paranoid about ESAs," said Bull. "And if his family was that paranoid, he could blame them for his own state of mind."

"True," said Grigory. "But we have one irrefutable piece of evidence. It's stated in his records. His ESA evaluators rejected him because they diagnosed him as a psychopath."

Emily had never seen Bull smile in response to anything he learned on a case. But he came as close to one as he possibly could.

"Congratulations," he said. "I think you just made our case stronger."

Once again, Andrei stood in the terminal with ESA Tam and watched *Halcyon* boarding. She was somewhat worse for wear, but she was still beautiful. Her lines were sleek and fast. He hoped within a decade to have two more of her.

But as he looked at her, his heart was heavy. More evacuees were leaving. They would board one of his remaining ships, *Monitor*, leaving him just one ship, *Hurricane*. *Monitor* was supposed to return again if it could, to bring news and badly needed equipment. But Andrei would have forbidden its departure if he could have. He was losing some of his best-trained technicians and scientists, people he desperately needed. But *Monitor*'s crew intended to leave, with or without these passengers—and Andrei was forced to admit defeat.

He understood why they felt compelled to go. They were embarking on a journey far more perilous than the one that had brought them to Belarus. If there were no surviving colonies along their route, they would have to stop to mine asteroids and moons, to replenish supplies. If the ship broke down, they were stuck. Lost in an immense universe, just as Belarus was. They would try to make contact with what was left of the Republic, and he would have to train new people to fill their places. Not an enviable job from either point of view.

Andrei turned and saw Agent Bullman approaching. The man gave him the briefest of smiles, then stopped to shake his hand.

"I hope you were able to gather some useful information from this case, at least," said Andrei.

"I think we did," said Bullman. "Possibly even something that will let us catch the next one *before* he attacks one of our team members."

"You saved lives, Agent Bullman. Your attention to the case put the heat on John, He stopped killing because you were looking for him."

"Hard to say." Bull pulled out a cigar but didn't light it. "I've gathered more data for the profile, but I don't really believe that John represents the full spectrum of possibilities for superkillers. He was able to escape detection because he made himself indispensable to powerful people who helped him slip through the cracks. Everything gets better, Andrei, that's the way evolution works. Predators adapt. I still haven't found the smartest killers. But I will."

"That sounds almost optimistic," said Andrei. "You must believe the Republic has survived."

Bullman nodded. "Part of it, somewhere. I work for the president of the Central Government, whoever that may be now. I need to make sure that what we learned from this case is passed on to the central database."

Andrei didn't ask him if he had family to look for. He must.

"Good luck to you," Andrei said. "And thank you."

"You're very welcome," said Agent Bullman. He nodded to Tam, then turned and went out of the terminal, out onto the tarmac and into the line waiting to board *Halcyon.* He lit his cigar on the way out, leaving puffs of smoke behind him like a train.

"A lot of good people are getting on that ship," remarked Tam.

"Too many."

"Maybe they'll be back someday."

"Not in our lifetime," guessed Andrei.

"You're a good guy," said Tam. "That's why I'm sticking with you."

Andrei almost missed what she had said, she spoke in such a bland tone. "I'm glad to have you," he said.

"Don't mention it," said Tam, her face wooden.

*Halcyon* took the last evacuees up to Archangel, where they boarded the *Monitor*. After it had jumped, Jones called Andrei.

"That's the last of them," he said.

"All right," said Andrei.

"I'm sorry, old friend."

Andrei smiled at him, a sight Jones had seen perhaps twice in two hundred years. "This is the hand we've got, Mark."

"Two mining stations left," said Jones, "one half-crippled, only one-fifth of our mining craft still functional, one starship left, and one shuttle. It's a weak hand, Andrei, at least from up here."

Andrei knew it already. He listened to Jones's complaints with the same Slavic stoicism he had always displayed in the face of disaster. "We're alive," he said. "That's more than most of the Republic can say now. We're limping but we're still kicking."

Jones sighed deeply, then nodded. "Anyway," he said. "They're safely off and good luck to them."

"Save some for us," said Andrei.

"I'll try," said Jones. He signed off. His shift was over; he could take a hot shower and drink a beer from his stash. He had fifty of them left, with no more due anytime soon. He wanted to make them last, but it seemed like a good time to indulge a little.

Before he could get up, his com buzzed. Even before he took the call, he knew it was bad news.

"Commander, this is Captain Smirnov."

"You don't sound happy, Captain."

"I'm not. We've got a problem with *Halcyon*'s cooling system. I don't think it's safe to make the trip back into atmosphere until we make some repairs."

"Take whatever you need, manpower and supplies," said Jones wearily.

"Commander." Smirnov's grim tone let him know the bad news wasn't over. "I'm not positive we can repair this ship well enough to keep it going back and forth much longer. What we need is a new ship."

"Do your best," said Jones. "You don't want to be stuck up here, do you, Smirnov?"

"Understood," said Smirnov. "I'll keep you posted."

Jones signed off. Now he was sure he needed the beer. In fact, he might want two or three, because now he was facing the ugly truth.

Belarus might make it as a colony. But they weren't going to have surface-to-orbit capabilities much longer. Not unless they got unexpected help from outside.

Jones had a feeling that wasn't going to happen for a very long time.

# PART FOUR

BELARUSIAN YEAR 17

Gadara knelt at the edge of her family's onion field and picked sun blossoms. Her tiny hands were full of them, they blazed against her skin. She stuffed the handfuls into her apron pocket and picked more, singing to herself.

"Stay close, little one," Mama warned. She was using a machine to harvest onions.

Gadara adored the blossoms. All winter she had looked out the kitchen window, pining for the spring. "When do the flowers come?" she asked Mama, every day. And after a thousand years, Mama had pointed to green shoots nosing aside the blanket of snow.

"There, Gadara. Spring is coming. Winter is over."

Spring warmed the days, and they planted their onions. Gadara waited as patiently as she could for the flowers to open their petals. It was almost as bad as waiting for the snow to go away, because she could see the buds for the longest time.

And now, she filled her hands. She got precariously to her feet and went to another bank of flowers.

"Gadara . . ." warned her mother.

Gadara heard a sound. She looked up and saw a person approaching her, his movements like those of some wild, graceful creature. She was transfixed. And then she saw two more.

"Mama, look," she cried. "How beautiful they are!"

"Yesus Christos!" Mama cried. She snatched Gadara from her feet. Holding her close, she ran with her, crying for Papa. "Armen! Armen!"

Behind them, mocking voices echoed, "Armen!" and Gadara heard strange, cruel laughter.

Mama was breathing harshly now. She made for the house.

She never got there.

Peter tried to pull on his only functioning danger suit. It wouldn't fit. He threw it across the room.

"Blast it—what am I supposed to do now!?"

He was glad he was alone, and able to pitch his fit in private. Lately he had felt like pitching a lot of them. He had just turned twelve, he was already five-foot-eleven, nothing fit, no one understood him, and he was starting to get pimples.

"It's not fair!" he declared.

But that was obvious. Probably a zillion people had said it before him. Not that it helped to know that. He sighed and picked up the suit. Sitting on the edge of his bed, he messed with the controls. There was supposed to be a way to adjust the size. Tally had shown him once, but he hated to bother her about it again. He was practically a teenager, he could do it himself.

If he could just remember.

He fiddled and fussed, tapping in various codes. He succeeded in lengthening the arms, but the legs stayed short. Finally he gave up and lay the suit on his bed. For today at least, he was going to have to wear ordinary clothes.

Not that those fit much better. Peter wasn't accustomed to wearing regular clothing, he only wore the danger suit or special clothing for sports, like his fencing gear or his judo *gi*. He had plenty of things stuffed in various drawers, but no clue which went with what. Finally he settled for a pair of blue trousers and a navy blue pullover shirt. He had a pair of boots that fit at least, and when he went to look in the mirror he was pleasantly surprised.

*Hey. I'm not so bad-looking.*

His com rang and he hurried to pick it up. He tripped on the way over. "Blast!" he said, blushing even though no one was there to see him. His feet had gotten too big and he couldn't seem to make them work right anymore. The only time he was any good was in sports, when he was too occupied thinking about the fight to remember to be awkward.

"Peter, you're fifteen minutes late," his tutor chided him. "What's wrong?"

"Couldn't get my danger suit to fit," he said. "I'll be right there."

He hung up before she could tell him to call Grigory. Of all the adults who ruled his world, Grigory was the one who made him feel the most—*unsatisfactory*. Not that Grigory ever said so, in word or gesture, it was just that he seemed to know everything Peter still had to learn, plus a million things more. It was hard to take sometimes.

He ran down the hallway, past security. No one said anything about his missing suit, that was a relief. But when he got into the elevator, Grigory was already there.

"Good morning, Peter," said the blind man.

"Morning," mumbled Peter. At least Grigory didn't call him *little tsar* anymore.

They rode the elevator in silence. But just as Peter was getting off on his floor, Grigory said, "Code 557788-arms-lengthen, OK, code 557788-legs-lengthen, OK/EXE."

"Oh," Peter said sheepishly. He had forgotten the /EXE. He ran off to school, stumbling twice on the way.

Natalia smiled as she handed the transfer slip to Andrei. "Repairs completed. Gas lines are functioning properly, geothermal systems working within acceptable parameters, solar energy systems are performing satisfactorily, all repairs on roads and buildings complete, and we even have some material left over for a rainy day. But I still can't make the trains run on time."

Andrei deployed the slip into his office com and tapped the display. He looked at the reports and graphs briefly, but only to admire her work. "You did it in five years," he said. "Two years sooner than we thought. Sit down, have some tea with me."

"I can't," she said ruefully. "I promised to meet with the prosecutor."

Andrei nodded sympathetically. Natalia was long healed from her injuries, and she knew precisely what she needed to say at John's trial. But that wasn't going to make it any easier. Even Andrei would be testifying. John's lawyer was going for broke.

"Later then. Peter and I would love to see you for dinner."

"I'll be there." Natalia smiled, then lost her humor. "Listen," she said. "John's lawyer called me last night. We had a long conversation."

"I'm sure it was fascinating," said Andrei. He had already conversed with the lawyer. He still believed in the Bill of Rights, but some of its ramifications were hard to live with at times.

"He talked about the important information John claims to have. Andrei, I think he really knows something. His information could prove to be critical to our survival."

Andrei studied her. Natalia was no coward. She would do whatever she thought necessary to save lives, even make a deal with John.

But Andrei wondered if *he* could do it.

"We haven't been attacked by the people who built the derelicts," he said. "Not formally, at least."

"We will be. You know I've been having dreams."

He had been present when she had awakened from a few of them. He didn't know if he believed in them, but he couldn't dismiss them either. Not with Natalia's track record. "I'll consider the option of a deal with John. But I won't accept one without consulting you."

"You can consider me consulted," she said. "I trust your judgment."

Andrei was honored by her confidence in him. But he wondered if she realized just how badly he wanted to take John by his neck and squeeze the life out of him.

"All right," he said. "We'll see what happens. Perhaps talk of a deal is premature. If John is convicted, he'll want a deal worse than ever. Perhaps he'll be easier to bargain with under those circumstances."

"He may not be convicted, Andrei."

Andrei tried not to think about that possibility. For five years lawyers had fought, courts had ruled, delays and postponements had dragged the procedure through a mire mostly of John's devising. Even in jail he could control people.

"Let me hold my cards a little longer," Andrei said. "Then I'll decide how to play them."

Natalia smiled at him before she left, but he knew better than to think she was comforted. He scanned her report again, admiring the meticulous work. She did everything that was necessary and nothing that was not.

Whatever his feelings, he must do the same.

"I don't know where your mind is these days." Ms. Kenyon sighed. "But I have strong suspicions. Are you thinking about your hawk again?"

"After classes I'll go see her," Peter admitted.

"And if it's not your hawk it's your horse, or your

archery, or your fencing . . ." She snapped her display screen off. "Go. Today is half a holiday for you. I'm not getting your attention anyway."

"Thank you!" Peter said, and fled the room before she could change her mind. He flew down the halls of the palace without slipping once on the polished floors or tripping over any of the carpets. When he was going where he wanted, Peter was as light as one of his beloved hawks.

The flight to the private estate just outside Zhukovka took only half an hour, but Peter begrudged every moment of precious, wasted daylight. Upon landing he raced directly to the stables and saddled his mare, Lada. She nickered happily, nosing his pocket for the lumps of sugar he always kept for her. He rode her from the stable and onto the wide path that wound through the back of the estate to the hawk compound.

The hawk master was waiting outside, a grim expression on his face. He held something in his hands. Peter couldn't make out what it was. He dismounted Lada.

"Peter . . ." Master Karel held the thing up for him to see. It looked like a large chunk of charcoal. "Alina—your hawk is dead."

"What?" Peter felt like he had been punched in the stomach. "How—?"

"I was hunting with her this morning," Karel said. "We went into the meadow that stretches down to Elbow Wash. She was circling something. Then I heard a strange sound—I can't describe it. I saw a streak of red flame as she fell from the sky. I couldn't believe my eyes at first. I searched for her body all day and finally found her an hour ago."

Peter took Alina from the master, handling her gently, as if she could still be hurt. She began to crumble as he held her. Tears trickled down his cheeks in a steady stream, but they hardly seemed enough. "Who would do such a cruel thing?" he asked miserably.

Master Karel scowled. "Your father still has enemies from the Civil War. He should have put them in jail. To do such a thing to a hawk!" He spat, as if speaking of them tainted his mouth.

Peter knew his father had enemies. But he couldn't imagine why one of them would take vengeance by killing his hawk. It didn't make sense.

"Master Karel," he said. "I think we should call Grigory. Please tell him exactly what you told me."

Ara Hovhaness put on his brakes when he saw the burned truck in the middle of the road. He sat and stared at it for several moments, observing the wisps of smoke that blew from its shattered hide. The driver still sat behind the wheel. Or what was left of him did.

"Is it someone we know?" asked his son, Evran, sounding more surprised than alarmed.

Ara couldn't tell. There wasn't enough left of the truck or the driver.

"What could destroy it so completely?" asked Evran. "Why didn't the driver try to get out?"

Ara pulled out his hand com and punched in the number for the highway patrol.

"Highway Patrol, what is your emergency?"

"I'm stopped on highway 17, southbound lane, about three miles outside Bolnisi. The road is blocked by a burned wreck, a truck. The driver is dead."

"Is the fire still burning?"

"No."

"Are there injured persons?"

"No." Ara didn't believe a passenger in that truck could still be alive. The driver looked like he had been flash-fried. His hands were still frozen to the wheel.

"What is your name and address?"

Ara told him. He also told them that he and his son were visiting his sister in Bolnisi, and gave her address and com number.

"We'll have someone there in approximately twenty minutes," said the operator.

"May I proceed to my sister's house?"

"Yes, but the officers will need to interview you."

"It's a small village, we shouldn't take more than a few minutes to find."

"I know. I live down the road in Oni. It's even smaller."

Ara chatted for a moment longer with the operator. As he talked his eyes roamed the countryside surrounding highway 17. Fields as far as the eye could see, full of waving stalks of wheat. At the side of the road, brilliant yellow wildflowers were growing. Ara looked to see if anything else was moving. Or any*one* else.

His eyes kept returning to the burned man. His jaws hung open, as if he were screaming. Ara couldn't get over the feeling that the man had been fleeing from something. He turned off his hand com.

Evran had never taken his eyes off the dead man.

"Okay," Ara said. "We're going to take a closer look, but there's not much we can do here. I want to get to Nairi's house."

"Papa." Evran's voice shook. "How come it's so quiet?"

"Always quiet out here," Ara said, but he wondered too. He drove his truck alongside the wreck. He and Evran peered in the window. The body had no clothing, no hair, and very little flesh. Ara couldn't even tell if it had been a man or a woman. The eyes were gone.

"His ring melted," said Evran.

A gold ring was warped around the withered index finger. Close up, the wreck and its driver had a powerful chemical smell.

"Let's get out of here," said Ara. He accelerated and drove down highway 17, trying not to speed.

Bolnisi had a population of approximately five hundred people. Many of them worked farms or herded animals, but Ara was accustomed to meeting at least a few other vehicles on the road, especially so late in the afternoon. He saw no one. They entered the outskirts of town and drove past the market. No one was there. Ara stopped again, in the middle of the road.

"Where is everyone?" Evran asked, his voice little more than a whisper.

Curtains flapped in the breeze. A door swung loose, and no one moved to close it.

"No dogs," said Evran. "No cats." He listened for a moment and said, "Papa—no birds . . ."

Ara's heart was a rock in his chest. He looked desperately for some sign of life. The hairs on the back of his neck lifted. A moment later, the breeze shifted, and they smelled it.

"Is someone having a barbecue?" Evran asked, puzzled.

Ara threw his truck into gear and made a U-turn so fast they almost went up on two wheels. He gunned the engine and drove straight down highway 17 the way they had come. They had only gone a short distance when he remembered the driver in the burned truck.

He had been driving away from town. Running away from something.

But they flew past the smoking wreck, and no lightning bolt struck them. Ara tossed his hand com to Evran and said, "Call. Tell them one car isn't enough. Tell them to call the army."

"What's happened?" Evran punched the numbers with trembling fingers.

"I know that smell," said Ara, and now tears were streaming from his eyes. "I smelled it on Vartan Prime, many times. During the Five-Month War. It's the smell of roasting flesh, son. Lots of it."

"Roasting flesh?" Evran said, and then suddenly understood. "Oh, God. Oh, my God."

Ara drove like a madman, hoping that whatever had killed the other driver was far away now, that he and his son might live through the day.

As Nairi and her family probably had not.

At 5:00 A.M., Emily convened the meeting.

The members of the duma were all present, as well as the governors, the prime minister, several admirals and generals, the administrators of the state and local police forces and the armed reserves, ESA Admiral Jorge, Andrei, Natalia, and Grigory.

"For those of you who don't know me," she said, "I'm Emily Kizheh, head of the tsar's personal security forces. I'm speaking to you today because of my background in homicide investigation. Since no one has officially declared war on us, we are forced to approach the massacre in Bolnisi as a mass murder. Here are the facts as we know them.

"The killings took place yesterday between 11:00 A.M. and 4:00 P.M. Within that time period, everyone who was within a five-mile radius of Bolnisi was either killed or taken. Three individuals were killed on the roads leading to and from the village, the rest of the known dead were slowly roasted alive in the town square. According to DNA analysis, the victims in this larger group were 92 men, 98 women, and 207 children."

There were murmurings in the audience. Emily paused to let them die down. She was grateful for the time to compose herself. She had seen the carnage firsthand; she wouldn't stop seeing it anytime soon.

"We don't know who the killers are, but found fluids at the scene, on a hunting knife we believe belonged to one of the farmers, possibly used to defend himself before he was disabled. We've analyzed it—it seems to be blood, but it's not human. We have company on this world, as some of us have long suspected."

That caused another wave of sound, this one a little louder. Once again, Emily waited for silence.

"We aren't ruling out the possibility that the killers are human," she continued. "We will pursue all leads. But so far the only evidence we have is this fluid I mentioned. If the killers are not human, it's going to be difficult to understand their motives. So instead we're going to focus our efforts on determining what happened and on trying to prevent it from happening again."

A flicker of movement at the back of the auditorium caught her attention. She looked for it and found Katerina, surrounded by her security force.

"We will continue to examine the evidence we've discovered on the scene and to treat this action as a homicide," she continued. "Though our ultimate response will have to be either military or diplomatic—or both. ESA Grigory and I have deployed our full staffs in the investigation, and will be coordinating with ESA Admiral Jorge. At this point, I will turn the podium over to Jorge so he can outline our plans for civil defense. Admiral . . ."

Emily was grateful to let Jorge replace her at the podium. She felt like hell, knew she looked it, and she doubted that she could have continued making sense much longer. She sat between Andrei and Grigory, and gave Jorge what was left of her attention.

He was a small, compact man with cropped hair, intense black eyes, and a voice that belonged to someone far larger.

"I know that nobody wants to hear this after we just started to get over the war that was supposed to end all wars," he began, "but we've got a vastly different situation this time around. We have no idea where these aliens are or where they'll attack next. When they hit again, there won't be time to wait for orders through the chain of command. So here are our priorities:

"First, we want to move as many children as possible away from small towns and villages where they're more vulnerable. This will be a massive effort, but once you've seen the pictures of what happened in Bolnisi you won't need to ask why. Obviously, many children are too young to be left without their mothers, and we'll be making accommodations for elderly and disabled adults as well. We'll coordinate these efforts through the regional National Guard—we don't want this to become a mad dash for the various capitals. For that reason, we need to be careful about what information is disseminated to the general population."

Emily noticed that the audience did not murmur after this announcement. She wondered if shock was starting to set in.

"Second, we must arm ourselves and be ready to fight at a moment's notice. We'll have to make sure that watch is posted twenty-five hours a day. We still have some surveillance technology functioning, but these aliens evaded it even when it was at its peak, so we need to start using our eyes and ears more. My sense, after viewing what was done at Bolnisi, is that this war—if that's what we've really got on our hands—will be fought mostly by ground troops. This is not to say that we won't be using the best of what we've got left in our weapons arsenal, but we still don't know where these people are, and that's the third priority we need to address.

"We've got to find them. That's what Emily Kizheh and ESA Grigory will be concentrating on, though intelligence will be gathered by people in the field as well. Once we know where they are, we'll be better able to deploy long-range weapons, even chemical warfare if necessary."

That woke the audience up. Behind Emily, someone said, "*Chemicals?* On a world where we're planning to live and raise our families?"

"Chemicals are only to be considered as a last resort," said Jorge. "As I said, most of you haven't seen the carnage at Bolnisi. I promise you, we will exhaust every other possibility first."

His eyes suddenly went tactical, and he paused. The audience stirred. But Jorge had no news for them yet.

"Each of you have been asked here today because you have a job. The chain of command you currently work under is in full force. You'll be receiving your first orders today. Please make sure that this line of communications is two-way—we welcome and need your input." He paused, regarding the audience with eyes that saw far more than their faces.

"You'd all better acquaint yourselves with the murder scene at Bolnisi. You need to know what we're dealing with. It's a dreadful sight, so be prepared."

*As if anyone could be*, thought Emily. *Even I wasn't, and I thought I'd seen it all . . .*

"I won't be answering questions at this point," said Jorge. "I know you have them, and I don't blame you, but there is a faster and more efficient way for you to get the answers we have. Use your links or your coms—some of you will be going straight into other meetings from here." He looked at Andrei, who had nothing to add.

"This meeting is adjourned," said Jorge.

Emily, Grigory, Tally, and Andrei stayed seated as the sea of people broke apart and began to make their way out of the auditorium. No one attempted to speak to them. Emily felt as if she were in a movie theater, sitting through the credits. She was content to sit for a while, letting the sounds swell, then diminish as people slowly left the hall.

Tally moved over to a seat next to Andrei and sat down. She looked ashen. Emily wished there had been a way to spare her from the carnage, but Tally was part of her team. She needed to look at it. She needed to use her intuition if she could.

"I hate to bring up practical matters," said Tally, "especially anything involving the stomach. But we need to eat breakfast. Choke it down if we have to. You're all invited to my place."

Emily suddenly remembered Katerina. She looked around, but the tsarina was gone. That didn't really surprise her; Katerina had grown increasingly distant over the years. But Katerina's presence had made her uneasy in a way she could not quite define.

"I'll be along soon," said Emily. "I need to sit and think for a few minutes."

"It's not your fault, Emily," said Andrei. He stared into space, but Emily knew well enough what he saw. "What has happened is not your fault. You have done everything you could to make a safe place here. Do not blame yourself."

"I could say the same thing to you," said Emily. "I hope you'll listen."

"I'll try," he said.

*Right*, thought Emily. *Me too. For all the good it will do us.*

Andrei offered Tally his arm, and the two of them went off to find some breakfast. Grigory remained seated next to Emily. He took her hand.

"These killers make John look like a slacker," said Emily.

He could have pointed out that massacres had happened on many human worlds, fully as terrible as the one in Bolnisi. Emily was grateful that he did not. He merely held her hand tighter.

"Tally was right," she said. "They didn't make a

serious move against us until they knew we couldn't get help from outside. And it's not enough for them just to kill us, they have to cause as much pain and fear as they can."

"Whoever drove them into hiding had good reason to hate them," said Grigory. "There's no sense in try ing to understand why they should be destroyed, only how."

"God help me." Emily closed her eyes, but opened them again when images poured into her mind. "I hated the Civil War. But I thought at least it meant we wouldn't have any more of that bullshit for a while."

"War never ends war." Grigory's voice was gentle. Emily never ceased to marvel at his range of expression. He should have been an actor.

But she was exactly what she ought to be. And she had work to do. Already her mind was plotting her next actions. "I feel like a machine," she said.

"And I look like one," said Grigory.

She laughed. "You son of a bitch."

He patted her hand. "You always do your best, Emily. And your best is very good."

She shook her head. "We shouldn't have settled here. But we did, and now it's our place. If we can't find a way to live with them peacefully, then I agree with you, Grigory. We have to wipe them out."

"If we *can*," he said.

*Oh, Christ*, thought Emily, glad that she was already seated. "Okay, give it to me straight."

"I'm not clairvoyant, like Tally," he said. "But since we've landed, certain possibilities have haunted me. At first I thought our neighbors might be employing a stealth technology vastly superior to our own. But it really doesn't take much to foil sensors, as you know. I have come to believe that they live underground."

Emily frowned. "That makes sense. It would be a lot easier to avoid detection that way."

"And then there's the matter of the six-eyed mammals. In fact, they're *not* mammals. They're engineered. It was tough for our biologists to classify them at first, but the type of life they most closely resemble is insect life."

Emily felt a stir of queasiness. Those animals are *bugs*?"

"Yes and no. They're hairy and warm-blooded; they have internal skeletons. But they also lay eggs in sacs and spin webs around them. One of our local forest rangers has hypothesized that they were adapted to serve as cattle. They have no known predators on this world, but something is eating them."

"So our neighbors like to eat bugs," said Emily. "They're even more charming than we imagined."

"Our neighbors *are* bugs."

Emily tried to back up to the part that would explain the comment Grigory had just made. "What did I miss?" she asked.

"As you said, those fluids we found have been analyzed. The aliens have a lot in common with their cattle. They're probably also warm-blooded, they must have skeletons."

Emily turned in her seat to stare at him. "Are you telling me some kind of—of horde of locusts descended on that town? *Bugs?*"

"For lack of a better word. They may not look too different from us. In fact, I think we've seen them since we've been here. But they didn't attract our attention. They may have been taken for strangers, but not aliens."

Images poured into Emily's mind, the ravaged town, the people trussed on spits, the children.

And then she remembered something else.

"Tally's agricultural sprite database," she said, squeezing his hand tight. It was like squeezing a piece of oak. "We spent all that time looking for one killer. They might be in it, Grigory."

"They might," he said. "I'll ask her to take another look."

"And get Tam to see if she can break into John's database. He might have images of them too."

"She's working on it, day and night."

Emily frowned, fiercely, working on the puzzle in her head. "Intelligent bugs," she said. "No compassion, no restraint."

"Probably not," said Grigory. "After all, we ourselves are not capable of compassion or restraint under certain circumstances. And there's John sitting in his cell. Such a fine example of human nature. But our problem is a practical one, it can only do us so much good to wonder how they think and feel. If they're bugs, it may not be possible to wipe them out. No insect species has ever been successfully wiped out, on any known world. That is what worries me. They were driven here, they went into hiding like locusts boring into the ground, laying their eggs and waiting for a warmer spring. And now the climate is ripe for them again."

Emily's mind was racing. Details ignored or forgotten were lining up for examination. "It must be warmer underground, they can generate their own heat and not lose it to radiation through walls."

"Some of our colonists have built their homes partly underground for the same reason," said Grigory.

"They only came out to kidnap people in the spring and summer. Grigory, they must need to hibernate during the cold months!"

"Possibly. John's killings all occurred during the winter and fall months. That might have been part of his clue game."

"He knows more about them." Emily frowned, thinking back to her long investigation. "I guess I'd better look over my notes."

"We must get him to talk again," said Grigory.

Emily sighed. "I don't want to talk to him anymore. I want to kick his teeth in. But you're right, we need to do it."

"I will talk," said Grigory. "You listen and take notes."

It was an intriguing suggestion. Grigory had not interviewed John yet. John had been terrified of him at the time of his arrest. He was sure Grigory would kill or injure him if no one else was there to stop him. Emily knew that Grigory would never attack a helpless person, no matter how much he hated him. But John did not know that, *could* not know it. Under the same circumstances, John would have delighted in hurting someone as helpless as he was himself.

"Good idea," said Emily. "Let's do that."

Emily seated herself in the observation room and waited. On the other side of the barrier, John sat in his cell. His face was bland, just as it had been in the days she had known him as a weapons tech. His eyes had been replaced with glass ones, but his lids drooped over them. She tried to remind herself that a brilliant mind lurked inside his carcass. She thought it odd that he never seemed to move in there, never tried to exercise, according to his jailors. Only sat, slept, ate, and crapped.

*Rot, you bastard,* she thought, then shut her hatred down as Grigory entered the cell.

John twitched like a sapling hit by a gust of wind, but stayed rooted in his seat. "Well," he said, his voice featureless. "It's finally come."

"I have come," said Grigory. "I don't know about *it.* Were you expecting something else?"

"No. But now that I can smell you, I detect some desperation."

"I have a keen sense of smell too, Johnny."

John didn't move, but Emily got the distinct feeling he didn't like to be called *Johnny*. There was probably some deeply rooted psychological reason behind it, some trauma from his past. But she didn't really give a rat's ass.

"I won't talk to you without my lawyer," said John, as if that ended the conversation.

"You fired him," said Grigory.

"You'll have to wait until I get another one."

"I don't want to wait. But I give you the option of calling the man you just fired. We'll all talk together."

John didn't answer. Emily was amazed. The man who had been working for him most recently was top-notch. But he hadn't secured a deal with Andrei, so John fired him. That was why he fired all the others as well. Maybe he thought he could do a better job himself.

"I don't need him," John decided.

"When you arrived on this world, you noticed our neighbors," said Grigory. "That's what your clumsy clues were all about. But you did not expect to get caught, Johnny. You thought you would be free to defend yourself when they finally attacked."

"Ah," said John, and this time he definitely sounded smug. "They've started. Amazing creatures, aren't they? I studied their methods."

Grigory's face tightened into a death's head grin. "You weren't a very good pupil."

"You don't know whether I was or not," said John.

It never ceased to amaze Emily that serial killers could present such a cold facade, and yet could be so susceptible to insults.

"None of your weapons were good enough for me," said Grigory. "I reviewed all of them, and not one was acceptable."

"You did *not* review all of them," said John, his voice fraying around the edges. "You reviewed what I presented to you. I only showed you the weapons I wanted to sell you. The best stuff I kept to myself."

"The best stuff," mocked Grigory. "It's done you a lot of good in here, hasn't it? No, Johnny, the only thing you have to offer me now is small satisfaction. I'm happy to know you're rotting here. No one will speak to you, no one will give you an opportunity again in your life. This is far better revenge than just killing you outright."

"What about that fucking Bill of Rights Andrei was always pushing?" John said. "They evaporated pretty fast under pressure."

"Only for you," Grigory said lightly.

John's face had developed some tics. Emily wondered if he wanted to strike Grigory. How he must wish he had his danger suit to make himself invisible, and his hand-claws so he could tear at the blind ronin. But maybe even that wouldn't be enough to bolster his courage.

"I could help you fight them," John said, trying to match Grigory's light tone.

"No, your usefulness has ended," said Grigory.

John started to smirk, but stifled it. He reminded Emily of a boy who thought he had gotten away with some vicious prank.

"I have a cloud of chiggers in orbit," he said slyly.

"Chiggers," Grigory said, as if he didn't know what John meant.

"One of my favorite designs. Not very practical for war, but lots of fun."

"Chiggers are insects, yes? I've never seen them."

"No, these are tiny machines. You wouldn't see them, not as individuals. Not mine, anyway. I confess I've never been exposed to the insects I named them after."

"Led a sheltered life, have you?"

"Very." John looked confident again. His face had smoothed, and his voice carried an underlying, purring quality. Grigory was giving him a chance to brag about himself. "I've been comfortable. I've had to learn everything by doing."

"So you have your nice little cloud," prompted Grigory. "And it's lots of fun."

"Would you like to see?"

"Yes. Show me."

John laughed. "Perhaps another time. I'd like you to see it happen to Peter. He has such perfect skin. My chiggers dig underneath and lift the skin off—that's how I did Vanda Chudzik."

"You didn't do Vanda Chudzik. They did. Why do you take credit for someone else's work?"

John frowned. He had probably hoped to excite Grigory's interest with an apparent confession. But it was empty, he could not be prosecuted for Vanda's murder unless they found a body. Grigory wasn't even going to humor him on that account.

"As I said," John spoke as if he had never mentioned Vanda, "the chiggers aren't very practical. Though they're not useless either. A commander could be kept very busy trying to save his skin when he should be concentrating on other matters. Still, the deployment of such a weapon during battle would probably be self-indulgent. War happens so quickly these days."

"Relatively speaking," said Grigory.

"Nothing relative about it," said John, missing the joke. "You have to make your most important moves within the first fifteen minutes. Who has time to deploy chiggers under those circumstances? They're really outmoded."

"The chiggers you speak of," said Grigory. "I think they actually belong to the aliens. Again you try to take credit for someone else's work. They've used them against our machinery and our sprites for years. They don't lift the skin off, as you claim. They burn."

Emily thought that might be true. John's face grew pale. His mouth was a straight, bloodless line.

"It makes sense when you think about it," said Grigory. "The aliens are bugs, they use buglike weapons. Chiggers. So what do you really have in reserve, John? Anything?"

"Forget about using drugs on me," John said. His color was returning to normal.

*Careful*, Emily prayed to Grigory.

"I can't be tortured. I'm too thoroughly enhanced. Drugs will just shut me down, I don't feel pain for more than a few seconds. I have weapons that you could use against the aliens, I'll bargain with you for them. Your survival is at stake, Grigory."

Grigory smiled again. Emily had thought his previous smile terrible. This one was worse. It was really too bad John couldn't see it. He could hear it, though.

"My survival has always been at stake," said Grigory. "I have my own weapons. They serve me well. And so I have no bargains to offer you."

John was silent, his face completely blank. But Emily knew he must be thinking fast. He had been alone in his cell for three years, with no sound of human voices. The man who brought him meals three times a day was deaf and dumb, selected especially for the job. John was alive, so he still must hope. Even he was that human. He would be desperate to change his situation.

"You have to act fast," he said. "If they go into hibernation before you find them, you'll miss your chance to wipe them out."

"We can find them," said Grigory, "now that we're looking for them."

"No you can't," John said flatly. "They're too far underground. You don't have the devices you'll need anymore. The Civil War crippled you. You need me."

"We need you," said Grigory, "to rot. So do your job, Johnny. I suspect rotting is your greatest talent."

He turned and exited the cell.

"You're running out of time!" John called after him, getting to his feet. He rushed the cell barrier and smacked into it face first. "God damn fucking shit!" he spat, and pounded it once with his fist.

"Good job," whispered Emily.

She did not wait to see whether John would continue his tantrum. She turned and left the observation room, leaving John to his curses and his twitches.

<Grigory,> ESA Tam called, <big news. We found John's hidey-hole. And it wasn't even underground.>

<Don't make me guess, Tammy.>

<It was a camouflaged shack near Grey Forest. We don't know if it's the spot where he did his killings or not, but I did find one important little thing. His laptop.>

Grigory smiled, though she couldn't see him.

<I've already accessed a directory,> she said. <I found a very interesting file in there. It's called WILDFIRE.>

That was a surprise. Quite a profound one. But he had other matters that required attention too. <Now that you're in, I have another file for you to look for, Tammy. It might be called CHIGGERS . . .>

The map was fresh off the press, an old-fashioned hard copy. Andrei could smell the ink. He rather liked that. He and Grigory spread it out on the big conference table and tacked down its edges. Then Grigory handed him a box. Andrei stared at its contents, bemused.

"Stick pins," said Grigory. "We'll use them to mark events on the map."

Andrei nodded. It wasn't as good as the old tactical functions that had been available to him, but he had known he might lose them. He was adapting as well as anyone else.

"I'd like to use different colors for two different kinds of events," he said. "We'll mark all the spots where people disappeared. I think we can safely assume that those people whose bodies were never found were taken by the aliens, not John. Or at least most of them."

"All of them," said Grigory. "John was proud of

what he did, he wanted to make sure he got credit for his killings. But let us also mark the spots where he left bodies. He was trying to give clues."

"I'd like to go and shake some answers out of him," said Andrei.

"You're a kind man," remarked Grigory. "I'd like to *burn* some out of him."

Andrei stared down at the continent he had developed so carefully. It was beautiful beyond his dreams. "They seem to go for the unprotected ones," he said. "People in small villages, remote places."

"We have so many of those," Grigory said.

"We can't cover them all, but we can arm the citizens. Perhaps if we do that, they'll be less likely to—"

Grigory raised a hand. Andrei stopped talking and waited.

"Did you get any of that message?" Grigory asked.

"No."

"Three more villages have been hit. All of them lie within Russian borders: Donskoi, Semikarakorsk—and Nikolina Gora."

Andrei stuck a pin in the spot where Nikolina Gora used to be. It was only a few miles from his private estate.

Where Peter liked to hunt with his hawks.

"The hawk that was burned," said Grigory, "must have flown over them. Maybe she was after prey they favor themselves. The King Raptors who are native to this world won't touch those six-eyed mammals, but our birds think they taste just fine."

"These villages are far apart," said Andrei. "I can't see a pattern yet. We'd damn well better make a plan soon."

Grigory raised his hand again. Andrei clenched his jaws so tight he thought his teeth would break. But then Grigory went to the com and snapped it open. "You just got a message," he said. "I think you'd better see it with your own eyes."

Andrei joined him and read the brief message.

*Andrei,*

*It's time we met face-to-face. Leave your blind ronin at home. I'll allow you your danger suit, but come unarmed.*

*B.Y.*

“She probably won’t eat you,” said Grigory. “But I wouldn’t accept any food or drink she offers you.”

“It doesn’t look like a dinner invitation,” said Andrei.

“Don’t count on it.”

“I’m not even counting on the meeting. She didn’t say where or when.”

“Hold on,” Emily interrupted, her eyes unfocused. She blinked. “We do know where the meeting is,” she said grimly. “My office just received a call from Mr. Klebanov. He spotted that walking metal hut. It came right up to his southwest pasture and stood there for several minutes, like it was waiting to be noticed. Then it turned and walked back into Grey Forest. He followed the giant prints the feet left, damned if they aren’t sort of like chicken prints.”

She fell silent, giving him her disapproving look.

Andrei did his best to ignore it. “I’ll go. Alone.”

“Don’t do it,” she warned him. “You don’t know who she is.”

“If she wanted to kill me, she could have done it years ago.”

She gritted her teeth, as if fighting off a massive

headache. "You don't know that! Those letters may not even be from the same person all these years. Andrei, you've survived the first wave, now we're getting ready for the second, and who knows what the hell we've got here. The sprites couldn't see her!"

"That's exactly why *I've* got to see her," he said, his tone final.

She glared at him. "Be lucky one more time," she finally said.

"I shall try," he promised.

Andrei landed his flyer in Mikhail Klebanov's southwest pasture. The farmer waited for him on the fence that bordered his property. As soon as he saw Andrei he stood and tapped out his pipe. He placed it in his breast pocket and went to meet Andrei halfway.

"See?" he pointed as he drew near. "It had feet like a giant chicken."

Andrei looked at the print. It was at least six feet across.

"In all my days, I've never caught a glimpse of Baba Yaga's hut," said Mikhail. "But on strange worlds, who knows what you will see?"

Andrei felt an excitement growing in him. It was exactly the same way he had felt three centuries before, when his father and he had followed a certain trail.

But Mikhail did not appear to share the feeling. He was gazing at the night sky with a stoic expression. "The black Veil covers half the galaxy this time of year," he said. "It is a shame that we are such fools, we cannot see such a plain message from God."

"What message do you see?" Andrei asked softly.

"That half the Republic is dead," said the farmer.

Andrei thought of David, and could not speak.

"It happened so fast," Klebanov said softly. "I've been in microwars that lasted years, but the War To End All Wars was over in four days. Only God could move faster than that."

They stared at the Veil together. Andrei didn't tell Mikhail the Veil was where he had hidden the fleet that saved their lives. Besides, the farmer was right, anything could hide in the blackness, either good or ill.

"Which way did she go?" he asked softly.

Mikhail pointed toward the forest. "The trail is there. But once it enters the forest it changes. No more chicken prints, instead it looks swept away."

"Like the marks of a broom someone has dragged behind?" asked Andrei.

"Just like that. I'll show you."

They walked side by side to the forest's edge, until Andrei could see the trail. It was much more obvious than it had been three hundred years before. Someone has swept the velvety leaves, exposing the ground. The trail led deep into the forest. Andrei switched on his flashlight and started forward.

"We won't need that," Mikhail said, falling in beside him. "At night the forest is a darker shade of gray, but you can see."

"You've been here at night?" asked Andrei.

"Once."

And he was right. The flashlight did not make it easier to see the trail, it washed the scene out. Andrei switched it off and stuffed it back into a utility pocket.

They followed the trail for close to an hour, never speaking. Andrei was puzzled. The hut must be large, yet he could see no signs of its passage on the roots or trunks of the Giants. Perhaps the trees were so hard they couldn't even be scratched. But if they were that hard, how did the machine get past them? It should have been stuck. Yet the trail continued unbroken.

At last they entered a clearing that seemed half again as large as the one in which Natalia had made her grisly discovery. The trail went into it, but came to a sudden end about two-thirds of the way through.

Nothing moved in the clearing.

Andrei turned 360 degrees, searching for the slightest sign of movement. When he was halfway through, he met Mikhail doing the same, and they exchanged tense looks. When they finished, they were back to back. Still nothing moved.

"Hello?" Andrei called reluctantly. He immediately regretted it. His voice did not belong there. He thought about Peter's suggestion that they should build a tree house city in the forest. It had seemed so charming at the time. But no one could have lived in such a place.

He wondered if he should call Emily. Maybe Baba Yaga had left another message, some directions from this point. But he wondered if trying to call his security would scare the old witch off; she would surely be aware of it.

Mikhail drew a sharp breath. Andrei turned, ready to see just about anything. But Mikhail was looking up, far over their heads.

"It perches," he whispered.

Andrei looked up. Approximately fifty feet over their heads, the metal hut was perched on a giant root like a bird. Andrei scarcely had a chance to credit his eyes when the hut bounced on its legs and leaped to the ground. A tremor passed under Andrei and Mikhail as the hut landed not more than twenty feet away from them.

Andrei's heart pounded like a jackhammer, but he didn't move. He vividly remembered what he had asked his father all those years ago. *What if she steps on us with her hut?*

It swayed on its feet like a living thing that could see them, smell them. It was all Andrei could do to keep still. He was grateful that Mikhail did the same.

Then it settled slowly to the ground, its legs folding under its body. It was as big as Andrei's summer cottage in Zhukovka, hardly a "hut." It might contain several rooms, but God only knew where it housed its star drive, assuming it had one. The star drive might be parked in orbit somewhere, but he couldn't even see a thruster on the damned thing.

A door opened in the "hut," and a metal ramp extended itself toward Andrei and Mikhail. Its end settled lightly at their feet. The hairs stirred on the back of Andrei's neck as he tried to see into the interior of Baba Yaga's domain. There was a dull, red glow, but it did not illuminate anyone or anything.

"I have to go alone," he said.

"Little father," said Mikhail, "I'll wait for you here."

Andrei met the farmer's eyes, not as a tsar looking at a subject, but as a family man regarding another family man, fervently hoping they would both see their loved ones again. He saw that Mikhail understood him. Then he fixed his gaze on the doorway and walked up the ramp.

Andrei paused at the door. A warm breeze flowed over him, from an even warmer interior. The outside of the hut was perfectly smooth, a work of superior technology. But the inside was like the home of a wealthy farmer. Andrei peered down a short hallway that veered off to the right, out of sight.

In the corner stood a broom.

"Very funny," Andrei said under his breath. He stepped into the hallway, and followed it around its turn.

Tapestries on the wall were in perfect condition, but Andrei had a feeling they were old. The floor was covered in Persian carpets. They were thick and muffled the sound of his boots, but he was sure she could hear him coming.

"Andrei," said a brittle voice to his right, and suddenly he smelled pipe smoke.

A doorway had materialized when he wasn't looking. It opened into a parlor furnished in a very old-fashioned country style. Baba Yaga was there, a tiny, ancient figure perched on a padded, silk-covered chair. Eyes like polished black stones watched him as she puffed away at her pipe, which she clutched in teeth that were tiny and sharp as those of a predator.

The eyes could have been artificial, the teeth filed, but somehow he doubted it. She had skin the color and texture of old leather. Her embroidered clothing was that of a wealthy tribeswoman. Her grey hair was tucked under a scarf, her slippered feet rested on a stool. A samovar steamed on the table next to her chair, and at her back, a flock of golden cranes took flight against a red sky. The smoke swirling around them made them look as if they were fleeing from a fire.

Another, larger stool waited near her feet. Andrei suspected it was meant for him. He went to it and sat down.

Her eyes glittered as they followed him.

"You like the warmth, Grandmother," said Andrei.

"I am old," she replied.

For several moments, Andrei could only gaze in wonder. Close up, some disturbing details were making themselves clear. She clutched the pipe with one gnarled hand and gripped the skull carving that tipped the arm of her chair with the other. Her fingernails were iron-grey, round and sharp like a cat's—and apparently retractable.

"I'm honored to meet you," he said at last.

"Yes." She puffed twice. "You are. Your father was honored as well, your grandfather too, just before they were assassinated."

He gave up trying to read her expression. Her style, at least, was as it had always been.

"Andrei Alexandrovich," she continued. "I have some advice for you." She paused, taking several more puffs on her pipe. The smoke had a sharp but pleasant odor.

*No wonder she prefers to write letters,* thought Andrei. *It doesn't interfere with her smoking.*

"Do not waste your time with diplomacy," she said.

"Prepare for war. You think you have fought hard already, but that was nothing. These Enemies could kill you all, and it would not be an easy death. As it is, even if you fight with all your skill and your wits, you could lose almost everything."

Andrei let her take several more puffs, since he needed the time to gather his wits anyway. "So we must fight again," he said. "Will you help us fight these Enemies?"

"No," she said flatly.

"Why?"

She jabbed the end of her pipe at him. "You are not here to ask questions. You are here to listen."

Andrei rubbed his beard. He tried another approach.

"I think I've misjudged your concern," he said. "All these years I believed you were Russian."

She showed her pointed teeth. "I am Russian. I was there at the beginning. I was there when men used the word *Russe* to describe their Viking overlords."

"A long time," mused Andrei.

"A long time," she agreed. "Without the benefit of science to keep me alive. Otherwise I would look young like you." She cackled, and her black eyes gleamed. "But there is a certain wisdom that comes with old age that you will never learn if your body stays young. I value wisdom more than vanity. Have some tea, Andrei."

A saucer and teacup floated at his elbow. The steaming contents wafted a light, fruity perfume. As far as Andrei could tell, nothing supported the saucer, no sprite or gravity defying machinery. The china was decorated with a Persian design. It looked fine, almost transparent in its fragility.

Andrei accepted the cup. It felt almost as if hands were giving it to him. For the first time he thought to wonder if they were alone in the room, or if people with incredibly sophisticated danger suits attended them.

He knew better than to ask.

She set her pipe on an ornate side table and accepted another floating cup and saucer. She drank the steaming contents without pausing to blow the steam off.

Andrei sipped his own tea. He could picture Emily's cold blue eyes, watching him with disapproval. But he believed it was safe, at least for the moment. Baba Yaga had not cultivated him for three centuries simply so she could poison him over tea.

"Delicious," he said.

"I drink only the best." She set her cup and saucer on the end table, picked up her pipe, and resumed smoking. "You're a cautious man—though you have your bold moments. There is a question you must ask, now that we have seen each other. Ask it."

Andrei had *many* questions he wanted to ask. But he thought he knew what she was getting at.

"What are you?" he asked.

"A *dezhurnaya*," she replied between puffs. "Like the old women who sit by the elevators in buildings and watch all the comings and goings. Only I watch the galaxy."

"You may be that," Andrei said, trying not to scald his tongue with the tea, "but my question referred more to what you *are* than what you *do*."

"But what I am is what I do," she said. "*Dezhurnaya*, Baba Yaga, grandmother witch. Do you see? What I do is what I am."

"Grandmother," said Andrei, though he hadn't been given permission to ask another question, "are you human?"

She puffed until Andrei could see a red glow above the bowl of her pipe. "What is human?" she fired back.

"Are you of my species?" he persisted.

"I am of Earth," she replied. "That is all I will say about it."

Andrei's tea did not seem to be growing any cooler,

nor he wiser. But he thought about the concept of the *dezhurnaya*. She watches. All who live in the building know and fear her, because she will tell someone of their doings. But who will Baba Yaga tell of the doings in the galaxy?

"I have watched the people of Russia scatter into the stars like seeds on the wind," said Baba Yaga. "They mix with others, they change, just like their ancestors did. They are threatened on all sides, and that is when Russian blood runs true. You are threatened, Andrei. But you are a clever man, the son of clever men. You are chased by the horsemen of the Apocalypse, yet you have put down roots. Those roots must grow deep, and you must fight your worst Enemy. This must happen. I will not stop it, and I expect you to win. You need not kill them all to do that, and I have one more piece of advice for you."

She paused, puffing as if she needed the tobacco like others needed oxygen. Andrei began to wonder what exactly was in that pipe.

"You won't like it," she warned, and puffed some more.

"I believe you," he said. "But I will listen."

"When this is done," she said, "you will have your lives, probably little more. This new Enemy will survive as well, and over the centuries they will become your old and worst enemy. After a long time of fighting and hating, you will get to know them. That is the only way. You will know them, and they will know you. Once you have done that, you will learn the other truth."

She studied him, looking for what, he could not guess. It was unsettling. For a moment, he dared to suspect that something frightened her.

"You will learn," she said at last, "that they are *not* your worst enemies. Those—you have yet to meet."

Andrei did not try to sip any more of his tea. He gazed at the old creature who perched across from him, the cranes flying at her back, the skulls leering under her hands, her finely embroidered clothing and the brilliant colors that surrounded her, all singing of an ancient and fabulous past. If the old legends were true, she was neither good nor evil, but she was always dangerous, like a natural force.

"Are you done with your tea?" she asked.

"Yes, Grandmother."

Invisible hands took the saucer and cup from him. He let it go without looking after it.

"I've said what I wanted you to hear." Baba Yaga puffed. "Go now."

Andrei stood. He half turned, fighting the urge to take one last, and much more thorough, look at the room.

*Be lucky*, Emily had said.

Andrei turned to face Baba Yaga again. "I didn't come expecting to hear good news," he said. "I think you know what I hoped for when I started this project. If there is any advice you could offer that would help me ensure the survival of this colony, I would be grateful to hear it."

She frowned, and he knew he may have taken too great a risk. But he also knew what he had already lost. He would fight to keep from losing more with everything he had.

"You recall the riddle I told you," she said.

Fortunately he did. " 'What do booby traps and six eyed mammals have in common?' "

"Engineers," she said. "That's what they have in common. And that's your ace in the hole, Andrei. When you face your darkest day, remember the engineer."

Andrei had no idea what to make of that. But he bowed to her. "Thank you, Grandmother."

She waved him away. "Go! You know I can't stand sentimentality. Back to your team. Go put together your puzzles. Away!"

Andrei obeyed. He turned and left the room, his back itching, his curiosity itching even more. He would have loved to stay and examine the inside of the hut. But he could feel her presence looming behind him, as if she were ten feet tall. He had no doubt her eyes still saw him as he made his way down the hall and out the front door.

Mikhail waited at the foot of the ramp, his eyes bright. Andrei descended. He heard a soft *click* behind him and knew the door was shut again. As he stepped off the ramp, Mikhail said, "Little father, it is pleasant to see you again."

"It is pleasant to be seen," said Andrei. "Let's go. Before she changes her mind and steps on us."

The ramp was withdrawing back into the hut. Andrei and Mikhail started across the clearing. Andrei looked over his shoulder at Baba Yaga's dwelling. It had already reared up on its long legs again. It leaped from the clearing and up onto the giant root. In another moment, it leaped again, and was gone from his sight.

When they emerged from Grey Forest and were walking across the meadow toward Mikhail's south pasture, the farmer asked a question.

"Tsar Andrei, what do you want me to do?"

Andrei considered. Mikhail had addressed him as a soldier does his C.O., not as a subject would his tsar.

"I'm appointing you commander of your fighting forces from this village. You'll answer to your constable, but I doubt you'll have time for chain-of-command if you're attacked. You'll need to step up your patrols, starting tonight. Within a few hours you'll be receiving grenades and more rifles."

"Yes." Mikhail sighed. "I knew it. I'm the fire warden after all. I accept your charge, little father. But I have a suggestion."

"I'm always willing to hear those."

Mikhail drew on his pipe, though not as enthusiastically as Baba Yaga. "We can't let them lead us around by the nose the way they have. We can't find them, they attack at random, we run to the other end of the continent, and they attack somewhere else."

Andrei nodded. "We'll assign ESAs to possible trouble spots. They'll help the survival rate, I think."

"There's a way we can bring all your ESAs together to strike at these killers. I know many men who are veterans of other wars. I am one myself. We know how to fight as a unit." He paused, as if weighing the risk of his next remark.

"I'm desperate, Mikhail," Andrei said softly. "Tell me your plan."

"You could be bait," said the farmer. "You could put out news that you're going to visit us on a particular day, part of a goodwill visit to all your provinces to reassure your people in the wake of these new troubles. You know best how to say it, but I think it might be good to suggest that the leader of these killers is a coward, that he is afraid to face you, that if you had him in sight you would kill him with your own hands."

Andrei suddenly realized who Mikhail reminded him of. "My father would have liked you, Mikhail. I'm sorry you never got the chance to meet him. As for me, I'm not sure an alien could be provoked the same way a human could."

"Yes." Mikhail humbly lowered his eyes. "As you say, we are desperate."

"I'll implement your plan," said Andrei. He noted that the farmer did not seem terribly surprised by this announcement. That only made him like Mikhail more.

"Get your men together," said Andrei. "I'll assemble my team. Come to St. Petersburg tomorrow and we'll discuss the plan. I think it best if we only discuss the idea in person, out loud, without using communications devices that can be eavesdropped upon."

"Yes, very wise," agreed Mikhail. "I'll do as you say, Tsar Andrei."

"Then I'll see you tomorrow after breakfast."

Mikhail grinned at him. "You probably mean 8:00 A.M.," he said. "For me, breakfast is at four."

<ESA COM ESA.>

<Go ahead, Tam.>

<Problem, Grigory. I broke into one of John's files. I wasn't sure what would happen, so I picked one that seemed disposable, one of the weapons he designed for me that I don't use anymore. Good thing, because it self-destructed.>

<You're the expert. What do we need?>

<We need a fucking password, that's what.>

<I'll work on it. Right now, we've got other business.>

Deep inside the earth, the Swarm raged.

Ayat-ko stood like a stone at the edge of the cavern, watching them whirl like leaves in a windstorm. Pipers played wildly, urging them on to even greater frenzy. She observed their elegance, their grace and ferocity—and she was untouched.

In her long life, she had never seen the Swarm reach such a fever pitch. Intellectually she could appreciate the beauty of it, but she felt compelled to clinically examine what drove her kind. Just as the ritualistic movements of the Dance drove its participants to battle, the frenzied movements of the Swarm drove the clans to slaughter. She saw them moving toward a magnificent extinction. Her race was like a sun. The brothers craved pain and pleasure, continual conflict. The Witnesses needed stability and continuity. A good clan leader was supposed to balance the two forces.

But the Cousin clan was out of balance. It was the luck of the draw, that Kami-te was awake at the wrong time.

And suddenly he was there, a leaf blown out of the storm. He swayed before her, most graceful of all Dancers, and his beauty evoked a chord of despair and regret in her as deep as the thrust of a blade.

"Slip the bonds of your cautious nature!" he cried. "Dance with us!"

"Sterile sisters do not dance," she reminded him.

He only laughed, drunk with passion, and flew back into the fray.

Like stone she was, like the cold, stiff sleepers before she woke them. Ages had passed while the cycles turned, the galaxy expanded, the universe shifted its moving parts. But all suns must ultimately burn up their fuel. The Cousin clan would give up their life in a supernova.

Without the te clan to keep their bloodlines clean, the ko clan would grow cold. They would retire to their tombs and sleep until time wound itself down.

There had to be another way. But she would not find it with the te clan.

*Dance*, she thought as she looked upon them for the last time. *Amuse yourselves. I will witness you no longer.*

She turned and left them, the wind at her back.

Andrei and the local constable walked through Mikhail Klebanov's wheat field. Two of his Cossack honor guard brought up the rear. "We've had no trouble here," said the constable. "We're too well armed. They don't attack people who might fight back, they are cowards."

"It's just as I thought," said Andrei. He listened to further commentary, nodding at appropriate moments and making the proper replies. He kept his eyes straightforward.

They passed men in the fields. Andrei remembered all of their names. Mikhail had introduced them before the light of dawn touched the sky.

"This is Vartan Karayan, he fought in the Vishnu war and the Red Hand war. This is Yuri Chapaev, he fought at Agamemnon, that one lasted ten years. Jacob here grew up as a guerilla in the Spider catacombs before he finally escaped and emigrated here."

The list went on and on. The men were all ages, different ethnic groups. They shared two things in common: farming and war. As Andrei passed them in the fields, they looked like ordinary field hands. But their eyes gave them away.

All week Andrei made loud noises in the media about this trip, where he was going and when he would be there. During that time two more villages were gutted. In both of them, the men who stayed behind had been impaled in a most ingenious and sadistic way. Andrei could only be glad that the women and children had already moved to safety.

He thought the new killings were a deliberate challenge. In a way, he hoped they were. He did not want to chase this enemy in the dark any longer.

"If they attack us here," the constable said in a normal tone that carried well, "they will be cut to pieces."

*We can't show them everything we've got,* Grigory had warned. *Just like you did in the Civil War, we've got to hide the aces until they'll do us the most good. I'll be close, I can get to you fast. Tam is scouting, and twenty other ESAs will back Mikhail's people up.*

The grass was only up to the tops of Andrei's boots. It waved in the mild breeze. He continued to nod, to keep his eyes pointed forward.

*Use projectile weapons. They pack a lot of punch in a small package. And they have no energy signature. Besides, I hear you're a marksman.*

He was, thanks to his mother. He saw nothing moving ahead. But once they had reached the pasture where Mikhail had spotted Baba Yaga, Andrei felt eyes on them.

"Steady on," he said mildly to the constable, "I think the weather is changing."

"Everyone complains about the weather," said the constable, "but no one—"

Something shrieked past Andrei's ear. He saw the smeary lines of an ESA in superfast motion, and blood sprayed him. The blood was lavender-blue.

Andrei and his escorts drew automatic pistols and began firing at pale forms. One of the aliens already lay dead at his feet; it had attacked him so quickly he never saw it. Twenty feet away, part of the field exploded, and more lavender blood rained down.

But that was a lucky hit. They were moving so fast, Andrei wondered if they had their own version of danger suits. His own was switched onto maximum; he used it, running and firing more quickly and with more precision than the farmers could.

A flash of white-hot light blossomed behind him and a wave of heat dazzled him. He threw a look over his shoulders.

One of his Cossacks was a smoking corpse.

A creature out of a fairy tale flew past him, slashing with something he couldn't see that tore his outer clothing and exposed the danger suit beneath. He was spun by the force of a blow that should have torn him open if not for the suit. He went with the force of the turn and let it bring him around to face another attacker in time to shoot him four times point blank in the chest.

Apparently they had vulnerable organs there.

Andrei hit the ground and ejected the spent cartridge, slapping the new one in, all within seconds. He fired again at attackers moving almost as fast as ESAs, felt things slash his clothing to ribbons, saw the constable and his other Cossack go down to lie twitching. A pale form swooped down on the constable and whisked him away.

Andrei shot the kidnapper before he could get more than five paces. The constable lay with the dead alien, still twitching.

Andrei emptied the second clip and reloaded again. After this one there was one more. Then he had his knife. He began to fire again, but instantly realized that too many of them were coming for him. If he ran, the constable and the Cossack would be at their mercy. Andrei began firing again. In another second they would be on top of him.

A giant, metallic claw descended from heaven and

slammed into the ground, crushing his attackers, shaking the world, and knocking him off his feet. Andrei sprawled backward and got an excellent view of the underside of Baba Yaga's hut. It danced back and forth on the metal claws, coming down with killing force on pale, running forms. It crushed a few more, but they ran from it like gazelles, past Andrei without taking notice of him. The chicken hut leaped in his direction.

*Papa, what if she steps on us . . . ?*

It came down three feet from his head and kept going. Andrei rolled and watched it shoot blue-white bolts from weapons ports he couldn't see. Every pale form it struck shimmered in the afternoon breeze, then blew away like smoke. The hut took thirty-foot steps, firing at aliens the whole time.

Andrei felt the tremors pass under him when it came down, growing weaker as it moved away from him. It leaped over a barn and lurched out of sight, still firing. Slowly the sound faded in the distance.

He lay there with his ears ringing like the bells of Moscow. But he did not spend any more time looking after Baba Yaga. He looked for his men. He saw some, crouching or prone as he was. He saw others—or parts of them. No ESAs were near.

He looked for aliens. He found only one crouching nearby. Andrei looked into that one's cold, green eyes and knew he was looking at their tsar.

He gazed at this personage, feeling vaguely ill. Grigory had been right, the aliens did look almost human; in fact, by human standards they were quite beautiful. Yet the air of menace that emanated from this creature belied that illusion. The man was far more slender than any human could be, his features long and pointed, his skin far more pale and his hair so black it had a blue sheen to it. His clothing fit him as snugly as if it had grown on him, and its colors were the subtle shades of Grey Forest.

Andrei stood. The other did the same, far more smoothly. Andrei took several slow steps toward him. The alien waited.

When Andrei got close enough to hear a response over the ringing in his ears, he stopped. "Who are you?" he asked. "Why have you killed my people?"

The alien smiled. Even Grigory could not make the gesture look so terrible.

"We are your Enemies," said the alien, his voice soft and musical.

Andrei felt an unbearable urge to lunge at the creature and grab him by the neck.

"We wished only to live in peace," he said. "We never offered you harm. Had we known you were here, we would have left and found another world."

"That's not what *we* would have done," answered the Enemy.

"Why have you attacked us, why have you kidnapped and tortured my people?"

"Precisely what is it about the situation you do not understand?" asked the alien.

"I understand none of it."

"Then we have no common ground, except that on which we will kill each other. If you Dance well, we will honor you. If you do not, we will leave you where you fall."

"We will not fall," said Andrei. "It is you who will lose. You will pay a terrible price for this war. We must talk out our differences and reach an agreement."

"Talk?" The alien was excited by the word, Andrei was sure of it. "You will offer a gift?"

Andrei frowned. He didn't want to make any promises he couldn't keep. "What would you consider a proper offering?" he asked.

"Someone strong, of course. Someone you value. A favored brother or sister who will provide fine entertainment."

Somehow Andrei had a feeling he wasn't talking about someone who could sing and tap dance.

"Once this favored brother is dead, we will taste his liver. If it pleases us, we will talk."

"I wish to understand you," said Andrei. "You want me to give you a person as a gift, for you to torture to death. And then you will eat that person."

"Yes. We are civilized beings, we will observe the proper protocol."

"Why should I do such a thing?"

"You are the one who wants to talk."

Andrei showed his hands, palms up. "You have had years to watch us. You speak our language. Surely you have learned something about our nature."

"A great deal," said the alien, his eyes unblinking. "I have eaten your livers. That is why I stayed here and let you speak. I know what you want."

*Bug*, thought Andrei, fighting rage and disgust.

"So you have eaten us," he said. "What could that teach you?"

"Only the emotions your people felt as they were dying. Some of them tried to bargain. I think that's what you want to do now."

"I won't offer bargains I can't keep," Andrei said. "But if we are to be at war, then we should understand why."

"You speak only of yourselves again."

"I think not. We are alien to each other. Isn't it possible that you have misunderstood us?"

"Not anymore," said the Enemy. "It is only you who lack understanding."

"Then a formal meeting could benefit both of us. Bring your advisors, I will bring mine. We'll meet in a neutral place—"

The Enemy's eyes suddenly grew dark as his pupils expanded like exploding stars. In another instant, they had retracted to pinpoints again. "You never offered the gift," he said.

*"The gift,"* Andrei echoed.

"To show your good faith and your respect," said the Enemy. His voice had taken on a softer quality. "I think you know how we take our pleasure. Offer someone who you value, a strong and brilliant person who will survive our ministrations for many days. After we have experimented with that one to our satisfaction, then we will be willing to talk about—*talking*."

Andrei's heart was a stone in his chest. "There is no hope for peace between us," he said.

"I have eaten so many of you," purred the Enemy. "Yet I will never understand why you should want such a thing."

"I believe you," said Andrei. "But know this. You have chosen the wrong enemies. If it is your nature to kill, then you shall be killed in return. You have left us no other choice."

Green eyes watched him with inhuman interest. Andrei held himself firmly in check. He would not be lured as he had lured the Enemies into ambush.

"You've provided some pleasant diversion today," said the Enemy. "I didn't know you could Dance so well. I doubt I could make you understand how happy you've made me."

"Soon your happiness will know no bounds," promised Andrei.

The Enemy smiled. And then he was gone. The tall grass waved where he had passed.

Andrei stared at the field, looking for movement. There was none. The aliens who had attacked had died, or run away.

Grigory was at his side. Andrei had a feeling that was why the Enemy tsar had left so quickly.

"We lost twenty people," Grigory said. "They lost twice that, but only because of Baba Yaga's intervention."

Cranes had flown at her back, and the smoke of her pipe was like the smoke of burning villages.

*Will you help us fight these Enemies?* he had asked her.

*No*, she had said. But she had changed her mind. Perhaps she needed him to live a little longer.

*You are a clever man, the son of clever men . . .*

"How many of them did we kill on our own?" asked Andrei.

"The same number they killed."

"So. That's what it will cost us. We lose as many of our own as we kill of them. Did we lose ESAs today?"

"Not today."

Some men, like the constable, lay unable to move or speak, as if they had been injected with a drug. Andrei hoped their blood could be analyzed and an antidote found. In any event, it seemed to be wearing off as he and his guerillas picked up the wounded first, then began to tend to the dead.

Andrei and Grigory looked at the Cossack who had been burned.

"Just like the motorists outside Bolnisi," said Grigory. "Nothing left but charred flesh stretched over the bones."

"Did you see the weapon they used to do this?" Andrei asked grimly.

"Yes. I suspect these were the *chiggers*, the tiny weapons John bragged about. He said you can't see them until they swarm in large numbers. They must move as quickly as our sprites once did, and I don't think it takes many of them to combust something. I recorded their action, I will analyze it."

Andrei looked at the body of his dead honor guard and felt such hatred as he had never felt before. It burned in him as brightly as the heat that had consumed the Cossack.

*Vengeance is mine, Bug. You will answer for this, I swear it.*

"Tsar Andrei!" called a deep voice.

Mikhail and another were dragging a dead man between them. At first Andrei thought it was one of his young comrades. But then he got a closer look at the body.

"We thought you might find this helpful," said Mikhail. "Perhaps you can study it, find out its weaknesses."

"We'll try," said Andrei. "And when we're done, we'll put its head on a stick and leave it here." He nodded toward the fields. "As a *gift*."

<So, Grigory,> said Tam, <before we were interrupted by aliens and walking chicken huts I was telling you about some problems I'm having with John's database . . .>

<I remember. Did you find a file marked CHIGGERS?>

<Nope. But I found one that might be helpful. It's called BUG SPRAY.>

<This day has inspired my thought processes,> he said. <I'd like to propose a visit.>

<Do you know another database wiz?>

<Someone more interesting than that. I think it's time we paid a call on Basilisk. There are some things she may be able to tell us.>

When Tam was recruited as an ESA, her mentor gave her some advice.

"Don't look at the universe in tactical all the time, Tammy. Every day, put time aside to gaze at something with the vision God gave you."

It was interesting advice to get from a blind man, but Tam believed him. That was when she started collecting flowers. Most of the day her visual field was enhanced with grids, footnotes, heat patterns, and/or light from the extreme end of both spectrums. But for two hours every day it was enhanced by lavender flowers, roses, flowering vines, lobelia, hundreds of species of daisies—the colors and shapes of nature.

Twenty years later her sprites were disabled, and the tactical vision she now used was a shadow of its old self. But she was beginning to realize that the human face could reveal just as much without grids and heat patterns. Fancy was a cool one, but her feelings were made plain by the set of her jaw, the tight lines around her mouth and her eyes, her formal posture.

Still, Tam had to admit, the woman had class.

She deployed John's laptop and waited for Emily and Grigory to question the duchess.

"Welcome to my home." Fancy sat with self-conscious ease on the parlor couch, her body turned toward Emily at the other end. But she was looking at Grigory, who stood near Tam's chair. "I must say I expected you long ago."

Grigory did not employ his famous scowl. He spoke gently to the duchess. "Recent circumstances have made this discussion necessary."

Fancy's facade cracked a little, and Tam saw puzzlement. "How long have you known that I am Basilisk?" she asked.

"Twenty years," said Grigory. "I made you a special project after meeting you on Canopus."

"How flattering to be considered special."

Emily leaned toward her. "We're not here to accuse or punish you. We need to find out all you can tell us about Loki."

Fancy closed her eyes, her composure slipping further out of place. When she opened them again, they shone with unshed tears.

"I didn't know he was killing girls," she said. "I thought he was a weapons expert, nothing more."

"Tell us about him," said Grigory. "From the beginning."

Fancy took a deep breath. "I am a double agent," she said. "My family owes a heavy financial debt to Andrei's uncle Nikita. But my father and Alexander were friends, and *that* debt runs deeper. I worked for Nikita Mironenko, but I pursued my father's agenda."

"I understand," said Grigory, managing to make his gravelly voice sound sympathetic. "That is why you were allowed to emigrate here—and why ESAs were willing to work for you. But your work as a double agent is over, and there are things you must tell us. Your knowledge of Loki may be the key to our survival on this world."

Tam thought Fancy was starting to look a little ill. She wondered how she would feel in the same situation, then decided that sort of speculation wasn't a good idea at the moment.

"I pitied him," she said. "He was so cold, his social skills were poor, but he was so arrogant he didn't know it. I brought him to Lucifer in my private ship, about a year after Archangel arrived there. I withdrew beyond the orbit of the tenth planet and waited two more years, until I could seem to arrive with the first wave of immigrants."

"I would like to examine that ship," remarked Grigory. "Its stealth features must have been very advanced."

But Fancy shook her head. "To the best of my knowledge, it left this solar system with another agent."

Tam wondered if Fancy would be fool enough to lie to Grigory. She didn't seem the foolish type. Fancy took another deep breath, and it seemed to steady her. "I could not risk communication with Loki within those first three years," she continued, "but I sent TachyGrams to Nikita Mironenko. I urged him not to assassinate Andrei, painting as bright a picture as I could of Belarus. I knew the war was coming. I knew if I could delay covert action long enough, war would force the Mironenko family conflict out in the open where Andrei could deal with it properly. I had been told that Loki was developing a weapon that could cripple sprites, but I did not believe he could do it. I had no inkling that he could wreak such havoc."

"When did you see him again?" asked Emily

"Never," said Fancy. "I exchanged a few messages with him. He always treated me like a child, he could not seem to take me seriously. I confess that his attitude of me shaped my attitude of him. I thought him a fool. I thought he was too deeply buried in the abstract concepts he was pursuing to understand the real people around him."

"All of us thought that about John," said Emily. "How did you communicate with him?"

"A code," said Fancy.

Tam restrained herself from doing cartwheels on Fancy's polished wood floor. "Did you relay messages for him to your bosses," she asked, "or did he do it himself?"

"I did," said Fancy. "They didn't trust him."

"Did you send files?"

"Yes."

"Did you send one called BUG SPRAY?"

"Yes," said Fancy distastefully. "I assumed it was some sort of chemical warfare."

<If she sent that file,> Tam told Grigory, <Andrei's uncle Nikita must have known about the aliens on Belarus.>

<Which explains why he was willing to strand us here rather than trying to wipe us out,> replied Grigory. <Perhaps they hoped the bugs would do their dirty work for them.>

It was a weird piece of luck. Fancy transmitted files to their enemies, and now BUG SPRAY might just save their asses.

But only if they could find the Bugs.

Fancy's information got Tam into the file. She read it, and her heart sank.

"Okay," she told Grigory. "I know what it is. A cloud of tiny machines, just like John told you. They really are in orbit around Belarus. But they don't burn anything, they deploy a poison that reproduces in atmosphere. It has a time limit, which is fortunate for us. It's formulated to kill the aliens instantly, but it would kill us too, given time. Deployed underground in the nests, it shouldn't cause us trouble, but there's a big problem. I can't arm it or control it. We still need a code."

"Then get it," he said, but Tam shook her head.

"No go, Grigory. Only one guy can get us that code. And he's locked up for attempted murder."

She could not read his expression. Usually that meant he was thinking too hard to have one.

"We may have to offer him a deal, Grigory," she said. "I hate it, but we need that code."

"I'll pass on the suggestion," said Grigory.

Tam couldn't tell whether he agreed with her or not.

Kami-te sat in his thinking chair, but he already knew what he would do. He had known the moment he laid eyes on the Enemy clan leader.

That one was no weakling. He was truly a clan leader, and that had surprised the te. He had thought the aliens to be kin to the cattle who ate the weeds. His model of the universe was flawed, he could see that now. The eyes of his Enemy had Challenged him. But the Challenge was not a struggle for authority. It was a threat of extinction.

*Know this, you have chosen the wrong enemies . . .*

Kami-te had to admit the Witness was right in some respects. Her long life had taught her more than he would ever learn. But his instincts told him what his intellect could not. If his Enemies were not cattle, then he must Dance with them predator to predator.

*You have left us no other choice.*

The aliens harbored undetected resources. The walking tank was an unpleasant surprise. But Kami-te also had resources at his disposal. It was time he used them. He had hoped for extended foreplay with the aliens, that was how he liked to Dance. But he could change tempo again.

*Soon your happiness will know no bounds.*

"Perhaps," said Kami-te. "Perhaps not. Happiness is an illusive thing. Yet I am compelled to pursue it."

He called his favored brothers to his side. They came quickly, their eyes bright, ready for another foray. But he did not call the pipers.

"Playtime is over," he said. "Now we must go to war."

Tally opened her eyes. She was surrounded by Giants.

Grey Forest was still grey at night, but darkly so, like charcoal. Massive roots twisted over and around her, hemming her in. Trunks like skyscrapers shut out the world. Tally could only see straight up, where half the sky was obscured with the darkness of the Veil.

*Something in there. Something hiding.*

Tally lowered her gaze and saw two small girls standing hand in hand. She knew them. They were her sisters.

"No," she choked.

Their eyes were merciless. They could not be otherwise, because they were dead.

"Not you," said Tally. "No more ghosts, I can't bear it."

Their response was to run at her. Tally stumbled backward, and with each step she shrank until she was their size. They seized her hands and pulled at her, dragging her into a run with them. She went, because a sound had started behind them.

*Tic tic tic tic tic tic tic tic tic tic tic tic . . .*

Tally ran as fast as she could, but her sisters pulled

still faster, forcing her along at an impossible pace. They dodged under and around roots, or vaulted over them. Behind them, the noise got louder.

*TIC TIC TIC TIC TIC TIC TIC . . .*

Tally looked up and saw the stars sitting among the branches. They were falling, the darkness taking over the sky. Inside it something was hiding no longer. It came for her. Tally knew that without her sisters, it would catch her. They had to run, had to warn, had to get away from the sound that was changing, not clocklike any longer, becoming a shrieking, tearing sound like a giant Grinder.

Tally's sisters dragged her faster than she could go. She lost her footing and was pulled along like a kite. Behind them, the noise became louder, gigantic, devouring the world. Suddenly her sisters flew off in two different directions. Their hands came off. Tally fell to earth and tumbled, still holding fast to the hands. She stopped with a jolt against one of the massive tree trunks. The hands came to rest in her lap, palms up, as if in supplication.

The grinding sound passed directly overhead. Tally looked up and saw what was making it.

When Tally woke she instinctively reached for Andrei, but he was still working in his office. She shoved a rasta-link into the jack near her bed.

<ANDREI! EMERGENCY! ANDREI, IT'S TALLY, EMERGENCY!>

But she couldn't get through to him instantly that way. She was being shunted through Emily's office first, there would be a delay of a few minutes. She leaped out of bed and sprinted to her office, where her com was.

She switched it to audio, sound on full blast. "Andrei!" She yelled, "It's Tally! Emergency! Andrei!"

After she had shouted for half a minute, she got an answer. "I'm here—"

"The derelicts are moving!" She had to make herself slow down to get the words out coherently. "Warn the miners, warn Jones!"

"Stand by," he said.

Tally did. But she slipped her rasta-links into surveillance of the system and got the best view of Luci fer that she could, through a drone. She also linked into the emergency broadcast system and space-to-surface communications. A babble of voices filled her head. What she heard made her heart pound.

<Alert, alert—>

<—are moving, something strange is—>

<Jones, red alert, something's up with the derelicts!>

<Commander Hilmi here, Mining Station Beta, we have movement from the derelicts, patching in visual . . .>

Tally saw the thing from her dreams, and screamed.

The derelicts were moving, leaving orbit and coming together to form one machine. Instantly Tally knew what it was for.

<Andrei, tell *Hurricane* to fire now, before it completes itself! They've got to hit the separate parts with everything they've got!>

Andrei passed on the order. *Hurricane* was the only chance they had, most of their military hardware from the last war was gone. Military ESAs could only watch helplessly, like Tally, as the lone ship rallied to defend the mining stations.

<Targeted, ready to fire.>

Tally clenched her fists. The derelicts had become just like the clockworks they had always reminded her of, with so many moving parts she could not tell where one began and another ended. But there was a flow to the movement, an order. The thing was metamorphosing into something huge and flowerlike, its center moving at a different pace and in a different direction than its outer edges.

<Deploying slammers.>

*Hurry,* pleaded Tally, a sinking feeling in the pit of her stomach.

And then the thing was gone. A wave of disruption passed harmlessly through the spot where it had occupied space.

<It tunneled, it has a star drive.>

<Where is it?>

Suddenly Tally was looking at a four-way image of the orbital stations. Then Alpha Station filled her sight. The thing hovered over it, big enough to swallow it.

<It's right on top of us, one thousand yards and—>

<Yesus Christos!>

The machine struck the station broadside, tearing and shredding the hull like a buzz saw, a wood chipper.

*Eating* it. Blowing the debris out its other side.

Communications from the station fractured, Tally could no longer make out whole words. The effect was terrifying. She watched helplessly as the hull was breached and explosive decompression began. But the Grinder didn't stop there. It continued to devour the station, all the metal and flesh together.

<Is anyone close enough to fire at the damned thing?> demanded Andrei.

*Hurricane* emerged from jump, moving once more to deploy its slammers.

But Tally knew it was too late. She wept with frustration as *Hurricane* hit the Grinder with everything they had. Some debris peeled off the edges of the thing, but its grinding motion did not pause. It went through Alpha Station, sucking in the last sections and blowing them out its other side in tiny bits.

Then it turned on Andrei's last warship.

<*HURRICANE,* GET OUT OF THERE!> Andrei commanded.

<Something's got us. We can't jump, our systems are burning up.>

Tally wished she could stop seeing. But she refused to disengage. She watched as *Hurricane* was drawn into the maw of the Grinder.

<Engaging auto-destruct,> said Captain Dolinski. <We'll try to blow a hole in the damned thing. Good luck, Jones, see you in hell.>

*Hurricane* swelled into a ball of blue light. Tally held her breath. And then the Grinder jumped again, leaving the light to fade in empty space.

<We have no weapons . . .> Commander Hilmi said.

The Grinder dropped out of warp, a dreadful flower blooming over Beta. It closed on the station like a shark after a wounded seal.

<Allah is merciful,> said Hilmi.

And then the Grinder tore into him. It ate its way toward the center of the station. When it got there, a sun blossomed in its mouth.

<Hilmi blew the jump engines!>

The Grinder's maw began to wind down. Bits spun away from it. And then larger parts began to separate, but these were not shrapnel. Tally already knew what they would become. There would be four of them, possibly smaller than they had been before, but somehow essentially the same.

<It's dead. Hilmi stopped it.>

<We've got trouble,> Jones said. <Archangel Station is losing hull integrity. Stand by . . .>

Tally suddenly lost the image of the derelicts. Archangel Station appeared in its place, a view that included Belarus. But both were tactical images, and arrows pointed to spots on the grid. A cloud of dots was converging on Archangel Station. Several others descended into Belarus's gravity well.

They were burning into Archangel's hull faster than spores could have done it, and they didn't need slammers to weaken the alloy first.

<Grigory,> demanded Andrei, <are those the BUG SPRAY machines?>

<No. Those are still orbiting. These are something different. These are the weapons John tried to take credit for, the "chiggers.">

<Where the hell are they coming from?>

<They're tunneling,> ESA Admiral Jorge broke in. <Just like sprites. They could be coming from anywhere.>

*Anywhere,* thought Tally as darkness began to fill her mind. But it wasn't just anywhere, it was one place, the place they had always lurked, the place from which they had been wreaking havoc since the sprites had first arrived at Lucifer seventeen years before.

<The Veil,> she said. <They've been hiding in the dark . . .>

The chiggers attacked the surface of Archangel Station, burning, flaying, slowly eating their way inside. Millions more poured out of jump tunnels like gnats swarming from a swamp. They attacked technology, the automated systems that Belarus had managed to salvage and rebuild, the machinery that separated Andrei's fragile colony from the stone age. Though crafted by aliens, their priorities were exactly like those of humans in a war. Tally remembered something Tam had said to a stuffed shirt in the Hermitage, years ago:

*Both sides try to take out all the automated systems. Sometimes that's all it takes to decide the winner. Who still has machines that work?*

*And what will they do to us,* wondered Tally, *when we no longer have ours?*

The chiggers sought and destroyed technology. But alloys and chemicals were not their only targets. Soon a second priority was discovered.

The destruction of flesh.

<I'm getting reports of civilian casualties,> warned Jorge.

<The sprites!> Grigory broke in, and the grid in Tally's mind was invaded by another swarm of dots.

* * *

Sprites closed with chiggers. There was very little left of the minds they had once possessed, but one basic piece of programming still survived: the compulsion to protect. Sprites were still able to understand the defensive goal, and they had a simple plan for carrying it out. Locate each chigger, attach to it, activate its automatic systems.

Die with it.

On the streets of St. Petersburg, people were stirring for the day. In the hours just before dawn, only the night shift moved on the streets, people who ran systems that worked twenty-five hours a day. But when the sun began to throw light over the horizon the city woke and began to prepare itself for the new day.

Peddlers in the farmers' market were just laying their goods out when the alarm sirens began to sound. It rang through the streets, freezing everyone in their tracks. "The shelters!" officers cried. "Get to the shelters!"

No one had expected another war. But no one was surprised to get one. People ran for the shelters, leaving only officers and a newly roused force of state troopers in the open. These watched the sky, sick to their stomachs with anticipation.

Irina Khariton pushed her cart of books out of the elevator and onto the fifth floor of the St. Petersburg public library. She passed other shelvers in the hallway, some yawning and bleary-eyed. But she liked the early-morning shift, and she had two cups of coffee inside her. She pushed the cart past one of the large picture windows overlooking the public gardens. Glancing out, she saw the first flashes in the skies.

Irina stopped. A moment later, she heard the sirens and knew that fate had finally caught up with her. She was not afraid. She stayed where she was and looked out the window as the rest of the people in the hall raced for the doors to the bomb shelters in the basement.

Irina loved the library, she would die with it. She worked there as an assistant and was studying to get her degree in library science. Every night when Marta chided herself for luring Irina to Belarus just in time for her to be stranded by another war, she told her, "You were right, Marta. I am better off here. I miss my family yes, but they would be no better off with me where I used to be. I'm happy, don't be sorry!"

The two of them shared a two-bedroom apartment; they had more space than either had ever dreamed of. But when the big war came and they lived through it without a scratch, Irina became suspicious. *Something* bad should have happened. No one had such good luck. Bad luck must be waiting down the road.

And here it was. She gazed out the window and saw the flashes begin. They were small at first, like fairy lights. But then it began to look as if the entire sky would ignite.

*What are they doing?* she wondered. *Burning up the oxygen? Will they never cease to think up terrible weapons?*

But she could still breathe. She smelled ink and dust, leather and paper. It was the smell of civilization and she would not give it up.

*Come*, she told the fires. *I won't leave this place. It is where I belong.*

<This is Commander Jones, all personnel evacuate outer ring! Hull breach imminent!>

Tally thought about the bodies in the burned-out cars, Andrei's dead Cossack guard, and the machinery that had been mysteriously fried over the years. The chiggers didn't do exactly what John had said they did, but it was close enough. No defensive system could stop them—except maybe the sprites. But it was going to be a toss-up to see who ran out of tiny machines first.

Krasna Kopecky saw a man fried to a cinder before her very eyes. It happened so fast she felt like she was watching a movie with special effects. But she felt the heat from his combustion, and that was real. She threw herself to the pavement and prayed.

*Please, God, I'm only fourteen, I don't want to die!*

Something zoomed right over her, singeing her coat. Krasna cried out, then went back to her praying.

Suddenly the world was full of flashing lights. She saw them even through her closed lids, they filled her skull. She stopped shivering, and suddenly she was not afraid.

She opened her eyes. A few of the golden lights still lingered. They were as tiny as fireflies. One flew close to her, as if concerned for her welfare. She got a good look at it.

*Sprite. That's a sprite. Those things whatziznаme is always preaching against on the news. And they just saved my life.*

"Thank you," Krasna whispered to the tiny machine. It whirled in a few cheerful loops, and then flew away.

Irina watched the flashes spread across the sky like a magnificent fireworks display at the very end, when they set them all off at once. Then the flashes diminished. Finally she saw only a few errant sparks, and then the sky was blue.

The birds began to sing again. Then she remembered they were rodents.

But that was better than nothing.

It was very odd listening to a simple audio transmission from orbit.

"We got a signal," said Jones. "Some of Beta's miners were in their rigs when the station was destroyed. They're too far away to get back to us safely, and they can't survive for more than a few weeks on their own. They sent messages for their families."

"Understood," said Andrei.

"Archangel is still alive, but barely. We can maintain stable orbit for now, but we may lose life systems. Those damned chiggers ate through some critical systems. I don't know if we can repair enough of it to keep ourselves going."

Andrei's orbital mining operations were dead. *Hurricane* was gone, *Halcyon* had been severely damaged by chiggers. All that remained of their space technology was Archangel Station. And they had no way to get to it. Their remaining sprites had sacrificed themselves. Only a few survived, and they were tiny, crippled things.

On Belarus many of the communications relays were still working, ESAs and other enhanced individuals could still use it to talk, to see in tactical—but it wasn't as reliable. Worst of all, they had lost most of their heavy industry. It would take the colonists of Belarus a century just to get started back on the path to their lofty origins. And that would be too late to help the people on Archangel.

"I know what you're thinking," said Jones. "It's tough luck for us, Andrei. But it could have been a hell of a lot worse. We're spacers up here, it's where we belong. Understand?"

"I think so." Andrei wished he could see Jones's face. "You've sacrificed too much for me, old friend. I won't forget."

"I know you won't," said Jones. "And I'll keep you posted. We're not dead yet."

Not yet, Andrei agreed. But it was certainly time to start making out the will.

No dancing without music. —Russian proverb

John smelled perfume, and his heart began to slam in his chest. He sat perfectly still. He heard nothing, but the scent came closer, until she must be standing opposite him, right outside his cell.

"You know who I am," said Katerina.

"I do now." John turned his head so she could see his ruined eyes.

She was silent. Probably terrified, the stupid slut. He had entertained himself for the endless, unknowable time he had been locked up with fantasies of things he had done, or could have done, and she had been a recurring character. But apparently it was for the best he had never touched her. She was bringing possibility back into his life.

"What do you want?" he asked, as if he were some blind prophet and she a penitent asking for his visions.

"I have one question," said Katerina.

"I don't answer questions." He didn't like her tone, never had. She was imperious as only a stupid cow could be. She had a rich husband, so she elected herself tsarina.

"I think you will answer mine," she said, and for one burning moment he almost flung himself at the bars. If he moved fast enough, he could grab her throat. But that would get him nowhere. John was desperately sick of nowhere.

"Tit for tat," he said calmly. "You have a question, and so do I."

"Ask what you will," she said, like a queen granting favors.

John knew then that he must find a way to hurt her.

"How long have I been here?" he asked.

"Almost five years."

Only five. In all that time, no one but lawyers and interrogators spoke to him. The man who brought his meals was deaf, and could not hear his questions. John never left his ten-by-fifteen cell. The only thing he had to break the monotony was audio books, which he could request through a terminal on the wall.

"Five years I've been waiting in the dark," he said. "With no trial, no hearing."

"You are guilty," said Katerina.

"You're really annoying me. I have another question. Has Andrei gotten Tally pregnant yet?"

"I don't know," she said with no trace of anger, or even curiosity. "Other matters concern me."

Despite himself, he was getting curious. "Like what?" he asked.

"I have heard that the Enemies will not parlay with us. It is not their custom. They do not wish for peace and they have no diplomats."

John kept silent. If she wanted information about the Enemies, he was definitely going to screw her around. That was his ace in the hole, he wouldn't give it up.

"I have also heard," she continued, "that they will talk with us on only one condition. We must offer a sacrifice."

John tensed. Was she suggesting *he* should be the lamb offered for slaughter?

"I wish to be that sacrifice," she said.

That was the last thing in the universe he would

have expected from Katerina. He was astounded. But it did not take long for possibilities to occur to him.

"Very noble of you," he said. "How will you accomplish that if you can't find them?"

"You know where they are."

"Maybe. But I wouldn't tell you."

"You needn't reveal their location," she said, her voice so calm it spooked him. "I have another idea. For years, they have kidnapped my people. Tell me where I might go to be kidnapped."

He considered her proposal. It was surprisingly intelligent. The fact was, he could tell her what she wanted to know without giving away the location of the aliens. And even better, he could do to her what he had always wanted to do. True, someone else's hands would enjoy the work, but just the knowledge that he had set the machinery in motion was enough to feed his starved soul.

Magnificent.

"You can make your offering the same place I did," he said, and waited for her to figure out where that was. After all, the clues he had left were so blatant.

But she was silent, waiting for him to finish. He sighed.

"The cavern of the dead dancers," he said. "Wait there. They'll come for you after dark."

He waited for her to thank him. The perfume evaporated, leaving him alone. He gritted his teeth, willing himself to say nothing, do nothing.

She might do it. She might chicken out. But one way or another, he had planted the seeds that could lead to her undoing. Now all he had to do was wait.

Which was what he had been doing anyway.

*I've been waiting . . .*

Katerina had scarcely been able to contain her astonishment when the monster uttered that phrase. It was her own experience, waiting in the dark, and this foul creature was showing her the way out of it. The sign was unmistakable. If she had ever doubted her decision, that doubt was gone.

She cut off her hair, dressed in sack cloth she had prepared herself, and took the shoes from her feet. She would go humbly to God, she had no more need of finery. As a child she had walked barefoot in a world of wondrous light. It was fitting she should go thusly to her death.

She moved easily through the escape routes. She knew them well, Andrei had made sure of that. She knew how to drive, as well. No one tried to stop her, no one looked for her to escape from her own home. Their eyes were turned toward Enemies. Katerina's eyes were turned toward God.

Yet she glimpsed herself in the rearview mirror. With her hair short and curling around her head, she looked like Peter. Her heart ached when she thought of him.

*For you, my son*, she promised, and that strengthened her resolve.

She moved past convoys on the road, refugees coming in, fighting men and women going out. Katerina went with the flow of the traffic, but she was alone by the time she pulled onto the highway that would take her past the caverns. A long drive, but she didn't mind. Soon it would be over.

No more waiting in the dark.

Katerina went to the cavern of the dead dancers.

She carried nothing but a flashlight, and at first she feared she might get lost. Then she saw the crime scene tape.

Katerina could not help imagining the dreadful tableau that had greeted the investigators. But her ability to think about the matter stopped there. She could not conceive of the mind that had committed such acts, let alone the acts themselves.

"I am here," she said humbly. "I am the offering."

No one answered her. She aimed the pool of light upward, illuminating her face in a cone of brightness.

She waited in the cold, in her sack cloth, her feet numb. She prayed, but the verses echoed in her mind as if someone else spoke them. Worry began to creep into her thoughts, spoiling the litany. What if she was not a worthy offering? What if God did not find humility in her heart? She shone the light once more around the cavern. Shadows scattered and danced. But some were not shadows at all. She shone the light on them again, and they grinned at her, their teeth gleaming.

Katerina froze, transfixed with wonder at the graceful movements of the predators who came to claim her. They were beautiful, like angels. Katerina was blessed. When they seized her, their fingers bruised her skin, but this was to be expected. There would be pain. The path to heaven was difficult.

Their smiles were dreadful. They were like domovoy in their secret, underground world. Such beauty was not for human eyes. Katerina would have crossed herself had she been free to do so.

She was spirited through passages that sparkled with strange lights, through chambers decorated with magnificent items, peopled by beautiful creatures in clothing so fine it put Katerina's best wardrobe to shame. She was not surprised that her mind could not fully grasp the subtlety of their work. She was pleased to wear sack cloth at her final hour. She stumbled as she was dragged forward, but was hauled to her feet without regard for her ability to keep up. In a small corner of her mind, the Katerina who used to be was saddened. Such creatures were incapable of compassion. Beauty was empty without it.

"You are damned creatures," she told them. "But we have sinned, or you would not be a scourge upon our world."

"Do you understand what is going to happen to you?" one of her escorts asked in flawless Russian.

"I understand," she assured him.

"None of the others did. Why should you be different?"

"I have God to light my way."

"We heard you talking to him. Many of the others spoke the same way. They cried for him, but he did not come."

"He is here already," said Katerina.

That did not please them. They stopped grinning at her. They pulled her along until she felt bruised and sore. Her prayers became meaningful to her again.

They walked for miles. At times, Katerina was dragged along. She found her feet when she could, but always lost them again. She never uttered a complaint and she did not wish for an end to the pain. It would come. Through miles of tunnels and fantastical chambers she was dragged, until they pulled her upright to look into the face of their tsar.

His beauty awed her. "How odd," she said.

His green eyes fed on her like locusts on an ear of corn. *"Odd,"* he said. "I know the feeling. What a strange little face I see before me. I have never seen its like." He touched her with long, perfect fingers, turning her head this way and that. "I think I'll keep it. I shall place it where I can gaze upon it."

"I don't care what you do with it," said Katya. "I won't need it anymore."

He did not frown as a human would have done. He did not blink. He was a devil, with no human feeling.

"You are not afraid," he said. "All of the others were. Why are you different?"

"I am their tsarina," she said. "It is my duty to stand for them. I have seen what God intends for me, and I am glad."

"I don't think so," he said. "You won't be glad, no one is glad. Not even I shall be."

"You will not be glad because your spirit is not bound for heaven," she said.

"You will change you mind when you feel the pain," he said.

"I will not," said Katerina. She was glad she could confront him on her feet. "You have burned my people and made martyrs of them. I will suffer, I can do no less. And you will face God's judgment though you don't know Him."

The dark centers of his eyes expanded, reminding Katya of the images of the Grinder with its devouring center. "You are wrong," he said. "I shall prove that. You don't know it yet, but I will teach you." He stood. "Come." And he walked away.

Katya was dragged behind him. She did not protest or disagree. She knew she would not change her mind.

She did not change it even when she saw the chamber of torture. Her eyes moved over its devices, all gleaming and perfectly polished. They surpassed her imagination—she did not try to grasp their design any more than she had tried to understand the art or beauty of these alien creatures. They would hurt her. She would scream, but she would not cry.

He looked again at her face. "Yes, I can preserve it," he said. "The rest does not matter."

"None of it matters," she corrected him.

She wasn't sure why, but he seemed surprised. "We begin," he said.

<Clan leader.>

Andrei dropped the chess piece, startled.

"Papa!" Peter stared at him, wide-eyed. "What's wrong?"

"Someone's forcing a message through," said Andrei. The message had circumvented his security force. He shouldn't answer it. But he did anyway.

<I'm here.>

<She did not last, your gift.>

Andrei's stomach clenched tighter than a fist. Peter watched him, white-faced.

<I sent you no gift, Enemy. I told you I would not.>

<Not true. I'll show you.>

And the image filled Andrei's mind. He had no power to shut it out. He saw Katya standing in the cavern of the dead dancers, barefoot, her hair shorn, wearing nothing but sack cloth. "I am here," she said. "I am the offering."

"No," said Andrei.

And then he saw her bound. He watched as they began to remove her skin.

<She lived less than an hour,> came the message, cutting the images short. <Some of the other subjects

we took lasted several days. There was one who lasted two weeks, and he was not even fully grown. Send me one like him, and we will meet face-to-face. As it is, I will grant you this conversation. Ask me what you will.>

Andrei saw his own rooms again, and Peter's frightened face. Peter had pulled his com out of his collar and was talking into it. Andrei's heart raced in his chest as if he had just run five miles. But only one question occurred to him.

<Where shall I send the next gift?>

There was a delay in the answer, and Andrei held his breath. But then he had an answer.

<To the same place you sent the last one. Send a better one this time. One who lasts.>

<I will,> promised Andrei, and felt the contact end.

Grigory and Emily had joined Peter. He saw Natalia coming in the door. He heard their questions, but could make little sense of them at the moment. He knew that Peter must learn about his mother's fate. He would attend to all of that. But at the moment, he wanted only one thing: a face-to-face meeting with his Enemy.

That was the only way he would ever get his hands on him.

*Andrei,*

*The monster told me where I must go to offer myself as sacrifice to these Enemies who are killing our people. This is the cavern of the dead dancers. That is the point at which you should begin your search for them.*

*I pray that I shall have helped you. I have no fear to go with God. Please see that Peter continues to make proper observance of his lessons and his prayers.*

*—Katerina*

"Those are the details we know," Emily said.

Tally had the earpiece plugged firmly into her right ear, so only she could hear Emily's briefing. She looked through the open door of her office into the living room, where Peter sat wringing his hands. Tally wasn't crying yet, but she knew she would soon. She had to stay calm long enough to tell him.

"Do you want me to come over and help?" Emily said, her own voice ragged.

"No," said Tally. "You have enough on your shoulders. I'll handle it."

"Call me if you need me," said Emily, and signed off.

Tally went to the door. Peter looked up and saw her. He jumped to his feet.

"Tally, what's wrong? Papa won't tell me what's wrong!"

Tally went to him and put her hands on his shoulders.

"Your *face*," he whispered. "I have never seen you this way. Tally, it is something terrible."

"Baby," Tally said, as clearly as she could, "your mama is dead."

"No," he said, as if she were mistaken. "That's impossible."

"It's true, Peter. She was killed by the Enemies, in the war."

"We have bodyguards," he insisted. "No one can get close enough to hurt us."

"Peter." Tally squeezed his shoulders gently. "You mother went to them deliberately. She offered herself. She was trying to help us."

"No." But this time he believed her. His face was beginning to crumple, his shoulders to tremble. "Not her, Tally. She's my angel."

"I'm sorry, baby." Tally felt tears forming. "Your papa is too hurt to say it."

"But she's my angel," Peter said, as if he hadn't heard her. His eyes were going blank with shock. Tally hugged him tight.

"Stay with me," she said. "Peter, do you hear me? You've got to stay with me."

He shook like a leaf. He gasped as if he were drowning, and Tally's shoulder grew wet with his tears. The sound tore at her heart. She held him tight and wept with him. It was all they could do.

*This would have happened no matter what we did. We could have fled to Canopus, and still this would have happened. We've been in a trap all this time, and it finally closed on us.*

They wept until they were almost too weary to stand. Tally patted his shoulder and ruffled his hair. "She's my angel," he said again, but the idea seemed new to him. Then Tally realized what he must mean.

Katerina really was his angel now, because she was in heaven.

After many hours, Peter fell asleep out of sheer exhaustion. Tally tucked a blanket around him.

He was becoming a man, but she could still see the small child he used to be. She remembered a night years before, when Peter was only six years old. He had stayed for a sleep-over, and the two of them had camped out on the couch and watched a succession of ancient movies. They ate popcorn until their bellies were bulging and they giggled at the wonderful naiveté of those early times. But they were also filled with wonder at echoes from the past, the images that were both familiar and strange.

Peter had fallen asleep in the middle of a Russian movie, a fantasy called *Sadko*. It was corny when measured with modern sensibilities, but Tally found it charming. She was fascinated by the fact that such a fanciful movie could have been made during the Communist regime in the early twentieth century. She watched it into the wee hours, dozed, and then awoke to a scene of astonishing beauty.

"Take us to the Bird of Happiness!" the hero, Sadko, demanded of the sultan after defeating his champions. So Sadko and his men were escorted into a dimly lit chamber. A giant bird sat on a perch, her wings tucked around her head. Sadko lifted his lantern, illuminating her. She stirred and raised her head, peeking out from behind her feathers. Tally gasped when she saw the Bird of Happiness bore the head of a woman.

She was like one of George's harpies brought to life. But someone dreamed her a thousand years before George did. Some of the other effects of the movie were clumsy, but not this bird woman. She looked real. Something about her large, Byzantine eyes was familiar.

The Bird of Happiness let her wings fall away from the rest of her face. She was astonishingly beautiful. She began to speak to Sadko and his men in soothing tones. "Lay down the cares of this world, forget your pain," she urged them. "Sleep. Sleep . . ."

Tally almost woke Peter then, so he could see the bird lady, but suddenly she realized why the Bird of Happiness had such haunting eyes.

They were just like Katerina's eyes.

Peter, six years old and already troubled by his complicated life, slept in his nest of pillows with his head against her breast. He looked so happy. If he saw the Bird of Happiness, he might see the same resemblance Tally had. It would remind him that his beloved mother was as remote from him as a bird locked in a tower.

So Tally didn't wake him. She preserved his happiness a little longer. She gazed at him in the long hours before dawn, feeling as if the moment would last forever.

But it couldn't. The Bird of Happiness would haunt him forever, because she was never real to begin with.

*Sleep*, Tally urged Peter. *Forget, at least for a little while.*

His face was troubled, but his breathing sounded even and his color was better. Tally rubbed her own face, knowing that sleep would not come to her for a long time. She moved quietly away, back into her office. She had no notion what she was seeking when she went in there, but by the time she was behind her desk she had a plan.

She slid her links into the system.

Crippled though it was, it had worked for the Enemy tsar. If he could talk to Andrei, then someone else could talk to him. She sorted through her options.

The answer was so simple it made her ill. They could have found the Enemies this way years ago. She needed to place a call, but didn't know the code. Yet he must be in the system. So she simply eliminated everyone else on Belarus and instructed the system to place her call to whoever was left.

<Motherfucker, I know you can hear me. Answer me.>

<I can hear you,> the answer came instantly. <I can see you too.>

Tally's mouth went dry. Had the Enemies been observing them since the beginning? If he could see her, maybe he could see Andrei and his staff as well. She would have to warn Grigory about that.

<That word you called me, *motherfucker*. I perceive it to be an insult. Is this so?>

<I don't bother with insults,> said Tally. <In this case, you can consider it a prod.>

<I know you. You visited me once. How did you find me?>

<A dead woman guided me.>

He didn't answer. Tally wondered if she had lost him, making such an obscure reference. His kind probably didn't believe in spirits, otherwise they might feel haunted by their victims. She waited, wondering how she might goad him into speaking again. Her rastalinks stirred restlessly.

<Those data links you have in your head,> said the Enemy tsar, <are fascinating. I have never seen them employed in such a fashion, right into the brain. At least, not as a communications device. Unless one wants to think of the conveyance of pain as communications.>

<What a dreadful mistake you've made,> said Tally.

<I perceive no mistake.>

<You fight with us because that's what you do with your own kind, what your instincts tell you to do. But instincts should not rule intellect. You could have gained so much by keeping peace with us.>

<I wonder, do you consider this a meeting?>

<You'll get no promises from me. We're going to fight a war, Enemy, I'm not afraid of you.>

<You fascinate me. Your data links inspire thoughts of innovative communications. The great sadness in life is that all pleasure and pain must ultimately end, because flesh is weak. But all pleasure and pain begin and end in the brain. Your links could be used to stimulate you to indescribable heights of perception.>

<Don't threaten me.>

<You seem so eager to talk, to make me understand your point of view. I offer a proposal.>

Tally was afraid to answer.

<If you will consent to be the gift, I will take you for three of your weeks. I will find to what heights and depths you can be driven, and then I will return you physically unharmed. You have my word as a clan leader.>

<You still don't understand,> said Tally.

This time he was the one who did not answer.

<You have crossed a line,> she said, <and now you must die. No matter what happens to the rest of us, you are doomed to that fate. If you want to save the rest of your people, you still have a chance. But you're not calling any shots here.>

<That sounds like a Challenge.>

<It's a prediction. I can see the hour ahead, Enemy, that's how I found you in your lair. It wasn't my body that visited you, and I didn't use a device. My spirit found you and I see your fate.>

<If that is the case, there is no need to talk with me. You may simply sit back and enjoy it.>

<I enjoy nothing about it. I warn you. Heed me.>

<I don't heed my own Witness, but I admire her grace, just as I admire yours. Perhaps my offer was unwise, I might be tempted to know you with my hands if you were in my grasp. And with my palate. You must be a rare dish.>

<You could open negotiations even now, you could save the lives of your own kind.>

<They don't need me to save them. I don't need to speak to your clan leader face-to-face.>

<Are you afraid?> challenged Tally.

<Never.>

<But you know the emotion.>

<I have seen it in your kind.>

Tally held her head high. <I don't believe that you don't feel fear. Any living creature must, it is a survival trait.>

<There is so much I could teach you. Consider my

proposal. Perhaps I will change my mind about a meeting.>

<Your time is running out.>

<Good night, beautiful engineer.>

Tally did not move for several moments. Then she left the office and crept to Peter's side again. She watched him just long enough to make sure he was sleeping peacefully. Then she went to Thoth's door and let herself out into the hall. Once there, she placed a call through her portable com.

"Grigory, where are you?"

"Andrei's office," he answered.

"We need to talk someplace that isn't bugged," she said.

There was a long silence. Then Grigory answered her. "Meet Andrei and me at the door to my quarters."

Tally looked around Grigory's front room and was a little disappointed. He had no personal effects at all. His rooms seemed even more utilitarian than Emily's did. Then she remembered he was blind and felt like a fool. She took a deep breath and smelled the subtle fragrance of spices and aromatic woods.

Grigory led them into his office and closed the door. "I confess I'm taking a calculated risk," he said at a normal volume. "But my office is probably the most secure in the palace."

"I agree," Andrei said. Tally was startled to see more lines around his eyes than she had ever noticed before, and strands of grey at his temples.

Grigory turned toward Tally. "What has happened?" he asked her.

She swallowed. "I called that bastard that killed Katya."

"You *called* him?!" demanded Andrei.

"I eliminated all known codes in the system and told it to call anyone who was left. He's got a site. Even if he eliminates it, as long as he keeps calling us, we can find him the same way."

Andrei still frowned. "You're afraid he can spy on us in here?"

"He said he could see me. He described me. He was interested in my rasta-links, said he could torture me without putting a scratch on me."

"What else did he say?" Grigory spoke before Andrei could.

Tally thought back. "He's not interested in peace. Either he thinks we can't beat him, or he doesn't care if his people all die. I suspect the former. He said if I become the gift, he'll consider talking to Andrei. I told him no."

"Why did you call him, Natalia?" Andrei asked softly. He wasn't angry anymore. He looked impossibly tired.

"I wanted to call him *motherfucker* to his face."

"Ah," said Andrei. "I understand." His tone softened. "How is Peter?"

"Crushed." Tally's voice broke, and she cleared her throat. "Sleeping peacefully for now. For what it's worth, I think that at least he knows—he's loved."

Grigory looked more preoccupied than Tally had ever seen him. "Your bugs will be gone within the hour," he said. "This I pledge. Andrei and I are discussing a few theories. You said the right thing, Tally."

"Thanks," she said, almost losing her voice again. "I won't keep you any longer. I'm going to pull up a chair next to Peter. If I can't sleep, at least I can look at him. That'll help a lot."

"Sleep well," said Andrei.

Her eyes stung, then overflowed. "I'm so sorry," she said. "I wanted to tell you so."

"I know. Now you can ease my worries by watching over Peter and resting yourself."

"I'll do my best," she said. "Good night."

She was escorted out the door, which then closed with a puff of wood-scented air behind her.

Tally went back to Thoth's door and let herself in.

She knew the Enemy tsar might be watching her. She didn't care. She only wanted to be with Peter.

She pulled up a chair next to him and dragged a knitted throw over her legs. She gazed at his sleeping face the same way she had years before. Once again she found herself in the hours just before dawn. They still seemed like they might last forever.

They still couldn't

*"You recall the riddle I told you?"*

Andrei remembered it. *"What do booby traps and six-eyed mammals have in common?"*

*"Engineers,"* she said. *"That's what they have in common. And that's your ace in the hole, Andrei. When you face your darkest day, remember the engineer."*

Tally was an engineer. And the Enemy tsar wanted her. She might be the one Baba Yaga had meant.

But John was an engineer as well. Andrei need not sacrifice his queen.

"Come on," he told Grigory. "Let's go buy some Bug Spray."

"John," said Andrei.

John twitched, then instantly controlled himself. It was possibly the most difficult thing he had ever done in his life, but he managed. This was his moment of truth, he couldn't drop the ball now.

"Who's there?" he asked.

"You know who."

John fought to keep his voice steady. "I'm in a vulnerable position," he said. "So I'll wait to hear your terms."

"No terms," said Andrei. "Just questions."

John was not as inclined to be flip with Andrei as he had been with previous interrogators. "As I said—I'm in a vulnerable position."

"Your position doesn't concern me. Your work history does. We have suffered certain crippling attacks. I wonder which of them you engineered."

"I did more to defend this world than I did to harm it," said John, feeling a twinge of sore pride.

"Did you engineer WILDFIRE?"

"Well, yes, of course. But I didn't do it for fun. The sprites had to be curtailed somehow, they had an agenda. Machines should never have an agenda."

"Is there a cure?" demanded Andrei.

And here it was. After so many years of silence, in the dark, they were coming to *him*.

"There are some things you should know," said John. "First of all, you cannot torture me. I am modified. You can ask Emily about that, she has my medical history."

"I've heard about it," said Andrei. John thought he sounded intrigued.

"My modifications are very specialized. When I wasn't accepted as an ESA, my parents decided to remake me themselves. They hired some very talented bioengineers. You will *not* force any information out of me—but I will consider selling it to you."

"State your terms," snapped Andrei.

John didn't like the tone, but the content pleased him. "My demands are simple. I wish to have my eyes replaced. It will be almost impossible for me to survive without them, because I would like you to move me to one of the islands in the south. A small one will do, I can suggest a few. I will accept exile from your continent in exchange for my freedom and a few simple supplies."

"And what will you give for them?" asked Andrei.

"The cure to WILDFIRE. The code to some of the weapons in my arsenal that were never deployed. And the location of your Enemies, along with suggestions about how to kill them."

Andrei was silent for several moments. John could imagine the frustration he must be experiencing, and he tried not to feel too good about it. After all, the deal wasn't signed yet.

"You want to strike a bargain," Andrei said at last.

"No bargains," John said quickly. "You have my terms."

"I think perhaps we have had a cultural misunderstanding," said Andrei. "I am Russian, I am accustomed to a certain amount of haggling. I always feel compelled to get the best price."

"I'm not Russian," said John.

"No. You are the prisoner of a Russian."

John didn't like the controlled, confident tone he was hearing. This was not the way he had imagined this meeting would ultimately go.

"Right," he said. "But I can't imagine there's any way I can change my terms."

"You don't have to change them," said Andrei. "Perhaps we can discuss the timing."

"Timing," John repeated dully.

"We need the information you have, there is no doubt about it. But there is a matter of bad faith between us. I hired you to defend my people, not attack them."

John was wise enough not to express his opinion about the loss of a few bitches.

"You have spied on me and invaded my privacy." The cool voice teased his nerves. "And of course, you gave my wife information that led to her death."

John clenched his teeth, bracing himself for an attack.

"I think I shall need proof of your good faith," said Andrei. "But I won't ask you to give me all your aces. You mentioned certain weapons. I will accept one. I will test it, and if it works, we will consider your terms."

"No." Despite his best efforts, John's voice shook. "I'm not going to dole weapons out to you one by one. Not without some sort of reciprocity."

"You want reciprocity?" said Andrei. "Here it is. Give me one code. I am a man of honor, I will consider granting your requests in exchange for the vital information you hold. In exchange for the code, I promise not to kill you with my bare hands."

John's heart sank. To his horror, he was close to tears.

"Understand me," Andrei said, and this time John did not fail to hear the iron behind his soft voice. "You sent my wife to her death. I do not trust you.

Give me a code. Prove it to me. If the weapon is useful enough, I will consider your request for exile."

John knew he was screwed. Yet he couldn't help hoping that it might still work out. "I can give you one," he said. "It's called BUG SPRAY. You'll find it very useful right now."

"That remains to be seen," said Andrei.

It irked John more than he liked to admit when people doubted his abilities. He gave Andrei the code. "I'll wait to hear from you," he said. "It shouldn't take long."

There was no answer. Andrei was gone.

John knew he had just been outmaneuvered.

"Secrets, Mironenko," said Grigory.

He and Andrei stood alone on a plain below the Urals, near the entrance to the Gem Caverns. It was just before dawn. Andrei adjusted his new suit against the morning chill.

"From me?" he asked softly. "Or from you?"

"I will tell a few." Grigory's face was turned toward the east, where the sun would rise in minutes. "First: you are not my patron."

"I think I always knew that," Andrei said. The first rays of morning were beginning to lighten the sky. Andrei watched the Veil fade in the brightening air. "So," he asked. "Who *is* your patron?"

"That you will have to learn from God," said Grigory.

"Another item to add to a long list," said Andrei. He stared hard at the blind man's face. Grigory's eyes glowed red as the sun peeked over the curve of the earth.

"It's time," said Grigory.

"If I don't see you again—" Andrei said.

"I think you will. Then we'll see if there are any more secrets to learn."

Grigory turned without another word and climbed toward the entrance of the caverns.

Grigory smelled death in the cave, but it was old. It belonged to those innocent dancers who could never be avenged. He stood in their circle, feeling them around him. He promised them justice, if he could find it.

Soon a new smell teased him. He remembered it from the farmer's field. Then he had also smelled them before any of his mechanical systems could warn him.

"I am the gift," he called.

They approached him warily. And well they should. He knew where every one of them was.

"You are blind," said one.

"I manage very well without my eyes," he said.

"They're very pretty," said the speaker. "I think I'll keep them."

"Perhaps you can earn them," Grigory said.

The other answered by trying to put his hands on him. Grigory heard bone crunch under his deflecting blow. "Keep your foul hands off me. I will walk under my own power."

He smelled the other's breath and imagined lips curling back from teeth in a snarl. The odor was tinged with carrion. But the other did not touch him again.

"So you're a Dancer," he said. "We shall see. Come with me, blind one."

Grigory moved in the center of the pack. They moved deeper into the caverns, to a place he had been once before, when he had searched the crime scene for evidence. It was a dead wall.

But apparently it wasn't. It dissolved under a touch, and they all went through. Someone else gestured, and the wall formed again, like sand flowing backward into an hourglass.

*Interesting trick,* thought Grigory, filing it away for future reference.

* * *

The aliens took Grigory deep into the earth. Andrei managed to slip in just before the wall became solid again. If he had hesitated one more second, he would have become part of it.

*They will not see you in this,* Grigory said. *It is much like the one John designed to allow him to spy on them. But it's better than his.*

*How do you know?* Andrei asked.

*Because it's mine,* Grigory answered.

Andrei was invisible. Many times Grigory had counseled that they should not reveal the full extent of the technology they had at their disposal. Apparently Grigory was an old master at hiding his capabilities.

He followed the pack at a distance, his eyes in tactical. It wasn't the same tactical he was used to, but it worked well enough.

*The suit was designed for military ESAs who would not have the benefit of sprite helpers in battle. It will interface with your tactical vision enhancements very well. You will find your capabilities are as good as what you used to have.*

In some ways they were better. Andrei was able to build a map in his head of where they were and where they had been. He knew what alloys were used for structures in the tunnels. He could see energy signatures and avoid alarm sensors. When it was dark, he could see infrared. Grigory gave off heat, but the aliens gave off even more. They glowed like torches ahead of him.

They moved fast, but he kept up easily thanks to the suit. At last they came to a great juncture, precisely of the sort Andrei had hoped would exist in the underground maze. He stopped and let them go on ahead. It was time to relieve himself of his burden.

Andrei had worried the Enemies might detect the BUG SPRAY machines if he tried to send them in after Grigory, so he had felt compelled to employ an extra measure of stealth and security. When Grigory and his captors disappeared from view, Andrei lowered his face shield and undid the front of his suit.

Anyone who could have seen him at that moment would have thought him a portly man. But as Andrei's secret payload poured out of his danger suit, his size would have appeared to rapidly shrink. His suit emptied, and he was surrounded by the cloud.

He gave an order: <Maximum dispersal.>

The cloud dissolved like smoke. They would spread themselves throughout the hive and await his last order. Andrei tapped the controls on his right forearms. His field of vision shifted to grid tactical. Grigory's beacon began to signal. Andrei replaced his face shield and ran, using the speed function in his suit at maximum.

Grigory had to admit there were some pleasant smells in the hive. They passed several females along the way, and these had a pleasant, musky odor. He smelled blossoms, scented wood, and spices as well. But the scent of carrion always returned, sometimes fresh, sometimes ancient and ghostly.

No one spoke to him, but he heard them speaking among themselves. This sound held a sort of beauty, but also an insectile quality. The words they uttered were often like dry wings rustling against carapaces, oddly jointed legs rubbing each other.

*No pity*, he thought as he kept up with them. They never tired of testing him, trying to confuse him. *They are what John wanted to be.*

He stayed with them, matching their pace easily. But he was careful not to exceed their speed; he moved slightly slower than them, as if they had surpassed his limitations.

The open air of a large cavern suddenly surrounded them. He heard many voices rustling like dead leaves. The cavern was full. Apparently he was going to be the main event for the night's roster.

"I am the gift," he said again.

"We know what you are," answered the alien tsar, his voice carrying from the center of the cavern.

Grigory walked slowly toward him. No one attempted to stop him. He halted ten paces from the tsar. "Before we begin," he said, "answer one question."

"Is this in the order of a last request?" the tsar said, his tone light. But his odor had sharpened.

"You'll find it simple enough," Grigory said. "I simply want to know if all your breed is as stupid as you are."

In all his long life, Grigory had never heard a silence as taut as the one that followed his question.

"At last," breathed the alien tsar. "One who understands the true role of a gift."

This remark was followed by the sound of musical instruments, pipes that emitted a noise almost like the sound of mating cicadas. The creatures around Grigory began to move. He felt the wind of their passage all around him, and he understood that it was finally time to demonstrate his true capabilities.

Andrei paused at the edge of the cavern, gazing at the tornado of bodies that swirled at its center. Were it not for his tactical vision, he would not be able to make out what was happening at all.

"Silence!" he roared, but his voice was swept away. Once again, he would need the suit to amplify his abilities. He ran to the eye of the storm and tried again.

"SILENCE!"

This time he achieved results. For a moment there was a lull, and he could see the rivers of purple-blue blood on the floor. Andrei lowered his helmet and switched his suit to visible.

The storm halted as if turned off from a switch. Andrei saw Grigory on one knee, a dead man in his grasp. But the dead man was not the alien tsar. That one stood mere paces from Andrei.

"I told you," said Andrei, "that you had chosen the wrong enemies."

Wide green eyes stared at him with distinct astonishment.

"I, Andrei Alexandrovich, have killed you. This is for my people, the men, women, and children you murdered."

Even as he was saying that he gave the order: <Deploy payload.>

Throughout the maze, millions of mites let loose their poison. Andrei touched his controls to raise his mask again. Before he could do it, the alien tsar slammed into him like a freight train, knocking him from his feet. Andrei twisted in the other's grasp, rolling with the fall and pulling the other with him.

They landed in a tumbled heap against a wall. Andrei stabbed at the other's neck.

But the Enemy was already dead.

All around him, others were falling. Andrei moved again to touch his controls, but saw Grigory still struggling to get to his feet.

Both of them had breathed it already, it was too late. Aliens were dropping like flies around them. Some were trying to get to the door. Futile, since the poison now saturated their burrow.

*If you breathe it, even a small whiff, you're screwed*, Tam had warned him.

Andrei went to Grigory and helped him to his feet. The two of them limped out the door.

"They didn't hurt you, did they—you tough old bastard?" asked Andrei.

"No," said Grigory. "I'm just resting. I think I need to rest right here, Andrei."

He was bleeding badly and Andrei had nothing to stop the flow. He lowered the ESA to the floor of the corridor. Grigory could not sit up, so Andrei helped him to lie down.

His wounds were terrible.

"Some danger suit," said Andrei thickly.

"Tough bugs. You breathed the poison?"

"I had to make a last statement before I killed them. It cost me."

Grigory did not move. He seemed unable. But his voice was almost as strong as it normally was. "It was fitting. A tsar must make a speech before he kills his enemies. Silence at such a time is unseemly."

"I suppose you're right."

Andrei heard little sounds like the scuttling of beetles through dead leaves. The sound sickened him. Now he knew what it was like to be inside a hive when the termites were poisoned.

"Andrei Alexandrovich," said Grigory, "remove my left eye stone and take it with you."

Andrei hesitated. But he did not doubt there was good reason for such an odd request. He touched the eye stone, tentatively at first, trying to find a way to grasp it.

"You must dig harder, my friend. Do not fear to hurt me."

Andrei obliged. He found that he had to dig much harder.

"Forgive me, Grigory Michaelovich. It is slippery."

"You've almost got it."

Suddenly Andrei heard a click, and the eye stone popped out of its socket. He almost dropped it. He turned it over; it was not a stone after all.

"This was plugged in," he said.

"Yes. But it was not an eye, like you're thinking."

Andrei studied the blind ESA. The eyelid drooped over his empty socket, but Grigory's face had not relaxed in any other fashion. "One last secret?" he asked.

"It's a database," said Grigory. "They call it an avatar."

"What does it contain?"

"Me."

Andrei understood. He dried the eye stone on the front of his suit and slipped it into a utility pocket. "I'll put it in a safe place," he promised.

"Not too safe," warned Grigory. "When the Republic returns, God knows when, they'll need an accurate account of what transpired here. Don't put it in a fancy necklace."

"I won't," said Andrei. "I'll let Emily decide how it should be kept."

"Wise." Grigory swallowed, hard. "I'm failing, Andrei. Don't be surprised by how fast it happens. I've been ready for some time. You've been a good patron, even though you weren't really mine."

"Thank you," Andrei said humbly.

"And a good tsar. I will honor your memory. Or at least, my avatar will. This was a good place for our last stand, and I can think of no better comrade with whom to fight it."

"Nor I." Andrei laid his hand on Grigory's shoulder. "I have been very fortunate."

"I won't wish you any more luck, Andrei Alexandrovich. But rest well."

"And you, my friend."

Grigory seemed to hear him. There was the trace of a smile on his lips. It was not a bitter smile, but seemed to hint at real happiness. Andrei felt the life pass out of the body under his hand, and Grigory Michaelovich became an empty shell.

Except for the eye stone in his pocket. Andrei touched it.

"Nobel ESA," he said, "I know where your mind resides. But your spirit goes where it will. Good journey."

He stood slowly. Already, the poisons were slowing his movements. without Grigory's injuries, he wouldn't go as fast as the ESA had. He might have a few days. He had to use them wisely.

He spared the chamber little attention as he passed through it. It contained things of glorious beauty, but he was rather glad he did not have the time to examine them closely. Like everything made by the Enemies, their beauty contained hidden barbs, tipped with a poison of the mind.

*Die. You will not prevail in the end. Your kind, your children, your legacy, shall be destroyed, I vow it in my last hours.*

Andrei stumbled through the poisoned chambers. He felt as if he were fleeing a tomb. He rushed down long, hot passages that grew cooler with each step, as if he were inside a body that had just died. He passed fallen Enemies, littering the floor like insects in a smoked hive. This filled him with a gladness and a peace he had not known for a long time. Or perhaps he had never known it.

When he emerged into the chamber of the dead dancers, he saw movement on the far side. He froze. He had no more weapons with him, and he doubted he would be much of a challenge. This was regrettable. He had hoped he might accomplish a few more things before he died.

Then he realized that the people who moved toward him were wearing sterile suits and helmets. "Andrei!" one called with Emily's voice. He stumbled toward her. She pulled a tank with a nozzle off her back and began to spray him with decontamination foam.

"Too late," he said.

She looked at him with sad eyes, but kept spraying.

The main power grid was down; now Tally's danger suit was losing power as well, and she had no way to charge it up again. Though it was warmer in the winter palace than it was outside, it was still colder than she liked it. She sat on her couch in front of the gas fireplace, a blanket draped around her. It was long past time for sleeping, but she knew she wouldn't go to bed anytime soon.

Suddenly she felt someone in the room with her. She looked up and saw Andrei.

For several moments she could not speak. She could only look at his face in the flickering light and wonder if he was really there or if he was already a ghost.

"Did you tell him?" she asked at last.

"Yes," he said.

Tally swallowed, hard. She was grateful she wouldn't have to tell Peter his father was dying. Because she doubted she could have done it.

"I've loved you all these years," she said. "And I wasted so much time."

"You wasted nothing," he said. "We had our time together. And we have now."

All of these things that needed to be said hurt her

terribly. But she was grateful. "Come sit next to me. I'm thinking."

He moved as if it hurt him, but he hadn't lost his grace or dignity. He sat next to Tally and put his arm around her. She snuggled against him fitting perfectly in the curve of his arm.

"I never thought about why we were doing it," she said at last.

"Why we were doing it?" he asked.

"Why we were building systems that wouldn't depend on power. I had just come from a project where we were doing exactly the same thing, it was so easy for me. Canopus isn't going to have any power at all, and I needed to design systems that would facilitate life. And when you told me about the farmers, and how they didn't like to depend too much on technology, I just took it as a challenge. And I wanted the same thing for people in the city, simplicity, practicality, good design that conserves energy, keeps the energy bills low. And now here we are in the dark, and I finally figured it out."

"I blame myself," he said softly. "Years ago I should have heeded the warning of the derelicts. If we had settled on a different world . . ."

"Maybe it had to be this way," said Tally. "Maybe a sun buster would have gotten us if we had settled somewhere else. My grandfather always asked me if I could see the hour ahead, but maybe I've always been too busy trying to *make* the future to really see it clearly. I get so focused on the details, on making things happen so other things can happen, I forget to stop and think about why. I can't see the forest—"

For a moment, patterns moved at the back of her mind. But then they were gone, all she could see was Andrei's startled face. She sighed, defeated. "I can't see the forest for the trees. Even now."

Andrei shook his head. "You have made such beautiful cities for me. I forgive you if you aren't omniscient."

Tally gazed into his hazel eyes and tried to understand that soon they would be closed forever. She couldn't. "We don't even know if we killed them all," she said.

"We killed the ones who were plaguing us."

"Sure. And summer is almost over, and fall and winter will freeze this world, and we won't know if they're going to bloom like flowers in the spring."

"You have some weapons left," said Andrei. "A few attack helicopters, some nukes, plenty of guns. You may have to use them."

"Yeah, we'll use them. And then we'll run out of ammunition, and we still don't have the industry in place to make new ones. The new stuff we make will be more primitive."

"Is this what keeps you awake tonight?" He squeezed her shoulders gently.

"Yes," she admitted.

"Let it be for now. You're right, winter is coming. You have time for restful nights."

Tally closed her eyes, fighting tears. This might be their last night together. She didn't want to spoil it. If she got started, she didn't know if she could stop. He was right, it was so peaceful to be together in front of the fire, safe and warm while the world cooled outside.

But her mind kept wandering back to the forest, those trees she couldn't see. Unbidden, the image of Lyuba Petrova's head came to her again. Her eyes were open, looking at Tally, aware. She lay in her bower in Grey Forest, the leaves so dead around her, so sterile. The dead dancers in the cavern had been sterile too. Tally remembered how Emily thought the killer meant it as some sort of clue.

*He was giving us pieces of a puzzle. I thought the picture would be of him. But maybe he had another picture in mind.*

The cavern of the dead dancers had been very close to the Enemy hive.

Again the patterns moved in Tally's mind, and this time she saw what pattern they were weaving.

"Andrei," she said. "There *is* another hive. And I think I know where it is."

Ayat-ko raced through the cold hive like a hurricane, breaking into sleeping chambers and biting their inhabitants. Her spittle carried a hormone that forced them to wake.

It would cut centuries from their lives. But the alternative was to die right now.

She woke the females first, who still carried the fertilized eggs from the last mating. Then she went straight to Solan-ko's chamber. She sank her teeth deep into his cheek. His flesh was cold and hard as marble, but she felt it stir.

"Wake," she told him. "Or our clan dies forever!"

His eyes flew open. "Witness," he croaked.

"We have minutes," she snapped. "The alien clan has found our hive. They have already killed the te clan. Wake if you can, I must rouse other males."

She left him to fend for himself. She had time to bite ten other males before her sensors warned her that time had run out.

"Make for the water hive!" she told those who could hear. "Get out of here!"

"That hive is long dead," croaked a newly awakened male.

"Then it will suit us perfectly," she told him. "For these are our end days. We have lost."

She spied Solan-ko among the refugees. He was fully awake. Later she would give him the details.

And the plan she had conceived that might save them, after all.

From the safety of her office, Emily watched Grey Forest erupt into a pillar of blue fire. Her screen almost shorted out when the electromagnetic pulse preceded the flash, but it recovered when another remote picked up the image. The pillar telescoped from both ends, then released a shock wave from its center that spread out from it like ripples on water, vaporizing everything in its path. The greatest force of the blast was directed down, into the ground where the bugs lived.

The sight scared the hell out of her.

"That was the last nuke," said Tam. "We don't have any more."

*Thank God*, thought Emily, and got up to tell Andrei the news.

John could see again. They had kept their word, they had given him new eyes!

But why was it so dark in his cell? It must be a sleeping shift. On Archangel, they had always toned the lights down so people could have the illusion of a daily cycle. He supposed he would appreciate that now. But he wondered how long he would have to stay locked up. After all, he still had other weapons they could use, and they still needed them.

"No they don't."

He jumped, his heart slamming in his chest. The voice was right next to him, and it belonged to a dead girl. He could see her in the shadows now, the ballerina. The outlines of her lovely face were clearly defined, but her eyes were pools of shadow.

"They don't need you anymore," she told him. "They defeated the aliens on their own. You're just going to rot here."

His hands itched to do things to her. But he had already done them, he had turned her into butcher's meat, made her a thing for amusement, discarded her parts.

"You were so jealous of us," she said, her tone soft and infuriating. "We had talent, we were admired. But they turned you down all those years ago, John, they said you weren't good enough. And you weren't."

"Shut up, bitch," he muttered. "You're dead, you're not even here."

"I'm here because of Tally," she said. "She's a medium. Because of her, I can visit this world one more time. I can do one last thing."

She looked so real. Real enough to touch, or to touch *him*. "I killed you once," he said. "I can do it again."

"No you can't," she said, and she held something up for him to see. It was his bedsheet, knotted and noosed. "You can only kill yourself," she said.

"You wish," he sneered, but his voice shook. His hands trembled so badly he had to clench them in his lap.

"You destroyed our bodies," she said, "but you still amounted to nothing, Johnny. Your mother and father tried to make something of you, but they failed. That's why they discarded you. That's why everyone has. What is left for you?"

"I've still got weapons they could use," he insisted. But suddenly he felt moisture in his crotch. He had wet himself.

She came closer, moving on the tips of her toes, the knotted sheet in her hand. She danced around him and draped it over his head. He felt it tighten at his throat.

"What are you doing?" he asked, and he was humiliated to hear the terror in his own voice. *She* was the one who had pleaded in terror, who had begged for his mercy. Now it was his turn and he couldn't help himself. He backed away from her, climbing up on his bed, trying to climb up the wall when he couldn't go any farther.

"Please," he said. "I'm sorry! I don't want to die!"

"Katerina did," she said. "But that's no excuse. Step off the edge of your bed, Johnny. You have to."

"No," he said.

And then someone shoved him from behind.

*I have one more piece of advice for you,* Baba Yaga said. *You won't like it.*

Andrei lay in his bed and felt death coming. He was sorry to go. He was sorry that his son would lose him too soon. But his thoughts were not of the afterlife.

*When this is done,* she said, *you will have your lives, probably little more.*

She was wrong about that. They had little technology, but they still had their roads, their cities and farms, culture and traditions. That was all he really wanted to save. Things had turned out better than he had feared.

*This new enemy will survive as well. After a long time of fighting and hating, you will get to know them.*

That would be Peter's legacy. He had hoped to leave his son a better world. He had hoped Peter would not have to be tsar at all. But his time for regrets was running out.

*Once you have done that, you will learn the other truth. That they are not your worst enemies. Those—you have yet to meet.*

Andrei would not meet them on this side of the Veil. Perhaps God would explain it all on the other.

But Andrei worried enough to call Peter to his side and tell him everything Baba Yaga had said.

"Who could be worse than the Enemies?" Peter asked, deeply troubled.

"It's a wide universe," Andrei told him. "There is room for everything. The Republic may reestablish contact with you while you are tsar. Or the Union we hoped for—or someone totally new. I rather hope they do not come too soon. I hope you will have time to grow your roots stronger here, to adapt. Baba Yaga may contact you. Be courteous to her, son, as if she were your grandmother. And be wary of her, for she is not."

Peter nodded, but he was frowning deeply. "Papa. You do not look well."

Andrei suddenly had to fight to keep his eyes open. He succeeded, for the moment. "My time is close, Peter. I'm glad you have come."

Peter's face seemed ready to crumple in misery. But he held it firm, stubbornly. "No, you just need to rest. You need to sip some chicken broth and have the fire turned up in here. I'll call the nurse—"

"No, Peter."

Andrei still had enough authority left in his voice to make his son sit down again. He looked at him with love, and more pride than he could possibly express. But there was still a matter to discuss.

"Peter," Andrei said. "I know your mother had a last wish she imparted to you. About the Russian church."

"Yes, Papa." Peter's eyes were bright with tears he could not shed.

"I do not speak of this matter lightly, my son. You will be tsar someday. You may have the power to claim this world for the Russian church. But I doubt you will have the power to keep it. And in the process you will cause friction between good people. You will weaken our united front, giving our Enemy something to strike at."

"Father, I don't want to be tsar if I can cause so much harm!"

Andrei squeezed his son's hand. "No one can do it without causing harm. I have chosen you because I know you will think of your people first. You will teach your sons and daughters to do the same. That is what my father asked of me, and that is what I ask of you."

"Papa—" One tear escaped from Peter's swollen lids, and he furiously wiped it away. "Don't go. You must live another hundred years, I don't want to say good-bye now."

"I've run out of choices, Peter." Andrei smiled gently. "I wish to stay with you too. But I have lived so long already—can I really complain? I'll tell you a secret, little tsar. There is a problem with immortality. It takes a long, long time. And I have run out of patience."

"But I have not. Papa—I have not!"

"That's as it should be. You'll take care of Tally and Emily, yes? You will remember your mother and me. We'll see you from heaven. Keep the letters I've given you—I'm there, and so are your grandfathers."

"Don't say good-bye," Peter pleaded. "If you do that, you'll have to go."

"I'm glad I can say good-bye. Always say good-bye when you can. And I love you. Beloved son."

"I love you too, Papa." Peter could no longer hold back the tears. But he held his head up and kept his eyes squarely on his father's.

"Sit with me," said Andrei. "It won't take long."

Peter held on to his father's hand, desperately. It was warm and dry, but not strong. He wanted to be the last image Andrei saw before he flew to heaven.

His wish was granted.

Tally ran to his bedside when she heard he was dying. But she was too late.

*This is how I want you to remember me,* he had said. And so it would be. Yet even as he lay dead, he was still the man she loved. His expression had smoothed, peacefully.

Tally did not touch him. *He's in a better place,* she thought, knowing it was true, tears flowing so heavily from her eyes she could not see. Someone led her away and sat with her in Andrei's living room until she could see again. Then she realized that the warm hand that held hers so tightly was Peter's. He wept just as heavily, just as silently.

"I have some things I must attend to," he was able to say at last.

"Me too," said Tally.

He kissed her cheek and left her there. Tally went into Andrei's office. She found a black box on his desk. It was accompanied by a handwritten note.

FROM: Emily Kizheh
TO: Tally Korsakova

*This is Andrei's correspondence database. Since you're the only one who still has a functioning data link, I haven't tried to secure it in any fashion, except to send it with a trusted officer. I think we should eventually seal it in Andrei's tomb, in the hopes that one day someone will contact us again. If that happens, they will have a better idea who he was and what he was trying to do.*

*But first I thought you might want to read it. We'll make hard copies of some of it—regrettably, that means you'll have to scrawl a lot of it by hand. It encompasses most of Andrei's life and contains electronic versions of all the letters he saved from his father and grandfather. I know we have hard copies of the letters to share with Peter, but the medium they're printed on wasn't made to last. Also, there are some things in here from the last few weeks that you should see.*

*Baba Yaga sent Andrei one more message, just before we lost the com link. It may be tough to look at now, but eventually I think you'll want to see it.*

Tally placed the box on Andrei's desk. She stared at it for a long time, then raised her eyes to his mother's portrait. The woman and the painting looked back at Tally with lively curiosity.

Tally's rasta-link slithered toward the data portal and established a link. She found the files and looked for Baba Yaga's last letter. A few seconds later, she saw it in her mind's eye.

*Andrei,*

*I hope you will see this before you die. It is not an indulgence I afford myself very often, but I am fond of you.*

*You have done well. I will not try to tell you that you haven't been used your whole life, because of course you have. But it was for something. You did what must be done to preserve what we love, yet you have saved more than that. You have sown the seeds that must be harvested by the inheritors of the Republic. This war that pared the Republic back so brutally, and the war you have conducted here in your mir, are but precursors for something far more difficult. There are greater terrors in the universe, and they will find humankind. You will not live to see it. You go to your last sleep as all do. Except for me.*

*Peace, Andrei. There is no rest for the wicked. But there is for you. You have earned it.*

*B.Y.*

Tally went over it so many times it began to be meaningless. When she disengaged again, new tears were flowing. Andrei had not been angered by the message. In fact, Tally believed it had comforted him. There was much she had not understood about him. And now she never would have the chance.

She sat for a time at the desk, thinking about the database. There were mediums upon which she could transcribe the material that would not be so perishable. She had an extensive database stored within her rasta-links concerning ancient methods used by the Egyptians, the Greeks, the Romans. The monks of Ireland had painstakingly transcribed manuscripts from those dead civilizations. She imagined herself bent over stretched vellum, gilding letters with gold leaf.

John had scoffed at the rasta-links, and Tally thought it ironic she had almost changed them for something more up-to-date. And now, all of the most newfangled technology was fried; Tally's clunky old links were all that survived. She could plunder the database stored inside for ways to help Belarus through its dark ages.

And they could help her with one other thing. She accessed her own files, found the letter from George. In another moment she was standing on the Avenue of the Sphinxes. She turned her head, and saw Andrei standing just a few feet away.

Watchful hazel eyes. And around the corners, even in virtual reality, the hint of a smile.

She couldn't touch him in there. But it felt good to look at him.

"Tally?"

Someone was calling her from far away. Tally looked across the avenue, into the golden light of eternal noon. The flock of birds flew up from the uncompleted temple, just as they always would.

"Tally? Can you hear me?" Someone touched her hands. Tally took one last look at Andrei and exited the file. Peter was standing beside her, massaging her cold fingers.

The gas lamp wasn't burning as brightly. How long had she sat lost in virtual memories?

"Where were you?" Peter asked. He looked sad, a

little worried; all of the childishness seemed to have left him. He wasn't thinking of himself at all.

"I still have access to my own database," she told him. "I can research ways to do things that won't take fancy machines."

"But you looked so happy," he said.

"Yes," she admitted. "I was looking at an old file. Your father was in it."

"Oh." Grief sat heavily upon him. He thought for a long time before he spoke again, still rubbing her fingers, which gradually warmed under his ministrations.

"I suppose it wouldn't have done me any good to get a sprite interface," he said at last. "Everyone who had it misses it terribly. I feel very sad for them."

"Me too," Tally said.

"We'll have to do things the old-fashioned way," Peter continued. "Maybe it's for the best. I won't have to unlearn a lot of things." He sighed deeply. "That's good. Because I have so much to do, Tally. So much to know."

Tally captured his hands and held them tight. "You won't be doing it alone, Peter." She didn't call him *baby*. He wasn't one anymore.

"Thank you," he said, his eyes shining. "Bless you."

*Bless us all,* thought Tally. *And God save the tsar.*

It was the first time she had prayed since she was a child. Tally knew it wouldn't be the last. She would stand beside Peter in the great cathedral, and pray with all of Belarus. They had survived. Now they had to figure out how to prosper.

"Come on," she said. "Let's see if Emily has an interesting puzzle to work on."

Tally picked up the lamp, and they left Andrei's office hand in hand. The light left with them. But on the wall, the painting of Martha Kretyanova Mironenko seemed to glow with its own inner light. She was painted on fine canvas, in a medium that was all but imperishable. Her eyes would watch the world for another thousand years.

There would be much for them to see.

# Epilogue

BELARUS SYSTEM, 870 YEARS LATER

Archangel Station still maintained a stable orbit. Captain Taylor could scarcely believe his luck.

"Deploy the drones," he told his team. "Time to explore another haunted station."

Union Survey Ship *Artemis* moved into a synchronous orbit with Archangel. Down below, the world slept in the tail end of an ice age. As they moved past the night side, they could see dim lights in some of the heavily populated areas from orbit, but there were no energy signatures and no one attempted to communicate with them.

"Gas lights," said Kym, his number one. "The old records indicate that Mironenko had a contingency plan in case everything got knocked out, which apparently it did."

Taylor nodded, sipping his coffee, but he wasn't seeing the lights anymore. The drones were sending him pictures of the dead command station. "Heavy damage," he said, looking at holes in the outer hull. "But so far it looks like the inner hull is intact. We might even be able to revitalize the old girl."

"That would save some time," said Kym.

But Taylor wasn't counting on it. His team consisted of thirty-seven specialists, eleven of them ESAs. They had enough sprites to accomplish survey and reconnaissance. To do any heavy building they would have to employ most of those sprites and most of their other machinery to build more of the same. Taylor was not eager to make their presence in the system any bigger than it already was. Caution was the Union motto. First, last, and always.

"Ah-ha," said Kym. "I've accessed the logs."

Taylor blinked, seeing her coffee-colored face for half a second before his system hooked up with hers. She guided him to the right file, a frozen image of a grim, gaunt man in uniform. Kym played the message.

"This is Commander Jones," said the man. "Twenty-three of us are still alive, but life support is failing fast. We're holed up in the medical section. Anyone who finds this message, be warned: there are hostile aliens sharing the world below us with our colonists. We fought a war with them and won, but they're not dead. They may still have weapons in this system somewhere, we don't know.

"The colony has been bombed back to the pre-industrial age, at least in terms of what's available to people for immediate use. They'll have to reestablish heavy industry, and they don't have the stuff they need to do it anywhere near the level they started out with. I hope Andrei managed to salvage some of his sprites, but I doubt it. We haven't been able to communicate with him for a couple of weeks."

Jones looked like he was suffering from both hunger and dehydration. But Taylor knew in his gut that wasn't what drew such deep lines in the man's face. It was the knowledge that his station was lost, his crew dying.

"I think we're down to just a few hours of breatheable atmosphere," said Jones. "My crew have made entries in their personal logs, you'll be able to access all of it from this site. There's a lot to tell you, and I won't try to do it now. I've just got one important bit of information to pass on. There's an ESA Avatar down below, probably in St. Petersburg. His name is Grigory, and you're going to want to talk to him before you do anything—I mean *anything* in the way of contact down below. Get as close to St. Petersburg as you can and broadcast this message on a wide band: *Watcher, where are you?* You should get a homing signal from him. But be careful with your sprites, assuming you've got any. You won't be able to use them to find the Enemies."

Kym froze the recording. She backed it up a few seconds, then played it again. But Taylor already knew there was no mistaking what Jones had said.

"—assuming you've got any. You won't be able to use them to find the Enemies."

"God damn it to hell," said Kym.

"Okay." Taylor came out of tactical and looked at the central viewscreen on his command deck. Belarus hung there, its city lights dim and yellow. "Get the records people working on those logs, and have engineering survey Archangel. I'm going to send my snooper down to look at the pretty lights up close."

Kym's left eyebrow twitched, an indication that she was biting her tongue. He almost smiled. Everyone on his team was champing at the bit for a chance to go down and look around this new long-lost colony. What were the people like, what did they remember of the old Republic? Were they pale skinned, the way few people were anymore in the Union? Would it be possible to ask them back in?

Probably not—most of the other lost colonies required a lot of study, and some couldn't accept the Bill of Rights, the cornerstone of the new Central Government. These people probably still had a tsar. And maybe other kings as well, if they were divided into opposing countries. They might think Taylor and his crew were monsters.

They might think the sprites were fairies.

"I'll be careful with my snooper," he promised Kym.

"Jones had something more to say," she reminded him. "We cut him off."

Taylor went back into tactical. He looked once more at the face of a man who was living a captain's worst nightmare.

"Just a few words of warning," said Jones. "This is a dangerous place. This world will try you to the very limits of your abilities. Look out, stay sharp, and always remember—things aren't what they seem." He stared at the screen for a long moment, as if there was a lot more he would have liked to say. But finally, he simply said, "Good luck to you. Learn from what you find on this station. It's the last we can offer."

And then he was gone.

Kym's worried face was back again. He didn't have to ask what she was thinking. She didn't want *Artemis* to end up like Archangel.

"First things first," he told her. "Snooper's already on the way down."

Taylor's snooper descended to St. Petersburg through a gentle snowstorm. He watched through its eye, enchanted. The city was beautiful and strange, colorful and anachronistic. He saw buildings that must have been built just after landfall. They still looked new.

But many of the structures had been built since, mostly from wood, and painted with colorful, intricate designs. The high level of craftsmanship was impressive. Some streets were paved with cobblestones, others with indestructible alloys. People moved about in the gaslight, bundled up in fur coats and hats. Taylor floated over their heads like a snowflake.

He wished he could spend a few hours people watching, but that would have to wait. He made the call to Grigory.

<Watcher, where are you?>

A beacon instantly began to signal. Snooper followed it, making its way to a magnificent building. Men armed with primitive rifles guarded the perimeter. Some of them were coming out through a door—Taylor flew snooper right past them, slipping inside like a spirit, undetected.

Obviously a colonial structure. Taylor had seen a few like it in his time, designed by masters. He flew past magnificent paintings, sculptures, elegant furniture in marble corridors. Finally he came to a door from another world. A heavy thing embossed with gold, it depicted Thoth, the Egyptian god of scribes.

It was closed tight. Taylor signaled again. He saw a line of code appear just to the right of the door. Then it swung inward, and Taylor flew into a tomb.

Light shone dimly from the corridor, glistening on the ebony skin of Anubis. Taylor saw a ceremonial barge. Beyond it was a sarcophagus. The signal was coming from there. He drifted closer, bemused, remembering Jones's warning: *Things are not what they seem.*

A woman's image was carved and gilded on the outer casing of the sarcophagus. Back on *Artemis*, Taylor drew his breath in at the sight of her. If the woman inside was anything like this image, she was the most beautiful woman Taylor had ever seen. She was dressed and painted to look like an Egyptian goddess; she wore the serpent crown of Lower Egypt.

In the serpent's mouth was a bloodred stone.

<Is that you?> asked Taylor.

<Yes,> said the Avatar. <Thank you for coming. We have much to discuss.>

Kunum-ko dined on the liver of his brother. It was a fine feast, though not nearly as gratifying as one he had enjoyed nearly three hundred turns before. That time he had eaten the liver of Solan-ko, the greatest clan leader of collective memory. He honored that dead brother, and tried not to regret that the greatest Dance of his life was past him.

"Curiosity," Solan-ko had said, just before he died. "You can taste it if you use your sharpest slicer. Remember."

Kunum-ko had tasted curiosity many times since then. But more often than not, it was his own. In the final years of their decline, his clan had done wondrous things, they had fought with Enemies whose numbers grew more every year, despite the slaughter. As he ate the liver of the failed challenger, he could not help but wonder if he was not, himself, a failure. A slow one, a magnificent kill.

*Curiosity. One cannot help but feel it at the end. But who will eat my liver, who will know my essence? None but time, and time will only taste ashes.*

His Witness stood at the edge of the hall, watching him. He beaconed her. "Ayat-ko. Come share this. You can appreciate it better than I."

She obeyed. He gave her his slicers and skewers, then watched as she ate. He learned much from the experience.

She sliced a fine piece and presented it to him. He took the bite, chewing slowly. He tasted agony. It calmed his nerves.

"You have news," he said.

"They have returned," she said.

"Ah," he said. "The end."

"Perhaps not." She sliced and fed him another piece. He chewed, his own curiosity overcoming the flavor of the meat.

"What do you suggest?" he asked.

"No more raids for pleasure," she said. "Now, all killing must serve our purpose."

She sliced another piece of liver, taking her time. He admired her grace. "I didn't know we still had a purpose," he said.

"Survival, my ko," she said, as the petal-thin slice floated onto the skewer. "And ultimately, *change.*"

He watched her as he chewed the offered slice. She was a great mystery to him, she always would be. But he shared one important trait with Solan-ko, whom he had out-Danced. He knew that this sterile sister held the key to the future. She was odd, her opinions uncommon—because she was brilliant.

"The Dance of Change," he said, entranced by the notion. "I accept your challenge, Witness."

She gave no flicker of alarm. The pupils at the center of her eyes expanded with pleasure. He smiled at her, knowing he was truly understood.

Such a comfort, in difficult times.

<TRANSMISSION FROM BELARUS, TIGHT BEAM, UNABLE TO LOCATE PRECISE POINT OF ORIGIN:

*Captain Taylor,*
*What took you so long?*

*—Baba Yaga*>